The
GUEST
ROOM

TASHA SYLVA

The
GUEST
ROOM

WELBECK

First published in 2023 by Welbeck Fiction Limited,
an imprint of Welbeck Publishing Group
Offices in: London – 20 Mortimer Street, London W1T 3JW &
Sydney – Level 17, 207 Kent St, Sydney NSW 2000 Australia
www.welbeckpublishing.com

A CIP catalogue record for this book is available from the British Library.

Hardback ISBN: 978-1-80279-314-7
Trade paperback ISBN: 978-1-80279-315-4
Ebook ISBN: 978-1-80279-316-1

Printed and bound by CPI Group (UK) Ltd., Croydon, CR0 4YY.

MIX
Paper | Supporting
responsible forestry
FSC
www.fsc.org   FSC® C171272

10 9 8 7 6 5 4 3 2 1

For Sally
my mother
and my
sweetest friend

'What you seek is seeking you.'

—Rumi

The sun is changing. When I set out it was white, that glare spot no one can quite look at. Sheer star. Now, as I dig, my fingers in damp earth, its warmth is gone. I twist round and it's curving into cloud. Dark orange. The colour of Spanish honey.

I glance at the grainy black and white image next to my foot. Through the grey I can make out an arm, two toes, the curve of a skull. Beautiful and misshapen.

Careful what you look for.

I pull out more earth. Birds hide in the trees, moving between branches. I keep digging. The birds call to each other, in their unknown language. Screeching behind me. A glimpse of black feathers. An eye, watching.

I turn back to the ground. They can keep their secrets.

I expose an earthworm – it squirms in the coppery light. If I put her here, she won't be so alone. Neither of them will.

The sun is almost gone, its afterglow in the sky. I stand up. My fingernails are dark with dirt. And she's in the soil next to a worm.

1

There's a shoe in the branches above. Laceless. One of those ambiguous hybrids – half heel, half trainer, with a gold sheen. It's glinting through the leaves, reflecting the dim city light.

A stray thing. Probably thrown up there. By a snickering friend? A teenage bully? The shoe could be a girl's. It's small enough.

Rosie said my thoughts were like corkscrews, coiling off in all directions. Something she liked to repeat, often with an eye-roll.

Movement draws my eye. A figure coming through the dark.

I can tell it's a man, even from a distance. The flat-pack frame is unmistakable. The heavy tread. He's under the muddy lamplight, walking through the shadows of trees lining the path. *Aha, here we go.* My heels click on the tarmac as I stride out towards him. A firm forward strut.

He's getting closer, his details clearer. One hand in his jacket pocket. Close-cropped hair. Pressure floats into my stomach. There's no one else around, no one to witness – I've already done a scan of the park. Just me and him. I can feel my hair on my shoulders, flowing in the warm night air. His eyes are shaded but I know he's looking at me.

Less than ten steps away. The pressure swells into my throat, a clench of nerves. He's staring.

I dare you.

His boots scuff louder.

Go on. Grab me. Almost alongside. Strong aftershave on him – amaretto, over-sprayed and bitter. I fix my eyes on his. His black irises are gleaming in the tawny glow. Then, just like that, they drop away. And he's past.

I feel the pressure pop and deflate, let out as I exhale. I glance over my shoulder but his back is receding through the shadows. *Come on, look round.* I'm all alone. Asking for it.

My left heel catches on a lump and I stumble forwards, landing on my palms.

'Shit,' I breathe.

I look back at what tripped me up. A root, bulging out of the path. When I hold up my hand I can see the graze, blood-dark, stuck with grit. I rub my fingers over it, the raw flesh stinging.

I flop onto the tarmac. Its hard surface presses into my bones. This is where I belong, on the ground in London late at night. Once, I sat in a park until four in the morning. People walked by, men glanced, one guy even shouted at me.

But nothing happened. Why her? Why not me?

Apparently tempting fate isn't easy.

I kick off my heels and stand up. The man has disappeared. His aftershave seems to linger – I can almost taste it. That bite into a bad almond.

It's quiet. Only the stir of leaves overhead. I look back along the string of trees. Which one was I standing under? I wanted to climb and have a look. Hold it, feel it in my hands. That lost little shoe.

Sighing, I step off the path into the grass. Hardly the lush green lawns people associate with England. More like straw and dried dirt. I can feel the cracks in the earth, the dust on my soles. Tooting Common stretches wide and flat before me. Deserted. No one in the dark – not a shape or shadow.

I saunter away from the lamps. Above, the stars are stained out by the glow of pollution, but here the air is black. I feel myself vanishing into it, swallowing up my body.

Ahead, I notice a pale shape on the ground.

It's small. A rag? A napkin? It looks pinkish but I can't distinguish it clearly. Unidentified object. Taking out my phone, I tap on the torch. The details glare in my eyes, spotlit.

It's crumpled and sodden, one corner soiled brown. The label sticking out, the words *Fine Egyptian cotton* clear on white. A nice expensive towel here in a heap on Tooting Common. My mind corkscrews: Whose was it? What did they use it for?

Rose-coloured – it would be, wouldn't it. There are traces of her everywhere. I avoid mirrors now, and windows as I walk down the street. Even in there, my face dimly reflected by the sun, features dark and unclear, I see her.

I blink hard, the torchlight flashing in my vision. I realise that my phone is acting as a beacon. *Here I am, come and get me.* The perfect drawing power. But I bet if I held it up high until the sun rose nothing would happen. It would be another dud.

I turn and walk back towards my rejected heels, heading for the night bus. Maybe there'll be a stranger riding the same way home.

2

The eggs are sizzling in butter when my guest comes into the kitchen. She smiles at me.

'Hi,' she says.

'Hi, Kamlai. All good?'

She's hovering. 'Yes, thank you. I'm going up the Shard today.'

'Enjoy it.'

She scurries out.

I prod the eggs and rub my upper lip. Sweaty already.

'Tess?'

I look up. Her face has reappeared round the corner of the fridge. 'Yes?'

'It's OK if I check out at eight a.m. tomorrow?'

'Sure,' I say, waving the spatula. 'You can go whenever you like before eleven. Just leave the keys in the room.'

'OK. See you.'

Her head zips back. The front door snaps shut and the flat drops to silence.

People are strange. I've been bnbing the spare room for three months and some guests I barely see, they're so stealthy in their avoidance tactics. Others want to hang out and chat. If I had to choose, I'd go for stealth. Ghost guests: come on in.

I cut off a corner of the egg white and pop it in my mouth, the greasy texture burning my tongue. The sear of heat feels good. A sharp stimulant against the numbness that blunts my body every morning. I can't remember the last time I had a dream. For the past few months my sleep has been stagnant, hollow, and sometimes when I open my eyes it feels like my mind's been wiped blank.

I take another bit of egg from the pan, accidentally puncturing the yolk. Amber liquid dribbles out and fries solid.

Rosie loved eggs. Her favourite was scrambled on buttery crumpets. I remember making it for her one morning last autumn. But when I put the plate on the table, she shook her head, saying she wasn't hungry. Her face was a cardboard colour, the skin under her eyes white. Minutes later, she grabbed a crumpet with her fingers and bit off a chunk, a violence to her chewing. But then she stopped, ran to the sink and spat it out.

The yolk in the frying pan is going brown. I turn away from the stove, leaving the gas burning.

Today I woke up thinking about that little towel. The image was there, vivid, still spotlit. I imagined picking the towel up, taking it home, washing it and folding it up. Clean and cared for. But I left it there, just like its owner. Discarded, forgotten.

* * *

Sunlight streaks through the corner of glass, my hand in the triangular beam on the desk. My bedroom window's open, letting in the dank air. I aim the electric fan down my back. My vest won't stop sticking to my skin.

It's been like this for weeks. The hottest May anyone can remember. Parks sun-baked, people sleeping outside in their gardens, melting tarmac. The lime-flash of parakeets might fool you, but London isn't equipped for Andalucían temperatures. I glance at my phone – 5th of June and 35 degrees, which is not normal.

I stare at the screen of my laptop, forcing myself to read the Spanish words lining the page. I never thought language could seem so dull. But working as a translator will do that. Words without sound, inflection or exchange.

My eyes lift from the medical report – *en el cerebro puede haber vías neurológicas más oscuras* – and look through the window. Across the street, the girl on the second floor is changing again, her lacy lilac bra on view. The flat below hers always has its curtains closed, limp netting behind flaky frames. On the ground floor, window-centre, there's a garden gnome. A potbellied old man stretched out in boxer shorts and a red pointy hat. Leering at me.

Who does that? Has such a tacky figurine as a showpiece?

I'm curious about objects like this – possessions. Their implications. What they reveal about people.

I check my phone for missed calls, even though I keep it at max volume. No notifications. I scroll down my contacts to Detective Sergeant Pettiford. My thumb hovers over his name. Our last conversation about Rosie was eight days ago, when I called him. His words just before he hung up like paste in my ears.

'You can trust us, Tess. We're making every effort.'

'But there are no new leads,' I said.

Background silence.

'Are there?'

When he spoke, his tone seemed damp, a drizzly sound. 'We're doing all we can. We'll find them.'

You can trust us. We'll find them.

But they haven't found them. The person who hurt my sister. The man. Who probably grabbed her from behind, snuck up on her in the dark.

I rub my forehead hard.

Four months on and the police still don't have a clear picture of the scene, of what happened. Only that there was a crack in her skull. Blood in her brain – a ruptured aneurysm. The news headline flashes up: *33-year-old woman found dead in a London park.*

My palms are wet. The sweat won't stop.

In the kitchen, standing over the open freezer, I twist the ice cube tray. The cubes crack off the plastic. I suck one slowly, until it's bean-sized, then put another on my tongue.

I'm still sucking, the cold burning my mouth, when I pause outside the guest room. A bar of light under the closed door. I shouldn't go in. I should respect Kamlai's privacy. Though it's my flat; I can do whatever I want.

I push down the handle.

It's larger than my room, wider, but has the same big window. Double bed in the centre, desk opposite, chair tucked under. All of the wood pale. The walls and bedding clean white. It's a toneless space, except for the faded blue rug. A fern on the windowsill in a chipped yellow pot.

I look at the door in the corner. The one to a small storage space. Locked.

There's a strain near the back of my ribcage. Whenever I'm in here, I feel it, round my lungs.

This was Rosie's room.

For two weeks after I moved in, I couldn't step inside it. I kept the door shut; the edge of her space sealed. Her energy coming from it each time I passed. Knowing that her stuff was everywhere, all over the floor – her paints, clothes, notebooks, cookie wrappers and empty packets of sultanas. I'd pulled it all out.

The police had searched the place in the first few days, looking for clues. When they didn't seem to find anything useful, I was allowed in. I stood in the living area, the air cold with silence. The radiators starting to click, heating still set to come on.

I combed my sister's things. I didn't stop until I'd been through every room. In desperation, scraping my hands around inside the fireplace. Nowhere else to look. Night outside. I stared at the black windows, condensation dripping down the glass.

Not long after, the bank called. Rosie had a mortgage. It needed paying off. Our grandmother's inheritance and Rosie's growing success as an artist only covered a small portion. There was debt. A fair chunk of it. My sister could be thoughtless – not in a selfish or uncaring way. More that her brain didn't seem to fire off thoughts most of us have. Rash in her excitement. Not considering things beyond a particular moment or action.

I'm not sure how she was paying the bank loan, now left for me to deal with – parents in Spain, my dad a shell, my mum broken, saying she couldn't talk to me.

The bank pushed me to sell, but that was impossible. This was Rosie's home. Her life existed in these walls. And there could still be something here relevant to the police investigation.

So I moved in, forced to rent out one of the bedrooms to help with repayments. I hated the idea of anyone else being here, especially in my sister's room, her most intimate space, among all of her possessions. I told myself I should take it – especially as it's bigger, nicer, and it looks out onto the back gardens instead of the road. In every way it made sense.

But sense was something my body wouldn't follow. I couldn't sleep and breathe where my sister had.

Nor could I leave it as it was, her stuff all over the room. I made myself walk through the door and shoved her belongings into boxes as fast as I could. Suddenly I didn't want to look at any of it. I grabbed traces of her from the bathroom, the kitchen, the living room. Packed them inside cardboard, hidden and sealed. Keeping just a few items, salient parts of her – a palette with dried oil paint, clothes, a wooden hair stick. Her painting, which I hung above the fireplace.

I considered asking friends if they needed a room. Except I didn't want a face I knew. I didn't want someone taking root, becoming too fixed.

I decided to open it up to strangers. More neutral that way, as a guest room.

At first it was hard, letting them in. Every noise and movement, every time they were in the kitchen, the bathroom, turning around to find them smiling at me – grating.

But now it doesn't seem so bad.

I wander towards the bed. There are a few bits on top of the duvet – a shirt, a book, a plastic bottle. Kamlai's suitcase is next to my feet. Unpadlocked and unzipped. Free for a rummage. My fingers tingle at the thought of having a dip.

Possessions. The word alone teases. Possess. What do you keep close? What are you hiding?

Some guests have humdrum basics. Clothes, underwear, toothbrush, jewellery, shoes. But others have unique items, like the American guy a couple of weeks ago who kept a tiny glass bottle of vinegar by the bed, or the Chinese girl last month with a broken cassette player from the nineties. Peggy, my third guest, left a shopping bag stuffed with empty cheese and onion crisp packets in the wardrobe. One man had a mallet. I found it wrapped in a pair of tights. Made of dark wood, small, almost toy-sized, but a weight in my hand.

I've already been through Kamlai's belongings and she seems to have a thing for seeds. First, I found a pot of tiny black bits. I couldn't work out what they were, thinking they could be dead insects. But then I smelt them. A herb or spice. Now, there's a small pile of apple seeds on the bedside table.

People have weird habits and attachments. Seeds aren't that kooky, I suppose, compared to what some of us hold onto.

It's not just possessions, though. It's the thrill of being in here, somewhere off limits the minute I welcome a guest. The risk Kamlai could come back at any moment. Catch me. And what would happen if she did? How would I explain it? I've never needed to because I've never been caught.

Tempting fate fails again.

The Spanish girl is chewing. I can't see what exactly, but I think it's a chicken drumstick. It looks sticky and dark, all over her fingers. Some kind of syrupy marinade. She licks it off her thumb and chews the meat, biting at the bone.

It was a few weeks ago when I felt myself being sucked in. I saw her face and my heart seized. As if a hand had reached into my chest with cold fingers, and pulled. My impulse was to run at her, then run away, then touch her shoulder and smile, feel the soft of her skin, the warm beneath.

I did none of these things.

Gradually the feeling has sunk into something else. Now it's in my stomach, this oily curd that rolls around. And when I see her, she stirs it up, creating a strange mix of emotions. Gnawing at me like that chicken leg.

3

A flurry of stale air blows over my face. Hot wind is funnelling through the open slits of windows as the train hurtles through the tunnel. That dry fume in my nose: diesel and dirt. I cough into my elbow.

The carriage is crowded for this time of day, before rush hour has got going. People are clustering about me. Two instincts pull on my muscles: elbow them out of my space or sit on the floor. Neither of which is socially acceptable.

I shift the box leaning against my leg. It's heavy and awkward, feeling like it might topple. Inside is a vacuum cleaner I found on a second-hand website. The old one's been broken for weeks, and after Kamlai left this morning I realised the flat's dust had reached slob levels.

The train jolts, swerving round a corner. My hand shoots out for the rail as the box pushes me off balance, but I miss and fall backwards into a tourist couple. The guy pushes on my shoulder to rebalance me, then slides his arm round his girlfriend.

'Sorry,' I mutter.

Two girls beside the door are looking at me. Both in loafers, handbags on their arms. They exchange a smile: knowing, smug.

Stupid vacuum cleaner. It's not even for me. It's for the new guest arriving today.

Arran Cole.

The little disc photo beside his name isn't much to go on. He's far off, face in shadow. The only thing I can distinguish is that he's blond and smiling. It's the same picture on his Facebook, with all other images and information private. But there are reviews on the bnb website and they're all positive, praising his respect, charm and friendliness.

He's booked the room for four weeks straight. In his original message, he said he'd been subletting his friend's room for two months while looking for a permanent place to rent. He hadn't found anywhere yet, so he needed another short-term room to be able to keep searching.

When I saw the request, I was hesitant – I've never had someone stay that long before. It goes against the principle that every guest is temporary. And what if he's weird or a nuisance? What if I don't like him?

In the end I decided to give it a go. It'll make my life easier for a month without the constant bnb admin tasks. But I should probably make an effort before he arrives, which is why I'm lugging a vacuum halfway across London. Good-as-new, a bargain, but collection only.

I look up from the mottled floor and meet someone's eye. A man across the carriage. He glances away, back to his phone, thumbs tapping. He's at least twice my age, wearing paint-spattered trousers.

I often used to sense men's gazes on me. Women's some-times, too. Recently something's changed. I'm less appealing, there's something off about me. When they meet my eye, I notice them shift, as if they've seen something uncomfortable.

Last week I held a pocket mirror up to my face, to check for milky pupils or bloodshot whites. It was only three seconds but

I felt something curl round my throat. Rosie's eyes staring back at me. I chucked the mirror in the canal.

People always commented on how we had the same eyes, that warm Spanish henna. *Mis gitanas*, our grandfather nicknamed us. Gypsy girls. Two years apart, yet when we were little he would pretend to get us mixed up. She hated it when he called her Teresa. More than once I remember her sulking because obviously she was older, obviously she was Rosa. Taller and more beautiful.

The train lurches to a stop and the automatic voice chimes: *This is Angel.* As I shuffle towards the door with my vacuum, I notice the man getting off behind me. He can look all he wants. He can follow me home.

* * *

It's seven o'clock and I've just snapped the cap off an Estrella Galicia when there's a knock at the door. I jump, the beer fizzing up over the lip of the bottle. The white foam runs onto my fingers.

I'm expecting Arran but the building buzzer hasn't gone off yet. I press my eye to the peephole and see a warped version of a man. Not a stranger. My neighbour. I yank open the door.

'Luke.'

'Evening, Tess.' He grins at me. He's in a skimpy vest and running shorts. A small tattoo clear on the hard curve of his bicep: optical illusion triangle. 'What's going on?'

'Nothing much. I would invite you in, but I'm just waiting for my bnb guest.'

'Another one, eh? Business good then?'

'Pretty good, yep.'

He hasn't broken eye contact, a grin still traced over his features. I may get ogled less by strangers but I'm not exempt from unwanted attention. Luke moved into the flat below six weeks ago. One morning, there was a huge box blocking the street door – only legs and curly hair visible behind it.

'So, are you heading out this evening?' he asks in a casual tone.

'Nah.'

'Aw, come on. You never go out.'

If only he knew. 'It's Thursday. Who goes out on a Thursday?'

'Everyone,' he says, opening his hands. 'It's the new Friday.'

I smile wryly. Luke's a nice guy, for a city boy. And not your typical management consultant. A gym-goer and climber, sure, but he also writes poetry. So he claims.

'How about dinner then? I can whip up something of my mum's.'

Within the first week, Luke had shown me his mum's book. She's from Malaysia and released a recipe book last year that hit big in Australia, now finding its way to the UK.

'I thought you were going out?' I say.

'I am, but my plans are flexible.' He shifts his weight, tilting towards me. 'You've never tasted anything like this before. I can guarantee that.'

To be fair, the book looks amazing. Celebrating the unique cuisine with all its cultural subtleties. I'm just not much of a cook. Something tells me Luke isn't either, despite his mum's talent.

'I just ate, I'm afraid,' I lie.

His expression slips, confidence not so smooth. 'One of these days, Tess—'

'What?'

'You're going to realise how much fun you could have with me.'

I highly doubt that. 'You enjoy the new Friday, Luke.'

He laughs in the back of his throat. 'Fine, I will.'

I start to swing the door shut.

'If you change your mind, you know where I am,' he says.

'Sure do.'

I go back into the kitchen and swallow a good glug of beer. It's cold in my throat.

Leaning over the plants on the windowsill, I look onto the street below. A little boy microscoots by, a woman's boots clomping after him. A teenage girl in school uniform ambles past.

No blond men.

My hand's in my hair, rubbing strands. I let it drop and there's a dark clump in my fingers. It started falling out two months ago, as if my scalp is coming undone. I find dusty wads on the floor. The worst is in the shower, the water drawing it out.

I drop the clump in the bin. I don't want to look at it.

Sitting on the sofa, I glance around the living area. At the Victorian fireplace, the worn spines of old Spanish books on the bookcase, the Moroccan mosaic lamp. On the coffee table is a congealed disc of wax, marking a dead candle.

It's peculiar, the concept of bnbing. Letting a stranger into your home, not knowing what they're going to be like. The door closes behind you and you're at the mercy of someone you know nothing about. They could do anything.

I sip some more beer just as another knock sounds. Two slow knuckle-beats. I'm already opening the door when I realise that wasn't Luke's usual *thump-thump-thump*.

'Oh . . .'

A tall guy with a duffel bag looks at me with dark blue eyes. They're fixed on my face for two seconds before they drop.

'Hello,' I finish.

'Hello. Sorry I'm late.' A northern accent.

I almost hold out my hand, but it stays put at my side. I smile instead. 'That's OK. Nice to meet you. I'm Tess.'

'Arran.'

It's silent, and I realise I'm blocking the doorway. 'Come on in,' I say, moving out of the way.

He hesitates. 'Should I take off my shoes?'

I glance at his desert boots. 'Nah, don't worry about that.'

He's still hesitant, as if wanting to do it anyway. But he steps inside and I push the door shut.

When I turn around, he's right behind me. I nearly bump into his backpack, expecting him to have moved further into the flat. But he's looking through the doorway to the living area. I wait, about to say something when he walks in, footsteps quiet.

He halts next to the sofa, duffel dangling from his fingers. It's navy with brown handles. A contrast to his vintage-worn jeans and dark teal cord jacket. Nineties revival. How is he not overheating in that?

He swivels round. Those eyes again. Something about them reminds me of a river – flow so soft it's almost imperceptible.

'You have a nice place,' he says.

'Thanks.'

'Quite lovely.'

I feel my brows twitch as I glance round. Lovely isn't how I think of this flat. Scruffy round the edges more like, with fossil floorboards and neat clutter. Though it does have that north-east London charm.

He blends in well. His wavy blond hair flops onto his temples, messy yet styled. His hands are big but with elegant fingers. There's something two-toned about him, as if he's hovering between edges. Confident-shy, intense-calm, muscular-slim. I'm not sure which.

I look up and he's watching me, a soft smile in his stubble. OK then: confident, not shy. And undoubtedly handsome.

I clear my throat. 'This is the living area, which you're free to use whenever you like. Same with the kitchen. There's an empty shelf for you in the fridge.'

He nods once. 'What's with the reptile?'

'The what?'

'The lizard.' He motions towards the floor.

I look down at the iron sculpture by the door. 'Oh, it's a gecko.'

'Hm.'

'I think it's supposed to be a boot scraper. Something my parents left behind.' I shrug. 'I needed something to keep the door open.'

'I see.' He leans down to get a closer look. 'Are you sure it's a gecko?'

'Yes.' Sixty per cent sure.

'Shouldn't it have pointier toes?'

'I don't think so.'

I've never looked at it that closely. Now that I am, it's actually quite ugly.

He straightens. 'All right. I trust you.'

A pause stretches between us.

He runs his fingers through the hair above his ear, then grips his backpack strap. 'I'm not going to ask about the T-Rex clock.'

I glance at the teethy dinosaur on the wall. No other guest has commented on either of these things before, and within two minutes he's pointed both out. I'm not sure if I like it or not. Most people aren't that observant, which generally works in my favour.

'I wouldn't,' I say.

'Funny story?'

'No. It's just my old clock from when I was a kid.'

'Which you still use.'

Not a question. Is he laughing at me? I search the humour in his eyes, but it's warm, not belittling.

'Don't worry,' he says, lifting the duffel bag onto his shoulder. 'I've still got my purple owl night-light.'

'Really?'

'Yeah, still glows and everything.'

I look at him, the casually balanced bag making him seem lopsided. There's something open and direct about him. Too open. I suddenly sense how close we are, standing over the gecko. I inhale and turn away. 'Come on, I'll show you the room.'

I twist my head to make sure he's following. He's there, behind me, steps silent. I push the spare bedroom door and go in.

'This is it,' I say.

Arran halts on the rug. He's side-on now, his face in profile. From this angle I notice the ski-jump tip of his nose and cleft chin. He makes me think of the beach – smooth white dunes, the sand warm between your toes.

The duffel bag drops from his fingers with a thump. 'Where have your parents gone?' he says.

'Sorry?'

'You said your parents left the gecko behind.'

'Oh . . .' Did I let that slip? 'They moved to Spain a few years ago.'

He takes his backpack off and gently places it down. 'How come?'

'My mum's Spanish. All her family are there so she wanted to go back.'

I look at the bags, wondering what's inside, waiting to be found.

He goes over to the window and feels the curtain. Then he glides it across, as far as the cloth will go. The room dims, losing its amber evening light.

He sits on the bed, bouncing the mattress with his weight. 'So you're all alone here?'

'What?' That's an odd question.

'In the UK – if your parents live in Spain?'

Rosie. The reminder a needle to my chest. She's supposed to be there, where he is, sitting on the bed. Smiling. Talking to me about a folk gig she'd just been to, or the nature of love, how many different ways there are to love and yet we have such a limited way of expressing it in language.

When I don't respond to Arran, he kneels down by his bags. My ears catch the sound: that squeaky-buzz of a zip. He's opened his duffel bag. His hand goes in and lifts out a T-shirt, then grips something else inside.

He pauses. Looks up at me. 'If it's OK, Tess, I'd like to get settled.'

'Sure,' I say, tugging my brain back. Bnb business. 'The Wi-Fi code and the keys are there on the desk. And the bathroom's just next door.' I point my thumb towards the wall. 'You can use the cupboard in there if you want.'

'Great, thanks. What about that?'

'What?'

He tips his head towards the other door, in the corner.

I glance at it. 'That's storage space. A cupboard where I keep some things.'

'Not for guest use?'

I shake my head.

'Good to know.' He goes back to his bag.

'Well, if you need anything, just ask.'

His lips are pressed together, widening his mouth. I turn and walk out, leaving the door ajar.

In the living area I pick up my beer. That was strange. The conversation so easy, about lizards and night-lights. Recently, talking to strangers has felt forced, an effort to listen and respond. Not with him.

I ruffle my T-shirt and take a swig of beer. It's airless in here.

A minute later there's a click: his bedroom door shutting.

* * *

When I get into bed that night, I haven't heard a single peep. He hasn't come out to use the kitchen or the bathroom. Any movements have been soundless. I'm drifting to sleep when I think I hear something, a scratch or a scuff. In the hallway? The wall? Our bedrooms share one, and it's thin.

I wait, listening, but there's nothing. Probably just wood expanding, or a pipe. Sometimes I wonder if there are sounds inside my head.

4

The gallery is hushed and cool. Temperature-controlled. The sweat from my short commute dried an hour ago but I can still feel it, cold on my skin. My body's out of balance. I rub my bare arms hard.

I'm sitting on a stool in my cubbyhole, staring at the photograph opposite. It's half a woman's face, eyelashes just visible, fingers in her hair. Black and white like all the others. Zoomed-in fragments. An exhibition called Women's Edges.

A chemical-cleaner smell hangs. There's a couple in the far corner. The only people in here. They start whispering, voices amplified by the lofty space.

The intercom in my hand goes off: a fuzzy female voice. I report no incidents. As if there ever would be – peak drama in this place is a gasp.

Two days a week I work as a gallery invigilator at the Barbican Centre. It was a mechanical thing. A reflex. One morning, without clear thought, I applied for a job. When I came for the interview, the manager stared at me, his pale eyebrows knitting.

'Haven't you worked here before?'

I shook my head. 'My sister.'

'Oh . . . yes, I remember now. Rosie?'

I needed to grip any rope I could reach – any thread of her. Make a seam between us and stitch over it.

The Barbican isn't one of the big-name galleries in London, but Rosie considered it a cut above what she deemed to be square, out-of-touch institutions. She loved how multicultural and progressive it is, crossing art forms and pushing boundaries, with a focus on interdisciplinary learning. More reflective of the real world developing around it, not stuck inside historical walls and canvases.

For me, it's the fact she spent hours in these rooms, her footsteps on the floors, rubbing her finger along her right cheekbone, just near the hint of blue eyeliner. She wore it almost every day, a subtle line on her lower lids. Until those last few months when she wore no make-up at all. Some days, I wanted to beg her to put that eyeliner on again.

I'm gazing at the wall, eyes focused on the sharp corner of a frame. Black point against white. Nothing's that clear-cut. I keep going over it, everything with Rosie, every look she gave me, everything she said – carving at memories, looking for clues.

There was one evening last year when we went to a Spanish bar on a cobbled street in Notting Hill run by a guy from Cádiz. I thought cold cerveza and an authentic Andalucían atmosphere might lighten her, refresh memories of summer holidays in Sevilla and Nerja.

It was a good day. Her mood was warmer as we sipped Alhambra beer and ate *pipas* – sunflower seeds in salted shells.

'You've started a life drawing class?' she said, as if she didn't believe me.

'Yeah.'

She slipped a *pipa* between her front teeth and cracked the shell open.

'What?' I frowned. 'You're the one who's always encouraging me.'

Her face smoothed. 'Really? You've been to a class?'

I nodded.

'Tess, that's great.'

Relief edged in. 'Is it?'

'Of course.' Her hand dropped onto my arm and squeezed. 'You know I want you to explore your talent. Biggest mistake of your life, giving up art at sixteen.'

There was a jokey note to her voice. My heart lifted at the touch of my sister's fingers. I could let my words flow a little looser.

'You could be right. Though I'm not sure bodies are my forte.'

She smiled, cracking another *pipa* in her teeth. 'Oh no?'

'No.'

'Knees, noses and toes – the hardest.'

'What about chins? Nobody warns you about chins.'

A ripple of happiness in my chest: she was laughing.

'I can see now why you stick to palm trees,' I said.

She elbowed me in the side. 'I'm very sophisticated.'

'I know. Sophisticated with a finger in her beer.'

She was trying to fish out a bit of sunflower shell that had flown into her glass. Her finger kept pushing it round. 'I can't get it out.'

The barman had noticed – he was smiling at her. He put glasses of *tinto de verano* in front of two girls and leaned on the bar to chat to them.

Rosie gave up, flicking the beer off her finger. She slouched against her chair and tilted her head backwards. Her face glowed in the lamplight from above.

'You just need practice,' she said. 'It'll come.'

'Sure, soon I'll be just like you with your paintbrush.' I mimed the action.

She'd lifted her hair into a handheld ponytail, arms up round her head. No reaction. I watched her, feeling the air between us sag. She let her hair drop down her back and started pushing her thumb into the *pipa* shells on the bar. A flat tone over her face.

'What did I say, Rosie?'

She didn't look at me. Just kept pressing at the shells, making them crackle. Then she got up from her chair. 'I'm going to the toilet.'

She walked off down the bar, disappearing into the low light round the corner.

I leaned forward and put my elbows on the counter. I couldn't understand. The frustration of it in my fists, knuckles digging into my cheek. What had I done? What was going on with my sister?

The cold white of the gallery makes me blink. *The barman*, I think. *What if it was the barman?* He was looking at Rosie a lot, he smiled at her. And – I remember now – his eyes had followed her as she walked past him.

I get my phone out of my pocket. I need to call Pettiford. The impulse is so strong my thumb is swiping the screen when I realise I can't. I'm not supposed to have my phone on me at work, and my voice would echo too loud.

I notice a text from my friend Nalika: *See you later. Really looking forward to it xx.* We're meeting for a drink this evening. I'm not in the mood, but I've already cancelled on her once. I'd much rather get home and unzip Arran's duffel bag. I didn't have a chance this morning; I slept through my alarm and had to run to work.

About to put the phone away, the screen lights up with another notification. I swipe and something inside my ribcage clenches. *New message from Oliver Barlow.*

I've been waiting days for that name to appear. My fingers feel weak gripping the phone. But I don't hesitate to open the message.

Please stop texting me.

Four words. I stare at them. Above, the message boxes are all the same colour – seven texts of mine in a row. Before I can stop myself, I'm typing a reply. I hit send and push the phone back into my pocket.

I gaze at the wall, rubbing the skin on my arms. The black and white portrait opposite blurs into grey. The woman's eyelashes merging while the words of my text stay bold.

I just want to talk.

5

I scrape my foot over the burgundy bricks of the Barbican's Lakeside Terrace. I don't know why they call it a lake – concrete pond is more accurate. A duck starts honking and flapping. I can feel sweat patches under my arms.

I look at my phone again. When I rang Pettiford, he said he was in the middle of something and would call right back. That was six minutes ago.

I scratch my left eye. I check my phone. That message from Oliver. *Please stop texting me.*

My phone rings. I jerk at the tremor and look at the screen: *Detective Sergeant Pettiford.*

'Hello?'

'Tess.' His deep chalky voice. 'Good evening.'

'Thank you for calling back.'

'That's OK. What was it you wanted to tell me?'

'I've remembered something. A night last year when Rosie and I were in a bar – the barman was looking at her.'

There's no background noise. Normally there are voices, other police officers talking, or subtle clinks of coffee mugs.

'Looking how?' he asks. 'Staring at her?'

'No . . . I wouldn't say staring.'

Specifics are important. That's what he said to me in the first few weeks, repeating it each time we talked, sinking it into me.

'It was more like glancing,' I say. 'He noticed her and smiled. Then a few minutes later he looked at her as she walked past, and again when we left.'

'Right, I see.'

Pettiford's tone is composed. His patient air filtering through radio signals. I can see him at his desk right now, papers in neat piles, mug always on a coaster. Wearing a white shirt and purple tie, brown hair receding.

'And who was he?' he says. 'This man – another customer?'

'No, the barman.' *As I already said.*

'Do you know his name?'

'No.'

'What did he look like?'

'He was Spanish. Black hair, brown eyes. With a beard.'

A scratching sound, pencil on notepad. 'Age?'

'About twenty-five.'

I hear him inhale, a wheezy breath. Then he sneezes. 'Excuse me, hay fever.' A rustly noise. He's probably using a tissue from the box on his desk. The one he keeps for people like me.

'And this was when?' he asks. 'Which month?'

'September, I think.'

Pencil scratching. 'Hm.'

Hm what? I want to say. But it was only a faint sound deep in his throat. I've heard it before. When he's thinking, when there are furrows in his brow.

'What was the name of the bar?'

'La Joya Roja, in Notting Hill.'

The pencil scratch goes quiet. 'OK, Tess. I can look into it.'

'Great.' I feel my arm muscles slacken.

Silence for a few beats.

'I'll be honest, though, I'm not sure it will lead anywhere.'

'How do you know? You haven't investigated it yet.'

'No.'

I wait. A *tick, tick, tick* inside my skull.

'From the details you've given, its relevance isn't apparent. It's worth pursuing at this stage, but I wouldn't like to give you false hope.'

Daniel Pettiford has a fireside voice. At first it seemed soothing, but now when I hear it – as he explains, retraces, consoles – it feels like my hand is too close to the flames.

'What about Oliver Barlow?' I ask.

'Rosie's ex-boyfriend?'

Who else?

'Tess, he has an alibi. There are no grounds to treat him as a suspect. As I've said before.'

'Surely he knows something.'

Other than me, he was the closest person to her. She broke up with him a few months before but he wouldn't let it go. He kept contacting her, bothering her.

Pettiford is quiet before he clears his throat. 'Let's keep things moving forward.'

I don't answer, staring at the rippled lake water.

'I'll keep you updated of course.'

A breeze swirls round the Barbican quad, hissing through the reeds.

'OK, Tess?' Pettiford says. 'I have another call I need to make. I'll be in touch.'

As I disconnect our call, I feel the familiar creep of cold disappointment. Low in my spine, following me around like back pain. It fades, duller at times. But then it flares, always from the same weak spot.

I stand there, doubt and frustration pulsing. It's a long shot but it *could* be him. The barman. He could have been there that night on Hampstead Heath. And Oliver – he's hiding something, I know it.

I arch my neck and look up at the sheet of early-evening sky. Woollen clouds drift over the buildings. Their white shapes are reflected in high-rise glass.

Nalika's late; it's almost six-thirty. I want to yank off my black shirt, this blow-dryer heat is too much. I'm thinking of dipping my feet into the lake when I hear her voice.

'Teresa Rivero Hartley!'

Nalika is striding towards me through the white benches, one hand gripping her handbag strap, other arm swinging. Her accordion skirt is lipstick red. Confidence blaring with each swish of material. I've always admired her bold colours, her indifference to fashion or trends. Her greatest pow-factor is her hair: straight down her back like a sword.

She opens her arms and encases me in a hug. 'Sorry I'm late.'

I breathe in her hairdresser smell. She only goes to the salon for the odd trim, yet somehow manages to waft that shampoo-scent around.

'Holy magnum, it's hot,' she says, holding my shoulders. 'You all right? You look a bit like roast turkey.'

'I need a drink.'

'Me too. Let's go.'

Five minutes later we're sitting in the shade of an umbrella with cucumber-infused gin and tonics. The green peelings coil through our glasses, offsetting the bitter tang.

The taste lights a lantern of memory – sitting on a wooden deck in Colombia with Rosie, looking out over the jungle. Sipping G&Ts and laughing about a monkey that had leapt onto the canopy walkway, making the man in front squeal.

'So, tale of the day,' Nalika says, shedding a layer to reveal skin and a skimpy vest. 'We were shooting this pancake stack and I'd just arranged the fruit and put a dollop of yoghurt on top. And when I reached for the maple syrup – the final flourish, you know – this little kid was drinking it. Literally pouring it down his gullet.'

I can't help but smile. She must have seen my expression as I stared at my G&T. The best thing about Nalika is she knows how to be normal. To not shuffle her feet around me or clear her throat in search of something to say.

'What was a kid doing on set?'

'Apparently he just got kicked out of nursery, so his mum had to drag him to work with her.' She shakes her head, sweeping her hair over the back of her chair. '*Maple* syrup. You know how much a bottle of that costs?'

Nalika is a food stylist. She spends her days arranging food and taking photos of it. Whenever anybody tries to make light of it, she spouts a fierce defence, arguing how much skill is involved. Most don't realise that she cooks it all herself.

She's an amazing chef, completely self-taught. The kind that glides round the kitchen in dresses and has no need for an apron. Sides always clean, onions chopped into mathematically perfect cubes. When I cook, there are spilt grains of rice from ripping the packet, pans boiling over.

In late January and February, in those first few weeks after Rosie's death, Nalika cooked for me. She knew I wasn't eating, so she'd make big batches of stew, curry and lasagne for the freezer. Often, she'd stand over me, force me to put the fork in my mouth. 'You have to eat, Tess. You're getting too thin.'

Her words a parrot-echo of mine as I sat with Rosie just a couple of months before, watching her until she'd swallowed something.

I pushed Nalika's food down my throat. But I couldn't taste any of it. Her restaurant-worthy meals were like card.

'Hey, what did you do to your hand?' Nalika asks, interrupting my thoughts.

I glance at my palm. The skin is crusted, scabby, still red with blood. 'Oh, I fell over running to catch a bus.'

Nalika looks at me from behind seventies-disc sunglasses, the lenses mirrored. I can't tell her the truth – that I grazed it on Tooting Common at two in the morning.

'Looks a bit grim.'

'Thanks,' I say.

'I mean it looks *painful*. Have you heard of first aid?'

'Yes, obviously.'

She purses her lips before sipping her drink. 'What about your job here at the Barbican – any children drinking syrup? Trying to chew on a painting?'

'No, thank God. Just respectful exhibition-goers and sweat-free rooms.'

'So you're enjoying it then?'

I shrug.

'And translation work – how's that going?'

'It's fine.'

I hate it a lot of the time, in truth. But I know I'm lucky to have it as a source of income, to have had that freelance work the last few months. If I wasn't bilingual, I'm not sure what I would have done, how I would have managed.

'Have you thought at all about going back to work at the Holcomb Group?' she asks.

I shake my head. 'I can't go back there.'

Until earlier this year I worked in financial PR. I thrived off the challenge, at my desk by seven-thirty, leaving after nine, nailing projects and getting promoted sooner than my colleagues. But after what happened to Rosie, smog settled around me. I'd blink and realise I'd been staring at a blank document for thirty minutes. I'd drift from the coffee machine to the printer and sit at the wrong desk. It was like strings slipped down from above and hooked themselves into me. Someone else steering.

Nalika spins the bracelet on her wrist. 'You were so good at it, though. Such a jammy PR dodger.'

She's nudging, an unwelcome pressure. But I can't do the things I did before.

'You know,' she says loudly. 'Viv, our intern, bloody loves Jammie Dodgers.'

'Oh yeah?'

'Yeah, buys them all the time. A grown woman obsessed with chewy childhood biscuits.'

I smile at my friend. Noticing the uncomfortable shift of my body, she switches to Viv the intern and biscuits.

'I can't remember the last time I had one,' I say. 'They were so good though.'

'Not anymore – not as much jam as there used to be. And they're about half the size. Another thing that's getting shitter.'

She plonks her handbag on the table and starts rifling inside the black leather. A small box with a picture of a camel drops beside her glass, followed by a lighter.

'I thought you'd given up.'

She slides a cigarette between her lips. 'You sound like my mother. Pretending to my parents is enough of a bore.'

Nalika's parents are committed Hindus, and her brazen personality has always clashed with their expectations and values. They're two of the sweetest, caring people I've met though – not at all the tyrannical picture she often draws.

She flicks at the lighter, noticing my expression. 'I'm allowed one a day, OK?'

I give in as she inhales her first drag.

'Besides, if anyone has a bone to pick, it's me.'

'Why?'

'For flaking on me last time. And then not replying to my messages.'

Her tone is light, only half-serious, but this is her hitting back. No point arguing – because she always wins.

'I know. Sorry.'

'Silence for almost two weeks. You had me worried, Hartley.'

Her sunglasses are like fly eyes. I wish she'd take them off.

'I was thinking of ringing your mum. But then I realised she'd have even less idea where you were or what you were up to.'

Nalika doesn't know about my night wanderings. Nobody does. And it has to stay that way – no one can find out. Not Pettiford, and definitely not Nalika. If she did, she'd shout at me, tell me I was fucking crazy and probably insist on sleeping over at my flat. She'd try to stop me.

'You were right,' I say. 'Would have been a wasted phone call.'

A plane drawls through the sky.

Nalika blows smoke slowly from her lips. 'When was the last time you spoke to your parents?'

'Dunno. A few weeks ago.'

I spin my glass, making the light-pattern on the table swirl, the sun refracting through crystal.

'Do you know when they're next coming back to the UK?'

'No.'

I can feel her concern saturating the air between us.

'They're dealing with their grief in their own way,' I say. 'I understand.'

'*I* don't. Who stops talking to their daughter? Asks her not to call. Not to come to Spain.' She thumps back against her chair. 'It grates my goat.'

She's always said that phrase wrong. A Nalika-ism I've given up trying to correct.

'You know why it is, Nalika.'

'Yeah, yeah,' she says, waving her cigarette hand. 'It's too painful. They can't be near you or London because it reminds them too much of Rosie.' Her tone compresses, reciting my own words. 'Doesn't change the fact they're being selfish.'

'My mum's having therapy, apparently. That's what she told me in her last text. Her doctor is treating this as personal trauma.'

'What about your trauma?'

I fix my gaze on the table, willing her not to suggest I try therapy. I can't have that conversation again. Another plane flies overhead. Nalika's silence is noisier than the unseen metallic drone.

'It's not cool,' she mutters. 'I've a good mind to fly over there and give them both a smack.'

It bothers me less than it ought to, my parents being in Spain. And what they said to me before they got on the plane after the funeral. What my mum said. Because my dad wasn't talking, he just stared at the floor. He couldn't look at me. He couldn't wait to go back to a country she'd had to drag him to seven years ago. I could sense it as I hugged him good-bye. And my mum – desperate, face rubbed raw by tissues – gripped my hand and whispered those words, her voice like cracked clay.

We'd disagreed about where the funeral should be. My mum wanted it to be in Spain, she wanted Rosie near our family, buried near our home. But I said this was Rosie's home. She was born in England, she'd lived here most of her life. My dad quietly supported my mum, even though I had the sense he agreed with me. My mum was angry. But I wouldn't budge. I was closest to Rosie, and I was sure she would have wanted to be here.

Since then, in cold night moments, awake in the dark, I've questioned whether that's true. If Rosie would have preferred to be in Spain. If I was as close to my sister as I thought.

'It's fine,' I say to Nalika. 'They've been gone so long the distance feels normal.'

Smoke curls up past her face.

'And I want to be here, in London. I need to be.'

'I don't like to think of you being so alone, that's all.' Nalika's voice is quieter.

'I'm not alone. I have you. And my bnb guests.'

'Oh yes, I forgot. Your house squatters.'

I sip my drink. The gin is tart on my tongue. Another flicker of memory surfaces, our feet side-by-side on the rail, Rosie's toes longer than mine but our nails painted the same colour.

'I don't know how you do it,' Nalika sighs. 'Having strangers in your place, making your kitchen dirty, blocking the shower drain with their hairs.' She's mentioned this before.

'It's quite easy. They pay me a big whack of money.'

'There is that.' She taps ash into the tray with one sharp finger.

'I've just got a new guest.'

'Where from?'

'He's English, though he looks kind of Scandinavian.'

'*Does* he now? Correction – I'd be willing to put up with pubey drains for a handsome Scandi.'

My finger stops twisting in my hair and strands slip out.

'How old is he?' Nalika asks.

'About our age, I think. Difficult to tell exactly.'

'Interesting.' Her eyebrows flick above her sunglasses. 'And what's he like?'

I look at her, at her dark blue nails, cigarette perched between them, a strange feeling coming on. I'm not sure why, but I don't want to talk about Arran.

'He only arrived last night,' I say.

'Hmm, you'll have to keep me updated.'

The breeze fans past Nalika and I catch her fruity hair-salon scent again. 'Let's talk about you for a change.'

'Nah, boring.'

'No, let's. How's Chris?'

She squashes the cigarette into the ashtray. 'We broke up actually.'

'*What?*' My tone rises a couple of decibels. 'You're not serious?'

'I am.' She drains her G&T, ice jangling inside the glass. 'It's not a big deal. I'm fine with it.'

I stare at her. It's been Nalika and Chris for five years. I thought they were going to get married. 'When?'

'Nearly a month ago.'

A month? That proves how far I've drifted. How far I've let our friendship slip. I feel a pinch of guilt, deep in my side. Nalika is like granite – the rock that's stayed hard and firm underneath me while my other friends crumbled away. A group from university, after graduating we all moved to London, going to clubs, parties, dinners. But what happened to Rosie made me shrink back. I stopped going out, stopped calling or texting. And now they have too.

Except Nalika.

'But . . . why didn't you tell me?' I ask.

Her shoulders lift as she extracts the cucumber from the ice. 'I didn't want to bother you with it.' She bites into the pale green ribbon. 'It's no big deal,' she repeats. 'It was time.'

'Why? What happened?'

'It just wasn't working anymore. No passion. We felt like friends.'

'Was it mutual then?'

She's still chewing cucumber. 'Sort of. Though I started the conversation.'

'I'm sorry, Nalika. I . . .' I don't know what to say. I've been so consumed by myself, by Rosie. Sucked into a current I can't swim out of.

'It's OK, Tess.'

'It's not.'

I glance at the sky. It's a beautiful evening, the sun arcing down below the buildings.

'Tess.' Nalika touches my arm. She's taken off her sunglasses, her deep-set eyes looking straight at me. 'Is there any news? Any progress with the police?'

I shake my head.

'So there are no leads? Still no evidence or suspects?'

The backs of my eyes start to sting. 'No. But it could be this guy . . . this barman I remember looking at her.'

Nalika semi-smiles. 'That's something.'

'Pettiford's already poured cold water on the possibility. I don't know why I bother. Sometimes I wonder whether he's on my side. On Rosie's side.'

She's quiet.

'It's been over four months,' I continue. 'How have they not caught the guy? Not got *any* further?'

Her chin is resting on her fist. Sadness gleaming in her eyes. 'I don't know.'

A lump pushes into my throat, hard and acidic. *I don't know.* That's all people ever say, like birds lining up on a wire, squawking down at me. If I could reach, I'd grab them by the wings, press their beaks shut until they can't make another sound.

When I think of Tess, I always think of her shadow. It was the first thing I saw, falling across my feet. Darkening my toes. Something liquid about it, long and curving from her body. That's how it always is. Stretched between us, blackening the sunlit ground.

6

I'm out of breath. Nearly home. The moon is a white shell against the deepening blue of sky. Anticipation is building as I approach my door. Maybe Arran won't be in. Maybe I can have a snoop in his room.

As soon as I step inside there's the smell of baking bread. I halt, surprised, then head into the living area. No sign of Arran. But that smell. Opening the oven, I'm hit with warm air. On the shelf is a round loaf, crusty brown. I can't believe he's been *baking* – most guests barely use the kitchen. Just a small bottle of milk in the fridge or evidence of a takeaway in the bin.

When I go back into the hallway, his bedroom door's ajar. I can't see him in there. I lean round the frame and the space is empty. Out, it seems. He can't have left that long ago, if the oven's still warm. Unless he set a timer.

I don't waste time wondering. I sneak into the room.

At first glance there are only a few signs of occupancy – a small travel clock on the bedside table, a tube of hand cream, laptop on the desk. I run my fingers over the matte metal. It's cold. Beside it is a pencil. The top end is splintered, as if it's been snapped off.

I open the laptop. Password protected.

His duffel bag is at the foot of the bed, zipped shut. I check the wardrobe first, in case he's unpacked. There are two things hanging: a set of peach-red towels, and a garment carrier with a navy suit inside. I pause – he didn't have any suits or carriers with him when he arrived. Did he?

Sometimes details seem slippery. Things I think I can remember, but they're like soap. There's no grip and I'm not sure if I made them up, or perhaps missed something altogether.

I push away the doubt. The duffel bag awaits.

I check the door, listen for a second, then kneel and slide the zip. I almost expect it to catch, but it flows right to the other end. So accessible. Some guests padlock their suitcases. Others have all their stuff arranged in travel storage bags. Others leave passports and money lying around. Arran seems near the middle of the scale.

This is the best bit. What will my fingers brush against in the dark?

Once I remember reaching in and feeling something scratchy. My hand flew out again, a reflex with that spark of fear. But when I looked closer it was just a squashed straw hat. That was Fillip, a guy from Poland who wore socks with sandals.

I feel around in Arran's bag.

Clothes, folded in stacks, which is unusual for a soft bag. But no bother – I'm always careful not to disturb the order of things, putting them back in the right place.

To leave no trace is quite a skill.

The first time, with my very first guest, Jasmine, I wasn't careful enough. She noticed that her facial wipes weren't inside her make-up bag, where she always kept them, and pointed this out while putting white chocolate spread on a rice cake. I told her I'd gone in to close the window when it started raining, and accidentally knocked the make-up bag on the floor.

Since then, I don't make mistakes.

I lift out a pile of Arran's shirts. Underneath there are T-shirts and tops, a beaded leather belt, an apple, striped swimming trunks, jumpers, a wooden comb. At the bottom is a selection of trousers – jeans, cords, chinos. A washbag is wedged at one end. Inside are bathroom staples including a retainer, a well-used toothbrush and fennel toothpaste, which sounds disgusting.

I pause for a moment, spine-straight, listening for sounds or movements of Arran. But there are none.

My fingers go for the separate pouches at either end of the bag. In one are socks and underwear. Nice boxers, loose cotton and colourful, with prints of elephants, flamingos and water-melons. The opposite pouch holds one pair of shoes – white trainers. The others are against one wall, in a row: desert boots, suede loafers, Birkenstocks.

I check underneath the duffel bag, in corners and creases, between the piles. I scour it all twice. Then I sit back on my heels. Seriously – that's it?

Disappointment leaks in. I don't know what I expected to find. Just *something*. Arran Cole, baker, owl night-light user. What are your secrets? What have you got tucked away somewhere?

Everyone has something they keep out of sight.

I check the desk drawers. Bare. I look under the bed. Nothing. I kick the duffel. It's only when I start putting every-thing back into the bag that I notice something caught inside a pair of boxers. I extract it from the turtle-print material and stare at this light object in my palm, neatly coiled. Two wooden pegs with a circle of wire between them.

This is a bit weird. A cheese cutter? Maybe he works in a deli. Or maybe it's for cutting something else.

There's a feeling in my stomach – a faint froth of fear. I unwind it, pulling the wire taut between my hands, still unsure what this object is, and why he'd have it with him.

After a moment I loop it back up, return it to the turtle boxers and replace all the piles, resetting the duffel at the correct angle.

Still no sign of Arran, I stand in the centre of the room, slowly rotating. Something about the wardrobe catches. Maybe that suit carrier. I go and have another look. Pushing the suit and towels aside, I see another bag. His backpack.

It has a pin buckle and a flap over the top. The buckle's undone – all I have to do is lift the flap.

I peer into the sack, nudging things about. There's a stainless-steel water bottle, a plastic bag scrunched up into a ball, a book on ceramics. In a small pouch are some plasters and tweezers. At the back of the main section is a laptop pocket. When I ease it forward, I spot something down at the bottom.

I pull it out. Thin between my fingers, light brown with a soft paper cover. A notebook.

I toy with the idea of not opening it. This is next level invasion of privacy. I should put it back and leave the room. But my thumb is already lifting the cover.

There's a thud below – the street door shutting. Footsteps coming up the stairs.

My heart thumps against my ribs. I drop the book into the rucksack, push it back behind the peach towels and dart out. I've just made it into the hall when the front door swings. Arran sees me as he's wiping his feet on the mat.

'Evening, Tess.'

'Hey.' My heart is still thumping. Adrenaline flowing round my body.

He smiles. 'I'm making some sourdough, as you can probably tell.'

He goes into the kitchen. I linger in the corridor, composing myself. He seems casual, no inkling that I've been in his room or touched his things. No suspicion. The oven door clunks as I take a deep breath and follow him.

Arran's beside the counter, tea towel slung over his shoulder. The rustic loaf on the chopping board.

He wipes his hands on the towel. 'Should let it cool down more, but I'm too impatient. Would you like some?'

'Oh no.' I'm still flustered. 'I mean, it's yours.'

'Please, it's for you as well. Bread should be eaten fresh.'

He opens a drawer and takes out the bread knife, finding it without needing direction. The smell's stronger, sweeter, released from the oven. I brush my knuckle over my damp upper lip. Arran looks cool and composed, not a gleam of sweat on him. I watch him cutting smooth slices. His hand is splayed over the loaf, long fingers stretched wide. He has incredible buttercream skin.

'There's apricot jam here too,' he says, indicating a jar with a chequered lid.

He takes a slice but doesn't touch the jam. Instead, he moves along the counter and drizzles on some extra virgin olive oil. The bottle's new, the crick of the lid giving it away. A Greek brand I haven't heard of, and organic.

I hesitate. I'm starving – Nalika and I didn't get any food, and the aroma is making my mouth water.

He's leaning against the side, chewing, watching me. 'Honestly, Tess, have some.'

As if on cue, a gurgly sound comes from my stomach.

Arran laughs. 'You have to eat it now.'

'Fine,' I say, smiling. 'I've been betrayed, so why not?'

I go over and spread jam on a piece. Strangely aware of his legs slanting down beyond my elbow, and how he's probably still watching me. I step back as I take a bite. The bread's warm in my fingers, the gooey jam spurting onto my tongue. Delicious.

'You like the crust?' he says.

'What?'

'The end piece?'

I look down at my hand. I took the crust without thinking. Rosie's favourite part of bread. She'd cut off her crusts like other people, but instead of discarding them, she would save them until the end. When we were teenagers, I'd sometimes take a bite out of one to annoy her. She'd either chuck it at me, laughing, or calmly cut off my saliva.

I swallow, the crust scraping down my throat. 'Yes. The best bit.'

'I beg to differ,' he says, flapping a middle piece and pressing his thumbs into the pale centre. 'Look at that. Light 'n' fluffy.' He picks up the knife I left in the jar and spreads jam carefully to the edges. I'm watching his hands again. I can imagine them on my body, fingers gliding down my back.

I step past him to get to the window. I need some air. A pigeon's sitting on a windowsill opposite. Top floor. A hand appears through the open gap and it flaps away.

When I turn back, Arran's sprinkling white crystals on his slice.

'What are you doing?' I blurt.

'What?'

'Is that sea salt?'

His hand's hovering. 'Yes, why?'

'You're putting *salt* on jam?'

'Yes. Haven't you ever done it before?'

'No.'

'Oh, you gotta try it.' He sweeps his palms together, then cuts off a corner and holds it out to me.

I take it. Our fingers don't touch.

I eye the white flakes before biting. The salt melts into the apricot, making the sweetness pop. 'Wow,' I say. 'Who knew.'

Arran laughs. 'Told you.'

I grab another piece of bread and start slathering on jam.

'Don't hold back.' Arran's voice is light-hearted – teasing.

'Sorry,' I say. 'It's too good.'

I shower salt on and take a big bite. There's a smile in his eyes, the dark colour shining.

Jam drips onto my thumb and I lick it off. His gaze glides over my mouth, catching on my thumb as it slips out. A split-second eye movement, but I see it. Spirals of attraction in my chest.

'Who made this jam?' I ask.

'My mum.' He says it freely. Then his expression turns sheepish. 'She sends me boxes of goodies sometimes.'

'You mean care packages?'

'S'pose so, yep.'

'When you're what – in your late twenties?'

His eyebrows lift. 'Thirty-one, actually. No shame.'

Thirty-one. The same age as me, which somehow feels significant. He doesn't look it. There are crinkles round his eyes when he smiles, but they barely leave a mark.

He pushes off the counter and wanders towards the living area. 'Who painted this?'

His head is tilted back, standing below the big canvas above the fireplace. It shows a glass-walled room, all corners and slanting lines, with spiky succulents and palm trees – their white shadows stretching off the edge. Seventies Florida-Cuba vibe. A chair near the centre, at water's edge, split between outside and inside. That's what she was exploring – the cross between interior and exterior.

'It's beautiful,' Arran says.

The bread's stuck in my throat, a lump of stodge. 'It's . . .' I don't want to say her name. This blocking feeling, as though the bread is pressing on my voice box. 'It's my sister's.'

'Oh? Wow.'

I fill a glass and gulp water, pushing the bread down. Arran's still looking up at the painting.

'I really like it,' he says. 'She's got great style.'

His hands are in his pockets, relaxed, elbows open. Slowly I move to stand next to him. Unbidden, an image of Rosie in her studio: the huge warehouse windows throwing sunlight across her easel, the long shadows like the ones on her canvas. Only the shadows she'd painted were white. Empty.

That's what she felt like to me: white shadows. As though a palette knife was secretly scraping her out from the inside. Leaving behind these gaps she couldn't refill.

I remember one night, leaping out of a taxi, asking the driver to wait. My eyes searching for her, probably on the ground. Splinters of fear in my gut. It was three in the morning, and she'd called me half an hour earlier. What if she wasn't here? What if she'd moved, or something had happened to her? But then I saw her sitting on the pavement, her back against a postbox.

'Rosie! What are you doing?'

I crouched beside her, gripping her shoulder. Her eyes reminded me of a pony's: gentle and wary.

'I just felt like sitting down.'

'Why? You're in the street. Look, your skirt's all dirty.'

She shrugged.

'Come on, let's get you home.'

Her legs didn't move, firmly crossed.

'You can't sit here,' I said, glancing around, conscious of someone loitering outside the corner shop. 'It's not safe.'

She'd turned away from me again. I tucked her hair behind her ear, to see her face.

'No one cares,' she said.

'I do.' I took her hand, trying to guide her upwards. 'Please, Rosie. Let's go. The taxi's waiting.'

She wouldn't get up.

The next day – sitting on her sofa when I'd finally got her home and into bed – I stared at those white shadows in her paintings. The same ones I'm looking at right now.

'Has she done any exhibitions?' Arran's voice murmurs.

My fingers are curled into my palms, nails biting in. 'A couple. Once at the London Art Fair.'

'I'm envious of that.'

I glance at him. 'Are you an artist?'

'Sort of.' His feet shift and he runs a hand through his hair. 'I'm a graphic designer, though really I want to be a ceramicist.'

Ah, that explains the wire cutter. For clay.

'Did you study ceramics?' I ask.

'No, graphic design.' His hand drops from his hair and slips back into the pocket of his jeans. 'But I've always practised pottery. I did it in the evenings after school.'

'So you work in graphic design?'

'Yes. I do some freelance projects for a company that has recently moved down here from Leeds.'

'Is that where you're from? Leeds?'

'Just outside.' He smiles. 'Yorkshire born and bred.'

That's his accent then. It's subtle, I couldn't quite place it.

'But as I said,' he continues, 'I want to set up as a ceramicist, get a website going. That's the dream anyway.'

Wind blows in through the open windows and I catch Arran's scent. It's coconutty, with hints of sun lotion.

'What about you?' he says.

'What about me?'

'Are you an artist?'

My mouth opens before I answer. 'No, not really.'

'Not really? What does that mean?'

He's angled a little more towards me. My shoulder is close to his upper arm. Why am I so aware of his body? His proximity?

'I've done a bit of art,' I say. 'Life drawing, painting. But my sister's the artist.'

'Who says?'

I feel my brow crease.

'I mean, who says you're not an artist?'

'No one . . .' I pause. 'I'm just not that good.'

'I'm sure that's not true.'

When he blinks, I realise our gazes have been locked for seconds. Too long. I look away first, walking back towards the kitchen.

'So where is your sister?' Arran asks behind me.

Blood pulses in my neck. I don't talk to people about Rosie – about where she is, about what happened. Only

Nalika and Pettiford and the other police officers on her case. In the first couple of months my mum would call for updates, demanding answers in brisk Spanish, but she grew quieter as I repeated the same thing. No solid conclusions. No convictions. One day in April when I rang her she asked me to stop. She couldn't listen to it any longer. *Don't call until you know – until you have facts, hija.* I haven't spoken to her since.

'What do you mean?' I say to Arran.

He's beside the bread again, a beige linen bag in his hand. 'Just that you didn't mention her yesterday. Is she in Spain as well?'

'Oh . . . no. She's in Australia.'

'On holiday?'

'No.' My hands are clenched into fists again. 'A one-year visa.'

'Lucky her.'

My heart twitches. I don't know why I'm lying.

'You really are all alone here.'

I look up from the floorboards. Arran's wiping crumbs into the bin, his back to me. Did he just say that?

A fly buzzes from somewhere, droning towards the food. It lands on the jammy knife. Arran waves it off, drops the knife in the dishwasher, then starts putting the bread away in the linen bag.

'I'll save you the end from now on.' He winds the linen strap round the folded material and ties it into a bow. 'Please have as much as you want.'

It feels like that lump of bread has lodged back in my throat.

He pats his palms on his thighs, resting them there. 'Well, I've got an early-ish start in the morning. Goodnight, Tess.'

He's walking out when I answer. 'Goodnight.'

I gaze into the doorway's empty space, my forehead tight. That was strangely intimate. Sharing bread and apricot jam and talking about Rosie's painting – so different to other guests.

It's been a long time since I had this sense of something with a man. Something more than surface chat. Even with my last boyfriend, Matthew, looking back, it somehow didn't go that deep. Rosie didn't approve of how quickly we moved in together, and she was right. It ended almost a year ago, after the realisation that he was never really listening to me. Since then, a man's touch has been a memory.

I hold the backs of my fingers against the linen bag. Still warm.

Arran's oil is behind, next to the balsamic vinegar and sweet chilli sauce. I'm looking at the olive tree on the label when I notice that my olive oil's not there. I had a litre bottle from Andalucía, and there was at least half left. Did Arran use it? Or throw it away?

I check the bin but there's no bottle in there. Nor in any of the cupboards. An uneasy feeling slides in my abdomen. The one thing I don't like about having bnb guests: when they move things.

His bedroom door shuts, the soft sound reminding me of the notebook. The uneasiness slides higher, mixing with anticipation, a need to know what's inside.

7

The door hovers, just at that point when the hinges sound – a pitchy scrape.

Arran left the flat about ten minutes ago. When I went towards the guest room, there was no light reaching through the doorframe. Now I see why: the curtains are drawn. I go over and open them. The sky is pasty, the clouds close to the rooftops.

I open the wardrobe and push past the peach towel. The backpack is here, but when I poke inside, the notebook's not. My fingers can't find it. Only a silky texture. When I pull it out – ribbon. A dark bronze colour. Thin, with a torn end. I look closer, noticing something else, dangling from between my fingers. A strand of hair. Long and fair. The same colour as Arran's, but clearly not his. A woman's.

I gaze at it, gleaming in the sunlight, my mind following its wavy form. Wondering whose head it came from, how it got into his backpack. Maybe someone gave him the ribbon, and the hair was caught in it. Maybe her hair simply fell onto the bag and found its way inside. I've found my hairs in weird places. My jacket pocket, inside a packet of pasta.

Even so, a woman's hair in his backpack is curious. A girlfriend perhaps? A one-night stand? A friend? So many possibilities, even a stranger passing him in a public place.

The ribbon itself is a question mark. Why he has it, what it means to him.

I leave speculation in the background as I return the ribbon and the hair to his backpack.

The notebook. I try his duffel bag again, feeling around the clothes. I pull open the bedside table drawer. Empty.

The book's not here. Did he take it with him?

Frustration creeps into my jaw. I want to open that book, see what he might have written or marked on the pages.

At the window, the air is muggy. There's a girl in her garden. Stretched out, her back against the grass, arms and legs wide.

I look at my palm – at the graze from Tooting Common. It's now dark and blotched. Itchy since that night. I scratch at it, pulling off bits of scab. Pain throbs through. The pink flesh turns red, weeping blood.

* * *

Unscrewing the bottle, I drop the lid and swig. The wine is thick, a dark taste in my mouth. Red and cheap. I picked it up in a twenty-four-hour corner shop without even looking at the label. The store was empty. Slow business at two in the morning. When I went to pay, a man in the back was watching me, eyes gleaming from the shadows.

I walk into the road and follow the white lines down the middle. My throat is dry. I swallow another mouthful of wine.

I've been roaming the streets for over two hours. I was in the flat all day, trying to do translations, but as the afternoon wore on, I couldn't concentrate. Dejection rising like water in a bath. I had to get out.

I went to a bar and sat in the corner sipping double vodka sodas. The place had that stale-beer smell. Everyone else in groups, in couples. I watched them, how the men leaned into the women, found ways to touch them, their eyes sliding over their bodies.

And I texted Oliver again, although his name hasn't appeared since that message: *Please stop texting me.* (Yesterday, 16:21)

My responses: *I just want to talk.* (Yesterday, 16:22)

Please, Oliver. (Yesterday, 22:34)

What's so difficult about talking? (Today, 14:08)

There's something I need to ask you. It's important. (Today, 21:23)

But nothing.

I can feel the hot weight of my phone in my pocket. The last text I sent was twenty minutes ago, just before I bought the wine.

Get over yourself. Rosie's dead. She's DEAD and you're alive. Why is that?

My thumb hovered over the send button before I pressed it. He deserves it. He's turned his back on me. The one other person who was close to Rosie. Who was weaved into her life, and possibly her death. He could have been there that night.

I drink more wine.

I have no destination in mind. But my feet have mechanically walked – I know where I'm going to end up. A pull I can't avoid.

The tarmac turns to grass as I step onto Hampstead Heath.

There are no lamps here. I start up the slope and walk into solid dark. It's thicker under the trees but my feet know the route. Each time I blink, inky shapes disappear and reform. I duck too late and scrape the top of my head on a branch.

My footsteps seem loud, soles scuffing the dry earth. Twigs crack. I don't glance around; I don't look behind. If there's anyone else here – teenagers making out in the bushes, the homeless, skulking men – they're undetectable.

The moon is bright in the sky, a headtorch through the branches. But it barely reaches the heath.

The wine bottle dangles in my hand, cold against my thigh. My breathing changes as I get closer, the air in my lungs tighter. There's that dank smell. The patch of soil that always seems to be moist, as if water is rising from below.

I reach a cluster of trees and stop beneath an oak. It's old and knobbly. Moss fuzzes round the base, a low branch curls out of the trunk beside me. The word CLIMB is carved into the bark above my head. I know this even though it's too dark to see.

I sit down between two big, curved roots and draw air deep into my nose. I swear I can smell it. Rosie's perfume. As though it's lasted all these months. A warm base with a sharper note on top, like lemon sorbet.

Yet it can't be here. It's been months, the police tape long gone.

The ground is still warm – I can feel it on my legs, the sun's heat lingering. When it happened, the ground was cold. There was frost on the grass. She was lying right here. This is where that middle-aged dog walker found her shortly after dawn. Where the paramedics crouched next to her, then pronounced her dead.

I swig from the bottle. The wine sticks in my throat, my head thick with it.

Was it the dog that smelled her first? Did she feel its nose sniffing in her hair? The woman with the dog said Rosie was unconscious, but she could have had some sensory perception. She could have still been alive at that point. If only she'd been found sooner. In winter, in January, the sun doesn't come up until around eight o'clock. She was out here for hours, probably the whole night.

Rosie called me that evening. She rang me three times. The log showing missed calls at 21:37, 21:50 and 22:18. Those times are burned behind my eyes. After the second one, at 21:50, she left me a voicemail. I've listened to it hundreds of times, I can remember it word for word. Every pitch and dip of her voice.

'Tess? Tess, are you there? I . . . I want to talk to you. I'm sorry I've shut you out. I'm sorry for everything. I'd just really like to hear your voice.' She coughs. 'I don't feel good. I feel like I'm reaching a point . . . I don't know. Everything's so screwed up. I want to be honest with you, I don't know why I haven't. We used to tell each other everything, didn't we?' A foot scraping. A loud sniff. 'God, I've had a horrible evening. And I think there's some—'

It cuts out. Right there. 'I think there's some—'

What was she going to say? Some*thing*? Some*one*? And that sniff – it sounded like she was crying.

Where was I? Why didn't I answer? Or call her back? Questions that have repeated so many times in my head they don't sound like questions anymore.

I was with some guy I'd met in a bar. It was our third date and I'd gone back to his place. In his bed, my phone in the next room, I didn't hear her calls. I didn't see them until the morning.

I know why my dad couldn't look at me the whole time he was here in England for the funeral. Because he blames me. I failed Rosie because I missed her calls. If I hadn't, she could still be alive.

The guilt is like a shard of glass in my abdomen. Stuck deep between two organs.

I want to hear her voice in my ear, chattering at me like she used to. I want to call her. But I can't even do that. When I try her number, it doesn't ring. No sound, no voicemail. As if her phone's dead too.

Where is it? Another echo of a question.

When they found her here, she had nothing on her. Only clothes. T-shirt and jeans – no rips, no blood. Unmarked other than dirt from where she'd been lying. She didn't even have a coat. Nowhere to hold her phone.

I searched for it everywhere, combing the grass and streets around the heath. The police found her purse and her bag in her bedroom. But not her phone. If we had it, it would be evidence. There might be something on it that would lead somewhere – messages, pictures, notes. Scraps Pettiford could use.

It's possible she lost it. Dropped or left somewhere. But it's also possible someone took it. Purposefully dismantled, smashed. Evidence destroyed.

There aren't even any digital scraps, because she didn't have a smartphone – no cloud, no data floating around, no social media. She hated *all that cyberspace crap*, as she put it.

There were things Rosie hadn't told me. And in her voice-mail, it sounded like she might have been about to. But I didn't call her back.

How do you define killing? Without witnesses, or evidence, the act is shaded. An imprecise thing. It's like there's a figure behind a window, breathing on the glass. I can see it. *Him*. But his breath has misted it up and I can't make out his face. Only an obscure smile.

I thought the carving on the tree could be something – a clue – but the police said it's been there for years. I thought he might be back, that maybe he prowls the heath. I've been coming here for four months. At night and in the day. Watching, waiting. But he hasn't shown himself again. He hasn't come after me. No one has.

* * *

I'm still here, curled up in the dirt, as the sky begins to lighten. The sun draws muted colour over the heath, shapes emerging from the grey. There's a dark red patch in the earth. And on my skirt. Wine, spilt, the bottle on its side.

The ground beneath me is cold now, I can feel it crawling into my skin.

What is she up to? Swarthy gal. Night wanderess.

In a skirt strangely the colour of smoked trout – not quite orange, not quite rust or pink. There's a hole in the back she doesn't seem to have noticed. A split that stretches open with each movement of her left leg. Flashing a tiny diamond of thigh.

White shoelaces undone, too. Stained from being walked on. Her feet are classically dainty (slender ankles I could get my fingers round) but her heels stomp, normally. Not so much now, ambling and swaying about. Obviously drunk.

Trouble likes her. I might have said she likes trouble, but I feel it's the other way round. As if there's metal inside her body she doesn't know about, drawing in the cold, the sharp, things that can cut. She's so unaware of eyes on her face. Of what's behind. No idea I was close enough to touch her hair.

She's also stupid, boring me with her predictability. At night, she leaves her window open. She thinks she's safe on the first floor.

All these invitations. The sweat that sits between her shoulder blades – one of them lower than the other, like a broken wing. And her emotions. She's so bad at hiding them, she doesn't know how. I like it when she cries, eyes smudged and cheeks wet: that's when she's most compelling.

8

My head feels heavy and congealed. When I try to swallow my tongue gets stuck, rough and dry. The curtains are open but the light in my room is faint, a draining quality to it.

Fumbling for my phone on the floor, the clock reads 17:08. I must have slept all day. And no messages, no missed calls. I flop onto the pillow.

I don't remember the journey home, how I got back, or what time. The wine and the vodka mixing, creating black in my brain.

My phone vibrates. Oliver? Pettiford? The screen glares in my eyes, the name Luke in bold letters. *Hey neighbour-stranger. Hope you're feeling better? We should hang out sometime* ;) *x*

That's weird. How does he know how I feel?

I lie very still for a while and the skull-pounding wanes. I need to drink something; it hurts to swallow.

I feel dizzy as I walk slowly through to the living area. Once I've downed a glass of water, I check my phone again. Tapping on Oliver Barlow's name, scanning our text bubbles. The last six are mine. The final one last night just before 2 a.m.: *Get over yourself. Rosie's dead. She's DEAD and you're alive. Why is that?*

I stare at my words. How can he just ignore me? The anger feels like a virus in my chest, inflamed cells dividing again and again. I type a text fast, to Pettiford: *Any news on the Spanish barman? Any other updates?*

I think back, skimming my memories. I scroll through old texts. One from Rosie reads: *Fucking fate. Life can be so irritating.*

That was in June last year. I'd replied: *What do you mean fucking fate?*

Her answer: *Just stupid stuff. This guy at the Barbican being an asshole. Why are some people so shit to each other?*

My reply: *Dunno. Maybe we should rename ourselves bastard beings?*

Rosie: *I'll say. This other guy just took the last cinnamon swirl in the cafe. We'd both picked up tongs and he got there first, grabbing it before I could. NOT happy.*

I remember laughing at that. Cinnamon swirls were Rosie's favourite pastry.

But then, twenty minutes later, another text: *Maybe fate isn't so bad. The guy who pinched the cinnamon swirl gave it to me.*

I scan these texts again. Just a passing chat about two strangers.

The police think it was probably a random attack – that's their most likely reasoning. In the months before her death, she kept wandering by herself at night. Through parks, dodgy areas, backstreets. She'd be found sitting in the road or curled up next to a telephone box – often by a concerned passerby, or by me when she sometimes rang. She kept putting herself at risk. Her luck was bound to run out.

But what if it wasn't random? What if she knew her killer? Pettiford assures me they pursued every trail, questioned every possible suspect.

I'm not convinced. They could have missed something. Someone.

I drink some more water and look round the kitchen. The surfaces are shiny clean, not a crumb in sight. The flat's quiet – only the digital hum of the fridge. Arran's sourdough is on the counter inside its linen bag. That bow on top.

His notebook. Now might be my chance.

The guest room door isn't quite shut. I listen for a few seconds. I can't sense a presence. Pushing the door, the room is empty.

The backpack is on the chair. I check inside. Then I see the notebook on the bedside table. I pick it up and pause for a second, conscience wavering. But I know I'm going to do it.

I open the first page. Small writing in neat lines.

A heartbeat and you.

I felt the air. That light wind blowing in through the door, past your figure. You didn't quite shut it. You weren't sure if it was supposed to be open or not. There was a moment, your eyes scanning the tables, then you went over to the window. A table for two. But you were on your own.

You put your bag on top of the sugar spoon – I heard it clink underneath. You didn't notice. Nor did you notice the few granules the waiter's cloth had missed, sprinkled by the little girl who'd been sitting there before. When you pulled out the chair you lifted it so it didn't scrape the floor. Before you sat down, you scratched your elbow.

I was staring. You were framed by the window, the sunlight on your dark—

Movement, a thud sound. Coming from the bathroom. *Shit.* I thought Arran was out. I put the notebook back and tiptoe out of the room fast. Glancing towards the bathroom, the door is shut. Why did I only notice now?

A shift, footfalls. I slip into the living area as the bathroom door opens.

Did he hear me in his room? And what's he doing now? My back's to the hall.

'Hello, Tess.'

His voice makes me inwardly start, but my body doesn't give me away. I turn. 'Oh hi, Arran.'

He's in the doorframe, in a white linen shirt. One of the sleeves is rolled up, the other hanging loose at his wrist. A strange temptation to reach out and fold it up over the toned muscle.

His gaze drops away. I glance down, suddenly aware of my sloppy appearance. My hair's matted and I'm in an oversized T-shirt that hangs on my bare thighs, just concealing my underwear.

'Someone knocked on the door earlier this afternoon,' he says.

I'm gripping the edges of my T-shirt, trying to pull it lower on my legs.

'I wasn't sure whether or not to answer it.' He rubs his finger behind his ear. 'It was your neighbour.'

No need to wonder which one. The woman who lives on the top floor almost never disturbs me. 'Luke from below?'

'Yes.'

'What did he want?'

'He said he'd come to check on you as you hadn't looked well this morning.'

Oh, I remember now. I bumped into Luke on my way home. He was with a girl who had long copper hair. Ivy, I think he said her name was. She smiled at me, showing small straight teeth.

'He tried to come in,' Arran says. 'Tried to push past me. But I wouldn't let him.' His feet shift. 'I told him you were out.'

I search his expression. He lied for me? Or did he really think I was out?

'Thanks.'

His head dips, a silent acknowledgement. The fridge is humming again, a background whine.

'I've just been really tired this weekend,' I say, trying to seem casual. 'Went out last night.'

'Dancing?'

'Uh . . . yeah a bit of dancing, with some friends.' The lies come easily. But with that near miss, almost being caught, I feel skittish.

'I was out too. A friend took me to a bar in Shoreditch.'

'The cool end of town.'

He smiles. 'So I saw.'

I'm pulling my T-shirt down again. I want to go and change, but instead I ask, 'So this is the first time you've lived in London?'

'Yes. Apart from last summer for a few months when I was doing a design project. And years ago I was an au pair in Kingston.'

'An au pair? Really?'

His smile is ironic. 'They call us bro pairs. We're quite a rare breed.' A pause. 'Family friends were looking for some help. And I love kids, so . . .'

He wanders towards the sofa. I run my tongue over my teeth. They feel furry. When did I last brush them? Luckily, he hasn't come too close today.

Arran's fiddling with the hem of a cushion. My brow tightens as I notice something behind him. The asparagus fern is on the coffee table – the one from the spare room. Arran must have moved it out.

He lets go of the cushion. 'I know this isn't really any of my business, Tess, we only met a few days ago. But I hope everything's all right?'

Do I look *that* awful? I glance down at my body again. There's a toothpaste drip-stain on my T-shirt. I feel the blush in my cheeks, and I laugh. 'Sorry about my appearance. I know I look a bit slobby.'

'It's not that. And this is your home, you can do what you like. Though you don't look slobby – you look lovely.'

Lovely? Is he kidding?

'I only ask,' he continues, 'because I heard you talking in your sleep on Friday night.'

A drumbeat thumps through me. 'That can't be right. I've never talked in my sleep.'

There's concern in his eyes.

'Maybe you heard it from the next-door flat,' I say. 'Or from the woman above.'

'No, it was definitely coming through the wall that divides the bedrooms. At one point you were shouting.'

My muscles feel rigid, cement round my bones. There's a question I have to ask, though I'm not sure I want to know the answer. 'What was I saying?'

He hesitates, rubbing his neck. 'I couldn't hear specific words. It was more like you were having a stressful or upsetting experience.'

A nightmare?

'I wasn't sure whether I should knock on your door or even come in to check.'

For a moment my ears don't pick up what he's just said – a delay in my hearing. But then Arran notices my expression.

'I didn't,' he says quickly. 'It seemed too presumptuous to go into your room. Intrusive.'

A bead of sweat trickles between my breasts. 'So I didn't say anything in particular?' I confirm.

He shakes his head. He's clean-shaven today, making his expression appear softer – more boyish, somehow.

'I just wanted to let you know,' he says. 'I'd better get on, Tess.'

He walks past me, footsteps light on the floorboards. The guest room door closes.

I stare at the spot where he was standing, trying to process this new information about myself. No one has ever mentioned me talking in my sleep, let alone shouting. Not ex-boyfriends or old flatmates, nor other bnb guests. Could he be mistaken? Or was I genuinely talking – perhaps during a dream that I can't remember. I feel something sneak up my back, past my shoulder blade. The danger of what I could say in the night.

I take a shower, letting the flow wash away all the dirt and sweat and anxiety, turning the water hot then cold, hot-cold-hot-cold, when a thought occurs to me.

He could be lying. He could be making it up. But why would he do that?

9

I'm exhausted but my eyes are stretched open. I couldn't sleep last night, yesterday's events ticking through my brain.

The gallery's quiet today. The occasional body drifting through. I don't engage with the visitors like I'm supposed to, I barely even see them. I called Pettiford again during my lunch hour. He didn't pick up until the third try.

Nothing to report on the Spanish barman. It doesn't seem worth pursuing, he said. My teeth were clenched, but I forced them apart to tell him about the text messages, the two men Rosie had mentioned. Asshole and cinnamon swirl. There was a draughty pause, then Pettiford suggested I forward the texts to him.

I close my eyes, the dark behind my lids calming. When I open them again, there's someone in the room. A man standing close to a photograph, staring at the back of a woman's knee.

My brain jumps to Arran.

Arran and that notebook. It's more than just an object I can look at or touch. More than any other possession I've handled before. These are his thoughts I have access to. A way into his mind.

And what he wrote: *A heartbeat and you.*

An unnamed *you*, but clearly a woman. Someone he's seen in a restaurant or cafe. Someone he doesn't know? It's strange to use the second-person. He could be a closet writer, a poet, playing with ways of describing someone. But somehow, I don't think so. It seemed more honest than that. Like this girl is a real person. From what little I've read – a fragment of the writing I glimpsed on the page.

As the day drags on, the air in the gallery staler, I keep going over it. That little brown book, the description of the girl. And I think: notebook might not be the right name for it. What if it's something more intimate?

A diary.

The prospect makes me look up from the floor. The ache behind my eyes a little lighter. That simple shift in language, in definition, giving it a deeper sheen. All the more intriguing. More appealing.

*   *   *

I squeeze onto an underground carriage among the hordes of commuters. Someone's bag pokes into my leg. The guy behind me is breathing on my hair. His breath smells of chives.

I close my eyes. I think of Arran's diary, the feel of it in my fingers, soft and bendy. The words inside, there for me to read. The secrets.

At the next station people press their way out of the doors and more cram themselves in. A woman in front of me is reading a newspaper. The front page glares before my nose with the headline: MISSING IN MANCHESTER: SEARCH FOR KATIE CONTINUES.

That girl's been missing for eight days. Is it all down to chance? Fate? Who gets attacked or kidnapped, and who doesn't?

My phone buzzes in my pocket. Odd, since I'm underground. I slip my hand past the newspaper and pull it out. When I swipe my passcode, the name Oliver Barlow appears. I open the text fast.

Do you know how many times I've thought about blocking your number?

The woman turns the page of her newspaper, glancing at me. Nearby, a young couple are whispering. My phone vibrates again in my hand. Where is this signal coming from?

You're not being fair, Tess. Every time your name pops up it brings it all back.

I stare at his words. *Not being fair?* The pain is firm and top-heavy, weights of it stacking up. There isn't enough oxygen in here. I'm snatching at breaths.

*   *   *

Arran is cooking. A spicy coconut aroma in the flat. Too strong, it makes my stomach churn. I go straight into my room and stand next to the window, the evening air wafting into my face.

When I feel cooler, I go into the corridor and linger by the guest bedroom. I want to sneak in. If Arran's cooking, he still needs to eat, so he could be in the kitchen for a while. Worth the risk?

Thud-thud-thud on the front door. I jump at the loud sound – a fist on wood. Luke. He's a bit like a puppy that needs regular attention. I don't feel like interacting, but Arran shouldn't have to deal with him.

'Hallelujah!' Luke cries, holding up his hands when I open the door. 'You're alive.' He's wearing shorts again – slim chinos tight on his thighs. And he's barefoot.

'Yes, you doomsayer.'

'Hey, I'm just being a friendly neighbour. What if you had a heart attack and collapsed and no one knew about it? I'd be your saviour.' He grins.

'Uh, I think Arran would notice a collapsed body on the floor.'

The grin wanes. 'So that's his name, is it? You know he wouldn't let me in yesterday?'

'Quite right, you're a stranger. You could've been a burglar for all he knew.'

'*He's* the stranger.' His voice is disgruntled.

I shake my head and turn towards the living area. Luke follows, slamming the door behind him. Arran's by the hob, an array of vegetables, fresh herbs and spices on the side.

'Arran, this is Luke. Luke, this is Arran. So now you two have officially met.'

'All right, mate,' Luke says. His chest seems puffed out, as if trying to make himself taller.

Arran gives a short nod.

We all look at each other.

'So what have you been up to, Luke?' I ask, breaking the silence.

'Oh you know – work, play.' He crosses his arms over his chest. 'Night-time shenanigans.'

Involving Ivy? I'm pretty sure she's lacy lilac bra girl who lives opposite. Images of yesterday after my night on Hampstead Heath drift back. She's freckled. She has an accent. Scottish or Irish. Nudging Luke with her elbow, in a tube top showing bare shoulders. Thick eyeliner.

'I have some news actually,' Luke says. He frowns at Arran – the noise he's making, cutting vegetables with professional speed.

'Oh yeah?'

'Just heard my poems are getting published in this literary magazine.'

'That's cool.'

He's smiling. 'And they've been entered into a competition too.'

I feel my eyebrows flicker in surprise. Luke and poetry have never seemed to square, like two cards in a game of pairs that don't match.

'Congrats, Luke,' I say, and I mean it. 'That's great.'

'Thanks.'

'I need to read your poems then. How come you've never shared them?'

He shrugs, eyes darting to Arran's thigh as he wipes the blade on his apron. 'Most writers don't share their work until it's ready. Or they never share full stop, choosing to write in secret.'

The irony of his words hovers in the space. As if he knows I've read Arran's diary, which is impossible.

'But your poems aren't so secret anymore,' I say.

'No.'

Luke smiles and pushes his glasses up his nose with his index finger. I've often wondered if he actually needs them, or if it's just useless plastic inside the frames. He's moved closer and I can suddenly smell his aftershave, too strong.

Arran's sipping from a glass of red wine, his Adam's apple prominent.

'That smells amazing,' I say, an excuse to move away from Luke. 'What are you cooking?'

Arran speaks into the steam coming from the pan. 'Tofu curry.'

Luke puckers his nose. 'Tofu? Are you vegetarian?'

'No. Vegan.'

Silence.

'*Why?*' says Luke.

Arran looks straight at Luke. A metallic stare.

'OK,' I say. 'You don't have to answer that, Arran.' I grab Luke's arm and pull him towards the door. His bare feet thump behind me. 'Could you be more tactless?' I hiss in the hallway.

'What?' Luke says. 'Don't trust vegans. It's like people who don't drink.'

'Luke, loads of the recipes in your mum's book are vegan.'

The look he gives me says *so?* Asking instead, 'Is he wearing your apron?'

I don't want to know how he noticed that. I open the front door and give him a push, but he doesn't move.

'That's it? I get to come in for three minutes?'

'If you're going to insult my guests,' I say. 'Now out.'

He sighs and steps into the stairwell.

'Seriously, Tess.' He leans in close to me, voice hushed. 'There's something about that guy. He has a vibe coming off him I don't like.'

'Right . . . sounds like you're threatened by him?'

He frowns. 'On what planet could *he* ever threaten *me?*'

'On this one apparently. And anyway, you've met him for less than a minute – you're hardly in a position to judge.'

'I'm only looking out for you.'

'Goodnight, Luke,' I say firmly.

'Night, Tess. I'll see you soon.'

I shut the door and go back to the living room doorway. Arran's still stirring the curry. He is wearing my apron,
strangely. The palm tree and sunset design bright against
his pastel T-shirt. An apron I can't remember ever using –
hanging permanently by the fridge.

'Sorry about that,' I say. 'Luke can be a bit insensitive.'

He shrugs. 'No matter.'

I get a can of ginger ale from the cupboard, then crack
some ice into a glass and pour it on. It fizzes up to the rim.

There *was* an awkward atmosphere between Luke and
Arran. It's lingering now. Something cold about Arran's
silence.

His stirring pauses and he looks at me sideways, through
his eyelashes. I can take a hint. He wants to be left alone. This
is my flat, my living space, and what if I want to cook? But it's
fine. He's making a vat of curry, so I can always slip in here
later and sneak a few spoons.

'Enjoy your dinner,' I say, walking out.

Luke wasn't wrong. Arran's vibe can be a little odd, which
is why I'm itching to read his diary.

* * *

Arran's backpack is gone. He went out ten minutes ago, into
the morning heat, but I'm not sure if he's taken the diary with
him. If I kept one, I'd always have it on me, just in case. Most
people are way too trusting. I know better. You shouldn't trust
anyone.

I look in his empty duffel bag, the desk drawers, beneath
the bed. Agitation mounting. Then I think – bedside table.
I slide open the drawer and here it is.

My fingertips hover over the recycled-style cover, then I grip the edges and flip it open, starting from where I left off.

I was staring. You were framed by the window, the sunlight on your dark hair.

I thought – where have you been? Breezing through that door into my afternoon. Two seconds and everything shifted.

You slipped one knee on top of the other and arranged your dress's floaty fabric. No skin showing. But I could see your feet through your strappy sandals and your toenails were unpainted and the skin all smooth – no cracks or rough bits. You can tell a lot about someone from their feet.

I forced myself to look away, to respond to something one of my friends was saying. Right then I wished they didn't exist. That it was just you and me, alone at our tables.

You rubbed your eye then took something out of your bag. A hairbrush. You used it, right there at the table. You didn't care. You didn't even glance around. If you had, you might have seen me. But you just brushed your hair without a thought. I wondered what shampoo you used, what scent it gave you.

Lavender perhaps. Shea butter. Grapefruit. I could only imagine over the smell of coffee.

I wanted to talk to you. To saunter over with some witty charming opener that would make you smile and invite me to join you. Not inwardly roll your eyes or think I was hitting on you. Even if I had already wondered whether or not you were wearing a bra, and how dark your nipples might be.

You went up to the counter, leaving your things at the table. The hairbrush was sticking out of your bag with tangled bristles. Next to it a ripped packet. My guess would be something sweet, but it could have been nuts. I couldn't see what was inside. Only a curved object pressed against its edge.

A tube had rolled out onto the table. Something for your lips.

I watched you order, your feet crossed, ankles touching. You took your coffee back to your table, the knock of ceramic against wood like an announcement.

Your food came and you ground salt all over it then squirted sauce on the side, dipping with your fingers. You licked them clean. You must have been in a rush, except you didn't seem it. Your body language was smooth. The only sign was you nibbling your index finger.

You got up, gliding back out of the door in your cotton dress and clicky sandals. Fifty minutes and you didn't look my way once. As softly as you'd come, you were gone.

I stare at the page. Barely a chance to absorb the words before I turn to the next entry.

I went back. I thought maybe you were a regular. I sat alone and drank coffee and ate lunch five times in two weeks. The barista asked me if I worked nearby. I lied. He tapped his nose, grinning at me with his white teeth and pierced helix. A twist of irritation as I gripped my wallet, not knowing what that meant, whether he was winding me up.

I don't even like the coffee there that much, but what else could I do? I hadn't had the guts to go over and talk to you, so my only hope was that you might come back.

When you didn't, I walked the surrounding streets, scanning women's faces. I checked other nearby cafes and restaurants, lingered at the three nearest tube stations. I'd never done anything like this before. I felt like a madman. But there was something about you. How could I explain?

Your perfect feet. Almond eyes. Sweet smile. Gold bracelet. Concealed legs. Elegant thumbs typing on your phone. Deep-toned skin.

Stop. Please stop.

If only I knew your name.

It's my own fault, my own stupid choice. We have all these life chances and this was a chance untaken. I could tell myself this would be my last mistake, that I would never make another again. Or at least not the same one. But I am human.

10

My brain feels like a beehive, buzzing over the honeycomb of Arran and his diary. I'm on a bench in some park gardens. The sky is lido blue, a long strip of chlorinated water. The sun feels like it's baking my skull through my hat.

This morning I scoured Arran's room. I was hoping he might have written again. But the diary was nowhere to be found. He must have taken it with him. Deflecting the frustration, I wandered here.

A football soars towards me and bounces on the grass near my feet. A young sweaty guy runs over to retrieve it, glancing at my bare legs.

'Nice hat,' he says with a grin.

I ignore him and the *thump-roll* of the ball. It's background noise while I ponder what I read in Arran's diary.

People talk about being struck by someone, lightning to your chest. I've never really believed in love at first sight. You can be wowed by someone's looks or feel a connection when you chat, but this girl didn't even see Arran. He was staring at her from across a room.

It's a shade of creepy – hanging around, hoping to bump into her. Stalker territory. But who hasn't drifted into it? With the internet we can all do it in secret. I remember Nalika

civica

Issued

stalking Chris for weeks on social media. And loads of people engineer chance encounters. I did once, with a guy at university. Finding out he was on the tennis team, signing up to the tennis club then loitering near him during lessons. We ended up together, for about three months, until I got bored.

Who is she, this woman?

Dark hair. Almond eyes. Details that could describe thousands of girls. I glance down at my wrist, my gold chain glinting in the sun. Another universal detail – almost every woman in the world wears a bracelet, gold jewellery of some kind. Yet for a moment I consider it.

It's possible.

I think of the last time I went out for a coffee, about two weeks ago. A cafe in Hackney on my own. Something faint in my torso stirs, a strange sensation. The idea of being watched, admired, unaware of Arran's gaze.

I didn't eat anything in that cafe though.

A fly burrs round my head. I wave it away.

Yet he could still be writing about me. There's an ambiguity to his words – to *you*. I've been to cafes alone many times, and there's no way to tell when Arran wrote these entries. There are no dates on them.

If I listen to level-headed logic, the girl could be anybody. One of millions in London. Or not even in this city. Leeds. Budapest. São Paulo.

I know very little about my guest. His life, his relationships. He could have met the girl by now, be dating her. I think of Arran with a girlfriend. Some beautiful almond-eyed woman with perfect feet. It doesn't tally. He gives the impression that he's not in a relationship, not attached to any one person or thing.

If Pettiford's taught me anything, it's that you can't make assumptions about anyone. My brain might be coiling off again, but the sensation is there, a kernel of it near my gut.

It's partly the way Arran was last night, what happened when he got back to the flat.

I was lying on the sofa, empty bottle of wine on the coffee table. He came in talking to someone on the phone.

'We're meeting in Regent's Park. She said she can't wait to see me, that she's missed me.' A pause before he laughed. 'You're a funny guy, David. I'm not thinking about that.'

I was concealed behind the sofa.

'Sure, dare to dream,' Arran said. 'Look, I should go. I'll let you know about next week.'

When I peeked over the top of the sofa, he was looking at his phone. He rubbed his forehead with the back of his hand.

'Hey, Arran,' I said, popping up.

His head zipped towards me. I yawned, feigning drowsiness.

'Hey,' he said, face pale with surprise. 'Sorry, I didn't know you were here.'

'Don't worry, I was just having a nap.'

His eyes were hesitant. They slid past me, towards the wine bottle. 'I woke you up?'

I shrugged and stood up, stretching. Arran's gaze skimmed down my body, then away. My vest was riding up, I realised, showing stomach skin. I dropped my arms.

He was looking at his phone again, thumbs tapping. As if he hadn't seen. Then he put the phone into the back pocket of his linen shorts.

'I envy you, you know,' he said. 'I wish I could nap.'

'You can't?'

He shook his head, taking groceries out of a bag. 'If there's a hint of daylight, my brain won't switch off. I could do with some tips from someone who knows how to siesta.'

'You mean from me?'

He was putting things in the fridge now. Sundried tomatoes, oat milk, broccoli, goat's cheese, hummus. 'Yeah. Looks like you're an expert.'

Arran smiled, one corner of his lips curved into his cheek. I realised that his mouth is slightly lopsided. It pulls to the left. And I noticed something on his hands, dried pale. I watched as he opened a packet, the cellophane crackling. Almonds.

'What's that on your hands?' I asked.

Arran glanced at his fingers. 'Oh, clay. I've just been at my studio.'

'Studio?'

'Yeah, my friend helped me find a space over in Hackney. So I can start making ceramics here.' He was holding one of his palms open. 'You've reminded me, I should wash them.' He stepped towards the sink.

'No, don't.'

His head swerved towards me.

I don't know why I said it. There was just something beautiful about the clay on his skin, in his palm lines and knuckle grooves.

'Sorry,' I blurted. 'Ignore me.'

A moment lingered before he turned on the tap and rubbed his hands in water. I searched for something normal to say, to dilute the awkwardness of my comment.

'What kind of ceramics do you make?' I asked.

'Stoneware mostly, but sometimes earthenware.'

'What's the difference?'

'The quality of the clay and the temperature they're fired at. Stoneware's better quality and fired higher. It's stronger too.'

I watched his hands as he dried them on a towel.

'But I won't bore you with in-depth pottery details,' Arran said.

'No, please, I'm interested.' I was staring, I realised too late. 'Sorry, I was thinking about something.'

The evening light glimmered in his eyes. 'What were you thinking about?'

'Oh, nothing, it was silly.'

He didn't look away. Beneath his gaze I felt a drop of discomfort, as if he could see my thoughts. Finally, he reached for the almonds and slipped one in his mouth. 'By the way, I've ordered a recycling bin.'

When I looked confused, he motioned towards the bin. Beside it was a growing collection of plastic, cardboard and glass in a bag – one of those clear sacks provided by my London borough. Which was weird, because I thought I'd used up the roll before he arrived.

'I have a thing about recycling,' he said, crunching. 'Don't like it all getting mixed up, or recyclables going into general waste. Especially glass – it can be endlessly recycled.' He paused and swallowed. 'The bin should be delivered in the next couple of days. I hope that's OK.'

Part of me wanted to snap, *No, it's not OK*. This is my flat and he's just a guest. What makes him think he can order things? Even if he pays for them.

'Secret's out,' he said, dropping the bag of almonds on the side. 'I'm a recycling nerd.'

Something about the gentle toss of his wrist and his humorous tone lightened my irritation.

He moved closer to the table. 'Hey, what's this? Have you been drawing?'

Alarm clenched my lungs. I'd forgotten – I tried drawing in the afternoon. For the first time since last year, I'd suddenly felt like it. I pulled out my sketchbook and drew plants, a frog, a leaf. Then hands. And in that nanosecond of Arran leaning over to look, I realised they were *his* hands. Unconsciously I'd sketched them.

I darted over just as he reached out to touch the sketchbook. His fingers got there first, but I grabbed the edge, jerking it from his grasp. Somehow I overshot and bumped into him, my shoulder against his chest. And I lost my balance. I felt his hand on my arm to steady me.

'Whoa,' he said. 'OK, Scrappy-Doo.'

I looked up at him, the sketchbook dangling open in my hand.

'You all right? Found your feet?' His palm was cupped round the top of my arm, fingers pressed into my skin.

For a few beats I couldn't move, disarmed. My heart pulsing in my neck. His face was so close I could feel his breath. He smelled of coconut milk and honey.

I stepped back, closing the sketchbook. His fingers brushed down my arm as he let go, as if prolonging the touch.

'I just don't want anyone looking at my drawings,' I said. 'They're not ready.'

The atmosphere in the room had changed. It felt thicker, hotter, like something had melted between us.

'I'm sorry, Tess. I didn't mean to look.'

There was a shade of regret in his tone. And colour in his cheeks, blending into the blond stubble. I held the sketchbook against my chest, embarrassed by my reaction.

One of his hands clenched inwards. 'I only glimpsed it, but it looked beautiful.'

'Thanks,' I answered. 'But I don't think you saw enough detail to—'

'I did. A glimpse is all I need.'

I thought of his diary – the girl. He only needed a glimpse of her. Gliding into a cafe and *bam*. I tried to think of someone I'd felt that for, someone who'd struck right through my ribcage. But I couldn't.

'I'd love to see your drawings sometime, Tess, when they're ready.'

There was only one person I'd shown my drawings to, and I didn't want to share that. It was something between me and Rosie.

His phone rang, a sharp tone cutting through the air between us. He answered instantly. 'Hi, what's up?' Walking past me. 'No, that's OK. I'm glad you called.'

The guest room door shut. The low murmur of his voice through the wall.

It's strange, the sensations he creates. Like when he touched my arm and his fingertips tingled down it. I can still feel it, sitting on this bench, a warm spark in my skin.

The brim of her hat casts a shadow over one shoulder. A *sombrero cordobés*. It's made of felt, flat-topped – a black pancake. White strip round the ribbon. Underneath, she has smoky eyes and soft cheekbones.

She's a curious one, isn't she? Rare and stimulating. Her curiosity on the edge of intrusive. Not unlike me.

Curiosity can kill, you know.

11

Arran's about to leave. Jacket hung over his arm as he pours coffee into a flask. I'm late for work but I want to peek at his diary. His words have got stuck in my head. The description of this woman, what he meant about mistakes. I need to know more.

I'm sitting at the table with a bowl of granola. The clusters have gone soggy in the milk while I wait for him to go, eating slowly, picking out hazelnuts. I look at one on my spoon. A memory of Rosie, wrapped in a wool blanket – handing her a mug of hot chocolate sprinkled with hazelnuts.

In December last year, not long before Christmas, Oliver had texted me saying Rosie had asked to meet him in a pub, but then ran out, and he didn't know where she was. I'd searched the light-lined streets and phoned her eight times. It was nearly one in the morning and I was waiting outside her building, with no way in.

I'd wanted to move in with her since she got rid of her lodger. When she first bought the flat in May of last year, I was living with my boyfriend, Matthew, so a friend of Rosie's took the second room. Oliver had raised the idea of living together as well, but Rosie told him it was too soon. They'd only been together a year and her independence was somehow primary to her – she got caught up in it, a fixation, stemming from her art practice, which then fed into all parts of her life and identity. I think that's why she impulsively bought this flat. It was like she had something to prove. This was her place, *her* space. Possessive about it.

She fell out with her friend, and when they left, she got a lodger in, a stranger, but that didn't last long either. The room was empty again in late August. Matthew and I had broken up a few weeks before, so it seemed like an ideal opportunity.

But when I asked Rosie about moving in, she stared at me, this dark glaze to her eyes before she looked away and said it wasn't the right moment for her, she needed time to herself. A murmur from her mouth that she couldn't share the space.

I tried to push it, thinking surely she needed the rent money for her mortgage. The hurt a spine in my throat – that my sister didn't want to live with me. She had already started acting strangely. Things she said, the way her face sometimes went grey.

So I let the spine sit there in silence and moved in with my friend instead.

I didn't have access to Rosie's flat – her home, her art and belongings kept protected. All I could do that night in December was sit outside on the step, staring along Ravengale Road, waiting for her figure beneath the lamps.

After two hours she appeared, hunched and staring at the ground.

'Rosie, where the hell have you been?'

She looked up – slowly, her recognition flat. She wasn't wearing a coat. No scarf or gloves like me, just a black V-neck sweater.

'You shouldn't be here,' she said, brushing past me.

'Why not? I'm your sister and I'm worried about you.'

She halted, head dipped. Who was this strange, diminished double in front of me? I wanted to shake some of my sister back into her. I wanted her to tease me again, laugh at the jokes we used to share. But I didn't touch her. The last time I tried she'd flinched. A reaction that had ricocheted through me.

Rosie turned back, only then seeming to take me in. 'How long have you been out here? You must be frozen.'

'What about you? Where's your coat?'

Her eyes were like marble in the street light. 'Let's just go inside.'

In the flat, I made *chocolate a la taza*. Melted Venezuelan chocolate with shortbread – our version of *churros*, when deep-fried dough wasn't available.

Rosie held the mug to her chest, steam swirling over her face. She was wearing lipstick, I noticed. Dark plum red. Mascara smudged around her left eye.

'Why are you doing this, Rosie?' I forced it out, under my breath, but she heard me.

'Doing what?' Her voice seemed diluted.

'Going out in freezing conditions without proper clothing? Wandering around at night on your own? Loitering in dodgy places?'

She blinked down into the mug. Her fingers looked so soft against the fired surface.

I know you're depressed. Words I couldn't say out loud, for fear of upsetting her, and because it would make them more solid, more true, stated in sound. *But why?* That's what I needed to understand.

'I need to feel something,' she said. 'I need something to happen, after . . .' Her head shifted. 'Anything would be better than this. Any experience. Raw, bitter, I don't care. Pain, even.'

The hot chocolate had burnt my tongue and while I tried to decode what she'd just said, it throbbed for attention. She wanted pain?

'What is *this*?' I asked.

'This?'

'Yes, you just said anything would be better than this. I want to understand what *this* is.'

Her eyes left me, staring out at the bronze-black sky. She sipped her chocolate before, 'I wanted to talk to Oliver tonight.'

The window she'd given me had closed again. If I tried to put pressure on it, the glass would crack. Fracture in my face.

I went along with her. 'That's OK, Rosie. You can talk to him.'

Her head shook. 'It's not OK.'

'He wants to talk to you.'

She dipped her shortbread in the chocolate and bit down hard.

'He loves you,' I said.

'No, he doesn't.'

'How can you say that?' It was clear that he adored her – anyone could see it, the way he looked at her, cared for her.

She turned away. 'Never mind, you wouldn't understand.'

Her words tore. 'What wouldn't I understand?'

She didn't answer, her fingers scratching at her chest.

I look at my own fingers now, the skin splitting round one of my nails. I reach for my phone. Oliver. I have to text him.

Please just meet with me.

I watch it send, that tiny tick beside the box. Then I type another message.

I need to talk to you about that night. Please.

I wait, eyeing the notification bar.

Arran leans past me to the fruit bowl. I blank the phone's screen as he selects a red apple.

'See you later, Tess,' he says.

He gives me that lopsided smile. Something about it I can't quite interpret. Sarcasm? Familiarity? He walks out, denim jacket swinging on his arm.

I check my phone again. No texts. The last one was from Nalika yesterday: *Let's meet one evening this week? I could come to yours, bring wine and custard tarts xxx.*

At the kitchen window, I watch Arran disappear from view. And I notice someone in a window opposite – in Ivy's flat. Not her or her flatmate, who's blond and bearded. It's Luke. Looking straight at me, black hair gleaming. He smiles and waves. I lift my hand then step back out of sight. My heart rate is faster, as though I've been caught watching Arran. But I dismiss the silly feeling. It's only Luke.

I head for the guest room and open the bedside drawer. The diary's here. I start flicking through and – yes, there's another entry.

I thought I saw you again yesterday. You were in a plant shop, looking at succulents. Your hair was wet, the ends had made your shoulders damp – dark patches on your hoodie. Underneath you were wearing a swimsuit. One of those plain sporty ones, with a palm-print sarong round your waist.

My heart was in my throat for five seconds before you turned to look up at the hanging plants and: not your face.

Her nose was longer, her chin squarer. Lovely, but it wasn't you.

I walked out and could feel the pit stains on my shirt and my molars starting to ache. I was clenching my jaw like I do in the night. I passed an ice-cream parlour and went in and got cioccolato fondente. The darkest colour inside the counter. It burnt my teeth.

It finishes there. But there's one more entry on the opposite page. My eyes glide over.

I rang Laura. I needed to speak to someone and I knew her voice—

My phone buzzes from the living area. I drop the diary back in the drawer and run to look. I'm holding my breath when I swipe the screen and see a text from Oliver.

All right, I'll meet you in an hour. Blackcherry Row in the city.

I can't believe it. I stare at the words until they blur.

I should be at the gallery today – I need the money. The bnb payments and translation work barely cover the mortgage and bills. But this is too important.

My hands are trembling as I type a reply.

I dress quickly and hurry out of the flat, my bag banging against my leg. Halfway along the next road I see two people ahead of me. The first thing I notice is the copper mane down her back. Ivy. Who I have met, though I can't remember the details – the encounter, what was said.

Avoid, my primal brain thinks, going to cross the road.

'Tess, hi!'

I turn to see a beaming expression. When I don't instantly respond, something flits across her face like a bird's shadow.

'Ivy. Hey.'

She smiles again. The guy next to her is watching me.

'Sorry,' I semi-pant. 'I can't really stop, I'm late for something.' I move to skirt round them.

'Oh, right, don't worry,' Ivy says. Burry r's and reedy vowels: Irish.

The guy steps to the side, bumping into a tree.

'This is my flatmate, Elliot, by the way,' Ivy says. Her make-up is serious: black round her eyes, winged in sharp points. 'Ell, this is Tess who lives above Luke.'

He nods as I pass.

'Hey, I think you dropped something.' Elliot's voice behind me.

I swing round, looking down where he's pointing. On the pavement is something gold. A tiny scallop shell. My bracelet has two charms: a bee and a celestial sun-moon. But not a shell.

'It's not mine, but thanks.' I hurry off before they can say anything else.

'See you, Tess,' Ivy calls. Then, more distant, 'I think I've left it behind.'

'Go back for it,' Elliot says. 'I'll wait here.'

Their voices fade as I run towards the tube. My feet clomping along the tarmac, my stomach frothy. A soda water feeling. This will be the first time I've seen Oliver since the funeral. This could be the day I discover something, the day Oliver's involvement in Rosie's death unravels.

12

I'm standing in Blackcherry Row. It's a cobbled side road near Monument Station, about a minute's walk from the Thames. Narrow and quiet.

I don't know why Oliver wants to meet here.

I check one way, then the other, the end of the street curving out of view. Brick walls either side – the backs of buildings. Where is he? The froth in my stomach feels more like wool now. Wiry fibres of excitement and uncertainty.

I sense something, my eye drawn to the far end of the road.

Someone's coming this way. In trousers. A dark jacket. I peer at them when they stop and half-turn. Two seconds, hovering, then they go back the other way, walking fast.

Something shifts uneasily in my gut. A seagull whines overhead – a thin cry. I jump as my phone vibrates.

A message from Oliver: *I've been held up by a client. Can we meet by Tower Bridge instead? At the dolphin fountain?*

I text *Yes* as I hurry towards the bridge.

* * *

I'm beside the fountain, breathing fast. I wipe my forehead and look around. I can't see Oliver. Tower Bridge looms overhead, bright against the muddy water of the river. The fountain is bronze, a sculpture of a girl and dolphin. Swimming together. Its tail is flicking, the girl upside-down with her legs in the air.

'Tess.'

A voice behind me.

I turn and Oliver's there, but he looks different. His hair's cut close to his skull, accentuating his widow's peak. Thick auburn beard round his jaw. Wearing navy jeans and a crisp shirt: a trim, well-groomed style. So far from his surfer messy-hair vibe.

We stare at each other.

Unfamiliar feelings stir in my chest. Rosie's boyfriend. The man whose face feels like it's burned behind my eyes.

'Shall we . . .?' he begins. He clears his throat. 'Let's sit over here.'

Oliver goes to the wall opposite the fountain. I follow without a word, sitting with a gap between us. Not too close.

For a minute neither of us speaks. A wand of water shoots up between the dolphin and girl, sprinkling into the circular pool below. *Say something.* Oliver is leaning forwards, arms resting on his legs. His fingers interlink then let go again.

'It's strange to see you, Tess.'

I swallow. 'You too.'

'I'm sure. But for me, you look so much like—'

'I know.'

He glances at me when I cut him off. His eyes shiny.

More silence. The fountain girl's hair is splayed like a fan.

Oliver's hands are kneading. 'You know, I thought I saw her the other day, at the Barbican.'

Alarm rushes through me.

'This girl at the other end of the main hall, in uniform,' he says. 'But it was crowded, and only a flash before she disappeared.' He gives a little laugh in the back of his throat. 'My imagination tricking me.'

There's no trace of ridicule or accusation in his voice. But the alarm is still strong. Why was he at the Barbican? He can't know about me working where she worked, slipping into more than her shoes. I'm wearing them now, her old suede brogues. And her denim culottes – snug around her waist just as they are around mine.

Oh God, what if he notices? I didn't think about the clothes I pulled on before I left.

When I risk a glance, he's gazing forwards, fingers knotted. Caught in his own thoughts.

Thank goodness I didn't put on my Barbican T-shirt. I called my manager on the way here, pretending to be sick.

Oliver unknots his fingers and puts his palms on his knees. I notice the tattoo on his forefinger: two tiny mountain symbols crossed sideways. The inguz; a Viking rune.

'What do you want, Tess?'

His question comes suddenly, his tone short. I meet his eyes and feel a twinge of irritation. *I want you to tell the truth, Oliver. Admit it.* Because even though he has a rock-solid alibi, even though Pettiford questioned him within hours of the discovery of Rosie's body, I think there's something he's hiding. Husbands and boyfriends are always the first suspects. The police treat them with suspicion when the investigation opens. But what about the last suspects? What about being suspicious of her ex-boyfriend now?

'I need to talk to you about Rosie,' I answer.

He stares at me, expression pale. 'What about her?'

'When was the last time you saw her?'

'December, that night she asked to meet me in the pub then ran out.'

'So you didn't see her at all in January?'

He moves one of his feet, the sole scraping the tarmac. 'No.'

'You're sure?'

'What kind of question is that?' he says, defensive. 'Of course I'm sure.'

I slip my hands under my legs, waiting a few seconds before: 'That day, that night of the twenty-sixth, did you talk at all?'

He doesn't reply for a moment. 'We've talked about this before. Why do we have to go back into it now?'

'I just want to be certain. Did you speak to her in those last few hours?'

'No.'

'Or in the last couple of weeks?'

'*No.*' His voice is loud.

He rubs his palm on the side of his head, through what's left of his dark auburn hair.

'What about any calls or messages?' I ask. 'Did she text you?'

Oliver closes his eyes. 'No, Tess, she didn't. I hadn't heard from her in over a month.' He looks at me, a pinkish shade to his eyes. 'Need I remind you that *she* broke up with *me*, for no good reason at all. Wham' – his hand thumps into his chest – 'out of nowhere, no explanation. Just *I can't do this anymore. It's over, Ol.* Pulling my life out from under me.'

I remember. I was surprised too. They'd been so happy, something yellow about them – their relationship a colour like saffron, warm and effortless. I'd felt envious. And Rosie dumped him as if discarding a packet of crisps.

More than once I tried to find out why, to uncover what was going on. But she didn't want to talk about it. Her voice like an answering machine making short, practised statements.

Oliver's breath grows calmer. I glance at him, his chest rising and falling. Why this outburst? Is he distressed and grieving? Or something else? A darker undertone. A hint of violence beneath the surface. I look at that black Viking tattoo, at his knuckles, and wonder what they're capable of.

When Oliver speaks again it's a murmur from his throat. 'You don't need me to tell you that she changed. She wasn't Rosie anymore.'

'You're right,' I say. 'She wasn't. That's why I want to ask you about anything she might have said that was unusual, that didn't seem right, especially towards the end.' I grip the edge of the wall. 'Since you didn't see her, perhaps texts?'

'She'd stopped texting me, as I just said.'

'OK.' I keep my tone calm. 'But what about the last few texts she sent? Or the last one? When was that?'

'The fifteenth of December, two days after the pub.'

The fifteenth. Did I see her that day?

'Want me to recite it?' he offers with a hint of sarcasm. 'Because I've read it hundreds of times, I could probably say it in my sleep. *I know you don't understand. But I've done things I can't explain to myself, so how could I explain them to you? It's not worth it, Ol. You should find someone else. Please leave me alone. I don't want to hear from you again.*'

His words ring in my head. *Her* words. What else might she have said to him? Or Oliver to her? Because his alibi was confirmed by multiple people – staff of the hotel he was staying at in Cardiff that night, colleagues at the work conference – a line was drawn through his name. He was out of town. But there could be evidence in their texts. Clues.

'Please can I see it? The text? Do you have your phone?' I'm speaking fast. Rosie's phone might be lost, but Oliver's is here – somewhere in one of his pockets.

He doesn't move.

'Please, Oliver.'

I'm not expecting him to do it. Why would he show me his phone? It's private. But then he sighs and takes it out. I watch his thumb on the screen, anticipation thudding. He finds the message and hands it to me.

My eyes lock on the green message bubble. It's just as he narrated, word-for-word. The name Rosie Hartley heads the conversation. Her text dated: *15 December, 14:37.*

Above and below her green bubble are grey boxes – Oliver's texts. *You have to explain what's going on*, I glimpse. *For fuck's sake Rosie, please.* Further up, the night of the thirteenth when they met at the pub. *Where are you? I'm worried.* Then late at 1 a.m.: *I didn't mean to hurt you. I love you so much. You know that.*

I scroll down to the texts after the fifteenth. Grey box, grey box, grey box. *Why are you doing this?* Another: *You can't just cut me out. I'm not some tumour.* Text after text from Oliver. *I'm sorry I called you a bitch. I was drunk, I didn't mean it.* In January: *Please call me back, Rosie. If you don't I might do something—*

The phone slides out of my grip. Oliver grabbing it from my fingers and pushing it back inside his pocket. There are pink smudges in his cheeks.

My hand is hovering in mid-air. What did I just see?

'This is insensitive of you, Tess,' he says, voice gluey. 'What are you hoping to gain from us meeting and talking about her?'

The colour in his face is deeper. Embarrassment? Guilt?

'She's not coming back.'

My hand drops to my lap, my skin going cold. *Not coming back.* No. But I can gain something. *I can get you.*

'What's wrong, Oliver?' Mockery flattens my question.

'What?'

'Why are you blushing? Being so hostile?'

His face is lined in a frown. 'I'm not. You're just . . . This is really hard for me, OK, Tess? I can't get a grip on it, I can't deal with—'

'What? My questions? Me striking closer to the truth?'

He stares at me.

'It was you.' The words come out whisper-sharp.

'What?'

'You were there that night on Hampstead Heath. You hurt her.'

'*What?* How can you . . . What the hell are you implying?' His tone is rising.

'You heard me,' I say, louder.

He looks as if he's hit glass. 'What the *fuck*, Tess?' He stands up, jerking round to face me. 'What are you saying to me?'

'I'm saying you did something! I know you were involved in her death.'

'How dare you.' His head is shaking. 'How could you ever . . . I loved her. She was everything to me, when she died—'

'When you hit her.'

'Shut up!' he shouts. 'Stop saying that.'

I glance around. People are looking at us, curious at his yelling.

'Look at me!'

I turn back to him with a flicker of fear. He's standing over me, his body blocking the fountain. The fountain girl's feet just visible above his head.

'This is me, Tess.' His palms are hanging open in front of me. 'You think I did that to your sister? Made her brain bleed?'

Those two words, *brain bleed*, make me grimace. My neck's stretched back to look up at him.

'You're crazy. Something wrong with your head.' He taps the side of his skull with a finger. The one with the inguz tattoo.

I stand up and face him, level. 'What's the matter, Oliver? Have I hit a guilty nerve?'

'*Jesus*,' he flares, lifting his arms. 'You're not listening—'

'Miss?' A man has approached us. In his forties, in a suit and tie, concerned eyes on me. 'Is everything all right here?'

'Yes, I'm fine, thank you.'

The man lingers a moment then carries on towards Tower Bridge. Its spires are glaring gold in the sun.

Oliver stares through me. The bones in his face seem gaunter.

'If it wasn't you, then who was it?' I accuse.

'How should I know? Don't you think I've asked that question a million times? Who the hell laid his hands on her? *Touched* my girlfriend?'

My girlfriend. As if they were still together.

His eyes are gleaming. He turns his head to the side, shoulders hunched over. When he looks at me again there's something else in his face. Something I'm unsure of.

'Where were you?' he says.

'What?'

'That night – where were you?'

I freeze, my throat tight.

'I've often wondered about that as well,' he says. 'What you were up to. What her sister was doing, especially when Rosie was so vulnerable.' Our energy has shifted. He's stepping on me, pressing me under his heel. 'When did *you* last see her, Tess?'

I clench and unclench my fists.

'You left her there. Let her stay out all night.' His voice is a sneer. 'If anyone killed her, it was you.'

Suddenly I can't breathe. His words like knife-points.

He turns to walk off.

'No, wait.' I grab his elbow. 'You're not leav—'

He rips his arm away, shoving me with the movement. 'I'm not listening to any more of this shit. It should have been you who died. Not her.'

13

'I need to speak to Pettiford.'

The woman on the front desk looks up, arcing her right eyebrow at me. Her mascara is so thick it looks like fake eyelashes.

'Ms Hartley,' she says. 'As I said when you first came in, Detective Sergeant Pettiford will see you when he's able.'

'But I've been here for nearly two hours. What's he doing? Where is he?'

'I believe he's currently out on another case, so you'll have to wait. Unless you want to come back tomorrow?'

I grit my teeth then release them. 'No. I'll wait.'

She clackers her keyboard – loud through the glass screen. When I don't move, she glances up again.

'If you could return to the waiting area until someone comes to get you, Ms Hartley, that would be appreciated.'

Grudgingly I go and sit on the bench-chair again, the metal hard against my back. Whoever designed this place must have been trying to make visitors more uncomfortable. Strip lighting, pale walls, diagonal floor stripes. And blue everywhere. It's too vibrant. Too cold.

I came straight to the police station, only noticing the dampness in my hair and clothes when I arrived. The spray from the dolphin fountain all over my body, traced with chlorine.

I press my arms into my abdomen. After twenty minutes I notice a man's eyes on me. They flick down to my jiggling leg.

Another twenty minutes before: 'Ms Hartley?'

A young uniformed officer with a shiny face leads me through security-door corridors into a small room with a table. No windows. A strange smell I can't quite place.

'Detective Pettiford will be with you shortly,' he says.

He has a pierced lobe, but no earring. The door thuds shut behind him and I have the feeling of being locked in.

Ten minutes, total silence. Is this room soundproof? I squint up at the halogen lights with their bluish glare.

Finally, the door opens and Pettiford appears. Wearing his classic purple tie, loose inside the collar. His hair even thinner than when I last saw him, white skin showing through the wisps. He smiles with lips pressed shut.

'Tess,' he says. There's a file tucked under his arm. He drops it on the table and sits in the plastic chair, heavily. He looks drawn. 'How are you doing?'

'I'm sorry to bother you, coming to the station like this, but it's important.'

'That's fine. I'm afraid I haven't got long – there's a team meeting in a few minutes.' He scratches his cheekbone with the back of his thumb. 'But please tell me.'

'Oliver Barlow.'

He blinks twice.

'He was the one who hurt her.'

Pettiford shifts in his chair, crossing his ankles. 'As you know, we investigated him. We spoke to him first, in fact.'

'But what if he secretly drove back to London? And he knew she was on Hampstead Heath?'

He swivels the file and opens it up. Rosie's file. A glimpse of her passport-style picture as he flicks through. I stare at all those bits of paper, resisting the urge to snatch the file from him so I can look.

'We have CCTV footage of him leaving a club in central Cardiff after one a.m.,' Pettiford says. 'Then returning to his hotel, walking through reception.'

'So? He could still have driven to London in the night.'

He consults the file. 'He checked out of the hotel at nine a.m. the next morning. I'm afraid it's almost physically impossible for him to have travelled to London and back within seven hours.'

'But it's not *impossible.*' I press my brogue – Rosie's brogue – into the floor.

'Well,' he says, flipping a page up. 'Granted, there is a window of a few minutes.'

My spine loosens as the paper floats back down. I'm tense. My hands feel hot.

'But what makes you—'

'I have evidence against him,' I declare.

Pettiford clears his throat. 'What evidence?'

'I saw him today, just now. I met with him.' My sentences sound robotic.

'OK, and what happened?'

'He was edgy and defensive, he shouted at me. And just before he left, he shoved me.'

'And why was he doing all these things?'

I hesitate, suddenly aware of how airless it is in here.

'What were you discussing?' Pettiford prompts. 'What did you say to him?'

'I accused him of killing Rosie.'

Something drops through his eyes. His fingertips perch on her file as he looks at the table. 'Quite an extreme accusation, Tess. Don't take this the wrong way, but it sounds like you were provoking him.'

So what if I was? Trying to provoke the truth, to draw out an acknowledgement. Isn't that what the police are supposed to be doing?

'I saw his phone,' I say, switching tack. 'He showed me the last text Rosie sent him in December.'

Pettiford is silent.

'And I saw some other texts of his which were worrying – obsessive and implying violence.' I pause, waiting. 'You never checked his phone, did you?'

'A colleague did look at it.'

'What?' He never mentioned that. 'Which colleague? Who?'

'Detective Constable Evans.'

Right, I think. *But not you*. 'I don't care if DC Evans already glanced over his phone, I'm telling you I saw some suspicious texts. He was disturbed and unstable; he wouldn't leave Rosie alone after she broke up with him. You need to read his messages, investigate him further.'

'OK, Tess,' Pettiford says, businesslike, taking a pen out of his pocket and clicking the top. 'What exactly did you see in his texts?'

I have to think for a moment, remember the language. 'In one of them, he called her a bitch.'

Pettiford scribbles in green ink.

'*For fuck's sake* – he wrote that. *I didn't mean to hurt you*.' I'm gripping my thumb. 'Oh, and in the last text I saw he said *Please call me back. If you don't, I might do something*.'

Pettiford keeps writing.

'There were more words after that, but he snatched the phone back.'

He full-stops and clicks the pen. Looks at the page a moment. 'All right, Tess, I'll look into this. Contact Mr Barlow and perhaps bring him in again.'

Emotion tingles through me – something close to excitement, hot and bitter.

'But you need to stay away from him, and don't contact him. It could compromise our investigation. All right?'

I nod.

'And, as before, I don't want you to pin all your hopes here. Or build the wrong impression about Mr Barlow before anything's been concluded. His alibi is concrete, and when I questioned him, he didn't seem . . .'

His fireside voice rasps in my ears. This again. Toning me down, guiding me back into my corner.

'Well,' his head tips, 'I'll follow this up and we'll go from there.' He pushes the papers inside the file. 'I'm sorry but I need to get to this meeting. Was there anything else you wanted to tell me?'

I inhale slowly, anticipation dulled by the way he's wrapping up. 'No, that was it.'

He gives me another compact smile. 'Good. I'll be in touch. Take care of yourself.'

* * *

My brogues scuff the tarmac. It looks black, a strange shade in the lamplit dark. London night never absolute.

I've been walking for hours. After seeing Pettiford, I felt feverish. I couldn't settle. The clash with Oliver, those texts on his phone, the fact that Pettiford's going to investigate him. Even though he minimised the likelihood, the police are now onto him. The investigation is picking up again. A lead that I think will actually go somewhere.

My clothes are damp, goosebumps on my skin. The road is wet and glowing, its surface reflecting coloured light. It rained half an hour ago. After weeks of sun and drought, spits of drizzle, then full drops on my face. And that smell. Rain on hot concrete, metallic.

I've been wandering through Haggerston, Dalston, Kingsland. Gentrification developing these areas by day, but a different story at night. Pavements scattered with rubbish, the homeless here and there, the odd person loitering in alleyways.

But nothing. No one bites.

I'm parading myself around, a woman on her own at night in a huge city. And no harassment. Not even a wolf whistle.

The lamplight is hazy, urban mist hovering over the buildings. It seems to dampen sound as I detect a strange purring behind me. I look over my shoulder and there's a car sidling past. A dent in the back door, windows blacked out. I can't see the driver, or anyone inside. This sense that they're watching me through the tinted glass. The hairs on my neck stand up.

The car accelerates off, disappearing round the corner. False suspense once again.

Then, two figures appear from behind a bus stop. One of them is hooded, the other big and broad-shouldered.

I quicken my stride.

The one in the hood has a pale face. He looks at me and his friend's eyes follow. My heart pumps against breastbone. The bulky one tips his head and says something to the hooded guy. A murmur I can't hear. Pale-face smirks, then bulky looks at me and does the same – a drawn smile.

Adrenaline flows to my fingertips. This is it.

Five steps away, my brogue slips on the wet tarmac, my leg sliding sideways. Pale-face bursts out laughing. His friend snorts as I almost lurch into his shoulder. They go straight past, laughter echoing.

The adrenaline drains away. Gingerly I step towards the wall and lean against it.

What am I doing? Why am I out here?

I don't have a simple answer. To get hurt, experience what Rosie went through. To feel *something*. The risk, the thrill. Or some kind of payback. The potential in this situation. I could hurt a man – any man. The next one I see, even. Take a rock to his skull.

I slide my back down the wall and sit on the pavement. The wet seeps into my culottes. Around me there are cigarette butts. Like Rosie, hunched up on a filthy street.

I remember one time she was sitting beside rubbish, tea bags and chicken nuggets near her legs. I was trying to talk some sense into her. Tired of worrying about her, of having to go out into the night to find her, of trying to understand why she shut me out.

The tether between us had gone slack. Her hands were letting go and there was nothing to pull on. I tried to get her to see a therapist. But she wouldn't. If I even mentioned the word doctor she'd shrink back.

Once she told me to fuck off. I'd come to get her in Finsbury Park at four in the morning and I said I was taking her to the hospital. Her eyes widened. For a split-second there was fear in her face, a grey-coloured dread. But then it turned to anger. 'No, no, not there,' she said. 'I'm not going there.'

The next time was in Greenwich after midnight; the next a Peckham backstreet. I couldn't make sense of her behaviour. I couldn't get her to stop.

There's a rustling sound, followed by a clatter. A plastic bottle rolls from behind a bin. It drops onto a drain cover and rocks still. I watch the zone for movement, blood in my ears.

After a minute someone appears, walking along the opposite pavement, body lurchy. White gangly legs. A girl.

I get up and cross the street towards her. 'Hey, are you all right?'

She looks round. Her face is thick with make-up, and her expression is clear: alarmed. She presses her handbag into her stomach.

'I just want to make sure you're OK,' I say, following. 'You're not lost, are you?'

'I'm fine.' Her voice is hoarse.

'Do you need some money?'

Her pace quickens.

'What are you doing out alone so late? It's not safe.'

She's jogging now, wobbly in her heels. Not drunk – just unpractised. A literal tenderfoot.

'How old are you? Fifteen?'

'Who the hell are you?' she hisses. 'My mother?'

'I'm only trying—'

'Leave me alone!'

She starts running and I slow to a stop. I watch her silky hair bouncing on her shoulders. At the corner she glances back. Her body language is unmistakable, as is her look. Anxious. Afraid of me.

14

Wind blows in through the guest room window. It's fanning the curtain over the frame, hot air on my face. The rain was brief – it came in the night like a secret.

Arran left early and I can't help myself.

The diary isn't in the bedside drawer. Where else might he have put it? There are two canvas bags beside the desk. One is printed with an oak leaf and is empty. The other has a shop-front illustration of Daunt Books, an independent London bookstore. Inside is *The Black Tulip* by Alexandre Dumas. I thumb through, but there's nothing tucked inside.

Or wait – there is something. A slightly bigger gap between two pages. I open it and blink at the creature lying there, beside the spine. A butterfly. Pressed into paper, powdery marks from its wings left on the page.

It's normal to press flowers. But insects?

The wide spots on the butterfly wings are like eyes, a cat staring out at me. Why would Arran want to preserve it like this inside a novel? Beautiful and dead.

I close it gently and replace the book inside the bag, refocusing on the diary. I scan round the room again. Under the mattress? I lift it up.

Bingo. The diary is lying on the slats. Why here? And why is he moving it around, to these discreet places? I feel a grip of worry that he could be onto me – that he knows I've been in the room, poking about. Or worse, that he knows I've read his diary.

But wouldn't he have raised it with me if so? Possibly left for another bnb if he was uncomfortable?

I don't know his character well enough to gauge how he would react. Whether he would challenge me or not. Nevertheless – what's he hiding?

I pick up the diary and flick to the next entry.

I rang Laura. I needed to speak to someone and I knew her voice would help. When I told her about you she said you sounded like a dream. Then she said I was a moron and I should have just gone up and talked to you and why didn't I? Women want nice guys to simply say hello and look them in the eye and make a real conversation. Unlike all the leering pervs out there who have no clue about girls and treat them like cushions they can sit on or chuck away.

I told her I got the idea.

She softened and told me not to give up, I might see you again. Maybe it wasn't coincidence we were both in that cafe. I want to believe her. I do.

But as soon as I hung up, I felt the glumness seeping in, a dark leaking feeling.

The entry ends there. I scan it again, then turn the page. More writing.

I've often thought there's a pathetic lack of imagination in this world. And it's been three weeks since I saw you, so I've been fostering mine, in stolen moments.

The flush in your face when you see me. Your wrist skin. Your pillow giggle. Talking for hours into the night. The clench of your thighs round my waist. Your scent after a shower. Dancing in the kitchen. Kissing away the tears from your cheeks. Warm in bed, body to body.

I could go on.

The brain is a powerful thing. Too powerful sometimes, it's annoying. These things about you are fantasy. Not real.

I went on a date a few days ago, with a girl called Sabine. She was pretty, telling me how I had to visit Canada one day. Her skin was dark. Against it her gold jewellery popped. And she had this cute way of rubbing her eyelashes and gently squeezing the skin under her chin.

But she didn't interest me, not like you did.

It's intriguing, what he writes. Observant, noticing the little details. He almost seems too good at it. Hawk eyes flitting over bodies, wide and watching. Or more like a deer: soft, cautious?

Gold jewellery again, on this girl Sabine. The other things in his imagination, which seems to be swirling, not unlike mine. He hasn't even interacted with this woman. What has him so captivated? They could have nothing in common, nothing to talk about. She might not even like him. Though I don't see how she couldn't. How she could not like having his eyes on her. His hands.

I turn to the next page and it's white.

A tug of disappointment. He has to write more. This narrative – a thread between us he's unaware of. A secret connection, all for me.

15

Nalika is coming over for a drink, bringing custard tarts. Those little puff pastry ones, *pastéis de nata*, from an authentic Portuguese bakery in Covent Garden. Since we visited Lisbon one university summer, they've been our thing.

When she texted me again at lunchtime, I felt a twinge. My conscience whispering, *You're a bad friend*. I've been too wrapped in myself, folding everything around me like package paper. I messaged her back suggesting this evening.

I'm sitting in the open living room window waiting for her, my back against the frame, one leg dangling out over the wall.

Across the road, the old man is dusting his gnome. The flat above still has its net curtains closed, except for a strip in the centre. The door to number 74 opens and someone steps out – a blond guy with a low hairline. He catches sight of me.

I offer a neighbourly wave. 'Hey, Elliot.'

He gazes up at me, unmoving, then lifts his hand. There's something hesitant about his stance before he walks off down the street. Swift pace.

I swing my leg on the wall, glancing the other way, checking the road for Nalika. And for Arran. He's been out all day. At work, I presume, or maybe his studio. Part of me is hoping Nalika will have left before he returns. I don't want them to cross over. I'm not sure why, I just don't.

There's a knock on my front door. A soft *tap-tap-tap*. I hoist my leg inside and go and pull it open.

Ivy is standing there, barefoot. She smiles. 'Hey, Tess, sorry to bother you.'

Her hair is tied up high, ginger strands scraped back on her skull. There's something white on her cheek, and on her black tie-front top. Presented like this on my doorstep, I realise how young she is. Early twenties I'd guess.

'I'm just baking a cake for Luke,' she says swiftly. 'The recipe says to sift the flour, but he doesn't have a sieve in his flat, so I was wondering if I could borrow one?'

I catch up with her gabbly words.

'I mean, who doesn't own a sieve?'

There are dark bits in her mouth, I notice. Multiple molar fillings. Not quite hidden behind her short front teeth.

'Uh ... sure,' I answer. 'You can use mine. But you know you don't really need to sift flour?'

'Oh. Really?'

'Yeah, it's just one of those gimmicky things.'

She blows air through her lips. 'I'm not really a baker. I kinda hate it.'

'So why are you making a cake?'

'It's a congratulations cake for getting his poetry published.'

'Uh-huh. What kind of cake?'

'Lemon drizzle, his favourite apparently.' She rolls her eyes. 'Most boring cake in the world if you ask me.'

'I'll second that.'

I'm looking at her top, wondering how she managed to get so much flour on herself. A hand print on the black material. When I look up, her eyes are on my face.

'Well,' I say, 'hope it turns out—'

'Actually, one more thing – you don't have a spare egg, do you? I need two and there's one lonely egg left downstairs.'

For a breath, I hesitate. 'Sure, you can have an egg, let me grab it.'

I didn't invite her in but she follows me into the living area, bare soles silent. When I turn from the fridge with the egg, she's looking at the bookcase. Her feet are so white. And small.

'I love these elephants,' she says, indicating the marble elephant inlaid with stones. 'From Agra, right?'

'How did you know that?'

'I've got one too. Same as everyone who visits the Taj Mahal.' She straightens, pushing her long ponytail over her shoulder. 'Ah, thanks so much.'

Her fingers brush mine as she takes the egg. They're cold.

'No worries,' I say. 'How come you're baking in Luke's flat anyway?'

'He's got some after-work drinks thing, so I'm cooking dinner as a surprise.'

I nod. She must have a key then.

'So are you guys together or . . .?' I'm prying now.

Her arms are folded, the egg tucked beneath her elbow. 'Sort of. I don't really like definitions or limitations. Men impose enough of them on us, don't they?' She's casual, in her face and posture. But there's something beneath it – a derisive inflection in her voice. 'Just a bit of fun, you know.'

'Hey, why not. Do whatever you like.' I'm in no position to judge.

There's a faint scent on her, almost grassy.

'Thanks again for this.' She holds up the egg between thumb and forefinger. 'You're an egg-saver.'

I laugh. I can't help it. She's witty, a sharp intelligence in her fern-green eyes. It makes me wonder what she's doing with Luke. Maybe because she's so much younger than him – by about ten years, if my estimation is right. Luke is thirty-two, a year older than me. Some people are drawn to older romantic partners, a kind of fascination or validation in it.

'If you hear any roars,' she says, heading for the door, 'I've either burnt it or it's turned into a lemon puddle cake.'

'Good luck.'

She smiles and goes back down the stairs, her feet silent on the steps.

I admire her kindness, making a cake like that. And her carefree air. Something I haven't been able to glow with since last year, and I'm not sure I ever will again. At least not in the same way as before.

Five minutes later, Nalika rings the buzzer.

'All right, amiga.' She hugs me with one arm, balancing a white box on the other. 'I've been guarding these tarts all the way from Covent Garden. A kid was eyeing them up on my lap, and some stupid guy with a tuba nearly squashed them. But fear not, they arrive unharmed and fresh from their Portuguese oven.'

I look down into the box where four little tarts sit. 'A tuba on the tube?'

'I know right? And at rush hour on a Friday, ironic moron.'

She dumps her bag on the sofa.

'White or red?' I ask.

'Ooh, white please.'

As I twist the corkscrew into the bottle, she plaits her hair. Thick and beautiful. She swears by aloe leaf juice, and occasionally mayonnaise. Perhaps I should try it.

'Damn heat,' she says. 'I can't handle it anymore. This is England, not Greece.'

'Talking to the sun there?'

'*Yes*, I am.' She holds up her arms to the sky. 'This isn't right, sun. We expect hot and humid in India, but London? What are you trying to tell us? You sick or something?'

Smiling, I pop the cork out and pour the pale liquid. Nalika is facing Rosie's painting, rubbing the back of her neck. I try to remember the last time she was here. More than a month ago – maybe two.

'Here,' I say.

She takes the glass and chinks it against mine. 'Cheers, Rivero.'

We both sip. It's smooth and melony.

'Now for the cream,' Nalika says, holding the box out towards me. 'Select your tart.'

I choose one with a big burnt-sugar blob in the centre. We bite into them, the custard gooey and sublime.

'Mmm, mm, mm,' she says, mouth full. 'Just so *good*.'

The custard is all over my teeth. 'Thanks for getting them.'

'*De nada*. I should have bought more. I could eat about ten of these.' She licks her thumb. 'So how's it going with your Scandi?'

It takes me a moment to realise she's talking about Arran. 'He's not Scandinavian, he's from Yorkshire.'

She points at the ground and mouths, *Is he here?*

I shake my head.

'Shame,' she says. 'So all fine then? You haven't caught any verrucas?'

'Not that I'm aware of.'

She smirks and sits on the sofa, pulling up her skirt to tuck her legs in. 'What's he like? Are you getting on well?'

I sit down next to her. 'He's uh . . . nice.'

'Nice? Elaborate please.'

I'm reluctant to talk about him. For no solid reason, just a feeling in my side. 'He's cool. We've had a few interesting conversations. He's a graphic designer and ceramicist.'

And I've read a few interesting things in his diary. Which I would never tell Nalika. For one thing, she doesn't know I snoop through people's possessions. For another, breathing a single word of Arran's entries would feel wrong. They're confidential, for my prying eyes only, however skewed that morality is.

'A ceramicist, eh?' Nalika says. 'He must have lovely hands then.'

'Why do you say that?'

'I dunno, I just can't imagine a guy with farmer hands or fat fingers making beautiful pots.'

She's right there.

'So, is there anything?' she asks.

'What do you mean?'

'Between you two?'

I frown at her.

'Do you like him?' She speaks slowly, as if I'm dim.

'What? *No.*'

'Sounds like you might.'

'Nalika.' A warning clips my voice. 'It's not like that. He's my bnb guest.'

'So what? There's no rule against it. Why not be open to the possibility? Maybe even flirt a bit to see how he responds?'

'Why are you asking me about this? Trying to push it?'

I can feel her eyes on the side of my face. 'I just worry about you. That you're quite isolated at the moment, closing yourself off from people.'

Closing myself off? It's others who drift away, who shrink at the first creep of shadow. Friends – like Sarah, whose flat I was living in when Rosie died, who showed barely a shred of understanding about me having to suddenly leave, unable to pay any more rent. Oliver. My parents. Rosie was the gleaming child, especially in my dad's eyes. She was closer to my mum. I was difficult when I was little. I used to get upset by the slightest thing. Oversensitive, they'd call it. I often ruined holidays or special occasions for everyone else. I would go quiet for days – they couldn't get me to speak, worried, eventually taking me to the doctor. My mum especially couldn't handle my moods.

There was a smoothness to Rosie's relationship with our parents, which mine's never had. I've always been something a little gritty in their mouths.

Rosie was our bond. The bridge in our family since they moved to Spain. Now that she's gone, there's nothing to hold the connection. Only limp ties. A stretching gap, wider than water and land.

'I have you, Nalika,' I state.

'Other than me.' She pauses. 'You haven't been in a relationship for a while. I think it might help you to have that support and care and . . . affection.'

She hesitated on the final word – she was going to say love. My conscience twinges again. She's just broken up with her partner of years and I didn't even know. I haven't been there for her. I look at her, trying to read her aura.

'Nalika, I wanted to ask you about Chris. How are you doing? I know you said you were the one who initiat—'

'I don't want to talk about that.' She straightens the large amazonite pendant on her chest. 'In fact, I've been on a few dates recently.'

'You mean online dating?'

'Yeah. I've got another one tomorrow.'

I take in her blasé expression, unsure if it's a front.

'You should give it a go,' she says.

'No.'

'Why not?'

'It's not for me.'

'But it's fun. It could—'

'Not everything's about *me*, all right?' I slump against the cushion, then pull it out onto my lap. 'I'm sick of me.'

Nalika's quiet for a moment, then says, 'Tess, you know I'm speaking as your friend. I only want to help.'

I soften. 'I know.'

'And it'd be good for you to get out a bit more, that's all.'

I think I get out more than anyone else she knows. Though I'm sure she doesn't mean skulking in dark streets after midnight.

I change the subject. 'I saw Oliver.'

'What? When?'

'Yesterday. He suddenly agreed to meet me.'

'How was it? Helpful to see him?'

'I accused him of killing Rosie.'

Nalika blinks at me. I've mentioned him to her a few times before, how I'm sure he knows something, he might have information, but this is my first use of that word – kill.

'What do you mean?' she says, tone quiet with surprise. 'You really think it could be him?'

I nod, squeezing the cushion.

She puts her wine down, the glass clinking on wood.

'He intimidated me,' I say. 'Shouted and pushed me. He looks completely different – he's not the Oliver that Rosie once knew. Not that sweet breezy guy. And I saw some texts on his phone.'

'Texts? How?'

'He let me look at his phone when I asked about Rosie's last text to him,' I explain. 'I wanted to know what she'd said, and he showed it to me.'

'That's a bit of a strange thing to do, to show you his phone. I wouldn't hand mine over to anyone. Especially not my ex-girlfriend's sister, if I might have . . .' She's silent, unfolding her legs. 'What did the texts say?'

'They were disturbing. His language obsessive, verging on threatening. I went straight to Pettiford and he's going to follow it up.'

There's a faint crease in Nalika's brow. 'Did the police not look at his phone before?'

'They did, apparently, but because of his alibi—'

A key scratches in the lock. We both turn as Arran steps through the door, wiping his feet on the mat. He looks up and sees us. There's a moment of suspension where nobody moves, then Nalika springs up.

'Hi, I'm Nalika.' She holds out her hand.

There's something pale and rigid about Arran's face. I can't read what it is. More than hesitation. He glances at her hand, seeming like he's not going to take it. But then he smiles and does. 'Arran.'

He's looking Nalika in the eye. She shakes his hand up and down, the movement lingering.

'I'm Tess's friend from university,' she says.

There's no clay on Arran's hands today, I notice, but he's wearing a T-shirt with finger smudges on the cream material.

'Nice to meet you,' he says.

His eyes finally leave her face, dropping down her body before he steps past and goes towards the kitchen. With his back to us Nalika points at him, mouths, *Oh my God*, then holds her mouth open wide. I expand my eyes at her. Then I watch him take a glass from the cupboard and fill it with water. Wondering what just happened – a weird moment.

'Would you like a glass of wine?' Nalika asks him, voice loud.

Arran twists his head over his shoulder.

'We're having some,' she says. 'You could join us.'

'That's generous. But no, thank you.'

'How about a Portuguese custard tart?' Nalika asks, indicating the box on the table.

Arran glances at it and smiles. 'Very tempting, but again no thanks. I'm heading out and need to go shower.' He tugs at his dirty T-shirt.

'Oh, where are you going? Big night out?'

Why does she sound so flirty? Although that was my thought – is he going to see diary girl?

'I'm going to a gig.'

'Rock 'n' roll?' Nalika asks before I can get a word in. She's leaning against the sofa, long legs on display. 'Hip-hop?'

Arran's eyes meet mine. In that instant, one of the lines from his diary flashes. *Warm in bed, body to body.* I imagine his body pressed against a woman's, his chest curved into her back. I blink and the impression is gone.

'Acoustic,' he says. 'A few different bands, I think. Folk, jazz, Cuban.'

'Hmm, eclectic mix.' Nalika looks round at me. 'So, Tess tells me you're a ceramicist.'

Does she have to so blatantly reveal that we've talked about him? I consider poking her in the back.

Arran swallows some more water. 'A budding ceramicist is the correct term.'

'Have you just been throwing some pots?'

'I have actually. A dipping bowl.'

'A what?'

He looks at me again. There's a little more ease in his face, though the stiffness remains in his body language. 'A bowl for soy sauce, dips, things like that.' He puts the glass in the sink. 'I'd better get on.' He strides past, skirting round Nalika's feet. 'Good to meet you.'

'You too, Arran.'

Pushing herself off the sofa and swivelling round, she leers at me. I focus on a clump of dust and hair beside my feet. I don't want to share the provocative curl of her mouth. I stand up and finish my glass of wine.

'Well, well,' Nalika murmurs behind me.

There's a niggle in my stomach. I've never thought of myself as possessive or grabby but, out of nowhere, the reaction is strong. Arran's mine.

She is a naughty thing. Does what she wants. Fingers things that aren't hers. Did no one ever teach her respect?

It's not that I don't like it. The creeping voyeur. We have things in common.

She hums while she works on her laptop, and sometimes when she's walking. I don't think she's conscious of doing it – a little tic, a quiver of her voice box. I hum to calm myself, when my body needs to soften or settle, the vibration through my skull. We both have attached earlobes and neat ears. I can't read her mind, obviously, but I'm pretty sure she has poisonous thoughts. Her soul is a sky lantern. Made of paper, hollow yet lit from within. Floating in salt wind or caught on a branch, flapping. She hates citrus. Which is strange, considering she's from the land of oranges.

And, there are things which are very different. Her lilting voice. The way she rubs the bones at the back of her neck. Her smell. She isn't scared of the dark.

And her lack of respect. I learned it a long time ago, when I was six, and I touched my mother's things. Silence, cold and cruel. Her eyes like boiled wool. When I got older, pierced by words. Sneered at.

I watch. I come close. But I don't touch.

16

I don't know where Arran is. My first thought was maybe he never came back after his gig. But he must have slept here and gone out again because there's a new entry in the diary. Four words surrounded by white:

Holy shit. It's you.

I stare at the page, those two words jutting out. *It's you.*

My immediate thought is: where? If he's come across her again. That kernel of possibility in my torso, wondering – in my doorway? On the bnb website?

In the previous entry, he said he hadn't seen the woman for three weeks. Which could work, if he first saw me in a cafe a few weeks back. It's still too vague though, a tenuous thing. We met before Arran wrote this line. Yet the sensation is warming, an odd sort of heat, with a kick to it.

He could mean here, in the flat.

But then – wait. What if he's referring to Nalika? The warmth fades fast, to cold.

The timing is too synchronous. Too close. She was here last night and he's written this. From the physical details he's given, she could be a match. The idea of it prickles.

* * *

Borough Market is congested with people. Everyone out on a Saturday afternoon, here for their street-food lunch or supplies from the stalls. It's stuffy under the old arches, the air thick with steam and frying and fat. I look up at the green railway vaults. Starlings chatter and squabble, darting between the beams.

I needed to come out, feel people around me. Be just another body in a crowd. It helped at first but now it's too busy. I push through the couples and groups, walking quickly under a low brick arch.

The last time I was here, I was with Rosie. She was eating fresh tortellini and a starling swooped too close, making her drop it. She shouted and waved her fist, one of those times when humour was still mixed into her anger. Eventually the humour seeped away. But that day Rosie looked down and said, 'Poor pasta. Look, squashed to death.'

The parcels had been stepped on, pumpkin smeared on the tarmac.

'Stupid birds,' she muttered, while I laughed.

Oliver. He reminds me of a bird. A corvid – something unnerving about their eyes, an eerie intelligence. His are like that.

No word from Pettiford yet. I resist the impulse to call him, the itch in my fingers to text Oliver. To pester or pursue him myself.

As I look up something catches my eye. Blond hair. That bright honey colour waving over an ear and cheekbone. I blink but the flash of it's gone behind faces and bodies. I shift my head, trying to locate the figure. But there's no trace of him.

I'm frowning. There are loads of blond men around the market – in a few seconds I can count more than ten.

I take a breath, trying to steady what's going on in my head. Since that entry, my thoughts won't stop coiling, stuck on Arran, twisted up with Nalika. I close my eyes for a moment before walking towards the river.

Clouds are hovering over the city, drifting in front of the sun. By the water the air feels cool, almost fresh, if it wasn't for that Thames sludge.

I follow the river path beneath Southwark Bridge, past Shakespeare's Globe, towards the Tate Modern. At the Millennium Bridge I decide to cross back over to the north side. A couple are coming towards me, the man's arm over her shoulder. I try to imagine that gentle weight around my body.

They've gone past when I notice someone behind a girl.

Arran.

I halt, shock in my legs. He's standing near the end of the bridge, looking out over the river. My secret-diary-writing guest, metres ahead of me. The coincidence is too much – bumping into someone you know in a city this size. Central London is a sprawl. Yet here he is.

I stare at the side of his face, at his body casually leaning against the rail, hands clasped together.

Was it him at Borough Market? If he's been following me, surely he'd be behind, not in front. Perhaps he saw which direction I was heading and nipped ahead. Perhaps he's trying to make it look like pure chance.

I don't trust chance, or fate. And seeing him here now, I feel that warmth seeping back in. The possibility of me in the diary. Not Nalika. Me.

'Arran?'

He turns, surprise lighting his face. 'Tess! Hey. What are you doing here?'

'Getting some lunch. At Borough Market,' I add, to see how he reacts.

He doesn't. Not a flicker in his features. I can't tell if the surprise a moment ago was genuine.

'How about you?' I say.

'Oh . . .' He hesitates, shifting his head. 'On a walk.'

Behind me?

'I was supposed to be meeting a friend,' he says. 'But she didn't show.'

'Why not?'

Something glints in his eye. An emotion too faint to discern. 'I don't know. People are a mystery.'

'People or women?'

A smile edges into his lips. 'Women, mostly.'

I'm not sure why I said that. Men are a mystery too, with Arran seeming greyer by the moment.

He looks away, scratching his skull. 'Someone told me recently about a place I had to visit, St Dunstan in the East Church Garden. Do you know it?'

'I think so, yes.'

'It's just along the river,' he says. 'I'm going to the studio and was planning to stop off on the way. Want to come with me?'

I gaze at this man, his shirt flapping softly in the warm river wind. A faint sheen to his forehead – the first sign of sweat I've seen on him. His eyes haven't left my face. I'm the one to break contact, a knotted feeling around all these threads of him, unsure what I'm meant to think or feel.

'Sure,' I say. Why not? An opportunity to interact in a context outside the flat – to read him a little deeper.

'Cool, come on then.'

We set off along the river, then turn into the road where the Thames path ends. Neither of us speaks. At first, I don't mind the silence. Walking side by side, his body in line with mine. Then, suddenly, I have an urge to bring up Nalika.

'Yesterday, I hope you didn't find Nalika too . . .' I nearly say forward, but I don't want to use that word. 'Direct. She has a lot of confidence. Sort of does what she likes.'

I wait for a reaction to my mention of her, but none comes. No awkward air or strange look like last night in the living area. He seems neutral.

'Not at all,' he says. 'She's a straight talker, it's good.'

'So you like people who are direct?'

'Generally, yes. Dancing round things can get tiring.'

I feel like saying, *You're a dancer*. Meandering and serpentine in his character – or characters.

'Nalika doesn't do that,' I say. 'I've often felt envious of her ability to go after what she wants, just say things, without hesitating.'

'That is an admirable quality. Not when it's in your face though.'

'She can get too close for comfort.'

I don't like saying anything negative about Nalika, but with that diary entry, the possibility of it being her, my *bad friend* mode has slipped back in.

I have always admired her audacity. I've watched her walk up to people under various circumstances. Kiss a guy she likes the look of within five minutes. Confront someone who's wronged her. Once, in a club, she grabbed a girl's arm. My necklace was hanging on her chest – the one I'd lost an hour before. Thirty seconds later it was in Nalika's hand.

'Have you known her long?' Arran asks.

'We met in our first year of university.'

'Oh yes, you mentioned last night, sorry.'

He skirts round a dog, the woman holding the lead looking at him. He doesn't give her a glance. Just steps back over towards me.

'How many years is that then?'

Why is he asking? When I'm silent for a fraction he looks at me. 'Thirteen years,' I answer.

'So you two are good friends?' There's a quality to his voice I can't place.

'She's my best friend, yes.' My only friend, now, in truth.

Arran's response is a faint nod. I'm not sure what that or any of this exchange means. The potential connection between the diary and Nalika like a slow burn on the roof of my mouth, beginning to smart.

We walk beneath a bridge, its low ceiling dropping shade over us. As my eyes adjust, I feel something brush my hand. I glance at Arran, but he's facing forwards, impassive. As though I imagined it.

Yet it felt like his fingers. Touching me in the dark, where I can't see. Sly contact. The knotty threads thicken. I can't straight-talk like Nalika, directly ask him. But I can curve round the diary, flex towards it by working something into the conversation.

'Have you ever done something you can't explain?' I ask. 'Something that makes no sense and you know you have to stop, but you can't?'

Arran looks at me, face still impassive, except for something about the set of his jaw. 'I think we've all done things like that. Following whims and energies beyond the brain's rationality.'

I'm aware of how pertinent this is – my compulsion to look through my guests' possessions.

'I'm glad it's not just me,' I say.

'What specifically are you referring to?'

I think for a moment, how to frame my lie. 'People watching, of a kind, I guess. Sometimes I see someone on the street and my attention gets stuck. I like to see what they're up to, listen to their conversations.' I glance at him, to see if my arrow towards the diary has any edge. It seems flat though. I can't make the point too sharp. 'It's nice to get lost in other people's lives for a while,' I continue. 'Is that weird?'

'No.'

He smiles – a subtle curve to his mouth. I return it as we walk past high-rise offices. A woman with a pushchair goes by, the little girl in it sucking a red ice lolly.

'Sounds like you're describing addiction, of a kind,' Arran says.

Addiction? That's a strong word. 'Perhaps. I could be addicted to strangers' stories.'

'I've never heard that one before. But there are worse things.' There's no judgement in his expression – more like curiosity, tinted with amusement.

I glimpse a glass skyscraper through an alley with a pub, then we come to a row of bollards. A sign reading *St Dunstan's Hill*. Up the slope are clustered trees and a church spire. I wipe the sweat from my cheek, hoping Arran doesn't notice. We walk up some steps towards the church, hanging with vines and leaves. I remember this place now – the sense that you could be in rural France, not London's dirty metropolis.

'What are you addicted to?' I ask.

Arran looks at me, the softness in his eyes from a moment ago suddenly gone. And I think – was this stupid? To work something so connected to his diary into the conversation? Will he see through me?

'That's quite a question. Not easy to answer.' His words are measured and quiet. 'I think addictions are probably one of the most intimate things you can know about someone.'

'Yes. You're right. I didn't mean to—'

'You didn't. It's OK.' The softness comes back with a smile.

He turns to go through the arch and I follow him into the church. It's roofless, trees growing inside the old walls.

'This is amazing,' Arran says. He looks up, the stubble over his jaw lighter in the sun.

'Yeah. It's beautiful.'

I look from the Gothic tracery in one of the windows and find his eyes. Something in his gaze makes my body go still.

He turns away. 'There's a rawness to these places, isn't there? Nature finding its way back inside. I like that.' He speaks towards the wall before wandering over to another doorway.

I go after him, and we're outside the church walls again. The trees seem to make their own roof, sunlight dappling the mosaic floor.

'It reminds me a little of that Tintern Abbey painting by Turner,' Arran says. 'You know the one I mean?'

'I think so. I can picture it, pale and washed out.'

'A watercolour.'

The walls are darker this side, I notice. Stained with pollution. 'I've never liked watercolours,' I say.

'Why not?'

'They're so . . . weak-looking. Bland. I prefer vivid colour and contrast.'

'Like your sister's painting?'

I feel my breath catch, forgetting for a second that we spoke about it. 'Yes. A bit like that.'

Arran nods. Silence between us before, 'That doesn't surprise me. You're not a watercolour.'

'What?'

'I mean if you were a painting, you wouldn't be a watercolour.'

My heart is stronger in my chest. 'What would I be?'

'I'm not sure.' He looks sideways. 'A Kandinsky, maybe. Or a Degas.'

His eyes come back to mine, a smile pulling into his left cheek. Then he breaks my gaze and walks further round the church. I watch his back disappearing through another arch.

When I follow, he's standing beside a small fountain – a bronze disc running with water. I stop next to him, my thoughts lingering on what he just said. And the similarity strikes me – of how I'm with another man next to a fountain.

Arran's still a stranger, a guy I met little over a week ago. Yet it seems like a much longer measure of time. There's a depth to it, an undercurrent I can sense. Already he's not just my bnb guest; I know more about him than he realises.

In contrast, I've known Oliver for years. But he feels like the stranger.

A child's yelp echoes from another part of the ruins. It would be amazing to have an open-air concert in here – an orchestra or just a singer with a guitar. Which reminds me.

'Hey, I didn't ask – how was your gig?'

'My gig?' There's a blankness to Arran's expression.

'Last night. You said you were going to a gig?'

'Oh . . . yeah. It was great.' He bites his lip. 'Look, Tess, I need to go.' His tone is cooler, something stiff about it.

A weight sinks in my stomach.

'Sorry. I need to deal with something. I've just had a . . .'

He doesn't sound sorry, and he's avoiding my eye. I scan the past thirty seconds, wondering what's happened, whether I did something.

Arran moves to go past me, stepping closer. For a heart-rippling moment I think he's going to lean in, maybe kiss me, but then I feel his hand on my arm. The soft touch of his fingers as he murmurs, 'See you later, OK?'

They leave my skin as he walks off. I stare after him, my heart still beating in ripples.

17

The diary isn't under the mattress.

There's a tickle inside my nose. I can't stop sneezing, a cold that came on yesterday evening. Throat sweets are useless, only effective while sucking – that bitter aftertaste of blackcurrant on my tongue. I rub my temples then go for Arran's backpack.

This morning I got up just as he was leaving, and he gave me a short nod. No words or smile before he went through the door. I stood there pondering it. Something cool about the look he gave me, dark and closed.

Yesterday, in the church garden, it felt like there was a connection between us, thrumming somewhere deep. But the way he turned, leaving so fast. What made him shift? It was jarring, strengthening my sense of uncertainty about him. How he seems to have multiple sides. Diary and man, with growing variations, obscure patches that leave me wondering.

I looked at Degas and Kandinsky paintings earlier on my laptop. I don't know much about art but they're beautiful. Moving and human. Something stirring in the images, the colours – it buoyed me. Until I thought of Nalika. The possibility of it being her in the diary still burning my mouth. I need to know more.

I try the bedside drawer again. Back where it was before. His hiding skills aren't brilliant, or very logical. But I suppose I've had more practice.

You. Here of all places, my favourite museum. I'd been looking at statues, then went upstairs into the minerals room, when I came out into the main hall. And there: your face.

I froze.

Looking straight up. Your arms folded, your hair in a loose ponytail. You walked beneath the hanging sculpture, neck arched back, then your eyes skimmed the upper levels, right past me.

I was in shock, thinking: it can't be you. Just there below me, in a completely different part of the city. I could so easily have missed you. If I'd gone into another room. If you'd arrived a minute later. If I hadn't spent so long looking at one particular thing.

But I did.

I found myself drifting down the stairs. You had your back to me. Steps away. Something so lovely about your head – hair sheening round your skull. A black moonstone. That's what it made me think of.

You let out a noisy sigh. Not as though you were bored – a sound I couldn't quite interpret. You looked around the room, your gaze seeming to catch on a woman. A girl with red hair. Then you turned and sauntered by. You still hadn't noticed me, but you were close enough to smell. Rosemary and apple. Too subtle for perfume – more like body lotion.

My eyes stayed with you.

You scratched your arm, slipped your hand inside your top and rubbed your back. I wasn't conscious of what I was doing until we neared the end of the hall. Following you, instinctively, my feet gliding silently on the marbled floor.

You went out through the main entrance. Your body behind glass.

I watched you walk away from me for the second time. My legs pushing but my mind holding them firm. How could I let you go?

I'm gripping the book tight, the page bending between my thumb and finger. I could be creasing it, but that kernel of warmth is rising, up against my diaphragm.

It's not Nalika. She doesn't go to museums. Appreciation of history isn't on her radar – she always says she has better things to do than hang out with the dead.

It could be me.

I think he's talking about the Natural History Museum. It's not one hundred per cent clear, but from his description it would make sense. I was there a few weeks ago. I wandered through the rooms, then stopped in the central hall and looked up at the whale skeleton hanging from the ceiling.

My fingers go cold. The nerve tips like a warning – this guy is staying in the guest room. In my home. And he's potentially infatuated with me. *Close enough to smell. My eyes stayed with you.* I didn't notice him, didn't sense his eyes on my body, even though he was there, behind me.

This is creepy. Not in a clear-cut scary way. The fear in my body isn't precise. A sense of exhilaration to it.

I relax my grip so I don't leave any marks or creases on the paper. Then, I turn the page.

I went after you.

Four words near the top. I stare at them, wanting more. This statement leaving me hanging again. Except I could be living the next part. I might not need to find out in the following instalment – I already know.

Pieces of it, at any rate.

Whether it is me or another woman, we were oblivious to Arran's presence, vulnerable. Unaware of what could happen.

I know what men are capable of. Arran's intentions could be shaded, darker than what he's shown me, which so far doesn't seem dangerous. But people hide things, like this diary. And what he's written – tones of it verge on sinister.

Although it *could* be read as someone falling in love, those early days when you get so caught up in another person. Interpretation is tinted. And the line between love and obsession is blurred; they blend into each other.

I look at Arran's writing in pencil. Scratched lightly on paper.

Attraction, pursuit. The primal part of ourselves. Always there under the surface, secret desires and true traits. Gradually finding their way out, like sweat on our skin.

*　*　*

I don't like the silence. It's too blank, too human.

It's been three hours since I read Arran's diary, and doubts have inched in. I don't know for sure which museum it is.

And it seems too convenient. For diary girl to be someone whose spare room he's staying in. Chance, again – I don't trust it. Could he have been stalking me online? Somehow finding details, my picture on the bnb website?

I sip some cider. It's a bad idea to drink when unwell, but I like the sugary apple down my throat. Intermittently, I can hear tapping from below. Luke up to something.

At the living room window, a glare catches in my eye – sun on glass or metal. From the middle flat across the street. Its net curtain twitches. Above, Elliot is near a window, something in his hand. He's watering their plants. And I notice that the old man's gnome has gone – replaced by a doll. An old-fashioned girl in a dress with blonde curls. Her head tilted to one side, staring out into the street with sightless eyes.

'Hey, Tess!'

I start. The voice seeming so loud, almost like it's inside the flat. But it comes from below. I look onto the road and Ivy is there, grinning. Street sounds often seem to travel in an unnatural way here, the open window like a funnel.

I don't want to interact right now, but Ivy waves. It would be too rude to ignore her. I wave back.

'How's it going?' she calls.

Reluctantly I shove the window wider and lean out. Over-sized sunglasses cover most of her face, black and square. She slides them down to the end of her nose.

'Fancy going to the beach?' Ivy asks.

She's in a bikini, I realise. Baby-blue triangle top visible above her skirt. *Beach?* I think to myself. We're in London.

'Southend-on-Sea,' she says. 'I'm dying for a dip.'

'Sounds nice, Ivy, but I can't today,' I lie.

'Only takes just over an hour to get there. Sunbathe, ice cream. Not tempted?'

If I wasn't ill, I might be. But it's a little forward – I don't know Ivy well, I'm not sure what we'd talk about. Or if I have the energy for her vibrancy today.

'Sorry, I have plans.'

She shrugs, pushing her sunglasses back on. 'Suit yourself.'

'Are you not going with Luke?'

'I might get him along.' Her tone is breezy, yet there's something hard about her stance. 'This is meant to be girl time though.'

'So you're going with friends?'

She looks up at me, expression obscured by the sunglasses. 'Yep,' she says. 'That's right.'

A cyclist curves past her. She's standing in the middle of the road.

'Cool, well enjoy.'

'Catch you later, Tess.'

Ivy turns, shifting the towel tucked under her arm as she walks off. Luke could probably hear our conversation, not that I care. I duck back inside and sneeze.

Within a minute my thoughts revert to Arran's diary. Should I be worried? *Is* it me?

I enter the guest room and scan from one side to the other. Everything's so neat – the bed made, his laptop parallel to the edge of the desk, shoes lined up against the wall. Some guests make the space messy, bed sheets slung sideways, suitcases spilling open, clothes on the floor. But not Arran. He's a tidy man. Clothes folded and put away. Phone charger in a loop on the bedside table, beside a tube of watermelon lip balm.

And there's nothing in the bin.

I peer at the bare wicker basket. How can he have created no waste? He's been here for a week and a half.

I repeat that timeframe to myself with a twinge of surprise. When he made the booking four weeks seemed too long. But now I have the feeling four weeks isn't long enough.

I wish Rosie was here. I can see her now, her dungarees flecked with oil paint, rummaging in the wardrobe for something to wear on her date with Oliver. Half-eaten toast balanced on top of the lamp with her teeth marks in it. At least three mugs on the floor because she used a new one every time she made a cup of tea. Muttering about the neighbours, the annoying girl playing loud music and doing aerobics in her garden.

I can hear her voice. Almost.

I get my phone and listen to that message she left me on the twenty-sixth of January, saved as an audio file. Her voice, yet not hers. I want the real thing.

I scroll down my contacts list to R. Rosie's name and number shining up at me. I tap on it and hold the phone to my ear, expecting blank silence.

It rings.

My breath falters. It's never rung before.

So many times I've tried calling since January and nothing, no connection. Now there's a *brr-brr*. For a moment the air in my lungs compresses, thinking she might answer. That I'll hear Rosie say *Hello?*

It goes to voicemail. The automatic words from the phone provider inviting me to leave a message. It beeps, recording, waiting for me to say something.

I hang up. There's a strange buzzing in my head, the space around me faded out.

I dial her number again. It rings. Voicemail.

Dial. Ring. Voicemail.

I scroll up to Pettiford and dial his number. He doesn't answer. I try him again. No answer. Squeezing my phone in frustration, I realise it's Sunday.

So what? The police shouldn't be affected by days of the week. Crime and emergencies can happen at any time. I picture him at a table with his family, eating roast lamb, sipping wine, laughing with one of his kids.

I try him one more time and leave a message. 'Hi, it's Tess. I'm sorry to bother you on a Sunday but something's happened. I need to talk to you as soon as possible.'

I stare at the fireplace, holding my phone in cupped palms. My skin warms the metal case.

I dial Rosie's number. It rings.

Someone has her phone. Someone's fingers have turned it on. They can probably see me calling right now, my number flashing up on the screen. My name even? The thought is like Alpine lake water, chilling yet bracing.

Tess in white letters. I see the person staring down at it. His hand with that tiny inguz tattoo. His face lit up by the phone's backlight.

She's ill. Poor little pip.

Does she not realise she's on display? How loud she is? It's surprising, what can be heard through old Victorian walls, through doors, open windows.

She's also messy. I don't mind that, too much, but she leaves things lying around that have value. It's irresponsible. Identity is gold these days, being mined by so many. The picture on her library card makes her look like a sloth. I've considered telling her, but I don't like to be rude.

Teresa. Beautiful name. Why doesn't she use it, I wonder? Much more rhythmic and tasteful. A grace to its form. Though grace isn't a quality she holds. Self-absorbed, funny, deceitful, weak. But graceful? She licks the pan as she's serving up, and her plate sometimes too, when she thinks no one is looking.

18

I'm standing beside the kettle, looking into a mug with a teabag in it. A woody-sweet smell in my semi-blocked nose.

'I noticed you like rooibos in the morning.'

Voice behind me. When I turn, Arran's choosing something from the fruit bowl.

I breathe through my mouth, wavering between when he noticed that and how nice it is he made me a cup of tea. From curt yesterday morning to this. The contrast.

My carton of milk is next to the mug, along with a teaspoon. 'Thanks.' I'm not sure what else to say.

A few minutes ago, I bumped into him coming out of the bathroom in his towel. Presented with his toned torso, clotted-cream skin damp from a shower. He gazed at me, calm, steady, before saying good morning and going into his room.

And now he's smiling, a nectarine in his hand. He puts it on a plate and starts cutting it with a kitchen knife, into perfect segments. I've seen him doing this with other fruit – pear slices, banana discs. He never eats them whole, never bites straight in. They have to be chopped.

I check my phone. Pettiford hasn't called me back yet. It's 9:30 on a Monday morning – how long is he going to make me wait?

I watch Arran's fingers extracting the nectarine stone. Behind him, the asparagus fern comes into focus. The one that used to be in the guest room.

'What's wrong with that plant?' I say, on impulse.

The knife pauses in the nectarine. 'Sorry?'

'That plant.' I nod towards the fern. 'Why don't you want it in your room?'

'I'm not sure what you mean.'

'The *fern*.' I squeeze the teabag, getting the excess moisture all over my fingers. 'It was in the bedroom and you moved it out. Do you have a problem with it?'

Confusion stiffens his features. 'No, it's lovely.'

'So?'

'Tess, it was never in my room. It was out here in the living area when I arrived.'

'What? No, it wasn't.'

'I assure you it was.' He bites into a segment. 'I'd be happy to have it in my room if you like.'

I try to force air through my stuffy nose.

'I'm a responsible waterer,' he says, still chewing.

I'm not sure what's got into me, why I'm trying to accuse him. Probably my cold mixed into everything else: impatience with Pettiford, Rosie's phone ringing, and all my twisted feelings about the diary. So what if he moved the plant?

Arran finishes his nectarine. 'I'm going out now – do you need anything? Food or medicine?'

'I'm fine.' I don't know why I'm refusing. Both would be helpful.

'A hug maybe?'

'Oh no,' I blurt. 'You don't want to come too close. You could catch this, and I'm all . . .' I indicate my ragged appearance.

His expression is unreadable. He shrugs. 'I'll catch you later then. Hope you feel better.'

He's walking out.

'Thanks,' I say, coughing.

Once my throat has calmed, Arran gone, the flat seems different – too much space around me. As if the walls have moved. The heat feels syrupy this morning. I tell myself it's that, and my cold. I'm not seeing things.

I try calling Pettiford again. Now his phone doesn't even ring. I don't want to go into the station again and have to wait for hours, I want to speak to him *now*.

I can't go to the Barbican today. My manager wasn't happy on the phone – I could tell he didn't believe me. I must have jinxed myself last week. I feel genuinely awful.

It's not good, missing another day. I need the income. I haven't opened any post for a couple of weeks, something sharp about the letters by the front door. I ignore the white envelopes and the background anxiety, and continue sipping my tea.

After a few minutes, holding the warm mug against my chest, disappointment drifts in. The missed chance to touch Arran, feel his arms around me. Why did I do that? Reject his offer of a hug? *Stupid, Tess.*

The reactions he provokes in me are unsettling – they surface randomly and throw me off balance.

I still don't understand about that plant. I keep one in the guest room to give it a vague homey feel, and so I have an excuse if I'm ever caught. *Oh, I just came in to check on the plant.* Not that I've ever needed to use it. Is Arran messing with me?

I go into his room and grab the diary from the bedside table drawer. *I went after you.* There's more writing on the opposite page.

I went out through the museum's doors but couldn't see you. Searching the street, skimming the faces for yours. Then a glimpse of your back through the crowd.

It was busy, bodies clogging the pavement, and I had to weave in and out, losing sight of you more than once. Fucking people, most of them mindless. Eating plastic food and eyes sewn to screens. One woman shouted at me when I kicked her dog. I didn't see it because it was so small. I heard the squeak though. It wasn't on purpose, even though the woman seemed to think it was.

I kept going, my focus on you.

I wasn't sure what I was going to do but I wanted to stop you and say something. Ask for your number. Introduce myself. Ask if you were so-and-so from x, as if I recognised you. I browsed my options, all the methods and pretexts we use to talk to women.

Which one to draw on?

Although that was the next stage. First, I needed to catch up to you. You were walking fast, almost jogging. I had to shove past a group of ageing tourists in little blue hats, my shoulder thumping against someone. I ignored their yelp. I kept my eyes on you.

You darted across the road through a gap in the traffic. I stepped in front of a car and made it brake sharply, the man behind the wheel lifting his hand at me. I had this voltaic feeling. I'd never pursued anyone like this before, my spine pulsing.

I used your green top as a marker until you halted outside a building. You bent down to get something out of your bag. Finally, you were within reach, but I hesitated. Nerves in my stomach.

Come on. Do it. Walk over and talk.

I took too long psyching myself up. Your bag was back on your shoulder and you headed for the doors.

Fuck.

Idiot.

But then, I looked up at the building you'd gone into. Somewhere you probably came on a regular basis, if my guess was right. Maybe this wasn't so bad.

I think back to what I did after the museum. I walked for a while, through crowded streets, but it's always busy in that part of London. I think I went to a library. Yes, I remember – a big one nearby. I go to libraries sometimes to get translation work done. A place where I'm not isolated, there are people all around, but no one bothers me.

Did he follow me there? Could that be the building he describes?

His feet are firmly in stalker territory now. That should make a red light flash, but there's only a glow in my mind, with an indefinable colour. I like the thought – the possibility that he's been following me, and writing about it. That vitalising fear. It makes me feel alive, the numbness since Rosie died a bit looser.

And, as before, it's how you read the diary. Between the lines and implications. Too nervous to talk to the girl – suggesting he's human, a guy constrained by shyness and social customs. What are you supposed to do if you see someone on the street and you feel drawn, you'd like to chat or somehow meet? You can't just go up to them. It's off limits.

Message a stranger online, within a phone app – fine. But speak to one in real life? It shows how distorted everything is.

There's a nagging doubt though. From the moment Arran was standing on my doorstep, he hasn't been shy. Nervous is not a quality he gives off. And what he said – kicking the dog, calling people mindless. These things don't seem like him.

I turn the diary's page, and there's another one-line entry:

You are so pretty it carves at my heart.

Carves. An odd word choice. His language is unusual – the connotations vague, hinting at concealed sentiment. I reread the line. Another way of saying so pretty it hurts. Which could be taken as sweet, sappy romantic. Or it could suggest something else.

His motivations are still murky.

Somewhere you probably came on a regular basis. That could apply to the library. He's guessing, after all. Was I wearing a green top that day?

It's possible.

Those two words a whisper, like someone's lips against my ear, breathing them into the canal. Tickling my mind.

* * *

There's a knock on the front door. I'm translating a long report about some strange behaviour of killer whales. Struggling, my foggy brain not flowing as it should, but I need to finish it. If I'm not at the Barbican, I can at least do freelance work. I shouldn't take the option and flexibility for granted.

I keep going, but there's another *thump-thump-thump.*

When I see the triangular torso on the doorstep, I frown. 'Luke? What are you doing here?'

'What's it look like?'

There's a carrier bag hanging from his fingers. I still have no idea. 'Why aren't you at work? It's the middle of the day.'

'I popped back for lunch, and I brought you some things.'

'Things?'

He swings the bag in front of me. 'Heard you were ill so I've got some goodies.'

'How did you hear I was ill?'

'Oh, it was just on BBC News,' he says, lifting one shoulder. 'The whole country's worried about you.'

I stare at him, patience fading fast. 'Seriously, Luke.'

'I heard you coughing yesterday. Sounded grim.'

I'd love not to believe him, but I can hear him a lot of the time – his sneezes edge on a roar.

'Come on,' he says, the smug smile slipping from his face. 'Do you ever let anyone be nice to you?'

How has he hit the button so squarely? I *do*, when I'm thinking half-clearly, but right now I haven't got the energy for this.

Luke frowns at me. 'Look, Tess, you need it. You're ill and I bet you haven't been shopping. So just accept the gesture.'

I have to cough, holding my hand over my mouth. My eyes must convey my resistance because he sighs.

'It's nothing, OK?' he says, rustling the bag. 'Just a few little things. It's not like you'll have to repay me.'

Fine. I take the bag. Anything to get him to go away. I'm being ungrateful, but it feels like he's overstepping.

'Good girl.' He shifts his tie. Irritated by that comment, I go to push the door, but then he says, 'One more thing.'

'What?'

He leans in, elbow against the doorjamb. 'I have an invitation for you.'

'For what?'

'A party. I'm having one on Friday night. Are you free?'

'Possibly. Depends if I'm better by then.' Even if I am, a party hosted by Luke doesn't appeal.

'Come on, it's Monday. You've got four days to recover, especially with these remedies.' He gestures the bag with his chin. 'Bring some friends if you like. Or just yourself.'

'Don't you need to get back to the office?'

He glances at his watch. 'Shit, yeah, I do. Final thing I have to tell you,' he says, pointing at me with thumbs up. 'You know you're adorable when you're cross and your voice is all nasal?'

I consider hitting him in the face with this bag. But instead I close the door.

His foot thuds are heavy down the stairs as I go back into the kitchen. I plonk the bag on the side and pour out the contents. No sense wasting anything now it's here.

Tomato soup, figs, Night Nurse, vitamin C, mac n cheese, waffles, vanilla ice cream.

Annoyingly, all things I would probably have bought myself. How does he know I haven't been shopping anyway? And how could he know that figs are my favourite fruit?

Which I almost never buy because they're too expensive. Perhaps they came up in conversation once, I can't remember.

* * *

'Tess. Hello.' That smooth granular voice – finally. It's nearly two o'clock in the afternoon and Pettiford's name has just flashed up. 'I apologise for taking a bit of time to call you back. Another case required urgent attention.'

Implying Rosie's case isn't urgent.

'What's happened?' He sounds tentative.

'Rosie's phone.'

'What?' His ears have pricked up.

'It rang.'

'What do you mean?'

'I tried calling it and instead of going straight to voicemail, there was a ringtone.'

Pettiford clears his throat. 'Right, OK.'

The silence between us thickens.

'So—'

'Just a moment, Tess.' There are muffled voices. He's never done this before – cut me off, made me wait while he talks to someone else. 'Sorry about that,' he says. 'You were saying?'

'Why is her phone suddenly ringing? It must mean something.'

'It is strange.' He sounds unmoved, as cool-headed as ever.

'What if the person who hurt Rosie has her phone? What if they've just switched it on again?'

'That is a possibility.'

'Maybe because it's been so long they think they're safe, or maybe they feel guilty. Perhaps they hid it somewhere and they've got it out again.'

There's movement, a rustle, as if he's shifting in his chair. 'Hm, yes, they could have. Or they could have put the SIM in a different phone.' He pauses. 'I'll pass this on to Detective Constable Evans.'

Why DC Evans? Why not him?

'But, Tess, as you know, we tried tracing your sister's phone at the time, and it gave no results. It was undetectable, which is more common than you might think. A device can be untraceable for a number of reasons.' He clears his throat. 'Especially a feature phone with no access to data.'

Sometimes I feel angry with my sister for having a basic block-type phone with buttons and a small square screen.

Pay-as-you-go, no contract. Only used for calls and texts. No GPS or internet, which we could have used. Of all the millions of people with a smartphone, Rosie had to be different.

I catch myself, the anger like a cut. Into me, but also into her. I can't hold a blade to her skin.

'What about tracing Rosie's phone now?' I ask. 'Since something's changed and it's ringing, can't you trace it?'

'Yes, we can try tracing it again. And we can look into any other activity.'

Silence, blood beating in my ear.

'Oliver could have it,' I say.

More beats.

'What's going on with him? Have you spoken to him yet?'

I hear Pettiford's breath. 'I have had an initial conversation with him, yes. He's scheduled to come into the station this afternoon, in fact. Once we've chatted and asked him some more questions, I'll have a firmer update for you.'

Why has it taken so long to get him in? I told Pettiford about Oliver on Thursday.

'That may sound slow to you,' he says, reading my mind. 'But I'm afraid a murder case came up the day you visited the station. A child's death. So I've had to focus on that over the weekend. I might not be on hand to speak as often as we have been, but we are following up with Mr Barlow. All right?'

My left hand is clenched.

'I'll contact you when we know anything more,' Pettiford says. 'OK, Tess?'

The muscle in my palm is starting to ache.

'Tess?'

'Fine, yes.'

'OK, bye now.'

He's gone. The low *bleep* of him hanging up.

A child's murder. Terrible, unthinkable. But what about Rosie? That child is diverting attention away from her.

Oliver's being questioned today, soon, in the next few hours. *Focus on that.*

I wish I could be there. A fly on the wall. Or better, a spider. They're silent. They can creep anywhere, through holes, unnoticed. I'd like to crawl onto Pettiford's shoulder and watch Oliver's face, see what happens to his eyes when they ask him about my sister.

19

Arran is writing in the diary.

He's on the sofa, his back to me. I can hear the soft scratch of his pencil on paper.

I've been in here for nearly ten minutes, drawing out kitchen activities: opening the fridge, a cupboard, rustling a packet, putting some oats in a pan for porridge. I saw the brown book the moment I came through the door, my eyes lingering on it as Arran said hello and asked how I was feeling.

I feigned a casual response before he turned back.

This is the first time I've seen him with it. Man and diary together. And he's writing in it with me in the room, behind him. The tension of it is buzzy, a pick-me-up while I wait to hear from Pettiford about Oliver.

I swipe my phone but there are no notifications. Latest activity a text from Ivy. *Hey Tess, heard you're unwell. Let me know if you need anything. I know a few good movies if you want any recommendations. Got the best popcorn at the ready too :) Feel better soon! Ivy xx.*

She must have got my number from Luke. Sweet of her to send a message. With both of them, though, it's a bit much. People aren't normally this nice, especially in London. Most neighbours don't even know each other's names.

The scratch of the pencil stops.

I hold the spoon in the pan, listening, then stir the porridge and glance at Arran behind me. He hasn't moved. The corner of the diary visible beyond his shoulder.

I hear him sigh before he gets up, stretches and leaves the room. The bathroom door shuts and locks.

I tiptoe to the sofa. The diary is on the coffee table. Resting on the old wood, beside a glass of blueberry smoothie. Surprising – for him to leave it here in plain view, but I don't care. Listening for any sounds from the bathroom, I grab the diary.

I stood near the entrance, watching the doors. At one point a woman was watching me. Manicured nails, glossy orange. Horrible hair. She had a rabbit in a cage. White fluff pressed up against the metal grate door, one ear almost poking out. I wanted to put it out of its misery. I can't stand those kinds of animals. Or anything in a cage.

The woman lifted her sunglasses and smiled. I ignored her, pretending to walk round the corner. Then I came back.

Sometime later you re-emerged. I was starting to think you could be in there for hours, or I'd missed you somehow. But there you were. Your beautiful legs walking out the door, sun catching the contours of your hair. You halted, on your phone, thumb-tapping the screen. Unconscious of the people around you. One guy looked at you as he went past. I noticed a girl staring, gaze flicking down and up your body, envy narrowing her eyes. No doubt comparing herself to you.

You stretched your arm backwards, swung it beside your body.

The urge again to go up to you. Smile, say hello. But I didn't want to spoil it. What if you made a face, shrank back? Shook your head and told me to get away. I'm not some creepy old guy, bad breath, standing too close. Some leering perv like Laura said. But still, that could be it. If it didn't go right.

At least from here I could watch you.

I wanted it to be natural. Not contrived or manipulated. There had to be a way, if I chose the moment. An innocent encounter.

There was no innocence about you. The tilt of your head. The way you held your body, ran your thumb along the waistband of your jeans. I could imagine you unzipping them. Gliding them down your skin. A confident depth to your eyes, dark in the sun. You didn't need to squint.

You walked off, tapping your phone on your thigh. I was torn again about what to do. Follow, see where you go. Or gamble that you would come back to this place.

I kept my eyes on you, pondering, as your shadow skimmed the ground.

Sounds from the bathroom. The toilet flushing. I replace the diary on the coffee table, at the angle he left it, then dash towards the cooker.

Arran comes back in just as I grip the spoon. My porridge has thickened, stuck to the pan.

'Can I smell burning?' he says.

I didn't add enough liquid, the milk's turned brown on the base. 'Just my porridge,' I say, my back to him.

When he doesn't say anything, I twist my head to look. He's drinking his smoothie, cool and composed. No hint of concern that I could have been near his diary – that he suspects me.

I drop my shoulders, trying to make my muscles relax.

Arran puts the smoothie glass beside the sink. 'Have you ever been swimming on Hampstead Heath?'

My hand stops stirring.

'The bathing ponds?' Arran says. 'My mate wants to go tomorrow as it's so hot. I've heard a lot about them, but this is my first time.'

The porridge is sputting up at me, the spoon suspended in the white mush. Arran's open face is waiting for a response.

'Yeah,' I force out. 'The ponds are great. As close to wild swimming as you can get in London.'

I used to love swimming there, but I haven't been once this year.

'Cool, I'm looking forward to it.'

The diary's in his hand, next to his thigh. I can see it in my peripheral vision. I stir again, the spoon scraping the bottom.

A few moments with his eyes on the side of my face. I can feel them.

'Well, catch you later, Tess.'

Five minutes later he leaves the flat, and I'm still mechanically stirring. *He's describing me.* That's all I can think, barely noticing my arm begin to ache. The fact that he was just writing with me so close, over his shoulder, I feel is a suggestion towards me. However risky or arrogant it is for him to do that.

It's bizarre, reading about yourself. Through someone else's eyes. The things they notice. *There was no innocence about you.*

The tone of this entry has slightly shifted. Something veiled about the language, hazy in its edges. Whether he did follow her. Me. My body and shadow.

I turn the gas off. The smell of burnt milk is nasty.

20

I'm on Hackney Marshes. The wind has a cool touch, feeling its way over the water. I wrap my jacket closer to my skin.

I've been following the river for half an hour. Canal boats line its banks. There are lights in some of the small windows, curtained yellow squares with people behind them.

I haven't seen anyone on the marshland. Alone, out for a night walk on common land in north-east London. Alone in my home. Alone everywhere.

Nalika's right. I have no one. My sister is gone and my family are in another country. I've lost most of my friends. Sunken holes I don't know how to refill. Just like Rosie's white shadows. Am I stepping into her silhouette, letting her blank shape outline my life?

Pettiford's phone call this evening echoes back at me. *After questioning him again, we gained no further indication that Mr Barlow is a suspect. There was nothing that gave us grounds to keep him at the station. We can see why you might think his texts could be suspicious, but his alibi is verified and there is no proof of his guilt.*

Innocent until proven guilty. *Right.*

A twig cracks behind me. Then a swishing movement, like a foot in fallen leaves. I halt. Both of these sounds were faint, a distance away. Noise travels further in the night's quiet. The swishing could have just been the reeds in the wind. But something tells me it wasn't. The sounds were human.

I continue along the river path.

I keep turning my head, listening, but there's nothing. I look back, peering into the dark, scanning the trees and bushes. I can't see any figures or movement. Only swaying branches.

I cut in towards the grassy park area. There's a dirt path through small trees. Darker here. My foot knocks into something heavy, making me lurch. A log.

I walk through to the edge of the wood. There, I see something pale on the ground. It's small and multicoloured. I pick it up. A glove, for a girl's hand. Winter clothing – strange to find in summer. The backs of my eyes sting, Pettiford's final words sounding: *We'll continue our efforts. We're in the process of tracing your sister's phone.*

I put the glove in my pocket. I'm not leaving it behind.

The centre of the marshes is open grassland with football and cricket pitches. I go past a goal. It's darker, I realise, and when I glance up patchy cloud has drifted over the moon.

Something behind me. A breath – a long sighing sound. I stop, listening. Then I walk on. There it is again, followed by a low thud. A foot on grassy earth?

I look behind but can see only black. Yet somebody's there, I sense it.

I change direction slightly, keeping closer to the trees. And I feel an unfamiliar fear. Not like before, all the other times I've been in parks or hazardous street areas at night. On those occasions I felt afraid, but it was muted, passive. Now it's different. The fear is stark.

My urge is to run.

I fight against it. Isn't this what I want? Someone following me, not knowing what their intent is.

My footsteps are quiet, the wind whispering in the leaves. I'm beginning to wonder if it was my imagination when there's a scream. A girl's screech, the sound piercing. She screams again, more muffled. Nearby, coming from the open field area.

I run towards it.

I don't know what I'm going to do. I just keep running.

Ahead I see movement, two figures struggling. One much bigger than the other. A woman shrieking, 'I promise I'll get it to you. I'll have it tomorrow. Please!'

'I want it now.' A man's voice, hoarse and aggressive. 'You hear? Give me my money, or you'll pay in other ways.'

He's pushing her down. She keeps struggling. I'm steps away when he holds up his arm. I don't hesitate. I sprint at him and slam into his shoulder. He's much bigger than me, but the impact of my body makes him stagger and fall. A heavy thump to the ground.

The girl gasps. Through the dark, I can just see that she's blonde, and young, maybe around twenty. Hooded, but her legs bare in a miniskirt.

Before I can say anything, she bolts.

The man is scrambling to his feet. I jerk away from him, backing up. He's broad, in a shiny black coat. 'You bitch.' He grimaces at me. 'Who the fuck are you?'

Run, Tess. A distant voice in my head. *Go.*

He comes at me, face contorted, and my legs are frozen. I can smell his hot beer-breath. *This is it*, I think. *Really it.* But then he halts, looking past me. His eyes focused on something behind.

He scarpers, boots thumping fast. His figure vanishing before his tread fades out of earshot.

Breathless, I turn to see what he was looking at. A weak gleam of light, like the glow from a phone screen – on a bare hand. It's gone in a blink, turned out.

My heartbeat feels like a drum as I watch an outline slip away, the back of someone disappearing into the gloom.

* * *

I peel off my denim jacket, drawing air sharply through my teeth. The end of the sleeve is damp and dark red. I drop the jacket on a chair and look at my hand.

There's a slice in the skin, stretching over the wrist bone. Somehow, I cut it. I didn't notice until I was back on the night bus.

I stood there in the silence after all the figures had vanished. Then I ran. Over the grass, through the trees, the brambles, stumbling on something, knocking into bridge railing. It was too dark to see on the marshes, but I didn't slow down until I reached the bus stop.

Surrounded by empty seats on the upper deck, I felt the moisture on my sleeve. Then the pain. In the waxy yellow light, the cut looked black.

I go to the sink and run water over my hand. It stings. Blood running down the drain, leaving pink drips on metal.

There's a sound behind me, a shifting scratch, the swing of a door. Arran appears in the hallway. Has he just got in? At one in the morning? Or did he come from his bedroom? I'm not sure. There's a shrill buzzing in my ears, leftover from the marshes.

'Tess.' He's in a T-shirt and soft denim trousers. His eyes drop to my hand. 'Christ, what happened?' He walks towards me fast.

I inhale as he touches my arm. Not from pain. His warm fingers are careful as he checks the cut.

'How did you do this?' he asks.

'I . . . don't know.'

He glances up. 'What do you mean? Where have you been?'

I shake my head. 'Out.'

'Where?'

He's still holding my arm. The feel of his hands combined with the waning shock of the marshes makes it difficult to concentrate.

'Tess.' The rawness in his tone makes me focus and look at him. 'Did someone . . . do something to you?' He speaks slowly, as though it's hard to get out.

'What? No.'

There's something grim about the set of his face.

'No,' I repeat. 'I tripped and fell into a metal bar on some railing. It was broken. I was unlucky.'

His eyes seem darker, with flecks of an emotion I'm unsure of. One thing I can tell – he doesn't believe me. 'Don't move.'

He goes out. I hear him in the bathroom. I do what he says, my weight against the counter. He comes back with my first-aid kit.

'This will sting, but the cut needs to be disinfected.' He opens the green box on the side, takes out a cotton pad and unscrews the lid from a bottle of clear liquid. 'Ready?'

I nod.

He presses the pad into my cut. I gasp as pain spurts through my hand.

'OK?' he says.

'Yes.'

He dabs the skin dry then squeezes some cream onto his fingertip. His face is angled down, hair flopping over his forehead. He rubs the cream into the cut with smooth circular motions. The antiseptic smell is strong. He glances up at me again but doesn't speak as he snips off a section from the bandage roll and starts wrapping it round my hand. A soft silence between us. It's warm in the flat, a nice temperature.

He ties the bandage into a bow, not too tight.

'There,' he murmurs.

'Thank you.'

He starts putting things away in the box. 'You'll need to leave that on for a couple of days. And try not to get it wet. After that you can use normal plasters.'

I like him instructing me.

'Keep applying this cream as well,' he says.

'You're very efficient. Seem to know what you're doing.'

'I've taken a few first-aid courses.'

The bandage feels good, the cut cooler, soothed. 'Are you a budding doctor as well as a ceramicist?'

'I did want to be a paramedic when I was a kid.'

'A bit like I wanted to be an archaeologist, then a vet.'

'Oh yeah?'

I nod. 'Then an opera singer.'

He smiles.

'I was a fickle child apparently.'

He zips up the first-aid kit and leans against the side. 'I think all of us are, to a degree. Children and adults. Uncertain of ourselves, and other people.'

Yes, Arran. I think of the diary, the most recent entry. Tailing the woman from the museum, waiting outside that building for some time. Watching her movements and mannerisms.

Is that threatening? Or just a guy pursuing a girl he's attracted to? It depends on what happens next.

'Sometimes I think it'd be great if we could hear what others are thinking,' Arran says.

I blink, aware of the thoughts I just had. 'Read minds?'

'Yeah.' He lifts a shoulder. 'But probably not a good idea overall. The world wouldn't be able to function. And there would be no mystery.'

'No secrets?'

It's a moment before he responds. 'No.'

He's closer than when he was doing the bandage. I know some of his secrets. We can't read minds, but diaries – they're a way in. A backdoor revealing tones of light and shadow.

His hand lifts towards my face. Blood pulses in my throat as his thumb brushes my cheek.

'You've got a small cut here too,' he says.

If I was a normal person, reading what my guest truly thinks of me, the things he's revealed in the diary, I ought to be concerned – on guard against potential harm. Even if it's what I'm looking for. The apprehension, the sense of danger. The *bangbangbang* of my heart.

But with his fingers touching my face, I'm not thinking of my own safety. My heart is banging with exhilaration and attraction.

'What have you been up to?' he asks.

His thumb skims my cheekbone, eyes fixing on mine. That dark blue, too deep to read. He leans closer. Then he looks down and I feel his hand on my arm again.

I sense something change – the comfy ambience between us shifting.

Neither of us moves. His fingers are holding my arm and I stay perfectly still. I don't want to be the one to break this moment. I can't see his face; it's slanted down again. Seconds of silence before he lets go and moves away.

'It's late. We should get some sleep.'

When his face turns it's pale and calm. I'm still propped against the side, searching for emotions or clues – about him, about what just happened between us. There are none.

'*Hasta mañana*,' he says. 'Isn't that what you say?'

I nod.

He scratches the back of his neck, half-smiling as he turns to go to his room.

She is so lovely.

Especially when asleep. Curled into herself, hair splayed around her head. She dozes off with the light on, sometimes, making it easy to see. I can stand there looking at her, perfectly still except for the breath in her chest.

Both of us make mistakes, it appears. We are not perfect. She doesn't look good in the morning, which gives me a shot of satisfaction. She is flawed down deep. She has done bad things.

I like a bit of fight in a girl, you know. *Una luchadora con potencial.* That's probably wrong – one of those shitty online translations. I don't know, I don't speak the language, do I. Something I might have to remedy.

21

I know it was you.

I watch the text bubble as it lights up green. Sent. 13:04. It's probably landing in his inbox, a *ting* on his phone. I can't take it back now. Not that I would. He has it coming, and I can do what I want. I don't care what Pettiford says.

I know it was you.

Five words accusing him. My sister's death, that night in January. But also last night. There was someone there on Hackney Marshes. That sighing breath, the lit-up hand, the figure slinking away.

Oliver.

He thought he'd escaped with his crime, wriggled through the system. But then I got the police onto him again. He's been threatened – so now he's following me.

I think. Because each moment I feel sure, my conviction wavers. Towards Arran. It could have been him, I realised when I woke up. In light of the diary and what he's been up to. Even though a rational voice says – why would he be following me on the marshes? What motive does he have? He can see me anytime he wants here in the flat.

Yet, the coincidence of him getting home that late, minutes after me, seems too much. He could have been in his room, watching something on his laptop, writing, reading a book. But I'm ninety per cent certain he wasn't – that scratch was like a key in the lock, and the swing was heavier than the guest room door.

Questions keep curving round my mind. I can't sort through it all, can't make these sketches of him into a solid portrait.

The way he took care of me, wrapped my hand. No other man has ever done something like that. And it had felt like he was going to kiss me. But then – his face unreadable. That half-smile before he went to his room.

I don't know what it meant; I'm not sure what kind of smile it was. Too ambiguous. That left slant almost sly. It's been getting to me all morning. I'm walking the streets of Canonbury, everything twining up together.

My hand twinges beneath the bandage. The bow Arran tied is looser, the cloth already fraying. I ignore the pain and look at my phone. No response from Oliver. I type another text.

I know you have her phone.

I almost bump into someone, our shoulders brushing. Too focused on my screen, not looking where I'm going. I half-glance round, too late to apologise.

I type one more message.

I know you were there last night.

Even though there's a chance it wasn't Oliver, I want to disturb him, make him crack.

The heat is building. I can feel it through my sandals, the sun seeping into tarmac. I get an almond croissant from a bakery. Outside, I take a couple of bites. While I'm chewing I notice someone go past. A woman in a bucket hat. Redhead.

She's hurrying, stooped, eyes on the ground. Trying to avoid me?

'Ivy?'

She halts, a beat before she turns. 'Oh, hey, Tess.'

'You all right?'

Her skin is all red. And she's clutching something, arms pressed into her waist.

'Yeah.' She tilts the bottle towards me, wrist at a funny angle. 'Just getting some aftersun.' Her whole aura is awkward, like she's attempting to shield her body. 'I got *so* burnt at the beach.'

I can see that. Between her freckles she's bright pink – her shoulders and arms the worst. She should cover up with the sun blazing down. Her hat doesn't look effective, some gauzy turquoise material.

'Such an idiot.' She gives a sheepish laugh. 'You'd think I would've learnt by now. I never tan. Just white, red, peel.'

I don't have that problem, fortunately. Her feet are shifting, edging away. No eye make-up today. Natural lashes pale and sandy – she looks so different.

'Sorry I never texted you back,' I say.

'Huh?'

'The get-well text you sent.' I've only just remembered it.

'Oh, yeah, no bother.'

It's obvious she wants to escape. I let her. 'Hope that aftersun helps, Ivy.'

'Thanks. See you later.'

She carries on down the street, scooting between people. That was a crack in her relaxed friendliness. People are always more complex than their outward display; they have more than one face. I know that already.

I take another bite of my croissant. Grease and powdered sugar all over my fingers when my phone rings.

Pettiford.

'Hello?' I say, swallowing my mouthful fast.

'Tess, hello. Good afternoon.'

Is this about my texts to Oliver? Could he already know about them?

'What is it?' I say. 'Have you traced Rosie's phone?'

'We've tried tracing her phone again, yes, a few times. But, unfortunately, we have no firm results.'

'What do you mean no *firm* results?' Why does he have to be elusive? Just say it. Straight.

'Well, it's possible to track a device approximately, and we know it's in the London area.'

'You mean it's here, in the city?'

'That's what our results showed, but it was a wide radius.'

So, Oliver could have it. 'You haven't got a location?'

When Pettiford answers, his chalky voice is measured. 'Not a precise location, no. For that we'd need a phone call to trace. An answered call, that is.'

'Have you tried calling it and tracing it at the same time?' I'm pacing on the pavement.

'As I said, we'd need the call to be picked up.'

'But . . . it's here. You know it's here in London somewhere.' My tone is lightened with hope.

I catch the sigh in Pettiford's breath. 'To outline all possibilities, the device could have been pirated. And down the chain someone could've bought it and is now using it with a new SIM.'

'But if that's the case then why is Rosie's number ringing when I try it?'

'Similarly, someone else could now be in possession of that number. And since your number is unknown to them, they may choose not to answer.'

The irritation and pain stretch, elastic bands pinging back. 'I can't believe you're saying that. It's like you don't even want to catch this guy. Like you don't care.'

'Tess, of course I care.'

I won't let my voice wobble. 'You don't.'

He's silent.

'You care about child murders and gang violence, knife crime and terrorism. You don't care about my sister.'

'Tess—'

'Why don't you just close the case?' I challenge.

'I know how hard this must be for you, losing your sister, and under such circumstances with no clear answers or closure. I have two sisters and—'

'Don't you *dare* say you understand.'

You don't, Daniel Pettiford. You have no idea.

Somewhere in the nearby streets, an ice cream van is playing its tinkly chime. I've never liked that sound. It's eerie, a tune for luring children.

'Tess, I'm sorry. Where are you? Is there anyone there with you? Your family?'

I shake my head, then realise he can't see it. 'No.'

'What about a friend you could meet? I think it's important you're not alone right now.'

'I'm fine.'

'OK.' He doesn't sound convinced. 'Otherwise, we could possibly arrange for someone—'

'I'm fine.'

Silence.

'Let's leave it there for now then,' Pettiford says, in his practised tone. 'We can speak again when you need, how's that? Or when there's anything new to tell you, of course. I really am sorry.'

I'm pressing the phone to my ear so hard it hurts.

'I'll be in touch, all right? Take care of yourself.'

He hangs up.

I stare at the ground, people walking past me. My half-eaten croissant dropped; flaked almonds scattered.

The vibration in my palm seems distant before I register it and check the screen. A text from Oliver.

Fuck you, Tess.

I blink at his words. Another text buzzes.

I pity you. How desperate you are. How sad. They should lock you up. Crawl back in your hole and leave me the hell alone.

Bile inches up, his message biting in my throat.

I'm not hanging around anymore. I'm doing something, taking this into my own hands.

22

I'm on Oliver's street. Leaning against a tree diagonally across from his building. He lives in a modern block of flats in Hammersmith – or he did. I'm presuming he hasn't moved.

I got on the train ten minutes after receiving his texts, headed straight here. Realising he was probably at work, I walked the streets, then along the riverbank. Killing time. A heron soared silently overhead, towards the wetlands on the far side. Parakeets cheeped from high in the trees. Too many birds, too many noises.

I feel edgy. It's 5 p.m. and I'm back outside his flat.

I have no idea when he'll get home, but I'm waiting. I want to watch him. Find my own evidence.

I wish I could somehow get inside. Look round his rooms and his things. See what he's hiding. I'm sure I'd discover something shady, something troubling. And Rosie's phone.

I've called Oliver six times this afternoon. He hasn't picked up, not that I'm expecting him to. I ring him again now. Nothing. I try Rosie's number, watching the window where I think his flat is, as if I might see it light up. It goes to voicemail.

He could be inside the flat, I suppose, if he was working from home today.

There are people in some of the windows, appearing through the wide glass. I glance around the street. A man walks by with bags of shopping. A girl has halted with her bike, on the phone. I probably look a bit odd – standing here beside a tree not doing anything for ages. *Y qué*, as the Spanish say. Who suspects or distrusts young women like me?

Commuters flock home, people in suits, a group of women dressed up going for drinks. I scour the men's faces, looking for that auburn hair.

My legs begin to ache. The clouds are darker, that gunmetal colour, like it might rain. But I'm not going anywhere.

Just after six o'clock – he's there. I blink and straighten, thinking for a second that I'm imagining it. But it's him. That near-shaved skull and widow's peak, hands in his pockets as he approaches his building.

I chose my position well – he doesn't see me. This tree with conveniently low branches.

He goes in through the door. I wait, thinking that could be it, I could have waited hours for this glimpse of him. But then I see him in the window. Not the one I thought – above it, on the third floor. I shift behind the tree, nerves flaring. When I check he's still visible in the glass, but his eyes aren't staring out at me. He's looking at his phone.

He disappears from view.

I think about ringing his bell, pretending to be a delivery person. Or slipping into the building when someone opens the main door and going up to his flat.

But then he comes out again.

Ten minutes and he's changed into jeans and a black jacket. He's walking fast, in the direction he came from before.

I watch his back, his stiff posture, his pale hands. I consider trying to get into the block, but these new buildings have so much security. Only one other thing to do.

I push off the tree and follow.

The bitter strain in my chest mixes with excitement at what I'm doing. Stalking Oliver. I'm not sure if it's actually a crime, to walk behind someone in the street, but it's a gamble I'm taking. For Rosie, and for all women followed by men. It could get me into trouble, but those texts Oliver just sent me were aggressive, callous.

He strides through the streets of Hammersmith. I hang behind, keeping at least one person between us, with his head in sight. He turns left, right, left. At street corners I pause to see where he's going, then catch up.

It's busy, all the people leaving work, and the tourists. I think of Arran following the girl from the museum. I'm doing the same thing – the same questionable furtive act. But for very different reasons.

Oliver slows a little, looking at his wrist.

Arran wrote about the nerves in his spine, the voltaic feeling. I see what he means. There's a similar sensation down my back. Enjoying this sense of power, of chase.

Oliver has halted outside a bar. A pub with groups of people standing round high tables, holding pints and glasses of wine. He looks around. For someone?

He lifts his hand – he's seen them. A woman.

She's smiling at him, flicking dyed blonde hair off her forehead. Curvy. Heavy make-up. The opposite of Rosie.

He points at the door, she's nodding, then he goes inside while she waits at one of the tables. She looks in her hand-bag, giving herself a quick glance in a pocket mirror. I don't know why she's bothering – she's not a patch on my sister. She adjusts her skirt slightly. Oliver comes back out with two glasses of wine. White for her, red for him. He smiles at her as they clink glasses.

I watch them chatting, the bitterness tightening. He made out he's oh-so-torn-up about my sister, that she pulled his life out from under him. And here he is on a date with another woman, just a few months after her death?

He laughs at something she's saying. He leans towards her, touching her hand. She flicks her hair some more and shows him something on her phone.

'You all right there, love?'

I glance round. I'm next to a restaurant over the road, using a parked van for cover. One of the waiters is giving me a quiz-zical look.

'Yes, fine,' I say.

I move away from the restaurant, pretending to do something on my phone while keeping my eye on them. On Oliver. Every smile, every moment and mannerism digs in, deepening my disgust.

Half an hour. I shift my position to further along the street, at a different angle, still able to watch. Forty-five minutes. She goes inside the pub. He glances around then gets his phone out. She comes back with more drinks. I don't know how much more of this I can take.

Ten minutes later, the woman puts her handbag on her arm. Saying goodbye? Her glass has some wine left in it. She kisses him on the cheek, his hand lingering on her waist. She turns and walks away.

Oliver drains his wine, then hers.

He stands there, his fingers gripping the edge of the table. Still looking in the direction she went. Then he moves, going the same way.

Is he doing what I think he's doing? I don't wait around – I go after him to find out.

I jog through people, catching up. Ahead of him I can see the woman. Her dyed hair and raspberry top visible beyond a family with two kids. Oliver's flat is in the opposite direction. He *could* be going somewhere else, but then she turns down a road and he turns too.

I can't believe what I'm seeing.

When I turn into the same road, I see Oliver is closer now. One man between him and the woman. I have to do something; I have to warn her. This could have been how it was for Rosie, followed without knowing. This woman needs to know she's at risk.

I run up to Oliver and grab his arm. 'Hey!' I shout towards the woman. 'Wait! Turn around!'

Oliver's face is astonished, then incredulous. I see it darken just before I yell at the woman again. She's half-turned at the noisy disturbance.

'Yes, you! In the dark pink top.' She catches sight of us – of me gripping Oliver's jacket. 'This man is dangerous! He's stalking you.'

Shock shifts her features. Oliver tries to pull away from me. 'What?' he says. 'No I'm not. I'm going to the dentist.'

'Be careful!' I shout, ignoring his lies. 'He hit my sister!'

The woman looks at Oliver, with fear.

'Ellie, I told you,' Oliver says quickly. 'I have an evening appointment. The clinic's just up there, Grove Dental Practice.'

'He's a killer!' I screech.

'Jesus Christ, Tess! What the fuck is wrong with you?' He's spitting at me. He grips my arm, wrenching it off him.

People are staring at us. The woman looks anxious. Skittish, like she wants to bolt. She does, turning and hurrying off down the road.

'Yes, run!' I shout. 'Get out of here.'

Oliver's clenching my arm, twisting it. 'You stupid bitch.' His voice is hoarse, low, glancing at the bystanders. The mother from that family is glaring at him. 'Are you insane?'

'What are you doing following her, Oliver? You were going to do something, weren't—'

'What the hell are *you* doing? Did you follow me here? From the pub?'

His fingers are digging in. I try to yank my arm out of his grasp but he's too strong. He starts pulling me along the street, away from the people watching.

'You're fucking twisted,' he hisses.

I struggle against him. His eyes are glassy – a pale sheen of hate and hostility.

'You're the one who's twisted.' I feel a hint of fear, but keep it out of my voice. 'I know what you did.'

'Will you shut up!' His fingers dig harder, hurting. 'Do you know what you're doing to me?' His voice rises. 'I can't take this. I ought to . . .'

'To what? Hit me? Crack open my skull?'

He lets go, pushing me away. My arm is pulsing with pain. His head is turned from me, his jawbone set hard. A muscle in it flexing. And I suddenly realise he's shaved. Last time I saw him, he had a beard. Is he trying to change his appearance?

When he looks at me again his eyes are wet. 'I don't hit women, Tess. I wouldn't hurt anyone.'

'Bullshit.'

He jerks his head. 'It's not bullshit. You know what's bullshit? *You*. Following me. Harassing me. Accusing me of being a killer and shouting at Ellie like that. You freak.'

I hit him. With a wave of rage, I swing my arm and punch him in the face. Or try to – it feels more like a whacking slap.

For a moment he's shocked, the impact of my knuckles making his features jar. Then he laughs. A cold snickering sound. He shakes his head at me and turns to leave.

I go after him. I grab him from behind, try to yank him back. I want to hit him again, the anger burning through my hand. But he shoves me with his shoulder, elbowing my ribcage and pushing me sideways.

I land on the pavement. My hipbone striking tarmac and my arm caught under. I push myself up, palms in the grit. A glimpse of his face – the wet on his cheeks – before he turns his back, leaving me on the ground.

She's screeching in the wrong direction. That poor guy, and the woman. Traumatised, probably. If I didn't know a lot about Tess, I might think she was losing it.

But she can't help herself, can she?

23

Arran is on the rug by the fireplace, dipping a Mars into a mug.

The curtains are drawn, the light in the room low. My mosaic lamp from Granada is the only one on, and there's a candle flickering on the coffee table.

He looks up from the flame.

'Hey, Tess. I hope you don't mind me closing the curtains. The evening sun's too bright.'

'That's fine.'

I go over to the sink. I need a moment to myself, to cool off. My knuckles are still throbbing with pain and anger. My arm too. The journey back across London seemed slow, everything stewing in my brain. That last glance of Oliver's face won't leave my eyes. He was crying.

I take a deep breath and run the tap, filling a glass. I can't let Arran see I'm upset. I don't want to appear vulnerable – not to him.

When I turn he's there, right behind me. I didn't hear him move. His footsteps silent from the fireplace.

'Excuse me,' he says, touching my shoulder as he steps past. 'Just getting some more milk.'

He's too quiet, I don't like it. Normally you can hear everything in this flat. Every movement or click or throat noise. It takes time and effort to do things so softly.

I let my heart settle while he pours milk into his mug and returns the carton to the fridge.

'Hey,' he says. 'What's that on your arm?'

'What?' I glance down.

He switches on the kitchen light and I see what he's referring to. Bruises starting to appear in the skin, where Oliver's fingers gripped.

Arran is frowning at them. 'What have you been doing now?'

'Nothing.' I shift my arm behind my body so he can't see.

'Tess, that's not nothing.'

When I meet his eyes, there's worry in them.

'Is your other hand hurt too?' he says.

My knuckles are pink, the skin around them swollen. Why does he notice everything?

'No, it's fine.'

He looks between my arm and my hands. 'Look, Tess, if you need help—'

'I don't.'

His river-water eyes sink into mine. I want to look away, but for some reason I can't.

'It's just that these injuries and marks—'

'It's none of your business,' I snap.

Arran gazes at me for a few more seconds, the T-Rex clock ticking in the silence, then he nods and goes back over to the fireplace. I watch him fold his legs on the floor. Dip his chocolate bar into the mug.

Sighing, I sit on the sofa.

'Are you a spy or something?' he says, his expression lighter. 'Secret cage fighter?'

I feel a small smile in my lips. 'No, sadly. I'm not that cool.'

'I beg to differ.'

He bites into the melting chocolate. Warm orange plays over his face, shadows bending round the bones. I look at the candle flame below, finding movement, quivering in air we can't feel.

Arran's phone rings. He looks at the screen and cuts the tone, declining the call.

'Not going to answer?' I ask.

'Not right now. It's my sister.'

Sister? A flash of a girl – honey-blonde, beautiful, smiling. Stretched out on a lounger with sunglasses pushed up into her hair. One arm above her head, a book balanced on her stomach.

A jab of realisation: I'm using a photo of Rosie on a beach near Marbella, projecting it on, morphing into a pale Scandinavian-looking sister.

'We just had a bit of an argument,' Arran says. 'I'll call her back later.'

Call her back. A sister who rings him, who he can call. I think of Rosie's phone, that voicemail, and my eyes start to sting again.

'She's pissed off with me,' Arran says. 'She wants me to come back to Yorkshire.'

What? *No*, he can't do that. I try to steady my emotions. They're coming out of nowhere again, from all angles.

'How come?' I say.

'She misses me, I guess.'

Another jab. I can't talk about sisters, not now.

'Is that tea?' I ask.

He's holding the chocolate in the hot liquid. 'Yes.'

'Mars bar in tea?'

'Yeah. Have you never tried it before?'

'You say that as if I'm the abnormal one. This is like salt on jam again.'

He smiles. 'Maybe so. But it's really good. Why only dip biscuits in tea when chocolate bars exist?'

I hadn't thought of that.

'Want to try it?' he says.

I lift my shoulders. Why not?

He gets up and sits on the sofa next to me, handing me the Mars. As I bite off a chunk I'm conscious of his teeth marks, and his saliva.

'Good huh?' Arran says.

I nod. It's delicious, the melting Mars sticky in my mouth. And something occurs to me. 'Wait, Mars bars aren't vegan.'

'What?'

'You said you were vegan and Mars have milk in them.'

His brow creases, then seems to clear. 'Oh, you mean when I told your neighbour I was vegan? I just did that to see how he'd react.'

I look at him.

'A lot of people are still weird about veganism,' Arran says. 'Guys especially.'

Now that I think about it, he's had goat's cheese in the fridge. Which I failed to pick up on. 'So you're vegetarian then?'

Arran nods.

Vegetarian, yet he doesn't seem to like animals that much? From what he's implied in the diary, about the caged rabbit and the dog he kicked, whether accidentally or not. Is this a hidden part of his personality? It doesn't follow the shape of the man here, on the sofa next to me.

He leans back. 'I'll admit I felt like winding Luke up. I know I'd only just met the guy, but he seemed a bit . . .'

'Full of himself?'

'Yeah.'

'That's Luke. Cocky and irritating.'

Arran's smiling. 'I got that vibe.'

We're both quiet for a moment. He lifts his foot onto the sofa, his knee tilting towards me. Beyond him, my mosaic lamp glows, its jewelled light on his body.

'I forgot to say – he's having a party on Friday night.' I don't know why I'm mentioning this. I'm not keen to go.

'Who?' Arran says.

'Luke. And he said everyone's welcome, if you want to come.'

Arran arches an eyebrow. 'He invited me?'

'Not specifically. But there'll be loads of noise, you probably won't be able to sleep anyway. So if you're around . . .' If Arran comes, that changes things.

'OK, thanks. I might have plans on Friday.'

'A date?' I say it without thinking.

'Possibly.' He's not looking at me, as if talking to the air. 'It depends how you define date.'

What a strange answer. Though his definition of a date could mean spending time with a woman without her knowing.

I glance at Arran. Then I watch the candle, wondering what the next entry might reveal about my enigmatic guest.

* * *

My fingers are sore as I grope inside Arran's backpack. Numb, knuckles swollen, I can't bend or move them fully. Much worse when I woke up this morning. But I'm not letting that deter me.

I try the canvas bag beside his shoes and find it. The diary resting against a book on birds.

Arran's gone out shopping. I don't know when he'll be back, so I thumb through to the previous entry, that final sentence

I kept my eyes on you, pondering, as your shadow skimmed the ground, and turn the page.

You made me wait. But it was worth it.

I was right about this place — it gave me the opportunity. To get close, while still at a safe distance. Intermittently I felt annoyed you didn't notice me. Other women did. More than once, I realised I was clenching my jaw or gripping my knuckles.

But your lack of perception also worked to my advantage.

I stood behind you in the queue. Saw you eat a baguette with dark meat inside. A moment of disappointment as I watched you chewing, red sauce caught in the corner of your mouth. One day an outfit that accentuated your form, clinging to the curve of your hips, the nip of your waist. I had to stop myself imagining sliding my hand inside the fabric, along the soft skin of your inner thigh.

You wandered to a park and lay on the grass, big toe hooked on the back of your ankle. Rolling over, you read a book, pages casting a diamond shadow on your face. Then you fell asleep. Not for long, but there was something so serene about you, a bee buzzing round your toes, up your body, seeming interested in your eyelashes, and the tiny mole on your cheekbone.

I considered taking a picture. Unsure if it was OK as I reached for my phone.

Another occasion, you looked round. Not at me. At someone saying your name. You knew the person, though the way you hung back, your smile weak in your eyes, and the fact the conversation didn't last that long, indicated you weren't close. The woman seemed a little fake to me. But I was glad your paths had crossed because I discovered some interesting things. Information I could look up, type into a search engine.

And I'd heard your name. I whispered it to myself, playing with the sound on my tongue. It wasn't what I was expecting. I'd imagined something longer, a little more refined. But I could get used to it.

I stare at the page, hairs on my arms lifting from the skin. Part of this entry has been scribbled out. Sentences and words I can't see. But what's here is edging closer, a gradual creep towards me.

Whispering my name. And *the tiny mole on your cheekbone.*

I still don't like mirrors. But I go into the bathroom and force myself to look.

My face is bonier. My lips pale. The pain in my chest isn't as sharp as I thought it would be. I lean closer. Some of the hairs in my left eyebrow are sticking up. I smooth them down. And as I turn my cheek – there it is, high on the bone. A dark spot slightly raised from the skin.

24

Rain is spattering on the tarmac, and on my face. I'm running. I need to move fast and unstick everything that's clinging to me.

Arran's in the flat. He came back from shopping and started making bread again. His phone on the kitchen table while he kneaded dough. I was staring at it, wondering: does he have a photo of me on there?

I had to get out. What I know from the diary, about me, about him – this perception feels like baggage, now impossible to unload. In conjunction with the last twenty-four hours, what happened with Oliver, following that woman, Ellie. Oliver crying as he walked off, whatever that means. The friction of it all is getting to me.

I push harder, sprinting, breaths heaving through my lungs. This stuff won't stop sticking.

I glimpse my arm again – the bruises in the skin. Darker than yesterday. Plum-coloured finger marks.

When I saw them earlier it jogged a memory. Last summer, hugging Rosie one morning, she'd winced. A few days later I glimpsed something on her arm. Pale blotches fading to yellow. When I asked her what they were, she laughed, saying she'd knocked into something in her studio and paint pots had fallen on her. She was often clumsy, so I let it slide.

They were bruises. The marks small, four little spots in the skin – like fingerprints. Almost identical to the ones on my arm.

When I reach Ravengale Road, my throat is stinging. I feel faint. I bend over my knees for a minute. The rain is more like drizzle now, dreary haze hovering over the buildings. I decide to do one more loop.

I cross the street. Rejoining the pavement and darting round a tree, I knock into someone. 'Whoa,' I yelp, our shoulders colliding.

I reel in shock as they stagger, the force of my running body enough to make them fall backwards. A blurry jolt before they're on the ground. I look down and see a man in a black coat.

'I'm so sorry,' I say. 'I didn't see you. Are you OK?'

He's on his side. As his head lifts, I recognise his bearded face.

'Elliot?'

His cheeks are red, embarrassment clear in his features.

'No, no,' he says, scrambling to his feet. 'It's not your fault, I wasn't looking. Too busy on my phone.'

His phone is screen-down on the wet pavement. He snatches it up. His hair is dripping and there's mud streaked on his arm. He's a thin guy, but tall. Surprising that I managed to knock his weight off balance.

'Hey, hey,' a voice calls.

Ivy is jogging towards us. In bright leggings, purple-white mystical print, with a gadget strapped to her arm. 'Fancy seeing you both.' Pulling out her headphones, she looks me up and down. 'Great minds, eh? I love running in the rain.'

She's clocked my outfit, only I'm not in fancy running shoes or fashionable activewear – I'm wearing old tracksuit bottoms and a white T-shirt, which is now semi-see-through, I realise, the outline of my sports bra showing through the damp material. I cross my arms.

'Do you run a lot?' Ivy asks. 'We should be jogging partners.'

'Not really. I often have to stop and walk.'

'Well, maybe when you get your fitness up.'

I've seen Ivy jogging a few times. Her toned arms testament to how fit she is. Something sinewy about her – muscle, tendon, with pointed elbows and a prominent collarbone. I get the feeling she eats very healthily. Kale smoothies, quinoa, plain chicken breasts. The kind of girl who snacks on raspberries.

'What about the gym?' she says. 'I go to a great one up near Stoke Newington. They have the best classes.'

'The gym isn't really my thing.'

'Oh.'

'I've never been to one in my life, if you can believe that.'

She tips her head and smiles. 'There's always time to start.' She looks at Elliot, taking in his dishevelled hair and muddy sleeve. 'What happened to you?'

He clears his throat. 'I wasn't looking where I was going and we had a collision.'

'You mean you fell over?'

He shrugs.

'Oh, Ell.' She shakes her head. 'You clumsy oaf, you.'

He doesn't seem to appreciate her teasing tone, turning his face away. She looks at me and widens her eyes. Humorous again – back to her animated self. I feel a nip of resentment at the open-minded ease she exudes. Except for yesterday outside the bakery, when she was so different. Her skin is no longer angry red, but it has a pink tinge.

'Did that aftersun work?' I ask.

She looks at me, deadpan.

'I hope your burns have been soothed,' I prompt.

'Oh *that*. Yeah, better thanks. No big deal, the lotion worked a treat.' Her light tone brushes off with a smile. 'Excited about the party on Friday? I'm in charge of snacks and music, so at least you know you won't go hungry and can have a good dance.'

I hope her idea of party food isn't quinoa and raspberries. 'Cool, I think I'm coming.' It depends on Arran. And Nalika, who I asked this morning via text.

'Brill,' Ivy says. 'Ell's coming too.'

I shiver, my wet clothes sticking to my skin. I don't feel like any more jogging now. Elliot's pale face and rigid posture are making me uneasy.

'I'm going to head in,' I say.

'Cool, see ya,' Ivy says.

I jog back towards my flat. Inside, the air is full of baked bread. A crusty nut-brown loaf on the side, untouched. The guest room door is open – Arran's gone out.

I'm just about to get in the shower when my phone rings. I left it behind. In my room, I thought, but the ringtone's coming from the living area, on the table. I grab it and Pettiford's name is gleaming on the screen. I have two missed calls from him.

'Hello?' I say. 'What is it? Do you have news?'

'Tess.' His voice is different. I can tell from the taut way he says my name. 'I was wondering when you were going to pick up.'

Something cold about his tone. It makes me stop shivering.

'This isn't an easy conversation for us to have, but unfortunately it's necessary. What happened yesterday?'

I open my mouth. I wondered whether Oliver would tell the police, if he would squeal on me. Part of me has been waiting for Pettiford to call. Hoping to avoid this. But why should I duck my head or shrink away? Look at the bruises on my arm – evidence of his violence.

'I saw Oliver.'

'What do you mean you saw Oliver?' Pettiford says.

'We had a disagreement. A clash of sorts.'

He's silent for a long moment. 'Tess, Mr Barlow says you've been stalking him. That you were probably outside his home, that you must have followed him to a bar where he met the woman he's been seeing. And you ran after her, shouting that he's dangerous, that he's a killer.'

'That is not true!' I exclaim. 'At least, that's not the whole story. *He* was following *her*. After their date I saw him go after her, walking behind her without her knowledge. They'd said goodbye, but there he was, like a shadow. I was concerned for her safety, worried that he was going to do something, so I intervened. I warned her.'

Pettiford sniffs. 'Right. Well, be that as—'

'I was only following Oliver because of these texts he sent me, threatening and aggressive.' My words spurt out. 'And he actually hurt me – he injured me. I have bruises.'

He's quiet before his stiff voice sounds again. 'Mr Barlow says you hit him. You punched him in the face, and when he tried to walk away, you ran after him and grabbed him.'

Why does he automatically believe Oliver's story? Even though it's true, shouldn't he let me describe what happened before deciding who to side with? I just said Oliver hurt me and Pettiford has skipped straight over it.

'So what? He shoved me onto the ground. He's violent. He's the one who hurt my sister, who hit her head and—'

'Tess, please stop for a moment. You need to listen to me. I'm going to speak very plainly now.' He inhales, a sound like an inverted sigh. 'You need to stay away from Mr Barlow. Cease all contact. Don't message him, don't call him and certainly don't show up at his home. If you do any of these things, certain measures may have to be taken. We might have to issue a restraining order.'

My nails are digging in where I'm gripping my thigh.

'Perhaps I should have been straight with you sooner,' Pettiford says. 'If I haven't, I apologise. I sympathise with your situation and the grief you must be going through, but you are not a detective. Your behaviour is jeopardising our investigation. What you're doing is not helping us get any closer to determining what happened to your sister, or who was involved.'

The rain falls harder, nicking on the window.

After another pause, he says, 'I'm very sorry for your loss, but this has got out of hand. I shouldn't have let you carry on in this way for so long. Again, I apologise for any lack of clarity. For giving you a false impression of the boundaries here.'

I consider hanging up but he keeps going.

'I'm referring you to someone who offers counselling, as I'm concerned that you need support. A Dr Vasilakis. I know her personally and feel that she could be very helpful to you. She specialises in . . .' He trails off. 'Tess? Are you there?'

I press my fingers harder into my thigh.

'Tess?'

'Yes.'

'She's going to give you a call in the next couple of days. All right? Please talk to her.'

I don't respond.

'OK, Tess. Just to reiterate – stay away from Mr Barlow. This is a warning.' He pauses, as if for emphasis. 'If we have any information or news, we'll contact you. In the meantime, please accept my deepest condolences.'

He's gone.

I stare out the window, watching a tree sway in the wind. I can't believe what he's just said. A weight seems to sink into me. This mass pulling me down, pushing me to curl up on the floor. Foetal position. Hugging my knees. But I can't do that.

It feels like everything's turning a shade darker, shapes sidling in front of the sun, blotting what little light there was around me. Flat black forms and faces.

I don't know how long I've been staring at the tree when I turn and notice the Mars wrapper on the floor by the sofa. That's uncharacteristically messy of Arran.

I look at my phone on the table, then see something else behind it. A stoneware bowl. It's next to the fruit bowl. Shallower, flat-bottomed. Unglazed and rustic with that mottled effect, the top half washed blue-green like a robin egg.

Arran's?

I lean forwards. There are cherries in it.

I go into the guest room. More ceramics on his desk. All stoneware. All Nordic sea colours. Varying blues, turquoises, grey-greens. Not bright – whitish pastel shades. He must have brought them back from his studio.

I pick up a small cup. I feel the smoother top and the rough base. As my thumb rubs, a strange feeling comes on, a grain of memory, like I've seen this cup somewhere before.

I glance over the other items, similar to a lot of stoneware. The bowls and plates I've seen in shops with that freckled farmhouse look. Yet there's something about the cup in my hand. The coarse texture, the teal pigment.

I blink and the feeling is gone. I put the cup back on the desk and focus on the primary object in here: the diary. Arran could have written in it again in the last few hours. I need to follow his trail, since my own has suddenly shrunk and stalled.

He's left it in the bedside drawer. Thank God – I don't feel like hunting round his room. And when I open it, there's another trickle of relief. He has written more.

You practise yoga.

I saw you go into a class, all these women in their neon crop tops and tight activewear. Unlike them, you have taste. Relaxed in plain black leggings and a loose T-shirt.

You attended the same class again. Here was my in. I was bored of hanging back, I'd had enough of the distance. It was time to make my move.

I went through two classes without any sign of you. Good thing I'd done yoga a few times before, otherwise I would have stuck out too much. I was already prominent as the only guy in the class. Drawing all the women's eyes, including the teacher, Alice. But your eyes were the only ones I cared about.

Third class, I was sitting on a mat near the centre of the room, watching the door for you. One minute to the hour you stepped through. My whole body stiffened as you breezed past. In the mirror I saw you unroll your mat then scoop your hair into a ponytail, revealing gold earrings that looked unsuitable for yoga.

The hour went slow and fast. Glimpses of your legs pointing into the air or your torso twisting in poses. You reminded me of a cheetah, long limbs supple, body stretching in soft curves.

At the end, I rolled up my mat slowly. You let your hair down again, tucking some of it behind your ear. When you looked up our eyes met in the mirror.

A split-second. But that was enough – you'd seen me.

I can't believe this. All of this he's just written. I'm blinking at the words, something fuzzy about them against the page. There's one more entry, with scribbled bits and lines crossing out.

I let you go after that class, after our eyes touched. Best to wait, talk to you next time – an organic procession of things.

You're eating into my mind.

That sounds weird.

I think about you too much. It's disturbing. Before you, I didn't know a person could saturate my thoughts like this.

You were there at the next class. And you looked at me, a blink of recognition. Your eyes finding mine in the mirror four times through the hour. In the final few minutes, while we lay on our backs in silence, I could feel the blood rushing round my body.

I sat up. You laced your shoes, hair a shield over your face. Hiding yourself? Shy? No. I could sense the attraction in you, the desire, undisguised in your look. Most women are like glass. Way too transparent. You at least weren't bare, you had a colour. Apothecary blue. Earthen amber.

Contact between us, there was no going back. You walked out and I went after you, and I was close enough for you to hold the door. 'Thanks,' I said.

You smiled. Honey low in my abdomen.

'That was such a good class, wasn't it?'

'Yeah,' you said. 'I love Alice.'

Your voice. Speaking to me. Finally. Thank fuck.

You'd been coming to this class for a while, I found out. You commented on how it's rare, guys who do yoga. I said I'm no pro but I enjoy it. You thought I looked pretty good. A glimmer of suggestion?

You smelled faintly of sweat. There was a strong odour round reception, something like incense – too much. I wanted to kiss you right there, wrap my arms around your back, push you against the wall. But I couldn't. Not yet.

I made a joke about yoga not being that macho. You laughed. A beautiful sound. You didn't mind my closeness, physically or emotionally. You said my secret was safe with you. The smile in your eyes had a gleam. I wasn't sure of what. Just as I wasn't sure if I was imagining the flush in your skin.

I held out my hand, introducing myself, and you told me your name even though I already knew it. Your hand was warm and I was no longer a stranger.

You said Arran's an interesting name, and I explained it's Arran like the Scottish island. You were rubbing that hollow between your collarbones. Your fingers brushed your necklace before they dropped. And you said, 'Well, maybe see you at Alice's class again.'

'Yes, maybe.'

There was something hidden in the shape of your mouth. 'Cool, good to meet you, Arran like the Scottish island.'

You walked out of the door, into the sunlight. I was surprised when you glanced back at me through the glass. A direct unguarded look. Then you slid sunglasses onto your nose and disappeared from view.

I'm staring at his messy writing, this horrible feeling crawling up my torso. Betrayal. Like a rat beneath my feet I can't see – yet it's been there all along.

I'm not the girl. I'm not *you*.

An urge to rip the pages, chuck the diary at the window. Even though I know it's nonsensical. Groundless. I'm reading Arran's diary behind his back and I've made all these assumptions, false connections.

Except they don't *feel* groundless, or false. There are details in the diary which seem to correspond to me. And the way Arran acts with me, his looks, his touch.

After everything that's just happened, I can feel an outburst beneath the surface. I put the diary down before I do something I might regret.

I'm shivering again. My clothes are still wet, my hair sodden and stuck to my neck.

I don't do yoga. I haven't had that conversation with Arran. Facts which undercut everything I thought was true. The building he was talking about isn't a library. It must be some kind of gym or exercise centre.

I go over his entries, everything he's narrated, and I try to picture her. This woman who isn't me. I try to form an image but nothing holds. The details are in bits that refuse to come together and crystallise.

Who the hell is she?

She bruises easily. I think she might be deficient in minerals, among other things. Perhaps I should sneak something into her water, or her beer. Her cuts take a long time to heal too. It doesn't help that she picks at her scabs.

25

I'm going to follow Arran. It might be crazy, it might be rash. But that's what I'm doing.

I've barely slept. I lay awake turning it all over, thoughts whirring and returning to the same point: who this girl is. This rival, hidden and nameless. There's only one way to find out. See her for myself.

The sun is already up, arcing into a cool milky sky. I'm on the sofa, dressed, pretending to work on translations. My days at the Barbican aren't set each week – on the rota I was down for today, but my manager switched me out when I said I was still unwell yesterday. A semi-white lie. My throat's still sore and I'm coughing a bit.

I glance at the doorway. I feel apprehensive, a little twitchy.

Arran's bedroom door closes and my spine straightens. 'See you later, Tess,' he calls.

'See you.'

Muffled footfalls on the stairs down to the street. I wait a second, still red. Two seconds, amber.

Green light. Go.

I bolt from the sofa. The street door bumps shut as I gently close the flat one. I hurry down the stairs and out onto the porch. Arran is walking along the pavement, already a distance away. I lean round the wall of the front area of our building, then step out and follow.

I'm more nervous than I was stalking Oliver.

I need to be careful. Keep well back. Even with caution, it could all go wrong. He could turn and see me, catch me out somehow. There are so many things beyond my control. Like right now – him halting. I panic and dart behind a car. Crouched low beside a drain, the smell of sewage is strong in my nose.

Maybe I shouldn't be so hasty, maybe I should go back, wait until I'm better prepared. But it's not like I can plan. The next opportunity will be just as unpredictable and dicey.

I peek round the wheel arch.

Arran is bending down. When he straightens there are bits of plastic packaging in his hand. Picking up litter? He carries on, so I skirt round the car back into the open. He drops the rubbish in a bin without slowing.

There's no wind. Not a hum or a distant siren. The quiet seems unnerving, for mid-morning in London. This city is never silent.

As I did with Oliver, I linger at street corners to watch where he's going, then jog after him. The timing is tricky at Highbury & Islington station, waiting to make sure he's gone through the barriers. On the escalator his blond head gleams below me and I feel precariously exposed. A colourful bird in a bare tree. Why did I wear red? I didn't think this through.

I weave through the people on the southbound Victoria line platform. Arran walks along, away from the crowd bunching at the entrance. With a tremor I realise the train is going to be more difficult to navigate. Should I get on the same carriage as him? An enclosed space means greater risk.

A train hurtles in and I'm still undecided, so I go for the nearest set of doors. Same carriage, opposite end.

Arran finds a seat but immediately gives it up for an old woman who shuffles on behind him. I'm squashed up against the rail. But this is good. I'm well concealed behind tall bodies, and from this angle I can see his leg and his hand holding his phone.

A few minutes in, I have an urge to cough. I let myself once then hold it down. I can't draw any attention. My eyes begin to water, but I stay strong. And my throat eases.

At Green Park alarm grips when he seems to vanish. But then I spy his denim jacket and ear beside the doors. He's getting off.

Back up towards street level, Arran heads for the exit into the park, his body silhouetted against the light. His walk is a saunter. I follow cautiously, a few steps behind, keeping one or two people between us as potential screens. That voltaic feeling is back, my body high-wired.

He goes up the ramp and halts near the fountain, doing something on his phone. I manage to navigate behind him, using a group of people, and as he starts to turn, I make it to the snack bar cabin selling ice cream and sandwiches. He slips his phone into his pocket and watches the station exit. The one I was standing in seconds before.

I lean against the cabin, in the shadow of its roof, keeping my head low behind the queues of people.

Arran takes his phone out of his pocket again, checks something, then returns it. He runs his fingers through his hair. I've noticed he does this when he seems slightly on edge.

Is he meeting someone here? Meeting *you*?

I have a strange desire to walk over, to feign amazement at such a coincidence. But I can't give him any reason to be suspicious. I have only one get-out-of-jail-free card and I need to save it for when I get caught. *If* I get caught.

Arran stands there, stroking his hair, then he jolts, pulling out his phone again.

'Hello?' I hear him say through the background chatter. 'Where are you?' He scuffs the ground with the toe of his desert boot. 'Just five minutes. It's important. We can't just—' He goes still. 'OK, but you know how much we—'

Who is it? And why do they keep cutting him off?

His voice is quieter; I strain to hear. 'I know that, but this can't wait.' He smiles. 'Yes. It'll be great. So?' His fingers pause in his hair. 'In five minutes? Yep, I'm coming.'

He hangs up and starts walking. To my horror, in my direction. I press myself into the cabin and use a bin as a shield, ducking down behind it. I'm expecting him to lean over and say, 'Tess? What the hell are you doing?' But when I dare to look, he's walked straight past. He hasn't seen me. And he's power-walking. I watch him go round the black railing up towards the road.

Out on Piccadilly the pavements are teeming, congested with tourists and shoppers and workers. Arran walks under the arcade of The Ritz. I follow him, hurrying beneath the glitzy letters of London's smartest hotel. A family with teenage children is blocking the space. I almost bump into the boy, trying to keep Arran in view.

The road is jammed with traffic. Lorries and red buses chugging, exhaust fumes in my nose.

Arran carries on down Piccadilly, past shops and patisseries, the Royal Academy of Arts and Fortnum & Mason's green clock. His long legs striding fast. I have to jog to keep up.

Piccadilly Circus opens out into tall Georgian buildings and huge gleaming screens. Arran crosses Regent Street into the central pedestrian area and this time I keep near.

He halts beside the fountain steps. I make use of a gang of French schoolkids, concealing my body behind their cluster.

I watch Arran, ducking when he seems to turn in my direction. One of the French kids notices and sniggers at me. After a few seconds I lift my head again. Arran is angled away. Looking for someone? When his mouth goes slack and his palm slides down his chest, I know he's seen the person. Whoever he's meeting is almost here.

I swallow. *Her?*

Arran smiles, bright and wide in his cheek. His arms move and I glimpse someone stopping in front of him. A girl. Dark brown hair and tanned skin. Anticipation bubbles up, soured with resentment – I can taste it in my mouth. *This must be her.* But her hair and skin are the only features I can make out. The French kids are shouting and jumping around, blocking my view.

With a spurt of frustration, I step round them, but still I can't see her face. Only her arm as it goes round Arran's shoulder.

When I finally have a clearer view, their backs are walking off. Too many people in the way. I collide with a woman, tripping over her shopping bag on the ground. She glares at me as I stumble.

Feet firm on concrete again, I can't see Arran's blond hair or denim jacket or any sign of the girl. I spin round, 360 degrees. There are so many streets intersecting at the circus, so many directions they could have gone in.

I stand there in the blaring noise and bustle, the giant screens flashing adverts and reds in my eyes. But I barely notice the glare. The glimpse of her is stuck in my vision, still searching for it in the crowd. Beautiful figure and curving waist. Silken hair on her shoulders.

26

I slam the front door so hard it rattles the crockery in the kitchen cupboards. I'm soaked through, my shoes sludging into my bedroom. It's pouring outside, water splashing on the windowsills.

The rain started as I walked along Shaftesbury Avenue, in case I might see her and Arran, since they'd seemed to disappear in that direction. But no luck. On my way back to Green Park it was mizzle, then a tropical burst from Highbury station.

I yank off my wet clothes and sit on the bed with my face in my hands. All that effort foiled by crowds, French kids and a shopping bag. For a mere glimpse of diary girl.

The pragmatic part of my brain tells me it's not surprising, losing someone on a busy city street. I've only got two eyes, I don't have a GPS tracker or superhuman abilities. It was naïve of me to think it could be that simple. And this was only the first attempt.

Still, it feels like an anticlimax. The disappointment is heavy and sharp, a stone of it in my stomach.

Naked, I walk into the living area to get some cranberry juice. I don't care if anyone sees me. Arran, if he walks in; the people in the flats over the road; anyone peeping through the webcam of my open laptop and watching me through cyber-space. What does it matter?

I've poured some cranberry juice when I change my mind. I feel like something stronger. I take out a carton of sangria and drink from it straight.

I get into the empty bath. I lie there for a while in the cold hard tub, sipping my sangria and staring at my skin against the white porcelain. Then I turn on the taps with my toes and wait for the water to fill up round my body.

*   *   *

I'm lying in a brimming bath, the waterline lapping the over-flow drain. My mouth is underwater. I'm breathing through my nose.

I sit up, sloshing water over the side.

I watch the surface of the bathwater swaying slower and slower to stillness. There's no reflection. Only the faintest shadow of my head. Unbidden, the glimpse of the girl returns. Taller than me? More beautiful than me?

Stop it.

I get out of the bath. My fingers are pasty and wrinkled. I don't need to analyse her fragmentary features. I can follow Arran again and see the whole picture.

When I go into the guest room, there's something different that makes me halt. A smell. Not immediately identifiable, but there – a subtle odour. Dusty, a little like sherbet. Not bad, just a room smell. A human smell.

This room has never had an odour before – no one's been here long enough. Arran's making his mark in Rosie's zone. The idea mixes up feelings. That she went between these rooms, her footsteps on the floorboards, her body shifting the air, leaving scents and traces – are they all gone now?

Also, Arran's already been here for two weeks. Time is running out.

His diary's not here. That's weird. He went out today without a backpack or bag, so surely he didn't take it with him? I look around and my eyes land on the bin. There's something in it now. Ripped pieces of paper. I pick one up and see writing. Lifting the other four pieces out and slotting them together on the desk, a page from the diary appears.

I lean down and read.

Something was different about you. As soon as you came into the class, I noticed. You were wearing make-up. I preferred you without it – far more striking.

'Hi, Scottish island Arran.' You were smiling. Flirting?

I flirted back.

You fiddled with your earring, spinning the gold stud. You were wearing a more fitted T-shirt, the curve of your breasts just visible through the fabric. I asked if you wanted to get a coffee. You blinked, but there was no surprise in your eyes. They flickered down as you adjusted the bracelet on your arm, then came back to me.

The cafe was one of those cool urban joints, all steel beams and exposed light bulbs. You didn't get your purse out or try to pay like girls always do, making men insist, say it's fine, I've got it. You just leaned on the coffee bar, angled towards me, ankles crossed. And I liked it.

Your smoothie was a dark speckled colour, and you sucked through the paper straw before we reached the table. I liked that too. You were self-assured enough not to wait.

You sat there opposite me, your legs almost touching mine, and we chatted and laughed. People watching, playing a guessing game about who they were, what their story was. I was only interested in yours. That and being able to touch you.

When I asked for your number, your energy shifted. I felt it. You tucked your hair behind your ear. I thought you were going to say no, make an excuse, the idea leaching, but then you told me to hand over my phone.

I watched you type it in before you stood up, saying you had to go. As you walked out, I sat there looking at your smoothie, an inch of it left behind. I picked up your glass, tasted the smoothie, wiped it from my lips. It wasn't enough. I needed more. I went after you.

I didn't know when I would see you again. That weird shift of your energy. Something skittish about you, something I couldn't hold on to, troubling.

That was my reasoning for following.

It wasn't so difficult to keep you in sight – you were ambling. Your hair was twirled on the back of your head, in a loose bun, downy strands dangling out. I was too close, I realised. Dangerous. What if you turned around? I dropped back, keeping a few people between us.

I followed you onto a train. It was crowded and I positioned myself behind two large men, but I needn't have worried. You didn't look round.

The whole journey my heart was thumping inside my skull. What I was doing was mad. I told myself to stop.

But then you got off the train and I'd come this far, so I kept going. The sun was going down. This butterscotch light on all the roofs and walls, and on you.

Giddy, I zigzagged your route through your neighbourhood. I snuck along your street and watched as you put your keys in your door. As it shut behind you.

I stare at the ripped page, seeds of uncertainty growing into unease. This is full-blown stalking – following her home.

This man who I picture leaning over his pottery wheel, fingers softly shaping the wet clay. Creeping behind a woman. His words here are possessive. Following as though he's mesmerised, powerless to his infatuation. He could mean no harm by it – he just can't help himself, he's so in love.

Except following someone is always a little threatening. A little weird. I know that myself.

I'm in no position to comment or disapprove. Stalking Arran and Oliver. Waiting outside Oliver's home isn't very different to what Arran's doing here. Yet the motivations are. I can't help wondering if Arran is everything he seems to be.

How much can I trust him? In person and in the diary?

I rub the texture of the paper between my finger and thumb. Why did he tear out this page – want to get rid of it? This entry about following a girl to her door.

I'm not sure how to evaluate it right now. I place the scraps of paper back in the basket, arranging them how they were.

I wander into my room. My phone is on the floor. It must have fallen out of my jacket when I pulled it off. I kneel down and swipe the screen. No notifications or messages. The most recent text from Nalika two hours ago: *Excited about the party. Is Arran gonna be there? Wink wink xxx.*

I turn the screen black.

When I look up, I notice something on my window. A smudge. From this angle on the floor it's clear against the daylight.

I get up and go over. Smeared fingerprints.

They could be mine, from weeks or months ago. I've never cleaned my windows. But when I press my hand into the glass, the smudge is bigger. As if it's from another hand. As if someone else has stood here and touched the glass.

I look beyond the mark and a person is crossing the street. Luke – coming towards our building. As I move back my hip knocks the corner of my desk.

My hipbone throbs but I barely feel the pain. I'm staring at the finger smear, a strange feeling beneath my ribs. A question thrumming in my throat.

Has Arran been in my room?

27

'*Buenos días,* Tess.'

I look up from the kitchen table. Arran is there, putting his backpack down on the floor. No footsteps or rustles of clothing. How does he do that?

His hair's darker. Just showered. He goes over to the cupboard and takes out a large jar of granola. 'Isn't that what you say in the morning?'

'Yes.'

'My accent's probably terrible.' Granola clusters tinkle into a bowl.

It wasn't that bad. The emphasis on the í, and the slight dropping of the 's' in *buenos*, which most people fail at. But I don't tell him this. I just watch him with his breakfast, questions pulsing.

Why have you been in my room? What were you doing?

After that torn-out diary entry, following her and watching her go in through her door – most women would be worried, to have the man who wrote that staying in their home. But it's not worry I feel. It's intrigue.

I need to see her properly, and I need to see Arran following her – witness it with my own eyes. Then I'll have a better idea. Of him and the risk.

My jacket's in the hall, ready for grabbing. But Arran takes his time. Leaning against the counter, eating granola. His stoneware bowl is in front of me, three cherries left at the bottom. Dark and shiny.

This is the first time we've been in each other's presence since I discovered the diary isn't about me. Stalking's not the same, of course, as it is here – with him close, sharing air and space. My chagrin in the background. I hope he can't sense it, but it's strong and difficult to hide.

I get up, scraping the chair legs on the floor. I can wait in my room until he leaves.

Arran's putting his bowl in the dishwasher when, out of nowhere, I feel his fingers on my arm. He grasps it, stopping me. 'If you need someone to talk to, you know you can talk to me, don't you?'

I'm so surprised, looking down at his hand.

When I don't reply he seems to hesitate. 'Maybe I've got the wrong impression or I'm being too forward, but—'

'No.' I find my voice. 'You haven't got the wrong impression.'

I want to talk, feel closer to him. But where would I start?

'Good,' Arran says, a soft smile in his left cheek. His hand feels hot before it slips off. 'It's an open offer.'

I have to swallow.

'So the party tonight,' he says. 'It's still happening?'

I nod.

'And I'm still invited?'

I nod again.

'What time does it start?'

'Nine.'

'No fancy dress theme or anything like that?'

'No, I don't think so.'

'Great, I'll see you later then.'

He's not seeing *her* tonight?

Arran bends down to pick up his backpack. I haven't moved when he pulls on his desert boots, deftly lacing them. *Be cool, Tess. Stop watching him.* I turn and pretend to wander towards the fridge. At the front door, he pauses to glance back at me.

'*Hasta luego?*'

I make myself smile. '*Hasta luego.*'

He goes through the door, his footfall on the stairs faint. I wait ten seconds. *Hasta luego* isn't quite right. For me it's more like *hasta pronto*. I grab my jacket and go.

* * *

Arran gets off the underground at Chalk Farm.

I've been screening myself behind a large man and a couple with a buggy. The man is smirking at me as I peek round his shoulder, shuffling off behind him. I dart after Arran.

On the street, his pace quickens. I speed up to match it before he suddenly stops, looking at his phone. Two seconds later, the sun breaks out between clouds, casting my shadow on the tarmac. It points towards Arran like a sundial. Too black, too sharp-cut.

Arran half-turns, and for a moment I think he's going to see me. But then he continues the way he was going, towards Camden.

The sun goes in again and my shadow disappears.

I'm on thin ice. I can feel it beginning to crack, however much I enjoy the adrenaline. Good thing I'm wearing plain colours today.

He turns onto a quieter cobbled street, then a main road teeming with people. The array of outfits in Camden is always diverse – people who don't give a shit, who feel able to express themselves however they like. I love that, but I don't love how busy this area is. Stalls all over the pavement, stuff spilling out of shops. I struggle to keep Arran in sight. He takes another side road away from the market, then crosses over and stops.

I stay on the opposite side. He's next to a building with big glass doors and a sign that reads Niyama. A board on the brick wall with smaller writing: Wellbeing Centre, Yoga, Pilates, Meditation, Workshops, Pool, Gym. The centre from Arran's diary, where he met *her*.

Envy spurts, blending with a weird sort of excitement.

Arran goes through the glass doors. I can just see his body, half-obscured, in the entrance area. Near the reception desk? He's there for a minute before he turns and comes out again. I move behind a parked van delivering plants to a florist. At the front end, I peer round the windscreen.

Arran is side-on. He glances around as if looking for someone. Perhaps they've arranged to meet. Perhaps she's in a class right now.

A church bell chimes somewhere. Midday. Arran straightens, looks at the entrance, then gets his phone out again. Something about this action makes my forehead tighten. The way he moved, jerky, too fast, like he's pretending to be busy on his phone.

The glass doors open and girls with mats spill out. They all have high swinging ponytails, neon-Lycra leggings and fashion trainers. I scan their faces and figures, looking for those features from yesterday. One girl with brown hair could be her. But no – she's too short and her hair's frizzy.

The door has stopped sliding, the flow seemingly dried up. It opens again and Arran's head moves. A short lift and drop, but I see it.

Through the door steps a platinum blonde, followed by a girl with dark hair and brown skin. Stunning. Flawless complexion, leggy yet curvy. All natural – no make-up, no hair dye, wearing plain black leggings and a loose T-shirt. She makes me think of a glossy-coated foal.

I notice Arran swallow, Adam's apple rolling in his throat. The platinum blonde is saying something to the girl. She nods, laughing, then looks over the blonde's shoulder, noticing Arran. Surprise fills her face. I see her lips move, saying 'Arran?' as she steps past her friend. Arran looks up and blinks. His surprise is slower to appear, but then blatant. Excessive, even, like he's putting it on.

She introduces her blonde friend. They stand there chatting, the girl beside Arran, smiling, nodding. She puts her hand on his arm. Touches him. A cold cavity feeling as I watch them.

The blonde girl says goodbye and walks off down the street. Leaving just Arran and her.

They're talking. Arran says something that makes her laugh. Clearly they have a connection. His eyes don't leave her face. They stop speaking for a moment, neither of their lips moving. She glances at the ground. Something more serious passing between them? Arran's gripping one of his backpack straps.

But then they talk again. Arran smiles, mouth pulling left, and she smiles back. Their voices get a little louder, but I still can't hear the words.

It looks like they're saying goodbye. The girl initiates the parting. Arran indicates Niyama, tipping his head and half-pointing, and she nods. They don't hug. But she touches his arm again.

She turns and walks off, yoga mat tucked under her arm. Hair gleaming on her back even though the sun's not out. I want to follow her. But Arran's still there, watching her go. Ten seconds and he hasn't moved. Hands in his pockets, staring.

Finally, he stirs. He glances at Niyama, in through the glass doors, then he starts walking. In the same direction as her.

When I move out from behind the van, looking up the street, I can see she's crossed over, now on the same side as me. Arran continues down the other pavement. They could be going the same way for different reasons. But something tells me they're not.

I jog after them.

The irony isn't lost on me – how similar a situation this is to Oliver. Although Arran isn't directly behind the girl. She's further up. Too far away, it's difficult to keep her in sight, trees and people obscuring my view.

I have to skirt round a bicycle, then a bollard. Scaffolding on a building is another obstacle, all the poles blocking my sightline up the street. Arran is there, diagonally ahead. I squeeze past a pole and it's too shaded. Is that her? I think she turns, goes down another road. Her jade yoga mat a marker disappearing at that corner. Once I emerge from the scaffolding I squint at the spot, but she's not there.

I look over the road towards Arran. I can't see him either. No blond hair or backpack or white T-shirt.

I cross the road and look both ways down the pavement. He's vanished. I wait, then cautiously walk a bit further, in case he appears behind someone, or at the bus stop ahead.

He doesn't. I've lost both of them. Again. And he was just here – I saw him by this tree. Where did he go?

This is what we're up to now, is it?

Stalking should be termed an art. It takes talent and care.

28

I'm staring at my face. In the bathroom mirror it looks back at me, cheeks and nose dead on, lips heart-shaped. Espresso-eyed. Spanish skin.

I lean forwards.

Even from a distance, diary girl's face was model-striking. I turn to the right, looking at the mole on my cheekbone. I wasn't close enough to see hers.

I flick mascara over my lashes, just enough to pass as natural. It's nearly nine o'clock – the party's about to start. And Arran isn't here.

After I lost them, I went back to Niyama and dared to go inside. I just wanted to have a look. It had a nice vibe, wood and plants everywhere, simple palm decor, an incense stick burning on reception. The girl behind the desk was filing her nails. She glanced up at me.

'Can I help you?' she said.

'Uh . . .' I hadn't intended to speak to anyone but this was an opportunity. I wanted to ask about the girl and Arran, what he wanted, what he'd said, but I'd sound like a lunatic. Instead I edged towards her and said, 'I've heard about yoga classes here. A particular teacher my friend recommended called Alice?'

'Uh-huh.' She'd resumed nail filing.

'Does she still teach here?'

'Yep, she has classes almost every day. She's one of our most popular teachers.'

I glanced behind, worried Arran might come back. 'What time are her classes?'

'Eleven a.m. and six p.m. are her regulars. I can print out a copy of our timetable if you like? It's also on our website.'

'I'll check the website.' I didn't want any potentially incriminating evidence.

She nodded and filed her thumb some more.

I was lingering, hesitant.

She looked up. 'Is there anything else?'

'Do you get many guys in classes here?' I blurted.

Her brow furrowed at me. 'We get a few, on and off.'

'What about in Alice's class? Have you noticed any men attending hers?'

The furrows deepened, the file balanced on her thumb. 'I'm not in a position to comment, I'm afraid. Client confidentiality and all that.'

'OK,' I wrapped up. 'Thanks for your help.'

I left and sped down the street into another road, nervous of being seen by Arran. Even though he'd disappeared.

When I got home I read the diary. Then read it again. There were still hours to kill before the party. I assessed outfit options and texted Luke in response to his previous three messages:

Are you coming to the party?

Are you coming tonight?

If you don't, I'll drag you down anyway.

I wrote: *Yep, I'll stick my nose in, and bring a couple of friends.*

Within ten seconds my phone buzzed. A text from Luke with two face emojis: wide toothy grin and smiling heart-eyes.

I looked at the hearts, and all the messages from him, wondering what he's playing at. Maybe it's not serious for him or Ivy.

I check my make-up in the mirror, adding a bit more mascara, then finishing with lipstick. It's plum-red, called Sunshade.

Nalika's due any minute. I go into the guest room. Arran said he was coming to the party. Has he changed his mind? Is he with her? I decide to have another look at the diary.

You took a while to text me back. You suggested going for a walk.

You wore a red floral dress. We went into a shop, looking at postcards. You grabbed one from my hand, snorting at my choice. A photograph of an apple. You hated these kinds of images, you said it made objects look dead. No such thing as a dead object. Life isn't still, you declared, it's alive, moving. I liked your reasoning. And I relished how close you were.

You let go of the card and twirled round to face me, the material of your dress swaying over your legs. I asked if you like real fruit, despite your abhorrence for fruity photographs. Your response was a smile.

At a market stall we got peaches and strawberries – you flat-out refusing apples when I suggested them – and we ate them in the park. You kicked off your shoes, sitting on the grass with your legs tucked under you. Coiling your hair round your neck and throwing a squirrel a strawberry, which it sniffed and rejected. Laughing. One of the peaches spurting juice down your chin.

The sky changed, drifting into that early-evening light, and you took my hand. We sat there quietly. I stroked my thumb on yours and felt a strand of your hair. Your fingers linked through mine before you did what I'd wanted to do since the cafe. You kissed me. Slow and exploratory at first.

We were still kissing when the sun had gone behind the trees, and you tasted of strawberries and peaches.

It's a moment before I close the diary. One thing glaring in my brain: how can I compete with that? With her?

No such thing as a dead object. Life isn't still. Her words reverberate through what I've been feeling the past few months. My life has been static. Going nowhere. Only starting to feel alive, moving, since Arran came to stay. Since the diary and *you*.

I'm ninety-nine per cent sure that was her today, outside Niyama. But was Arran following her?

He was on the opposite side of the street, quite far behind. That could be a tactic though. Precaution so he doesn't get caught.

Stop, brain.

I put the diary back in the pile and thump the books on top of it. I want to enjoy the party. Music is already booming from below, the bass thudding through the floor. For once I'm going to have some fun. I spent two hours getting ready, showering, blow-drying my hair, trying on clothes and staring at myself in the mirror.

He'd better come.

29

Nalika greets me with wide arms and a bottle of tequila. Her eyes taking in my dark red sundress.

'Don't you look a Spanish dream,' she says, hugging me. 'Love the buttons.'

'You look great too.'

She does. In a satin tie-waist jumpsuit, hair loosely plaited down her back.

'Arran here?' she says, going into the living room.

I shake my head.

'But he's coming, right?'

Why does she care? 'I think so.'

'Hm.' She opens the glass cupboard. 'Well, tonight is all about fun, OK, Hartley? We both deserve some of that. And the party has already started, so we need to *vamos*. But first, tequila.'

We have two shots each, then head down. A lot of people have already arrived, groups chatting in the living area and some outside in the garden, smoke from the barbecue floating behind.

Luke beelines over, leaving a couple of his friends mid-conversation. His gaze sliding down and up my body.

'Wow, Tess, you look incredible.'

He hugs and cheek-kisses me, his hand lingering a little too long on the small of my back. *It's not for you*, I think, as he steps back and admires me some more.

'Seriously, what a babe.'

'Scrubs up pretty well, don't she?' Nalika says, arm slipping round my shoulders.

'This is my friend Nalika,' I say to Luke. 'Nalika, meet my neighbour, party host and general gusher.'

'Good to meet you, Nalika,' Luke says. 'Welcome to the animal house.'

'Thanks for having me. Beastie fun is the best.'

Luke looks at me. 'I like her already.'

Nalika beams.

'Ladies!' he shouts, sloshing beer out of his bottle. 'Drinks. This way.'

He leads us over to the table, where bottles and dishes of food clutter the surface. In the centre is a huge pitcher of some pink concoction.

'Watermelon punch,' Luke says, ladling it into glasses. 'Courtesy of Ivy.'

It's delicious, if strong in the throat. All the food looks great too, an array of salads and canapés alongside dips, crisps and barbecued meat.

'How about a chocolate-dipped strawberry?' Luke says. 'My contribution, you know. Melted the chocolate and dipped them all myself.' His tone suggests that's meant to be sexy.

I roll my eyes and take one.

He bites hard into his, getting chocolate on his lips. He's wearing a cap backwards with a tuft of hair poking out of the hole. Nalika's round the other side of the table already talking to someone – a guy in a tight-fitting T-shirt.

'It's been ages, Rivero,' Luke says. 'Where have you been?'

I swallow my strawberry. 'Around.'

'You're obviously feeling better. My goodies must have hit the spot?'

I'm looking over his shoulder for any sign of Arran. 'Oh yeah, it was kind of you to think of me, Luke. And drop them over.'

'Is that a thank you I hear?' Mock-surprise pitches his voice. 'Mamma mía, blow me down.' His hand goes to his chest.

'What are you – a pirate?'

He laughs. 'Why not?'

Or Popeye. He's clearly been doing more gym work, biceps curving out from his T-shirt. He swigs his beer. He's looking at me with a funny expression, amplified through his glasses. I glance round the room again.

I can't shake Luke off for a while. People keep arriving and a guy comes over who he introduces as a friend from work. Eventually he goes to greet a couple of girls who have sidled through the door.

For a moment I'm on my own, Nalika still chatting to that guy. Then, 'Ah! You made it.'

Ivy glides in through the garden doors with a platter of grilled meat. Chicken drumsticks, sausages and burger patties.

'*Bienvenida a la fiesta,*' she says, plonking the plate down and lifting her arms. 'I hope you're hungry. I'm bloody starving. Luke's had me slaving away for hours.'

'You speak Spanish?'

'A little. Luke's been taking a course and trying to teach me the odd word.'

'Luke? Taking a Spanish course?' *Why?*

She gives a sarcastic smile. 'I know. I'm not sure languages are his forte.' She wipes her hands, clapping her palms together. 'If it were me, I'd go for French – much more alluring on the ears. No offence.'

'Why would I be offended?'

'You're Spanish, right? That's what Luke said. Or has he got something else wrong?'

'No, I am. Half Spanish.'

'Ah, makes sense. That lovely Mediterranean glow you have, unlike my Celtic pastiness.'

'Freckles are pretty.'

'You're sweet. But not *this* many.'

She picks up a patty and bites straight in, without bothering to make it into a burger. No bun or lettuce. Glancing over at Luke, who's still chatting with those two pretty girls. What else has he got wrong?

'Well, it's rare,' I say, trying to be nice. 'Makes you unique. And freckles are in fashion.'

She pauses chewing, looking at me. Then she swallows. 'Thank you for saying that, Tess. It means a lot.' She rubs her temple. 'I used to *hate* my freckles. I would scrub at my skin every morning, trying to get them off. Get them out.' She pulls what's left of the patty apart. 'I was bullied at school. They tortured me, those girls.' Her voice has shrunk, turned in on itself. 'So much worse than the boys.'

A strange sort of energy is coming off her, suddenly intense. I'm not sure where it's come from, or what to say.

'I'm sorry to hear that. Girls can be so cruel.'

'That they can.' She's fiddling with the meat in her hand. 'But, hey, karma's a bitch.' She dunks the burger in guacamole.

Then, to someone over my shoulder, says, 'Where have you been? So much for coming early to help set up.'

I turn to see Elliot standing behind me. He edges past, towards the table.

'Yeah . . . sorry. Got a bit caught up.'

Ivy gives him a pouty look. 'What have you been doing? Testing out your gadgets?' She turns to me. 'Ell loves all the tech stuff. A few weeks ago, his new toy was an electric skateboard. Now it's a camera drone.'

Elliot is pouring himself a gin. He downs half the glass, then rests his fingers on the back of a chair.

'Hey, is she coming?' Ivy asks him. 'He's got some secret girlfriend he won't let me meet,' she tells me. 'Always chatting to her online. I'm sure of it, though he won't admit it.'

Elliot stares at her, annoyance in his eyes. He shakes his head, then takes his gin out into the garden.

'Don't know what's wrong with him,' Ivy says, semi-apologetically. 'He's being weird.'

In the smoky dusk air, I can see him behind a few people, back half-turned. He's lighting a cigarette.

'Have you known each other long?' I ask.

'From uni.'

I look at her as she selects a sausage and dips it in barbecue sauce. What she just said jogs a thought. A time when Rosie mentioned the neighbours here – a guy with weird flat hair. Elliot?

'How long have you guys lived here?' I say.

She bites off a chunk of sausage. 'In number 74?'

I nod.

'Well, I've come and gone a bit. I sublet Ell's old flatmate's room for a month last autumn, and when he moved out in

March, I took it. Ell's been renting for a couple of years now, I think.'

I look out of the open doors into the garden again. Elliot's standing alone, dragging on his cigarette.

He was here when Rosie was. He was here in January. But so was his old flatmate.

'Who was his old flatmate?'

Ivy looks up from double-dipping her sausage in mustard and mayonnaise.

'Out of curiosity,' I say, keeping my tone casual.

'He was another guy from uni who I didn't really know. Paul. Bit of a weirdo, to be honest. I think Ell was relieved when he moved out.'

I feel my chest begin to tighten. 'A weirdo in what way?'

'He would do strange things with Elliot's stuff, move it around. Suddenly put loud music on late at night, blaring it from his room.' Ivy finishes the sausage. 'He didn't have many friends and kind of latched onto Ell in our final year of uni. Sometimes he'd knock on Elliot's door in the middle of the night, wanting to chat, as if that was totally normal and he wasn't disturbing Ell at all.'

'You mean he woke him up?'

She nods. 'And sat on his beanbag talking for ages. One time Ell came home and there was broken glass all over the kitchen floor – Paul said it was an accident, but it was about four glasses' worth of shards scattered around.'

'And Paul hadn't cleared it up?'

'Nope. Elliot thinks he smashed them on purpose.' She licks her fingers. 'As I said, Elliot was glad when he left.'

What else could this guy have done? Outside of his home. In a London park.

'Where did he go?' I ask.

'I think he moved to Newcastle. Although Ell said he's been back a few times, asking to meet up.' Ivy shakes her head. 'People are odd creatures.'

I look down into my watermelon punch, doubts stirring. To tempt a few more details, I say, 'Elliot seems like a nice guy.'

Ivy glances towards him. He's flicking ash onto the grass.

'He is. One of the sweetest.'

'What are his flaws?'

Her brow twitches at me.

I lift a shoulder, justifying my question. 'Everyone has flaws. They're a way to know the truth of someone's character.'

'Well, I wouldn't like to betray his trust, but he has a terrible temper. He full-on loses it sometimes. Though always in private. He's never shown it to me.'

How does she know then? Maybe she's heard, or witnessed it when he thought no one was around. How bad is it, I wonder. Even if not directed at a person – is he ever violent?

I hear Nalika's laughter and spot her within a group now.

Ivy sighs, looking out into the garden. 'I'd better go check on Ell. And the barbecue.'

I watch her go up to Elliot. He doesn't look at her, the tension between them clear as he fiddles with his cigarette. I wish I could hear what they're saying.

While I sip my punch, my brain ticks over what I just heard from Ivy. Elliot. Paul. Has Pettiford checked them out?

No. Stop. I'm here for fun. A good time. I don't need to speculate or try to solve my sister's murder. Not right now.

I could join Nalika, but instead I look round the room. Wondering where Arran is. It's after ten. Gloom and impatience begin to worm in. Only now does it dawn on me how much I've been looking forward to him being here tonight.

Images flash up. His arm round her shoulders. Sharing a pizza. Pushing up her top and kissing her stomach.

I feel like an idiot. All this effort I've made is for him. And he's with her right now, isn't he?

Luke shimmies over, making me dance with him. Nalika pulls me into the group she's chatting with, rescuing me. I keep glancing over people's shoulders, doing the rude party eye-wander. Luke turns up at my arm again. I feel his fingers grazing my skin, then brushing my waist. I need space. Air. Lying about needing to freshen up, I extract myself, using the mass of bodies as a screen before dashing upstairs to my flat.

I slice some lime. I pour myself a shot and sprinkle salt on my hand. The tequila burns all the way down my throat. My vision is already a bit blurry. That watermelon punch is powerful.

I cut another slice of lime and suck on it, the acidity biting into my tongue. Disgusting. I shut my eyes against the tang. I think of the diary. I think of her. The chain of pursuit today. A sudden wave of alarm. What if Arran did see me? What if he—

'Is this a habit of yours? Eating raw lime?'

I turn, heart seizing. Arran is leaning on the doorjamb, elbow up against it. Watching me with an amused look on his face.

The lime drops from my teeth. 'No. Definitely not a habit.'

He grins. And all the gloom and doubt dissolves, like salt in warm water.

'Party in full swing, I hear,' he says, sauntering towards me.

'Yeah, it's getting pretty . . .' What's the word? I can't think. 'Rowdy down there.'

'Fun rowdy, I hope.' He halts next to me and sighs. 'Sorry I'm late. I had a couple of errands to run, took longer than I thought.'

Errands? Involving her?

'Doesn't matter,' I shrug. 'You're here now.'

He's looking at me, one hand in his pocket. He's wearing a denim shirt with the sleeves rolled up. One of the buttons is undone.

'I've got some catching up to do.' He gestures the tequila with a chin lift. 'Mind if I have some?'

'Oh . . . sure.'

He gets a shot glass out of the cupboard and pours tequila. 'Will you join me?' The bottle is hovering over my glass.

I've already had enough. But how can I say no? The words *join me* vibrating in my brain. He licks his hand and sprinkles salt on. Then he holds the shaker out for me.

'Ready?' he says.

We tap the glasses, tongue the salt, down the tequila and suck the lime – all in unison.

Arran places his glass rim-side down. 'Delicious.'

I don't want to move away to get to the tap, so I lick the lime juice off my fingers.

'I thought you didn't like citrus?' he says. When I pause to look at him, he continues, 'You never have it, and you left the lemon wedge untouched in your fish and chips box the other day.'

Embarrassment trickles in. 'Oh, well you're right, I don't. But lime's necessary for tequila, and the least vile of them.'

'Hm.' He's silent for a few moments. 'You know, you were talking in your sleep again last night.'

My lungs go cold.

He's spinning his glass when he notices my expression. 'Don't worry. It wasn't bad.'

'Was I shouting?'

'Essentially, yeah. Mostly talking gibberish, but at one point you started speaking clearly.'

I suppress the panic before it can billow. 'What did I say?' *Please nothing about stalking him. Please nothing about the diary.*

'You said I like pineapples, so what? I'm a pineapple ninja.'

I process the words slowly. Ridiculous comical words. '*What?*'

He's smiling.

'A pineapple ninja?'

'Yep, apparently so.'

I'm laughing now. 'What even is that?'

His hands open, laughing with me. 'Who knows.'

I keep laughing. In relief and in drunken humour, getting the giggles. My abdomen starts to hurt and I cling onto the side for support. Arran is watching me, smiling. The room is warm and low-lit again. I only switched on one lamp when I came up, and the sun has set now, the sky turning dark.

'You did say something else after that,' he says in a quiet voice.

'Oh God, what?'

'*He can't leave. I need him.*' He pauses, spinning his shot glass. 'There was a gap when you were silent before, *And him – I'm going to get him. He's not getting away with it.*'

I stare at Arran, my lungs even colder than before the laughing.

'Then you started speaking in Spanish, which I couldn't understand.' His tone is steady and solemn. 'Though it sounded impassioned.'

Oh shit is on repeat in my brain. In English and Spanish. I can't look at him, my cheeks burning.

Then I feel his hand on mine.

'Maybe I shouldn't have told you. I was going to this morning, then . . .' He shrugs. 'You were probably just dreaming. Do you remember anything from last night?'

I shake my head. Of course not – a blank sleep as usual. I watch his thumb on the back of my hand, stroking. My heart beating harder.

'You have the softest skin, Tess. You know that?'

My throat's dry.

Shouts and cheers come from below, loud with the music. Disturbing the moment.

'It does sound rowdy down there,' Arran says, letting go and pushing himself off the counter. 'We should go before it gets too unruly. Do I need to change?'

'No. Why do you say that?'

'Just that, your dress, it's . . .' His gaze travels down my body.

'What?' My hand jumps to my dress, worried he's dropping a hint, like I've spilt something on it. I try to smooth the material and inspect the creases for lime juice or food.

Arran takes my hand again and lifts it towards him. 'You look beautiful.'

Oh.

'And I feel a little scruffy next to you.' He's smiling as he indicates his clay-spattered trousers. 'But so what? Come on.'

He pulls, leading me out of the flat. We walk down the stairs to the party and, as we go through Luke's door, I'm vividly aware of how he's still holding my hand.

30

'*There* you are!' Nalika cries, playfully accusing before she clocks Arran at my side. 'Arran. Hi. You made it.'

She goes straight in for a hug, widening her eyes at me over his shoulder. He lets go of my hand to return the embrace and I feel a twinge of annoyance.

'You've been missing all the fun,' Nalika says.

'I hope I'm not too late.'

'No, no.' She sweeps her arm round the room, towards all the people drinking, eating and dancing. She's tipsy. 'What have you two been up to?'

I grit my teeth, remembering how loud and indiscreet she can be. How she loves to be the life of the party.

Arran seems unperturbed, amused by her. He looks at me then shrugs. 'Oh, you know, this and that.'

'I see.' Nalika taps her nose. 'Hush-hush.'

It's hot in here, too many bodies. The garden doors are open. The barbecue still going, its smoke drifting inside and mixing with the sweat moistening people's skin.

Nalika looks down at Arran's hands. 'You, my friend, need a drink.'

She leads us over to the table and ladles punch into glasses, spilling it down the sides. She hands one to Arran and holds out another to me.

'I'm OK, actually.' I can't have any more. My head and stomach are swimming. I eat a tortilla chip, then go for a hunk of bread with hummus. I need to soak up the tequila.

'This is really good,' Arran says, tasting the punch.

'Well, thank you very much,' a voice chimes.

Ivy appears beside the table. She's wearing a different top to earlier. Before it was a mauve T-shirt. Now it's a black halterneck, cropped short, her stomach showing – flat and white. A piercing in her belly button: glittery diamanté.

'Mixed it myself,' she says. 'Careful though, it can be deadly.'

Nalika laughs. 'I'll attest to that. A girl already fell over, though Luke was there to catch her.'

Ivy arches an eyebrow. 'Ever the hero.'

'Ivy, this is Nalika and Arran, a couple of . . . friends.' How else to term him?

'Good to meet you both.' Ivy looks from Nalika to Arran, something shifting in her smile.

'You know, Ivy, I've seen you somewhere before,' Nalika says. 'I just can't think where.'

'We passed the other day in the building,' Ivy answers.

'Oh, yeah. That must be it.'

Ivy pulls her hair round one shoulder. 'I seem to have one of those faces, though, where I look like other women, or people think they've seen me before. I must have some generic features.'

Funny she says that, because her face is pretty distinctive. The point of her chin, her narrow nose and thick eyebrows. And that dark liquid eyeliner – something Egyptian about it tonight.

'Have you seen the garden yet, Arran?' Nalika asks. 'Let me show you.'

She takes him out, hand on his arm. Her fingers touching his skin bothering me more than it should. I watch their figures move into the darker air. Ivy is still beside me and when I look at her, she's watching them too, her eyes on Arran's back. A cold blankness over her face. Jaw chewing.

'Everything all right?'

She blinks and looks at me. 'Yeah. Sorry. Lost in my thoughts.' Her head shakes. 'And Luke's been annoying me.'

'When is he ever not annoying?'

'Good point.'

I notice a grassy scent again, like straw.

'Where is he anyway?' She scans the room, chewing gum. 'Haven't seen him in ages.'

'Not sure.'

I think I glimpsed his cap when Arran and I came in, though it was on a girl, not Luke's head.

'You know, Tess, I wanted to ask—'

Voices rise with a bumping sound. We both turn to see a guy on the sofa with watermelon punch all over his white shirt, drips on a cushion balanced beside the speakers.

Ivy rolls her eyes. 'Just a sec. Don't go anywhere.'

She heads over, edging through the groups. How many people did Luke invite? Maybe some of them are Ivy's friends. I survey the room, wondering which might be which, when I spot Elliot. He's chatting to someone, smiling, very engaged in the conversation. Much more relaxed than earlier.

The contrast seems strange. He looks the definition of friendly right now, yet he wasn't with me and Ivy. He glances up and sees me looking. His smile slipping before he focuses back on the guy in front of him.

I don't look away. That low hairline. Flat blond hair. Eyes a little too close together.

A shrieky voice draws my ears. I know that laugh. Nalika. I look into the garden and I can see her, standing close to Arran. She's blinking her thick black lashes at him, holding her glass up near her face. Arran is speaking before she leans to whisper something in his ear. He smiles, scratching his thumb in the corner of his mouth, and she laughs again.

In the past I've enjoyed witnessing Nalika's forwardness with men – how receptive they were to her come-on-strong approach and the impression she left.

But right now, she feels like a hook in my chest.

I start walking round the table to join them when Luke pops up in front of me, so close I bump into him.

'Tess! Babe. Now where did you run off to?' He waggles his finger as though I've been naughty. 'I've been looking for you everywhere.'

His shirt buttons are in the wrong holes.

'Where have you been?' I ask back. 'Ivy was looking for you.'

He waves his hand, a flapping motion. 'Never mind her. We've found each other now.'

I straight-face him. I'm not in the mood for his games. I glance towards Nalika and Arran. They're still out in the garden chatting.

'Wanna dance?' Luke says, shimmying closer to my body.

I can smell the beer on his breath but there's nowhere to step back, too many bodies around us. His hand slips round my waist and I push him away.

'Don't be like that, Hartley. I'm an excellent dancer I'll have you know.'

'Is that right?'

'I danced before I walked, according to my mum.'

'Your poor mum.' I try to get past, into more space, but he doesn't move.

He laughs, loud in my ear. Then he notices something and his expression sours. 'Hey, what's he doing here?'

I already know who he means. 'Arran?'

'Yeah, your little bnb boy. I didn't invite him.'

'You said to bring friends.'

'Obviously I didn't mean him.' He shifts his shoulder, huffy. 'You're *friends* now, are you?'

I take a moment to answer. 'Yes.'

Luke looks at me.

'Yes,' I repeat. 'So what?'

He snorts. 'Don't tell me you like him?'

I clench my jaw.

'Tess, he's your lodger. He's *paying* you to use the guest room.'

'So?'

'So of course he's going to be nice and polite and look after you and offer you food.'

I stare at him, irritation darkening with doubt. How does Luke know Arran's been like that? He's not that discerning, he can't be that good at reading people.

'Not necessarily,' I counter. 'I've had plenty of guests who do nothing for me, barely say a word and treat bnbing as the use of a bed and shower.'

Luke swigs from his beer bottle. 'Oh, come on. Don't be so naïve, Tess.'

'What are you on about?'

'I thought you were a clever girl.' He dumps his bottle on the table and holds his hand out towards Arran. 'A guy like that is only after one thing. It's so obvious. He's using you.'

I shake my head, unable to believe what I'm hearing.

'Look, *cariño* – loads of guys check into bnbs with beautiful women as hosts. They find a spare room in a girl's home and hope they get lucky before their checkout date. It's a ploy. They go for vulnerable girls who live alone and worm their way in, then ghost out of there.'

My arms are folded, hands gripping my elbows hard.

No. That's ridiculous. Maybe there are some guys out there like that, but not Arran. I'm glowering, I can feel the heat under my skin. I glance through the garden doors and Nalika's hand is on Arran's arm again.

'Do I have to spell it out?' Luke says, leaning his face into mine, breath rancid. 'He wants to fuck you.'

'You're full of *shit*, Luke,' I flare.

'No, I'm not. A great girl like you? So special, amaz—' He bites his words short, coming back all macho. 'Like I said, he's going to play it sweet and gracious, but it means jackshit, you understand, Tess? Whatever you're feeling, or whatever you think is going on between you – it doesn't mean he cares about you.'

I push past him. 'Leave me alone.'

I shove through a group of people straight out the doors, expecting to find Arran and Nalika. But they're not here. I look around, trying to make out the faces of the people in the garden. Could that be them over there by that tree? I go past the barbecue, the smoke in my face. Not them. It's a man and a woman giggling together, sharing a cigarette.

The garden's small but there are some overgrown bushes on one side, blocking a corner. I go to check behind them. Nothing, just dark grass and earth.

I turn back towards the barbecue, agitation churning. Where on earth did they go?

Someone steps through the smoke, blocking my path.

'Look, Tess, I just want to talk.' Luke's hands are out in front of him.

'I told you to leave me alone,' I say.

'I know.' He's half-silhouetted in front of me, his face in shadow. 'But don't you know how much I like you? Isn't that obvious?'

Yes, I think, tendrils of anxiety in my torso.

He steps forwards and kisses me, his hand gripping the back of my head. For a moment I can't move, the jam of his face against mine a shock. But then I taste the sour alcohol. Feel the squash of his lips.

I twist my head away, pushing on his chest with my elbow. His hand lets go. My foot hits a lump as I step back, managing to keep my balance.

'Can't you give it a chance?' His voice sounds strange. Thick and floury. 'Me a chance?'

'We're neighbours, Luke. Nothing more.'

Behind him, the couple with the cigarette have gone. A few people over by the doors. The tendrils climb higher – he's not budging.

'Come on, Tess.'

'What about Ivy?' I say, pissed off now. She's a flashing factor in this – an obstacle he seems to be disregarding.

'What about her?'

'You're seeing each other.'

'Yeah, *casually*. Friends-with-benefits vibe. Which were her words, by the way – insisting it's just about sex, but then coming over all the time, baking and shit like that.' He sways towards me again. 'She's got nothing on you.'

'Back *off*, Luke.' My voice is rising.

He takes my hand. His other hand sliding round my waist. The touch flaring something in me – though it's not grabby, a strange tenderness to it. Like a puppy again. But I don't want him to touch me. Not *Luke*, begging like this.

My reflex is fast, swinging my arm into his face. He staggers back.

As I'm about to run past him, a hand appears on his shoulder, jerking him round. I see Arran's face above Luke's head. Anger gleaming black in his eyes. He grips Luke by his shirt, pulling him up to his height. 'What do you think you're doing?' he says. 'Didn't you hear her?'

I stare in amazement, another shockwave numbing my body.

'Get off me,' Luke chokes, struggling in Arran's grip.

'Get off me?' Arran repeats. 'Now you know how it feels when someone won't let go.'

Luke scratches at Arran's arms, trying to pull them off. There are people behind, beyond the barbecue, looking over. Gathering in the doorway.

Arran shoves him away. Luke lurches and falls to his knees, thumping into the grass. Arran steps between us. He faces Luke as he clambers up again.

'Don't come near her,' Arran says, a warning in his tone.

Nalika runs over, taking in the scene – Luke's dishevelled hair, a dirt stain on his shirt. Arran's hand curved into a fist.

'Or what?' Luke says, spitting saliva on the ground.

'Arran, don't,' I say, touching his arm. 'He's not worth it.'

'Tess, are you OK?' Nalika asks, worried. 'What did he do?'

Arran's looking at me. His fingers start to uncurl.

'I didn't do anything,' Luke says, tetchy.

'What did you say?' Arran rasps.

'I was just telling Tess how I—'

Arran's fist crunches into Luke's cheek. The force sending him to the ground. Nalika gasps, some of the onlookers echoing the cry. Luke lands on his face, body sprawled.

For a second I can't breathe. The surprise clamping my airways. Arran's chest is heaving, the anger vibrating off him into the night air. The tone in his eyes is something I haven't seen before. He steps round Luke and strides towards the doors. *No. Don't go.*

'Come on, Tess,' Nalika says, arm round my shoulder. 'Let's go.'

Luke has pushed himself onto his hands. His glasses are on the grass next to him. I glance down at him as she guides me away, glimpsing his humiliated form, bitter vulnerability in his glower.

People stare at us, some trying to be discreet or half-pretend they didn't see. Elliot is inside, watching through the window. And Ivy is in the doorway, face white with unreadable emotion. Her eyes on me as I go past.

Shite.

I lost control, for a moment. One moment is all it takes though. And people will never look at you the same, something shifts in their eyes. Wriggling inside the iris, the colour that was there, the light, shrinking back. Grey all the way down to their heart.

It's happened before. Eyes that shone, sun on water – turning on me. Shallow and callous. Shaded with fear.

31

Nalika makes me sit on the sofa. She goes to check the other rooms, then comes back. 'He's not here.'

Where did Arran go?

'Jesus,' she says. 'Drama much. Do you need anything? Tea? A blanket?'

I shake my head, dazed. I can't believe what just happened.

'What the hell was that all about?' She sits next to me. When I don't answer, she asks softly, 'Tess, what did Luke do? Are you all right?'

I try to blink away the daze. 'I'm fine. He kissed me. And he tried to . . .'

'Force himself on you?'

It's a second before I answer. 'Not really. He didn't listen when I told him no. Tried to kiss me again.'

'That sounds like forcing himself. No wonder Arran punched him.'

I'm still trying to process it, how he stepped in, hit Luke. The violence of that act palpable in the sound his knuckles made against bone. The way Luke pitched to the ground.

'Little shit,' Nalika says. 'I would have punched him if he hadn't.'

'You would?'

A fold of my brain wonders whether Luke's behaviour warranted that? Among the indignation pounding through my body, the misgiving is there.

'Yes,' Nalika declares. 'Of course.'

I look at her. Her plait's looser, strands all over her shoulders. A drip mark in the satin of her jumpsuit.

'It was obvious Luke likes you,' she says after a moment. 'I could tell as soon as we arrived. The way he was looking at you.'

I take a deep breath, all the way into my lungs. 'He's a moron.'

'A sad truth,' she sighs. 'The world is full of morons and not-so-harmless morons, it seems.'

My arm is throbbing, I notice.

'Not Arran, though,' Nalika says, a different kind of sigh in her voice. Her hand is on her chest, fingers entwined in the chain of her necklace. The amazonite pendant hung low between her breasts. 'To have a guy like that defend you. Lucky lady, you are.'

'Lucky?'

She looks up at my tone. 'Yeah, I mean, having Arran fight for you – if it were me, I wouldn't mind too much.'

'*Excuse* me?'

She blinks. Surprised by the coolness in my voice.

I turn away from her, the resentment crawling back.

'Tess, I'm sorry,' she says, concerned. 'I'm not making light of what's happened, if that's what you mean. It must have been horrible, Luke pushing himself on you like that.'

I don't answer. Below, the music has been turned down, but there are voices through the floor. The party's still going.

Nalika reaches over, her fingers on my shoulder, but I shrug them off. 'Tess? What's wrong?'

I stay silent.

'What's going on?' she says. 'Please tell me.'

'I'm surprised you even noticed,' I mutter.

'What?'

'I said I'm surprised you even noticed me and Luke.' I turn to her then.

She's confused. 'What do you mean? Of course I noticed. I don't know what—'

'Oh don't play dumb,' I say, the pent-up bile coming out. 'Don't pretend, Nalika.'

'Pretend what?' She sounds baffled.

'You with Arran.'

Her puckered brow loosens as she registers my words. 'What – tonight?'

'*Yes* tonight. Just now at the party. You were all over him.'

Her head shakes, still unsure how to respond to my mini outburst. 'Tess, I was just being friendly. Chatting and trying to make him feel welcome.'

'Come on, you were being more than friendly. Touching his arm and whispering in his ear.'

'OK, maybe I was a bit. But why are you so upset? When I asked you about him before, even tried to encourage you, you said you didn't like him. You insisted it wasn't like that.'

She's right. When she asked me if there was any spark, I said no. But a lot has happened in the last week.

'So you do like him?' Nalika says into my silence.

It doesn't sound like a question.

'You must do, if you're reacting so strongly, blowing up at me like this.'

'*No.* I don't.' I pause. 'I mean, of course I like him. He's . . .' I don't know how to finish that sentence.

'Right, that's all you had to say. One word from you and I would have steered clear. Because you're my *friend*, Tess.' She's annoyed – I catch it in her tone.

I feel a nip of regret.

'And for your information we spent a lot of time talking about you,' she says, brushing something off her jumpsuit.

What?

'He was saying how great you are, how he'd never had such a good experience at a bnb. He hadn't expected to get on so well with a host or feel any kind of real connection.'

My ears are buzzing while she speaks.

'As in a real connection with *you*,' she says. 'He said how lucky he was he'd found you and that you'd accepted his request to stay.'

'Really?'

She lifts her eyebrows at me. 'And then he goes and slugs Luke, protecting you in the most physical way a man can. So you have no need to worry or get all riled up.'

Happiness and relief start to seep in, but then – I do have a reason to worry. Diary girl.

'It's pretty clear he likes you too,' Nalika says.

But in what way?

'If that's not enough for you,' Nalika continues, crossing her legs, 'he has zilch interest in me anyway.'

'How do you know?'

Her eyes veer towards me. Something sheepish in her posture. 'I have to confess – I kissed him.'

'*What?*'

'I'm sorry, Tess, it didn't mean anything.' She's speaking quickly, sincere with remorse. 'It was sort of an accident. Someone bumped into me and I was pretty drunk and I fell against him and I don't know . . .'

I'm barely blinking. *She's* kissed him? Diary girl and now Nalika too?

Nalika searches my face. 'But the important thing is it meant nothing. Arran moved away instantly, I apologised, he then walked off and that must have been when he saw you in the garden with Luke.'

I stand up. 'I can't believe this.'

'Tess, I'm sorry. I already feel bad, and now I know how much you like him—'

'Couldn't you have just left me this one guy? Like you said, it's been ages since I've had a relationship, ages since I've actually liked someone, and you have to leave your mark as always.'

I'm being unreasonable. I'm aware of it even as I shout at her, but I can't stop. A flood tide of anger and anguish around everything, taken out on my friend.

Nalika stands up, her height above mine. 'You're not listening to me, Tess. It was a dumb drunken thing and he didn't let it happen. He pushed me away. He doesn't want me.' She's upset, trying to mollify my outburst. 'And I'm really sorry. I would never do anything to intentionally hurt you. You're like a sister to me.'

A breath sucks into my throat.

She shifts her head, realising her blunder. 'I shouldn't have said that. I'm sorry. What I meant is – you're my best friend.'

'You'll never be my sister.'

'I know. I know I won't.'

I turn away from her, walking towards the fireplace.

'But that's the other thing – I'm so worried about you,' Nalika's voice spurts. 'Doesn't it feel like you're chasing Rosie's ghost around? Living in her flat, doing her old job? Even putting on her make-up?'

I meet her gaze then.

On my way home from stalking Arran, I bought navy eyeliner. I passed a cosmetics store and there it was in the window: a dark blue pencil. Rosie wore brighter blue, but something made me go in and pick it up, a strange whim. I felt like putting it on for the party. It's not like I used her pencil. It's not like I'm living in the flat exactly as she left it, with all her stuff around.

'And your parents,' Nalika goes on. 'You need them, Tess, whatever you may think. They could really help you – help you grieve and get over the loss of Rosie. Help you come to terms with her death.'

'Get over?' I repeat. 'Don't you dare, Nalika.' My words whip out.

Her eyes glisten, hurt. 'I only ever want to help you, Tess.'

'Get out,' I spit.

I'm glowering at her. She doesn't move.

'Tess—'

'I said get out!'

She looks at me for a long moment before she picks up her bag and walks to the door without another word, her plait disappearing last. I wait for the sound of the door snapping shut before I go into my room and sit on the bed.

* * *

My face is in my hands. The strain of the past few hours wrapping itself round me. I let the tears run down my cheeks, then scratch them away. *Stop crying.*

I'm not sure how long I've been here, hunched over my knees, when there's a thud and a scraping somewhere. The music's playing, people still down in Luke's flat. I don't think anything of the sounds – they're faint, dampened by party noise.

But then a *tap-tap* like a knuckle on wood. I look up just as he says, 'Tess?'

Arran in my bedroom doorway. Hesitant, a soft caution in his face and stance. And a bag of frozen peas on his hand.

'Can I come in?' he says.

I nod.

He comes forward and halts in the centre of the room. 'Are you OK?' His voice is low, pushing the words out.

'Yes, I'm fine. Thanks to you.'

'I'm not sure about that. I shouldn't really have ...' He seems subdued, a little self-conscious. 'I've never hit anyone before.'

'I'm glad you did.'

He meets my eye.

'Are you OK?' I ask back, indicating the bag of peas.

He glances down at his hand. 'Oh, yeah, I hope you don't mind. Peas seemed the best option for icing my knuckles.' He lifts his hand higher. 'Turns out punching someone hurts.'

'Funny that.'

He lets out a breathy laugh. 'Now I know how fake all those movies are.'

A thunk from below. Then a shout on the street.

Arran steps forward and crouches in front of me. The peas are right there by my legs, moisture glistening on the plastic bag.

'I'm sorry I wasn't there sooner,' he says.

I touch his hand. Arran is silent as I lift the peas up to look. His skin is all pink, his knuckles red and patchy. A trace of swelling round the bones.

'Looks sore,' I say, in apology.

'It's not too bad.'

Somehow he still smells of coconut. Not a hint of alcohol on his breath.

'And it was worth it,' he murmurs.

I look into his eyes. And, once more, they make me think of a river. Dark, smooth.

His hand lifts towards my face. My heart a sail flapping in the wind as I feel his thumb touch my cheek again. 'You've got a little mascara.' His thumb rubs gently. 'There. Gone.'

His hand drops away and a moment hovers between us. Him crouched there looking up at me. My brain thrumming with one thing: how much I want to kiss him.

I do it. I lean forwards and find his lips.

One second, two seconds. I stop to check his reaction.

He kisses me back.

His hands hold my face and he pulls me towards him. The peas drop to the floor. I hear the bag slap onto the boards but it's a faraway sound. I let the doubt go and forget everything. The party, Luke, Nalika, diary girl. It all drifts back as Arran pushes me onto the bed and I unbutton his shirt and he kisses my neck, his hands finding their way inside my dress.

32

Before I open my eyes, I can feel his body against mine.

Light reaches my retinas and the first thing I see is my hand on his bare chest. I look up into his face. He's already awake. Skimming his fingers on my arm while he waits for me to wake up.

'Good morning,' he murmurs, with a soft smile.

I smile back. '*Buenos días.*'

He kisses me, long and slow like Spanish guitar. Then he says, 'Don't move.' He pulls on boxers before leaning down to the floor. 'These peas have been a bit mistreated. Dropped and left to defrost.'

'Poor peas.'

He goes out.

I listen to his footsteps on the floorboards, moving about in the kitchen. I hear the clink of porcelain and the kettle boiling. A drawer opening then closing. The sun is streaming through a gap in the curtains. A yellow bar of light runs up the wall onto the ceiling.

'Room service,' he says, coming in with a tray. He puts it down on the bed and there's a single bowl full of tiny green balls.

I laugh. 'Peas?'

'Yes, isn't this what you ordered?'

'No.' I take a pea and put it in my mouth. 'But peas have a new charm for me now.'

He grins, eating a handful of peas before going out and coming back with the tray – this time with coffee and two bowls. Inside the bowls there's granola, sliced strawberries, blueberries and a big dollop of yoghurt.

'Real breakfast in bed,' he says.

'Thank you. How should I tip?'

'Hmm. I'll think about it.'

He passes me a bowl and leans against the headboard, pushing his hair back off his forehead. Silence between us. Not uncomfortable – easy, our shoulders touching. I look down at my bowl and notice the rough texture round the base. A Nordic turquoise rim.

'This is yours, isn't it?'

He glances at the bowl, colour in his cheeks. 'Yes. I was wondering if you'd noticed.'

'Of course.'

He's not looking at me, scraping yoghurt off the sides. A slightly strange expression on his face.

'It's beautiful,' I say.

His spoon pauses. 'You think so?'

'Yes. I love it.'

After a moment he smiles, putting his bowl on the bedside table. Then his eyes glide down my body. 'You know, it's dangerous if you don't put any clothes on.'

The duvet has slipped to my waist, my chest bare. 'Oh yes?'

'Yes.'

* * *

'I have to go.'

'What?' I twist to look at him.

Arran sighs, finishing his coffee. 'I'm meeting my mum and sister in Cambridge, for a sort of weekend excursion. Staying the night there tonight.'

My warm settled feeling wavers.

'It was arranged ages ago,' he says. 'And I can't flake on them, much as I'd like to.'

I can't help thinking – is this a lie? And he's actually going to see diary girl? Would he do that after what's happened, after what he's done in the last twelve hours?

'Sorry. It's bad timing.' He pulls me into his chest and I close my eyes. 'But I'll be back tomorrow.'

I listen to him showering, the sprinkle of water on his body. I pull on a T-shirt and finish my granola. It's lost its crunch, soaked into the yoghurt. There's a glumness in my stomach, among the soggy oats and nuts.

Arran comes back into my room, hair damp, backpack on his shoulders. He pulls me up from the bed into his arms. 'My train tomorrow gets in at seven, so I should be back by eight. I want you here, just like this.'

'You mean no make-up, hair a mess, in nothing but a T-shirt?' I say, keeping my voice light-hearted.

'Exactly.' He kisses me. His mouth tastes of mint. 'I'm going to miss my train,' he says. 'See you tomorrow, Spanish girl.'

The door shuts and he's gone.

I peek through the curtains, watching him. Luke's words from last night creep back. *They go for vulnerable girls who live alone and worm their way in, then ghost out of there.*

I go into his room and his stuff's still here. Shoes against the wall. Duffel bag beneath the bed. Stoneware, laptop and pile of books on his desk. Relief filters down my body, followed by a surge of bitterness, black and spiteful. *Fucking Luke.* Arran's not one of those men. I'm not a mark on his score sheet.

But then: diary girl. How do we slot together as two women? Where do I fit next to her in Arran's affection?

My eyes go towards the pile of books. The diary isn't there. I try the bedside drawer. I lift up the mattress and *yes* – here it is again. Flicking through, there's a new entry. I'm not sure when he had a chance to write it since yesterday, but I shelve the thought for now.

You came on another date with me. Dinner.

You suggested a Vietnamese place tucked in an alley. Small, low-lit, authentic. We sat on high stools at the bar and shared dishes, our chopsticks crossing and dipping together.

You traced your finger round my knuckles and asked about my family. A minute later you asked me if I'd ever been bungee jump-ing. You were like that sometimes, flitting from topic to topic, but I didn't care, we had so much to talk about, and I loved you leaning into me. You smelled so good, it made my head swim.

We said goodbye and you reached up to kiss me, slipping your hand round my neck as your lips found my mouth. It was exquisite, that feeling, delicate and delicious.

Afterwards, I wouldn't let go of your hand. You tried to pull it out, finding me charming, smiling up at me. You had to ask for your hand back before I loosened my fingers.

We met again two days later. Pasta making, you purposefully getting flour all over me, rubbing it on my apron and flicking it in my hair, laughing so loud the teacher of the class had to ask for quiet to give the next instruction.

At the end, the leftover ravioli in a little box, you took my hand and led me towards the bus. We sat on it in silence. You walking a fraction ahead of me along the road, a garlicky essence in your clothes, your hair. It was strangely sweet, the scent steadying.

As soon as we were inside you were kissing me. The door barely shut and the box of pasta dropped on the floor. You pulled off my T-shirt, guiding me towards the bedroom, and my hands were in your hair, then beneath your top and inside your jeans and under-wear. All of it a blur.

The best part was afterwards. You with your head on my chest, talking into the night. Your body curled into mine.

My eyes feel dry, his words like reverb in my ears. So much of this is a mirror of what happened last night. At least the last part, after the pasta drops. Like the peas. It's as if he's describing us.

Except it's not us. It's her and him.

Jealousy grows, magnifying in on his writing. There's more – another entry on the next page.

We had to keep it a secret.

That's what you said. After the bliss and sex and laughter and this energy between us. You wouldn't tell me why. You said this was only possible if it was concealed and we were careful about it.

'Please, Arran,' you said, after we'd showered. 'Don't ask me to explain. Don't ruin it.'

I pushed your damp hair off your face and kissed you lightly on the lips. I wasn't sure what to say. We ended up back in bed and I brought you breakfast there. You loved my homemade granola, and that day you asked for it with berries and peanut butter and chocolate chips.

Later, as you were leaving for work, you said, 'Do you want to see me, or not?'

You were half-joking, making light of it, but your expression gave you away. There was something going on behind your eyes, and behind our relationship. I had a few guesses of what. But I didn't push it.

I didn't care. Not really. As long as I could see you. As long as I could somehow have you.

I slam the diary down. I can't believe what I'm reading. Breakfast in bed, Arran bringing her his homemade granola with berries. Just as he did for me a couple of hours ago. The parallel feels sharp, these interchangeable parts like barbs. The lovely thing he did for me diminished.

My teeth are clamped together. I loosen them and look at the entry again. The question *where* floats up. Where these nights together are happening – at her place? Because it can't be here.

My brain shifts to when. Vietnamese dinner and pasta making – when did these happen? Could it have been since he arrived at the flat? Or further into the past? Arran said he was here last summer for a few months doing a design project.

I flick back through the pages and it dawns on me that in none of the entries has he actually mentioned London. I've just assumed he meant here. If it's another city, the diary could be retrospective, reflecting on a previous time in his life.

Yet it doesn't *feel* like that. It feels like London. It all feels present, somehow.

I look at the brown cover of the diary, shadow reaching into its pages. Then I look out at the sky.

This woman is here. I've seen her with my own eyes, talking to Arran. And she wants to keep their relationship a secret – why?

I think of her, outside Niyama. Yesterday, yet it feels like ages ago. So much has happened in twenty-four hours.

There are about thirty-three hours until Arran will be back. Biting my cheek against the spite, I picture her, framed in the glass doors of the studio. Long legs accentuated in black leggings, jade mat casually under her arm. What if she goes to another yoga class today? What if she's there?

I grab my phone and check Niyama's website. Alice is teaching at eleven again, the timetable tells me. If I hurry, I can make it.

Not a good idea, Tess.

But I can't ignore the jealousy. And if I go, I can see whether Arran was telling the truth about Cambridge. I can make sure he's not with her.

It's too tempting. The chance to see her again, up close. Find out her name. Maybe even talk to her.

33

The incense is still in my nose. Woody and spiced. I'm sitting on one of Niyama's black yoga mats, cross-legged, my heart bouncing like a ball. I just signed up for a week's trial at reception. I can't really afford it, even at the discounted rate. But it's necessary. That's what I told myself as I wrote my name down, smoke twirling from an incense stick into my face.

My gamble seems to be falling flat though. Two minutes to eleven and she's not here. No sign of Arran either, which is something.

Alice is arranging rocks around a Tibetan singing bowl. She lights a small orange candle. The class is busy, most of the floor space taken. I'm near the centre. Reasoning I'd be able to see all room angles from here.

Alice starts, getting us to sit and say namaste. We stand to do a sun salutation and disappointment leaks in. The next pose a swan dive. Just as we come back up, arms lifting, the door opens and someone floats in. I look over and my heart starts bouncing again.

It's her.

She mouths 'sorry' at Alice and tiptoes in, finding a gap near the front. Unrolling her mat with a neat movement of her arm, she ties up her hair into a loose ponytail, then joins mid-pose.

My hamstrings are tight and my body doesn't feel very bendy. I've only done yoga once before. I feel awkward, praying I don't look too out of place.

Diary girl is graceful and lithe. I try not to look at her too much through the hour. It's difficult though. She draws the eye just from her beauty, let alone the feelings stewing because of Arran. Not once does she look at me. Unaware of my gaze in the mirror.

At the end, lying flat on my mat, I can't relax. I'm more than playing with fire here. My hands are deep in the flames. The Tibetan bowl rings out, a burning sound in my ears.

We all say namaste to finish, bowing our heads, then I roll up my mat as fast as I can. Diary girl re-rolls hers and thanks Alice before going out into the foyer. I follow the ponytail swaying on her shoulders.

She waits behind a woman talking to the receptionist. Not the nail-filer from yesterday, thank goodness. I glance through the doors to make sure Arran's not out there, then pretend to be doing something on my phone.

Diary girl steps towards reception and says, 'Hi, I wanted to see when Marta is next doing a meditation class?' Her voice has a husky quality.

The receptionist checks her computer. 'Unfortunately, Marta is away at the moment. She'll be back in a couple of weeks. If you like, we can notify you by email when we have a date firmed up for her next session?'

'That would be great.'

'What's your name?'

'Joanna. Joanna Reynolds.'

When I hear it, my fingers go still on my phone screen. Joanna. Of course she'd be called something so classic and sophisticated.

The receptionist clacks her keyboard. 'OK, that's all done for you. You should get an email in the next few days.'

'Fab,' Joanna says. 'Thanks for your help.'

She turns and strides towards the main doors. The receptionist looks at me, wondering if I want something, but before she can speak I've gone, following long legs and a jade mat out into the street.

I check one more time for Arran, but his blond head is nowhere in sight. Maybe he really is in Cambridge with his mum and sister.

Joanna strolls along the pavement. It's windy today. The clouds are skimming the sky, the sun going in and out, intermittently lighting the concrete, and my tense feet. I'm conscious of every step behind her.

Her head is angled downwards. I think she's looking at her phone.

I'm not sure why I'm following. A magnetic pull from her back and iron filings inside my legs. There are fewer people on the pavement today, making it easier to trail her.

She halts. A moment later I do the same, closer than intended. Her phone is ringing. I can hear it over the background traffic. She doesn't answer. When it goes silent, she takes half a step forwards before it rings again. There's a frustrated sound at the back of her throat as the phone lifts to her ear. 'What do you want?' she says.

I turn towards the nearest shop window, pretending to look at the display. Puppets. Hanging from strings amidst delicate white china and dark mahogany.

'You can't keep doing this,' Joanna says. 'You can't just ring me and show up places I'm going to be.' She's quiet, listening. 'I *know*, all right? You don't need to repeat yourself. But this isn't—'

She turns, almost side-on, and I lean closer into the antiques store window. I hate puppets. These are wooden, limbs limp, with mock grins carved into their faces.

'I've told you how I feel,' Joanna says. 'Why are you making this so hard?'

Is that Arran? Calling her from Cambridge? The thought squeezes my throat, double-crossing me with her. Or her with me. I'm not sure which way round it is. Just that there's a cross between us that feels like a cut.

I twist my neck to glance at her. One of her arms is pressed into her side, squashing the yoga mat. A strained expression on her face, creasing her perfect skin.

'Look, it was only because Georgie was there yesterday—' She rubs her cheek. 'I do want to see you, you know that. I just . . . I'm not saying it again, OK? Please stop calling. I'll call you when I'm ready.'

She hangs up and drops the phone into the tote bag on her shoulder. Then she walks on. I wait a second before following.

Joanna is walking faster now, like she's going somewhere. Even from behind she's striking. A small part of me, in some dark ugly corner, wants to run at her. Wants to kick the back of her knee.

A disturbing impulse. Faint, but there.

A minute later Joanna stops again, with her hand on the door of a cafe called Cassia. Is this the cafe she led Arran to for their first date?

She pulls out her ringing phone, her face relaxing when she sees the screen. 'Hi, Lil. How are you doing?'

I use a postbox to half-hide behind, watching her beside Cassia's outdoor tables.

'Yeah, I'm all right. He just called me again.' Silence. 'I know, ruining my lovely yoga serenity.' She scrapes the sole of her trainer on the tarmac. 'Anyway, what are we doing tomorrow? Brunch?'

A man gives me an odd look as he walks by. I ignore him, focused on Joanna.

'OK,' she says. 'Wait, where? Apple & Adelaide?' Pause. 'OK, in Covent Garden, right? What time?' A bus rumbles past, making me strain to hear her voice. 'Can we do eleven-thirty actually?' She smiles. 'Cool, perfect. See you then.'

Joanna starts putting her phone in her bag again, looking at the bus pulling into a stop up the road. She glances at Cassia, checks the simple gold watch on her wrist, then darts round the tables, running for the bus. She steps on after an old woman. The doors slide shut behind her.

I watch it driving away, Joanna inside. I couldn't have followed. A bus is too small, too enclosed. I don't want her to notice me. She might wonder what a girl from her yoga class is doing on the same bus. She might grow suspicious, and that can't happen.

My annoyance is diluted by two things: I know her name, and I know where's she going to be tomorrow at 11:30.

34

I'm halfway along Ravengale Road when I see someone standing outside my flat.

Oliver.

I halt with a thud. He's beside the black railing, near the
front steps, looking up at the windows.

I haven't moved, question marks flaring. What's he doing?
What does he want? He moves forward onto the steps and he's
obscured from view. My heart is pumping when he reappears,
stepping back onto the pavement.

Has he already tried ringing the buzzer? Is he waiting
for me?

He glances up the road, the other way, and I step behind a
tree just as his head turns in my direction. One heartbeat, two
heartbeats, and I check round the trunk.

Oliver crouches down. He stands up again and leans over
the bins, shifting one to see between them. He tips an old
terracotta pot with nothing but soil in it. He's looking for
something. A spare key?

There's unease at the base of my throat. My sister's ex-
boyfriend is outside my home, searching for a way in.

He wipes his hands on his jeans. Then he looks over his
shoulder, checking the street again before taking out his phone.

He holds it up and taps the screen. The phone goes away and he rolls his shoulders before he starts walking – towards me. I duck down and shuffle off the pavement between two cars. To be safe I go further round, squatting in the road.

It's silent. No birds. No other people in the street.

I hear his footsteps coming. Louder, louder, until he's on the other side of the car. I'm beside the wheel and there's a small gap between the parked cars. His legs appear in it, one hand visible as he passes – the one with the Viking tattoo.

His footsteps begin to fade. He didn't see me.

As I'm squatting here, his footfalls almost out of earshot, I feel a surge of grit. What's got into me? Why am I hiding behind a car while he creeps about outside my flat? I'm not scared of him. I should stand up and say, Oi, what the hell are you doing?

But I don't. Something makes me stay very still.

That unfamiliar fear again, as on Hackney Marshes. Holding me back, making me hesitate. Perhaps Pettiford's last phone call, and what's happened with Arran. Or just that instinct to protect myself from harm, which I haven't felt for a long time. Doing the opposite – looking for harm.

A car approaches and I'm still in the road. The woman behind the wheel stares with a quizzical expression.

I hurry back to the flat. Just as I turn in towards the building, the door swings and Luke steps through the gap.

I stop short, the recoil in my body like cramp.

'Tess,' he says, colour dropping from his eyes.

Silently I swear. Could the timing be worse? Moments after Oliver, the last person I want to see. His nose is swollen, purple bruising round the eye socket. A prod of pride that Arran did that.

'I knocked on your door earlier.' His words roll together as a statement.

The sight of him like this, all sore and shrunken, makes me want to hit him again.

'I wanted to say how sorry I am. I was a fucking idiot last night.' There's sincerity in his face and in his voice, hangdog hurt. 'I don't know what I—'

'Yes, Luke, that's exactly what you are. A fucking idiot.'

He blinks at me, a gleam to his eyes. 'I would never hurt you, Tess.'

'Yet you did.'

My hostility snips, and his expression puckers. 'I was just trying to express my feelings for you. I went too far, I was stupid, yes, but—'

I step to go past him. I don't need this right now. I can't listen to it.

'Tess.' His hand moves in front of me, almost touching my arm, but then he pulls it back. 'Please. I made a mistake. But it wasn't . . .' He hesitates, clears his throat. 'Is what I did really that bad?'

There's something whiney in his tone that makes me loathe him.

'Get out of my way, Luke.' I say it slowly, through my teeth.

For a moment he doesn't move. But then he steps to the side, leaving a wide gap, the doorway clear. Without looking at him I go in and run up the stairs. Inside, I double-lock the door.

I look at it for a long time, listening. Then I move towards the window, stretching my neck to see below.

Luke's gone. I wait, watching, but there's nobody down there. No sign of Oliver. It's only when I sit on the sofa with a can of gin and tonic that I notice the skitter of my heart. And how cold I feel. These two men, one after the other.

Luke a nuisance, a bug. Oliver something more ominous. My mind pinning to the fact he was outside my flat while I wasn't home. I know I did the same thing to him, but there's something about him being just there, skulking around the bins. Could he have come here on other occasions? At night, for instance. Looking up at my bedroom window. At Rosie's window.

A memory loosens itself. Last summer, on Oxford Street with Rosie, walking through the crowds of shoppers. I asked her if she'd spoken to him.

'He got back from his course in New York last night,' she said.

'I thought he was due at the weekend?'

'He flew home early.' She sighed. 'Thought he'd surprise me.'

I remember now – his company had made him take some career development course that lasted a month. He'd asked to do it in London but the advertising agency was American, so they said it was New York or find another job. It started a week after I went to Spain to visit our family. Both of us away at the same time, by coincidence. But I'd been back for a few days when he popped up and surprised Rosie. Knowing full well she hated surprises.

'When I didn't scream for joy and leap into his arms, he got all huffy,' she said. 'Tried to make me feel bad by saying how shit the course was and how excited he'd been to see me. He stormed out then came back in the middle of the night, hammering on my door.'

I call Pettiford. It rings and rings. The damn weekend again. I wait two minutes, then try once more. If he's on that child murder case, he could be at the station. Come *on*, please pick up. To my surprise he does, on the fourth try.

'Tess—'

'Oliver was just outside my flat.'

'Sorry?'

'Oliver Barlow, lurking outside my home. And I haven't been in contact with him – no texts or calls at all. I haven't been near him.'

Pettiford is silent.

'Did you hear what I said?'

'Yes,' his voice comes. 'What was he doing outside your flat?'

'How the hell should I know? But I was coming home and there he was, looking at my windows, then rifling around outside, between the bins, as if searching for something.'

More silence.

'So what do you have to say? That's suspicious behaviour right there. I think he was looking for a spare key, looking for a way in.'

'What makes you say that?' His question is so neutral it sounds flat.

'Because of what he was doing, the shifty way he was looking around. And he took a photo of the flat on his phone.'

There are voices in the background. A door shuts. 'Look, Tess, I'm not sure how to ... I want to help you. Dr Vasilakis told me you haven't answered her calls, or returned them.'

What of it? I was too busy following Arran. And I don't need counselling.

'You need to at least try talking to her,' Pettiford says. 'Give her the chance to—'

'What about Oliver?' I snap. 'I'm not making this up. He was just here. And I remember Rosie talking about a time he showed up in the middle of the night banging on her door, angry. Surely that's evidence of his threatening unstable character?'

'I'm not saying I don't believe you, Tess.'

Yet he sounds like he doesn't.

'I'll contact Mr Barlow and question him,' Pettiford says. 'But nonetheless, I want you to talk to Dr Vasilakis. OK? It's important.'

'Fine.' I'm not talking to her.

'Good. Well, take care of yourself in the meantime. I'll phone you once I've spoken to Mr Barlow. All right?'

'Fine.'

I hang up.

There's a horrible feeling in my abdomen. Dark and slippery. Why would Oliver come here? Today or any time?

I think of last summer, going to Spain. Rosie and I went together every year, usually in May, but last year didn't work out. I hadn't been able to take time off work and she had to cancel her flights in July because of an exhibition showing her paintings. So I went alone. We barely spoke while I was away for over a month, and I presumed she was busy with her art.

On the way home from the airport, I called her. She picked up on the first ring, but she sounded different. I couldn't put my finger on how, yet her voice was tighter. Her laugh wasn't as rich or throaty. And she wasn't that interested in hearing about our *abuelo* or this sweet guy José I'd had a fling with. It was the same the next day when we met and I hugged her hello. She didn't embrace me like normal, her arms were looser. And she wouldn't quite meet my eye.

Was that when she changed? I can't remember her acting strangely earlier in the year, except for the occasional mood.

Did something happen while I was in Spain? I don't know why I haven't asked myself this before. Perhaps because her character shift seemed so gradual, so uneven. Some weeks she was Rosie, and others she was someone else. Patchy and unpredictable.

But now I have a feeling, a brick of it laid in my gut. Something happened while I was away.

My skull is throbbing. An ache behind my left eye. I press the heel of my hand into the socket then slowly lower my head onto a cushion. Staring at Rosie's painting on the wall. At all those white shadows.

* * *

It's dark outside when my phone rings. I open my eyes and detect the streetlight through the windows, staining the whites on Rosie's canvas yellow. I peer at the T-Rex clock. I think it says ten-something but my vision is bleary with sleep.

Then I take it in – my phone's ringing. I grab it from the floor. Maybe it's Pettiford. Maybe it's Arran.

I see the screen and my heart stops. *Rosie*, it says. Thoughts have barely flashed through my mind before I answer, swiping too fast, terrified I'm going to miss the call.

'Hello?' I say.

Silence.

'Who is this?'

No sounds. No background noises. The hairs on my neck stand up.

'What are you doing with Rosie's phone?'

Not a breath. Just blood pulsing inside my head.

'It's you, Oliver, isn't it?' My voice is something I don't recognise: malicious. 'I saw you outside the flat earlier.'

Silence.

'Answer me!'

I wait for it. A laugh. A snicker. His cold whispered words.

Nothing.

Yet the quiet in my ear is human. Someone's there at the other end, listening.

'What do you want?' I demand.

The line goes dead.

So. I have a confession.

The Spanish girl isn't the first Spanish girl. There was one before.

35

Apple & Adelaide. I see the sign ahead and feel another wave of nerves. The apprehension has been rolling over me. Since last night, since that call from Rosie's phone, I haven't been able to sit still. I couldn't sleep. I checked all the rooms twice, then the front door, sliding the chain across.

Then, half an hour later, I got up to check the rooms again, flicking on all the lights.

I was sure there was someone in the shadows, that there were footsteps in Arran's room. That I would feel fingers on my arm or a hand clamp over my face. Every sound made me sit up, straining to listen.

He doesn't have a key. He can't get in. I repeated this to myself. But it didn't help. I had to get up again, convinced he was here. Convinced that I would see Oliver in a dark corner, grinning at me. That I would open my eyes and Luke would be standing over my bed. Both of them swirling round my head, merging into one.

I tried calling Rosie's phone. No answer.

I haven't told Pettiford about the call yet. After talking to him yesterday, the uncertainty in his tone about Oliver being outside my flat, this would be next-level. Although I should tell him. What if Rosie's phone calls again and the police can trace it?

Early in the morning I thought about phoning Arran. I wanted to hear his voice. I'd already gone into my contacts list when it dawned on me – I don't have his number. I hadn't noticed before; I hadn't thought to text or call him. With bnb guests I use the website's messaging facility to arrange everything. We'd never exchanged any other contact details. There was no need to.

I stared at my phone, the name Arran missing from the list.

It was just after seven, still four and a half hours until Joanna would be at her brunch date. I didn't want to wait that long. I didn't want to be alone. And I wanted to see her again – my haunting competition. A wise inner voice told me I shouldn't go. Like I was going to listen to that. I'd already looked up Apple & Adelaide on the map.

I put the TV on for company, watching Sunday-morning shows, then took a long shower. I spent a while selecting what to wear. Kick-flare jeans with a casual broderie top, sleeveless and white to show off my skin. Gold jewellery.

Ten o'clock and I was ready. I could head for Covent Garden, maybe kill time at the market.

Just as I was unlocking the door, I heard voices in the stairwell. I relocked it then went to the living room window. Ivy's ginger hair appeared, crossing the road towards her flat. She had spent the night with Luke, it seemed, making me wonder what's going on with them. Any repercussions from the party? How does she feel about what he did?

I waited five minutes, then ventured out.

At Covent Garden I wandered the market, listening to the violinist in the cellar courtyard. Stringy notes echoing into the vaulted ceiling. I walked slowly to Seven Dials and stood by the sundial column. A coolness to the air, the weather turning. Apple & Adelaide round the corner, on a cobbled side street.

11:15 and I approach the entrance, jittery, with a sense of foreboding. But I go in. The waitress asks me if I have a reservation, which I obviously don't. She checks her tablet, saying I'm lucky, they have one spare table. All but three are occupied and she leads me to a small square one beside a wall.

It's a relaxed bright-coloured cafe. Tiled walls, painted coral floor, palm plants and wicker chairs. The menu tells me it's an Aussie-style farm-to-table eatery, with the best pancakes and poached eggs I'll ever taste. Despite this cheery atmosphere, it feels like I'm seasick.

11:26. I'm watching the door. A couple comes in. The waitress takes them to a table in the corner. Leaving only one empty – beside mine.

11:29. A woman's hand pushes the door and Joanna steps through.

I look away, pretending to study the menu. Seconds later the waitress leads her over. Their footsteps soft on the coral boards, coming right up to me. I'm rigid as Joanna says, 'Thank you.'

In my peripheral vision she takes off her coat, then slides onto the padded booth-style bench running down the wall. I can't believe it. She's close enough to touch. So close, I can smell her perfume: light and floral. I feel a little faint. At the luck and the chance of this.

She puts her coat on the seat next to my jacket, then sweeps her hair back off her shoulders. I'm staring at the menu. The waitress comes over and asks me what I want, and I order avocado toast and a black coffee. My stomach can't handle anything else.

Joanna seems relaxed, leaning back against the booth, legs crossed. Her foot pointing towards me. She's in jeans as well, though they're darker blue than mine. All of this in the corner of my eye, watching her obliquely.

She glances at the door. Whoever she's meeting is late. My eyeballs begin to ache, straining to see her without turning my head. My coffee arrives, then my food. The waitress asks Joanna if she wants to order anything yet. 'Just some water for now please? I'm waiting for my sister.'

My fork gets stuck in my mouth. Of course she'd have a sister. I force myself to chew and swallow.

After midday Joanna's foot starts to jiggle, her posture tensing with impatience. She pulls things out of her handbag, looking for something. Her keys appear. Two items on the keyring – one that looks like a piece of seaglass. The other a pink and green crescent moon. Jewelled, plastic-looking.

She gets up and goes to the bar. Over the beachy acoustic music and the blender, I can't hear what she's saying.

I peek at her handbag, still on the table. Sticking out is a feather. White, once. Now stained and squashed. As though it's been in her bag a long time.

A swan feather? I resist the urge to take it. Or touch it.

The barman is pouring green smoothie into a glass and handing it to Joanna. On a whim, I pretend to knock my fork off the table, not sure what the hell I'm doing as I step over and crouch to pick it up. Joanna's coming back to her table, walking round another customer, not seeing me on the floor, meaning that when I abruptly stand she bumps into me, my shoulder colliding with her arm. The one holding her smoothie.

I feel it before anything else. Thick cold liquid on my chest. And her voice making a surprised 'owh' sound. Then, 'Oh my God, I'm so sorry!'

Pine green smoothie is all over my white top. It drips from my arm onto my jeans.

'Shit, your blouse. I've ruined it. I'm so sorry, I didn't see you.' The remorse makes her husky voice higher.

'Don't worry,' I say.

She grabs her napkin, trying to catch the drips and wipe them from my shirt. 'I'm sorry. What a moron.'

For some reason humour bubbles and I laugh. This whole situation is ridiculous. Joanna – *diary girl* – wiping smoothie off my clothes. Engineered by me, albeit crudely.

She looks up at my laugh, relief softening her face.

'It's not your fault,' I say. 'Really. I wasn't looking as I stood up.'

Her hands are still dabbing. 'But your top. You'll never get the stain out.'

'Doesn't matter. It wasn't that nice anyway. You can stop.'

Her hands go still. 'Oh. Sorry.' She lifts the napkin away and gives a half-laugh. 'I'm a total stranger – patting your chest.'

The waitress comes over to clean up the floor, bringing more napkins.

'Don't worry about it,' I say, smiling at Joanna.

She smiles back. We both sit down again, side-by-side on the booth bench. Joanna lifts her bag off the table, out of view. Her smoothie glass is half full now. Or half empty.

'Suddenly I don't feel like superfood mush,' Joanna jokes, pushing her glass to the far side of the table. She's still embarrassed, even though it wasn't her fault. It was all mine.

'Perhaps I'll pour smoothie over the rest of my top,' I say. 'Dye it and create a new craze.'

She smiles, a note of sadness in her eyes. Strange. As if some underlying emotion is being brought out by our accident. She checks her phone before putting it screen-down on the table. She sips her water. Up close, her beauty is even more distinct. Natural, smooth, like driftwood. Her ears sticking out a little.

She looks at me and blinks, her brow drawing down. I pick up my coffee so I don't keep staring at her.

'I hope this doesn't sound too weird,' Joanna says. 'But have we met?'

My cup freezes in mid-air. I put the stoneware cup on its saucer and meet her eye. 'No. I don't think so.' My tone innocent.

Her brow is still drawn. 'It's just you look familiar. Like I've seen you somewhere before.'

A tremor of alarm. I thought she hadn't noticed me yesterday. Maybe she did glimpse me in the mirror, or by reception. 'It's possible, I guess. London's a smaller world than you think.'

She shrugs, her forehead loosening.

Silence. I don't want our conversation to dry up. I want to keep talking to her. So, without thinking I say, 'Do you do yoga by any chance?'

She looks at me again, realisation lighting her features. 'Ah, that's it! Do you take classes at Niyama?'

'In Camden?'

'Yes.'

Why did I say that? Tying a knot in my link to the yoga studio Arran visits.

'You must have been to Alice's classes?' Joanna says.

I nod weakly.

'The best yoga teacher.'

'I agree. She's fantastic.'

Joanna is smiling in amazement. 'How funny. And here we are sitting next to each other.'

Yes. Very funny.

'London *is* a small world,' she says.

Small when one of us is stalking the other. *Oh God*, what am I doing?

Her phone vibrates. She looks at the screen then puts it down again, checking Apple & Adelaide's door. 'I'm supposed to be meeting my sister for brunch but she's forty-five minutes late.' She shakes her head. Not annoyed – more of a breezy sibling sarcasm. 'I think she had a big night out last night and her phone must be dead, or she left it somewhere.'

The irony feels like a dagger. Her sister's phone. I grip the edge of the booth seat, attempting to smile. 'And on top of that I went and spoiled your smoothie.'

'Are you kidding? I spoiled your top!' She's almost laughing.

I feel a pang in my side. She's so *nice*. Charming, in fact. That should make me dislike her more, but it has the opposite effect. Against my own will I feel the affinity creeping in. No wonder Arran is so obsessed with her.

Joanna's phone buzzes again and this time she stares at the screen. Her fingers are pale, I notice. She sighs. A slow shaky sound through her lips.

'Are you all right?' I ask.

She glances at me. 'Yes, I'm fine.'

'Are you sure?'

She pushes her hair behind her ear and scratches her forehead, leaving pink nail marks in the skin. 'It's my ex-boyfriend. He's ... well, I've broken up with him, so he *is* my ex. But he's refusing to accept it. He says we belong together and ...'

Arran?

'He's making things so difficult,' Joanna says. 'I love him. He's an amazing person, but I just . . . I don't know, nothing's simple. All these other factors at play. His mum has multiple sclerosis and he got made redundant and he's been depressed, and it all just adds up to . . .' She puts her elbow on the table with a thump.

Maybe she doesn't mean Arran. He hasn't mentioned his mum having MS or being made redundant. He definitely doesn't seem depressed. Though people can hide that.

'I told him I needed time to think about it.' She's staring at the table, as if talking to herself. 'I suggested we have a break from each other so he can get used to the idea. But he won't stop texting or calling, even when I ask for space.'

Joanna's chewing her thumb. She blinks and looks at me, refocusing. 'Sorry, listen to me. I don't even know you and I'm jabbering about my problems.'

'No, it's OK. It sounds like a tricky situation.' There's concern in my voice, leaving some open space to continue. I want to hear about this. Curiosity and envy.

She presses her finger into the prongs of her fork, making it lift off the table. 'It's just . . . he's not who I thought he was. He seemed so charming at the start, but things changed. *He* changed. We had a few . . . problems. And now he's doing things like waiting for me outside my flat. Even following me.'

'Really?' The cords of all this are so matted, I can't separate them, but what's underneath is unnerving.

She nods, letting the fork ting back onto the table. 'A couple of times.'

I'm still not sure if she's talking about Arran. But it sounds like it could be him. That entry where he followed her home.

Her phone rings, an acoustic version of some nineties pop song I can't quite place. 'My sister,' she says, answering. 'Hi, Lily. Where—' She's cut off, listening. 'Wait, *what*? What do you mean it's brok—' She stops again. 'So you just came back and it was ajar? That doesn't make—'

Whatever's happened, it doesn't sound good.

'No, it's OK,' Joanna says. 'It's just so *weird*. That's never . . .' She's biting her thumb again. 'Yep, I'll come now. No, really, don't worry, I'm coming. See you soon.'

She hangs up and starts grabbing her coat.

'Is everything OK?' I ask.

She pauses as she's moving round the table, then she spreads her expression with cheery composure. 'Yes, fine, just a silly thing with my sister.' I can see the anxiousness in her face, like she's tried to spread butter over burnt toast. 'I have to go. Sorry again about your top, er . . .' She hesitates. 'I don't even know your name.'

'Tess.'

'Tess,' she repeats. 'I'm Joanna. Maybe see you at Niyama sometime.'

'Yes. Maybe.'

Already turning away, over her shoulder, 'Bye.'

Her figure is across the room and through the door in one smooth movement. I stare at it drifting shut. One thing gleaming out at me from all the thoughts and feelings of this encounter.

Why didn't I lie? Why did I tell her my real name?

36

I'm staring at a huge bunch of flowers on the kitchen table.

Roses.

The door buzzer went off ten minutes ago. I went to the window to check, thinking it might be Oliver. But then I saw the delivery van in the road and I buzzed the guy in. It was only as he was coming up the stairs that I saw the flowers.

'Tess Hartley?' he said.

'Yes.'

'These are for you.' He held the roses out towards me, their cloying scent in my nose. Nothing to do except take them. 'Have a good day,' he said, darting back down the stairs two at a time.

Why did it have to be roses? Not lilies or tulips or orchids. I dumped them on the table and stepped back.

There's no note. I check again between all the petals and leaves. No card of any kind.

Who sent them?

That question has been throbbing. My first thought Luke. It's just the kind of garish thing he would do. Only why wouldn't he acknowledge it, sign his name, if they're supposed to be some kind of apology?

Then I consider Oliver. The possibility makes me feel sick.

Third option would be Arran. Unlikely. It doesn't seem like something he'd give me, especially a peachy orange over-the-top bouquet. But how can I be sure?

As soon as I got home from the cafe, I had another look at his diary. That most recent entry where he wrote: *There was something going on behind your eyes, and behind our relationship.* I went back over what Joanna had said – in Apple & Adelaide, and what I overheard on the phone yesterday. I think it must be Arran she was talking about. Her ex-boyfriend.

I look at the flowers again.

The uncertainty is like mist. Each time it starts to clear, some new conviction like sunlight burning it off, another feeling drifts in, adding to the vapour.

The flowers are making me uncomfortable. I look up the meaning of orange roses. Apparently they symbolise desire. I want to chuck them out – burn them even. But I don't touch them.

* * *

It's after eight and Arran's not back yet. What if he has ghosted me? I go to the window and look out. The old man in 74a is sitting in his armchair reading a newspaper, that doll still there on the sill. Above, I notice Ivy. She's side-on in the window, holding something. I can't see what.

Her head turns and I'm not fast enough. She sees me. Face haloed by her hair, eyes in my direction. I step away from the glass, out of view.

The roses glower at me.

20:36 and there are footsteps on the stairwell. Light and smooth. My heart starts knocking against my ribcage. A held breath, thinking I might see Oliver's dark auburn hair. But the front door swings and Arran steps through.

I feel a rush of relief.

'Hey,' he says, with a smile.

He drops his backpack in the hall and shrugs off his cord jacket, then comes into the living area. Halting a metre away from me, seconds pulsing between us.

He steps forward and kisses me. His arms wrapping round my body as I kiss him back. He pushes me up against the doorframe, then into the hallway, guiding me into the guest room.

* * *

'I missed you.'

We're lying on his bed, bodies curved into each other. I feel the vibration of his voice box against my temple.

'I know it was only a day,' he murmurs. 'And it might sound like too much. But it's the truth.'

I lift my head to search his face. It's dark but I can see his eyes. Their sheen seems genuine. My response mirrors his, 'I missed you.'

He smiles. His fingers brushing up and down my back.

'How was Cambridge?' I ask.

'Oh, you know, good. Mostly. It's a beautiful city.'

'Mostly?'

He doesn't respond, his fingertips gliding on my skin.

'It was nice to see your mum and sister?' I want to coax something out of him. Any clues that might lighten the mist.

'Yes.'

That's not really an answer. 'What did you—?'

'You know, Tess, I just want to focus on now, on what I have right here.' His tone is warm. He kisses me again and I don't try to stop him.

* * *

In the morning, I wake up first. Arran's hand is on my arm. He's lying on his back and his breathing is quiet. There's a scar on his chest, I notice. A straight white mark about an inch long. I want to touch it but I don't want to wake him up. Pushing aside all reservations, I enjoy this moment, this man sleeping beside me while the sun comes up.

When he opens his eyes, he says he has to go to work. I protest but he asks, 'Don't you have work today too?'

'Yes,' I grudgingly answer. The Barbican. I can't miss another day. I received an email from my manager yesterday – a polite reminder that I'm expected at nine.

'Come on then, skipper.'

Twenty minutes later, when he comes into the living area, he looks at the roses on the table. Two seconds staring at them before he speaks.

'Those are pretty intense.'

I'm chewing a mouthful of sourdough, sweet with apricot jam. 'The flowers?'

'Yeah, who are they from?'

I watch him. His expression gives nothing away. He could be playing with me, gauging my reaction. 'I don't know. There's no note.'

His face is impassive as he goes over. Then I can't see it, his back to me. Roses visible either side of his elbows the bunch is so dense.

'A mysterious admirer?' he says, leaning down to smell them. 'Wow, that's overpowering.'

'I think I'm going to get rid of them,' I say, a little too loudly. 'Maybe give them to the woman upstairs.'

He presses his lips together, as if to say *fair enough*. Then he breezes towards me, slipping his hands round my waist and taking a bite of my toast. 'Hm-hm, who made this bread? It's so *good*.'

I smile. How does he do that? Make the stinging in my chest almost completely disappear.

He's grinning at me, chewing. Then he looks down and seems to notice something. The grin drops away. His hands slip off my waist as he steps back.

'What?' I say.

His forehead isn't quite smooth. 'You work at the Barbican?'

I glance down. I've got my work shirt on, *barbican* written inside the orange half-circle logo. 'Yeah, part-time.'

I can't read his eyes. Something floating beneath the river blue, only I can't tell what.

'I didn't know that,' he says, picking up the bread knife.

'Something wrong with the Barbican?' I ask, eyebrow raised.

The teeth of the knife crunch down through the loaf. 'No. It's a wicked place, especially for the arts.' He snaps down the toaster. 'Now chop-chop, missy, or we're going to be late.'

'What's so urgent?'

'I've got quite an important meeting today, as it happens.'

'Oh yes?'

'Yes, this afternoon, at two o'clock. And I need to prepare for it. You want me to impress, no?'

'You impress whatever you do.'

He grins again, blobbing jam on his slice. 'We'll see. The pressure's on. It's in another hipster zone of London.'

'Oh yes? Camden? Whitechapel?'

'Soho.'

I half-laugh. 'Not so hipster, you rookie.'

'What?' He speaks through the bread, chewing. 'What do you mean? Soho and Leicester Square are up there on the cool scale.'

'I think you mean tourist overrun.'

He swallows. 'Oh. Well, good thing I've got you around.'

I finish my toast, thinking, *Yes, it is*.

We walk to the station and he kisses me goodbye. 'I'll see you this evening. I can make dinner?'

I nod. Then I watch him disappear round the corner. I could have walked straight to the Barbican but I wanted to put off parting. I force myself to get on the tube, even though some of the muscle cells in my legs are itching to follow him.

I'm late to work, but no one seems to notice. I sit in my cubbyhole. It's too cold in here, the air conditioning still on strong blast even though the Mediterranean heat has gone.

The same photography exhibition is on: Women's Edges. On one wall, there's an image of a shoulder blade, light and shadow accentuating the contours of bone. To the left, part of a smooth freckled arm. In the far corner, hair curved round a breast.

My phone buzzes. I slip it halfway from my pocket, subtly reading the screen.

From Ivy: *Hiya Tess. It would be great to chat. We could go for a coffee? Or wine? There's a cute bar in Stoke Newington. Let me know. Hope what happened at the party wasn't too upsetting xxx*

I don't want to be dragged back to that again. It's inconsequential compared to everything else happening in my life. I blank the screen, shutting Ivy and Luke out.

There are goosebumps on my skin.

Thoughts slink in. Joanna. The diary. Her ex-boyfriend. Rushing out of Apple & Adelaide.

And just now – Arran mentioning a meeting. He didn't say what kind. I assumed he meant for work, graphic design or ceramics-related. But what if it was a different kind of meeting? What if he's meeting *her*?

37

I'm outside Leicester Square station.

Obsession, a little voice whispers.

I'm chewing my nails. I push my hands into my pockets and glance from entrance to exit to entrance. There are four of them.

I walked out of the Barbican without telling anyone. I pretended to need the toilet, then snuck through a back door. It's absurd, I could lose my job doing this. But once the thought was planted, its roots wouldn't come out. I need to know.

It's 13:23. I'm hungry and thirsty, but I'm not leaving this spot on the corner of the crossroads, between a tree and a bin. From here I have a view of all four station exits.

Arran said Leicester Square earlier, so I'm guessing this is where he'll travel to. I could be wrong though. I could have missed him already. It's insanely busy, and four exits are tricky to monitor.

My eyes keep hopping from blond head to blond head.

13:37.

Is that him? No, older and shorter.

13:41.

Very similar, but no.

13:46.

There. Arran. Coming out of the exit by the Hippodrome Casino. I almost can't believe it, the chances of spotting him are so slim. But it's him. Slipping wayfarer sunglasses onto his nose. He goes round the corner towards the square.

I hurry over the road among the hordes of people, weaving between them until I'm a safe-ish distance behind, close enough to shadow someone effectively.

That's what I feel like. Arran's shadow.

He strides through Leicester Square then turns right, passing Chinese restaurants. Strings of lanterns cross overhead. Chinese-style bunting, deep red. Arran halts, looking at his phone. I use a bunch of Mexican tourists for cover. But he turns right again, walking beneath the vibrant Chinatown Gate. He's almost going back on himself. As though looking for somewhere, unsure of the right way.

I half-trip on a loose cobble. His back momentarily vanishes before I follow it into Soho. My heartbeat is erratic, one thing driving me forward: *Don't lose him.*

Arran goes into a restaurant. It's painted black, decor dark. Low-lit inside. I can't follow. As desperate as I am to go in there after him, it's impossible. I stay on the street, using the stoop of someone's house for semi-cover. Arran is near the bar. I can just see him in front of glowing bottles. He's speaking to a waiter who leads him to a table. Arran sits down, out of sight except for one shoulder and the side of his head.

The outdoor tables have marble tops. Black sunshades. A smart restaurant called Foxcoal.

I keep checking each way down the street. Her glossy dark hair behind a tall man – but as she steps past him, not Joanna. Three minutes later, a woman in the other direction, side-on, half-concealed by a black van. Beautiful, but as her face turns – no. My tense shoulders drop a little. Maybe I'm wrong, maybe he's not meeting Joanna.

But then, within seconds, I see her.

A violin starts ringing in my ear. Watching her walk towards the restaurant, blue culottes swishing over her legs. I dart round the corner of a side street opposite Foxcoal to make sure she doesn't see me. Joanna goes inside. Her shaded figure approaches Arran's table, then disappears.

The pain is claw-like. Even though I knew already. Even though I've been reading about them, about *her*, in the diary. It doesn't make it any easier, witnessing them together.

Half an hour and I'm still in this alley, wide enough for one car. A van is parked at the end, giving me a little more concealment. I squint in through Foxcoal's windows, but the lighting is too dim. I can see Arran's darkened shoulder and head, and nothing else.

It's approaching an hour when Joanna steps out through the door. I hadn't noticed her leaving their table, the sha-dowed movements of people inside difficult to track. She's putting something away in her shoulder bag. I can't see what from this angle.

She walks off. I watch her in her heeled boots, gait gliding, like an African cat.

Then Arran reappears. He runs his fingers through his hair while the restaurant door drifts shut behind him. His expres-sion seems neutral. He looks up the street towards Joanna's back before turning and going the same way.

Is he following her? The question glows red as I tail him once more.

Glimpses of her blue culottes and silky brown hair up ahead, beyond Arran. She reaches the end of the street and turns left. Arran turns left too. I run round the corner onto a main road. It's busier, louder, but I don't feel flustered. Just hurt and resolute.

Joanna strides along the pavement and doesn't look back. Neither of them do.

The black and white framing of Liberty's department store comes into view – the old Tudor building with dark striped beams. Joanna crosses the road and goes into a stone building diagonally opposite. Flags hang from its walls, sticking out between the first-floor windows.

Arran crosses the road as well, dodging through traffic. I lose sight of him behind a big white van. I swerve my head to see. He's halted outside the building with flags. A lorry drives along the road and stops at traffic lights, Arran obscured behind it. With a spurt of desperation, I run to the front of the lorry where there's a small gap. Is that Arran's hair and backpack beside the building's entrance?

The lorry edges forward, blocking my view again. Its engine is a chugging growl.

I feel like swearing at the driver but instead I step between the lorry and a car. When I reach the middle of the road, a yellow van going the other way almost runs over my foot. I jump back. The van passes and I can see the entrance, a man with blond hair disappearing into it. Arran? I'm not sure, a bus goes past, and it was only a glimpse.

The lorry honks at me. A deafening horn in my ear that scares me senseless. I move further into the road, using a gap in the traffic to make it to the other side.

Arran's gone. No sign of him anywhere on the pavement. I look up at the gold sign above the door. It's a hotel.

My throat feels tight.

He walked on down the street – that's what he did. He's not going up to the hotel room where she's waiting for him, already undressing. That's not what's happening. I refuse to picture it.

While I try to steady my mind, think what to do, I move away from the main entrance towards a door that leads into the hotel's brasserie restaurant. I position myself between there and the takeaway place next door. It feels like Arran and Joanna are wringing my chest, their hands squeezing from both ends.

I rub my sleeve over my eyes. The breeze is getting stronger – I feel it on my neck. Cool fingers of it slipping down my back. I could look in through the hotel restaurant door, but as I step towards it, I see Joanna.

She's just come out of the main hotel entrance. After twenty-five minutes? That's not very long. And Arran's not with her.

She lifts her bag onto her shoulder and checks both ways before crossing the road. Still no sign of Arran. Joanna is on the far side now, walking towards Carnaby Street. I don't know what to do. Wait here or follow? I look at the entrance again, afraid I'm going to see him.

Joanna's almost gone.

Fuck it. I go after her.

A car hoots its horn as I dash across. I can just make out Joanna's head. Carnaby Street is congested with people. A man selling magazines shouts and waves one in my face, but I dodge round him. Then I realise that Joanna has stopped to look in a Liberty's window. She walks round the department store, looking in another window.

Back along the main road, wondering what she's doing, I get stuck behind a group of women in dresses and hats, as if they've come from a wedding. When I finally skirt round them Joanna's gone.

Just ahead is the Liberty's main entrance with flowers outside. A florist in the foyer spills into the street. Bunches in baskets and metal pots, arranged on chairs and ladder stands.

Did Joanna go in? I don't know where else she might have disappeared, but the street is so busy, it's possible she's further up. I curse all these people. Central London is so clogged everywhere.

Wary, I peer into Liberty's. When I look down at my feet, I see a stone lion. Beside it are red roses. I veer away and take a few more steps along the pavement, searching for blue culottes. I can't see her. The chase is over.

'Tess?'

The voice behind makes me freeze. It's surprised and throaty. I turn to see Joanna standing beside the flowers.

'What are you doing here?' Amazement overlays her face.

I look at her, my mouth open. *Think*, quick. 'Joanna, oh my goodness, hi!' I try to sound genuinely shocked. 'Sorry – I just can't believe this. The coincidence.'

Her head is shaking. 'I know. After Apple & Adelaide and now here, two days in a row.'

'Yeah. Bizarre.'

'Too weird really. The universe is so wacky sometimes.'

It's not the universe, Joanna. It's me.

'Especially outside Liberty's,' she says, glancing up at the Tudor walls and hanging coat of arms. 'It's my favourite department store in London.'

'It is lovely.' I clear my throat and lie. 'I work near here and I was just doing some shopping for my mum's birthday.' Luckily I had the foresight to change out of my uniform shirt before I left the Barbican. 'I was thinking about getting her flowers,' I round off.

'Oh, great. They do wonderful roses here.'

'Not roses.' I say it too fast.

She blinks at me.

'My mum likes tulips.'

'Right.' She smiles but there's no warmth to it. Slipping off her cheeks, it's clear something's wrong.

'Is everything OK, Joanna?'

Her eyes flick towards me. 'Yes I'm . . .' Burnt black toast again – I can see it. 'I'm fine. It's just . . .' She shakes her head. 'Never mind.'

'It's clear you're not fine. I know we hardly know each other, but . . .'

She shifts the bag on her shoulder.

'Is it your ex-boyfriend?' I ask.

'It's nothing. Don't worry. I've just had a strange day, that's all.' She's sweeping it under the rug. But I want the dust and dirt.

'Strange how?'

She tucks her hair behind a sticky-out ear. 'It's this guy—' She looks at something over my shoulder. Her eyes narrowing as she focuses on whatever it is behind me.

'What is it?' I ask, glancing round.

There are lots of people on the pavement, walking in both directions.

'I need to go,' Joanna says, words short. 'Sorry, see you.'

Before I can say anything she turns and walks back towards Carnaby Street, strides fast. I look behind again, scanning the faces. The men. As if expecting to see him standing beside Liberty's staring at me.

But Arran's not there.

I don't recognise anyone. Only strangers. And when I turn back to look for Joanna, she's gone.

I can picture her there, in Andalucía. I've never been to Spain, but I can feel it, taste it. Bread dripping with dark peppery olive oil, all over her fingers. Mountains alive with sunlight. Plucking figs from trees as she walks past, the sweet purple flesh filling her mouth. Wandering the Mezquita or the courtyards of the Alhambra. Dipping her hand into fountains.

I imagine us together too. She introduces me to her family. We make paella and white almond gazpacho. We share toothpaste. I run my fingers through her hair. We lie on the beach, towels touching, her hand reaching for mine.

I might have to do something. Soon. I can feel it in me, the clunk of disappointment. I'm beginning to wonder if she needs glasses. I was right there, behind her, looking at the back of her head, resentment in my teeth.

I've been patient. Now, my reward.

38

I open the diary and something falls out. It sails to the floor, followed by something smaller, fluttering. When I look down there's a piece of paper and a leaf. The paper has floated onto the rug and the leaf is on my foot. I bend to retrieve them.

A maple leaf, small, green. Still waxy and soft – it hasn't dried up yet. The paper is folded in half. When I open it, there's writing. An entry he must have written while he was away, then tucked into the book.

I'm relieved to have a new entry. I was expecting to read old ones, to try to decipher what's going on between Joanna and Arran. I need to know more. I need to understand and grasp answers, understand how I fit into all this.

Us together. Meeting in secret. Dates and park lounging and kissing and the occasional hotel room and sneaking into your flat when it was allowed.

It seemed fun at first. The risk, the stolen moments.

But then I got sick of it. I wanted the whole you. Walking down the street hand-in-hand, clear to the world. Together. I told you I didn't want to sneak around anymore. I told you I wanted to meet your friends and family.

I told you I loved you.

You said you loved me too but it wasn't that simple. You got pissed off. You ran out on me, telling me to stop pushing.

You weren't being fair. You were using me. I didn't deserve to be the guy you cheated with, behind everyone's back. In the shadows. I hated it, hated how you kept me there.

I challenged you, holding your face so you couldn't look away. I said I knew you had a boyfriend. You were shocked. You shook your head and said you didn't know what to do, you were confused.

I said you had to break up with him and be with me. I knew you didn't love him. How could you?

Joanna's ex-boyfriend is another guy. And Arran is her secret lover. They meet in hotel rooms – like the one today opposite Liberty's?

I feel their hands wringing me again.

Arran was following her for a reason. They'd arranged to meet at the hotel after Foxcoal. In which case she was aware of him, they were just walking there separately.

The threat for Joanna comes from another man.

But my mind jumps back to that entry where Arran wrote about following her home. Watching her door shut behind her.

How does that fit into this narrative, if Joanna's ex is the one stalking her? I go over to the bin. The ripped-out entry isn't there. The basket is bare again, no rubbish at all. He must have emptied it.

A dark corner of doubt – could that entry have been in my head?

No, here, the torn edge of a page is in the book. I run my thumb down the texture.

I look at this new entry. The language is possessive again. How much he wants her, a real relationship. She has to break up with her boyfriend. Be with him. It's not over with them, clearly. Yet Arran's been sleeping with me. Is he just using me while he can't have Joanna? Am I a convenient stopgap or distraction?

I slide the paper and the leaf back inside the diary. The roses are still on the kitchen table. I can smell them from here, filling the flat with their scent. I grab the bouquet. In the bathroom, I yank open the window and hurl the flowers out. I hear the rustled splat of them hitting the ground.

The bunch now on the grass of Luke's garden, splayed like orange paint.

*   *   *

I'm worried. Fear finding its way into my chest. It's nine-thirty and Arran isn't here. He said he would cook dinner. I can't call him – I still don't have his number.

It's not hard to guess what he's doing. With the diary and what I saw today.

Joanna.

The sting of that is fermenting with what if Arran saw me earlier. Alarm in my legs while I walked round the flat. They feel numb now, folded where I'm sitting on the floor. I stare at the empty hearth, bricks charred from long dead fire.

I get up to use the bathroom. The cupboard in here has a glass front – his washbag is visible inside. I open the door and there's a smell. Not bad, but something sour. When I lift the washbag the source is revealed. An apple core, shrunk and brown. Left on the shelf behind his things.

I wonder at people's rationale, their quirks.

Looking through his washbag, I nudge things around. A shaving brush. Natural deodorant, cedarwood and lime on the label, though it smells old – out of date. Silver gleams at the bottom of the bag. I move the toothpaste out of the way to see.

Sewing needles. A few of them, clustered together.

Confusion shades the question: Why does he have needles? In the bathroom? I don't think they're for sewing if he keeps them in here. No sign of any thread. They're all pointing the same way, near one end, a piece of plastic in the corner. Crimson and glossy. I take it out, holding it between my fingers.

I can't be sure, but it looks like a lipstick lid.

I shove it back in and close the cupboard, leaving the apple there to rot.

The radio's on loud, blaring classical music – strings and horns and drums – when Arran's voice cuts through the orchestra. I don't hear it at first. I don't see him in the living room doorway. But then I pick up the *s* of my name and glimpse his figure. I turn the symphony down.

'Wow,' he says. 'I didn't know Beethoven could make so much noise.'

I was trying to drown out my thoughts. It was almost working, but now they clap back on.

His face is shiny. Perspiration, overlaid with remorse. 'I'm sorry I'm so late, Tess.' There's a canvas bag on his shoulder. He goes over to the kitchen counter and turns it out, vegetables tumbling onto the side. A bottle of wine rolls into the bread board. He whips off his jacket and flings it over a chair. All of his movements brisk.

'I got caught up after my meeting,' he says, back to me, rattling through the cutlery drawer. 'Had to finish off a proposal for a design project. Took me way longer than I thought.'

I haven't moved from the radio.

He pauses to glance at me. 'Are you still hungry?'

Not especially.

'Do you want me to cook?' he asks, when I take too long to answer.

'Sure,' I force out. 'That'd be nice.'

'And wine?'

I nod. I go along with him, mostly because I haven't got the energy to object.

He twists the corkscrew into the bottle. The cork pops, the normally sweet sound somehow hard. Getting a glass from the cupboard, it tips sideways, chinking into others, as though his fingers are slippery. He pours dark wine and brings it over to me.

'Rioja for the Spanish girl.'

His eyes meet mine – only now since he came in. I take the glass. His hair is tousled, without its normal floppiness.

'Right,' he says, going back to the kitchen. 'Let's get cookin'.'

As he starts preparing the food, I sit at the table. I put my wine down on the wood without tasting it. Arran pours himself some and swallows a mouthful. One of his shirt sleeves is rolled up again, the other loose at his wrist.

It's only as he drinks more wine that I focus on the bottle. White and bronze label, the M embossed in glass so dark it looks black. Marqués de Minaya Rivero. A jog to my nervous system.

'How did you know I like this wine?' I say.

Arran's arm hovers. 'Minaya Rivero? I didn't.' He snaps cloves from a bulb of garlic. 'I went into a wine shop and they had about forty riojas. This Spanish guy spent ten minutes talking me through his recommendations. In the end, I went for this one because of Rivero in the name.'

I look at my glass.

'It's your name, isn't it?' Doubt enters his eyes. 'I saw it on one of the letters by the door. Rivero Hartley?'

'Yes.'

He looks relieved. 'You know this rioja well then?'

'It's one of my favourites.'

'Good. That's one notch in making up for being so late.' He rocks the knife through an onion. 'Mushroom pasta will give me a few more points, I hope.'

I stare at my glass, the black liquid with a ruby tinge. I think of the diary entry, him holding her face, telling her what to do. Joanna earlier, the way her expression changed when she looked behind me, colour draining from her skin. Shortly before, them together in a shadowed restaurant.

I try to blank my mind, but the images won't stop.

Pausing from the ingredients, Arran suddenly says, 'You're quiet.'

'Am I?'

He looks at me. 'I'm really sorry about this evening.'

I don't answer.

'Has something happened?' he asks.

'No.'

He turns back to the mushrooms.

I haven't touched the wine. I don't want that taste in my mouth. Not now, today. Black cherry mixed with mocha and oaky vanilla. Marqués de Minaya Rivero. A running joke in our family that we're related to the Riveros who make it, however distantly. My mum always has some in the cellar of our house in Sevilla. Gran Reserva 2011.

And here's a bottle my bnb guest bought, sitting on the side in my London flat.

I look from the wine to Arran. His demeanour and body language too confusing to read. Nothing clear or revealing – about today, Joanna, what's on his mind. Where he's really been the last few hours.

Within fifteen minutes, Arran sets a plate in front of me. It's delicious, but I can only manage a few mouthfuls.

'Don't tell me you don't like mushrooms?' Arran says.

'No, I do.'

He's quiet for a moment before he puts down his fork. 'Then what is it? Please tell me.'

There's worry in his eyes.

'Something's on your mind,' he says. 'It's obvious.'

For a beat, I imagine asking him what he was doing today. Asking him who Joanna is and what's going on here with us and what I mean to him. Demanding that he gives me the truth.

But I can't. Not without revealing that I've been reading his diary and stalking him. So I just smile and say, 'It's nothing.'

He doesn't believe me. I can see it in his face, but he doesn't push.

I make myself eat more pasta and sip some Minaya Rivero. Ignoring how heavy both sit in my stomach, I ask him how it's going in his studio space. He talks about making ceramics, firing in the kiln, and I immerse myself in his stories, in the amazing food, in his ability to make me smile even with my brain and heart knotted up.

I'm washing up when he comes up behind me. I feel his hand slip round my stomach. His fingers brush my hair from my neck and he kisses my shoulder. I turn the tap off. I close my eyes, savouring the touch. He slips my vest strap off my shoulder, kissing my right shoulder blade, lower down my back. Conflicted about Joanna, part of me wants to push him away. But I let him turn me round and kiss my mouth.

39

Arran has just gone out. He wants to make a jug this afternoon in the studio.

I don't feel like following him today. I can't face the strain of it all, the pulling in my chest. It's draining. And in the mornings, waking up next to him, I can forget. Let it all drift back and just soak in the warm feeling of us.

He kissed me goodbye, slow and lingering like a childhood memory, a little out of focus.

I stay in bed for a while, dozing. Then the thoughts sneak in. They're like insects. Silently scuttling, finding a way into our homes. Impossible to get rid of. Squash one and there's always another somewhere.

We slept in my bed last night. Arran was in his room earlier, getting dressed. The diary could be in there.

I try to resist. I have a shower. I ignore the third missed call from my manager, after two yesterday. I attempt to distract myself with some translation work. But his room is steps away, and the pull is strong.

The diary's in the bedside drawer, beside a pencil, a sharpener and a black phone charger. I open it to that loose piece of paper and the leaf and find more writing on the next page.

You said we couldn't see each other anymore. It wasn't working, it wasn't right.

I didn't believe you. It was bullshit.

You loved me. And you admitted you no longer loved him. He wasn't the person he used to be, when you first met. You assured me you were going to break up with him when the moment was good. But you also needed space. You needed time to yourself, to think. Then maybe we could be together. You asked me to leave you alone.

I couldn't not see you, not touch you, not feel the warmth of your body on mine. Surely you knew that. Surely you could see it in my eyes. But you didn't seem to care.

Turning to the next page:

LIAR.

That one word in capital letters. Below it, after a gap, he's scribbled more.

How could you not tell me? I found out by chance.

I'd stayed away, trying to respect your wishes. But then you asked me to come over. You said you needed to see me.

You didn't look good. There was something different about you, something worrying in your eyes. In your movements and mannerisms and voice. Something had happened.

I asked you if you were unwell. You shook your head. I sat with you, arms around your body, your head resting on my chest. Then I ran you a bath. You were just getting out when I saw a white envelope on the corner of your desk. I don't know what made me go and look at it. Just something about the paper, the way it was sticking out from beneath the books and general mess. Inside, a blurred black and white image that ripped at my heart.

You were wrapping the towel round yourself when I went in.

'What the fuck is this?' I demanded.

Your eyes filled with tears. You wouldn't speak for a few minutes, even as I asked you, 'Is it mine?'

You sat down on the bathroom floor. Then you screeched at me that you'd lost it. You'd lost the baby.

I held you then. Rocked you and rubbed your back as you cried. You said you'd tried to have an abortion. The doctor gave you a pill, but you couldn't take it.

All I could think was why hadn't you told me?

When you were quiet, when your body had stopped shuddering with sobs, I held your shoulders and looked into your eyes. 'Was it mine?'

Your dark irises seemed sunken, staring at me.

My fingers feel weak. I can't believe this. Joanna was pregnant.

*   *   *

I've been lying on my bed for two hours, gazing at the ceiling. The glow-in-the-dark stars a pasty colour in the daylight.

Arran's diary churning is through me. Connecting to something else Joanna said at Apple & Adelaide. *We had a few problems.* The way it seemed difficult for her to get the word *problems* out, her jawbone tight. Problems like getting pregnant and having a miscarriage?

There's something greasy about the idea of it, an inkling that it doesn't seem to quite slot together. Arran and Joanna and everything he's narrated in his diary. How long ago did he first notice her in that cafe? How long have they been seeing each other?

In that bnb website message, he said he'd been subletting his friend's room for two months while looking for a flat to rent. It dawns on me that we've never talked about that. He's never mentioned his room search or going to viewings.

Was it a lie?

Is anything he's told me the truth? From his mouth or his pencil?

Perhaps the diary is his way of dealing with the miscarriage. People say writing things down helps. Although I didn't find it beneficial when I tried. Nalika suggested it to me a few weeks after Rosie's death. *Just write whatever you're thinking or feeling. It doesn't matter what it is.* But it made things worse, even rawer.

I roll over, squashing the pillow beneath my head.

Then: *bang*. A thunk on the window.

I jerk upright. *Thunk* as something hits the window again. Whatever it was too fast to see, dropped and gone.

I watch the glass, heart beating at the base of my throat.

Probably just kids, I tell myself. Prankster boys sniggering and running off down the street. But what if it wasn't? I haven't spoken to Pettiford. He hasn't called me. Has he even questioned Oliver about being outside my flat that day?

I walk to the window and look out. No one there. I press my face up to the glass to look down at the front steps. Nothing out of the ordinary.

Yet someone just chucked something at my window. The mark is clear up close – a wet smudge.

I grab my phone. I type a text to Oliver and click send before I can change my mind. *Leave me the fuck alone.*

Then, pulling on my denim jacket, I run down the stairs. On the front steps, I look around. And I see it. There beside the black railing: half a lemon.

I go over. I pick it up. Bright yellow skin, pips in the mushy flesh. Squashed but still juicy. As though it's been squeezed by a hand. I look around the street.

It feels like there's somebody there. Eyes on me.

I chuck the lemon in the bin then start walking down the road. Just as I do, a door opens. Number 74. A glimpse at the edge of my eye: Elliot.

Since the party, he's slipped from my thoughts. Him and Paul. After what Luke did, Oliver outside my flat. And Joanna. I've been distracted from my sister, from the police investigation.

'Hey, Elliot,' I call.

He halts, eyes hidden behind sunglasses. 'Tess.'

I cross the road and stop in front of him.

'Are you OK?' he asks, with a note of sincerity.

'No, not really. Someone just threw something at my window. You didn't see anyone around in the last few minutes, did you?'

His brow is knitted. 'No, afraid not.' He pulls the second strap of his rucksack onto his shoulder. 'That's really strange.'

'Yeah. It is.'

Silence between us. Elliot's mouth opens a fraction, as if to say something, but then it closes again.

'I'm pretty sure a man's been hanging around outside my flat,' I say. 'Ivy mentioned this guy Paul who used to live with you, who did some odd things.'

I notice Elliot's head move on the word Paul.

'He hasn't been back recently, has he?' I ask.

It takes him a moment to respond. 'No. Not that I know of. The last time I saw him was more than a month ago.'

I wish I could see his eyes. I want to read what's in them.

'Did you know my sister?'

Elliot is very still, body static until he swallows. The throat movement his only reaction to my sudden question.

'I know what happened,' he says in a low voice.

'But you didn't know her?' I want an answer.

'No. I passed her a few times in the street. Knew of her, as my neighbour.'

He's got something in his hand. Small, hidden inside his fist.

'Look, Tess, I'm late for an appointment. I need to go.' He steps away, half-turned from me. 'But let me know if you need help with anything, OK? I'll keep an eye out for you.'

He goes off down the street, long legs striding fast. I watch his back before walking after him.

Following, Tess?

That voice in my head, asking if I should, if it's worth it. I don't know if I have the energy. Then indignation slices into me. Of course I have the energy for Rosie.

I quicken my pace – he's already quite far ahead. Reaching the next street corner where he turned left, I look down the road. I can't see him. He's gone. I don't understand where, scanning the buildings.

I exhale long and slow. Then I head for the convenience store at the end of the street, in case he went in there.

No sign of him. I decide to buy a few things. White chocolate cookies, hummus, breadsticks, Alhambra beer.

Outside, I check both ways down the road. No Elliot in sight. With a sense of deflation, I head home. I'm annoyed with myself for wavering and losing my chance. I push my hands into my pockets. There's something soft inside the left one. A glove. Cream with pink floral patterning. It takes me a moment to remember: the glove I found on Hackney Marshes. I haven't worn this jacket since that night.

I turn onto Ravengale Road, pausing for a moment to scan the area outside my flat, checking for signs of anyone loitering.

'Tess.'

I recoil.

'Whoa. Why so jumpy?'

My hands are clenched into fists, ready to swing my bag of beer and food into their face. Only to see freckles and bright green eyes.

'I hope you're not going to sock me with that,' Ivy says, one palm up.

I lower my hands, feeling stupid as the terror wanes. 'Ivy, you gave me a fright.'

'Sorry,' she says, though she doesn't sound it. 'Did you get my text?'

The bag is swaying from my fingers, knocking into my knee. I search backwards. Text.

'I wondered if we could talk,' she prompts.

Oh, that text. Which I never replied to, like the one before. 'Sorry, I've had a lot going on.'

A few beats of silence before, 'I wanted to see if you're OK.'

'I'm fine.'

'Really?'

'Yes.' It comes out too brusque.

She looks at me, something lifeless about her face. She's chewing gum again. I smell it on her breath.

'I was going to offer to . . .' She sighs. 'Never mind. Let's just say Luke's a dickhead.'

'Understatement.'

Ivy scrapes her sole on the ground. 'I can't believe he did that. To you. And to me.' She scrapes again, a kicking movement of her gold flatform high-top. 'You know, after you'd gone, I went over and hit him. Not quite like Lancelot, but I kickbox twice a week, so Luke didn't know what was coming.'

'Lancelot?' I repeat.

She looks up from her foot. 'Yeah, your knight in shining armour.'

There's something off in her voice – a vinegary humour, more acidic than normal. White elbows pointing out from her ribs, arms folded. The stringy texture of her muscles clear.

'So are you guys a thing or what?' she asks, chewing, a glimpse of pink gum.

'What?'

'You and that bnb guest of yours.'

I don't answer. The shopping bag is digging into my fingers.

'He seems to get so much attention. Girls were eyeing him up at the party – even my friend Bea. I don't see it myself.'

Ivy isn't looking at me, her eyes wandering. When she notices my face her chewing pauses.

'Oh God, sorry. I've said the wrong thing, clearly. I'm good at burning people with hot air, so my mam used to say.'

'Doesn't matter, Ivy.' It does.

She moves a fraction closer. 'He's not good enough for you, Tess.'

I step back. The soft murmur of her voice weirdly intimate, and her words surprising. Triggering.

'Excuse me?' I say. 'What about you and Luke? I saw you leaving his flat on Sunday morning. What are you doing with him?'

She takes a moment to respond, her jaw still. 'Believe me, Tess, I'm angry. I was fuming on Friday night. The fact that he likes you,' she says, shaking her head, 'kissed you—'

'I'm sorry, Ivy.' I feel obliged to say it.

'I don't blame you, Tess.' She shifts towards me again. 'It's his fault.'

'Yet you're still with him?'

She gazes at me, copper hair blowing over her face. Then she scratches her collarbone. 'Emotions aren't simple, Tess. I wish they were, but they mostly feel like snakes, squirming over each other.'

I can't tell if that's meant to be a joke. Even if it is, she's suggesting she still likes him. Loves him even? Her youth showing through – wide-eyed and a little crude. Yet she isn't naïve. The things she says, the air she gives off.

'Look, Ivy, I don't feel too good. I need to get home.' I start moving round her.

'Oh, OK . . .'

'See you later.'

I walk as fast as I can. When I put the key in my door, I check behind me. For Ivy, Elliot, Oliver. I have this sense I'm going to feel a hand on my shoulder. Relieved when the door closes behind me.

Inside, I check the rooms. Then I sit on the sofa.

Stop it.

I drink a bottle of Alhambra cerveza. I open another one. Slowly I feel calmer. It's too much. Elliot, Oliver, Arran, Joanna. Ivy's not helping, appearing from nowhere, saying things about Arran, with her birdy humour.

I put on some music. Spice Girls, for a nineties pop pick-me-up. Then a romcom on TV. To occupy time, I decide to cook. I open the fridge and there's almost nothing in it. I don't want to go out again. Checking my cupboard, I have the ingredients for cinnamon polenta cake – my mum's recipe with olive oil and ground almonds.

At seven o'clock, the cake's been cool on the rack for more than an hour. It feels darker than normal at this time. Slate clouds shading out the sun.

By ten I'm biting my nails. When Arran left this morning, he said he'd be back as early as he could. And here I am waiting for him again, late into the evening. No idea where he is. My fingers fiddle with my hair, a big clump falling into my palm. I look at it next to me on the sofa.

Anger threatens to swell. I push my knuckles into my eyes. I don't know why I keep doing this when I know about Joanna and the intensity of Arran's feelings, how he's pursued her.

I've drawn all the curtains. I don't want to look out of the window, not with the lights on. Anyone outside will be able to see me.

She is soft. Perhaps not quite as soft as her sister. She was a bit of a sap, as it turns out.

Tess has no one. Friends, family, all of them have dried up. Nobody to help her. Left with me, though she hasn't realised this yet. And I'm no puppet, no pawn on this chessboard. Forced to do things most people would consider disturbing. As if they know anything. As if they could ever understand.

How to explain? I have a certain weakness. But, for the record, they're no use to me dead.

40

The door makes a murmuring sound. I hear the low whine. I hurry into the hall and Arran is there.

'Where have you been?' I say, ready to flare *it's after midnight*. But then I see his arm. The sleeve of his shirt has been cut off at the shoulder. A bandage around his bicep. Cuts and grazes on his elbow, down his forearm to his wrist.

'My God,' I breathe. 'What happened?'

His face is pale. His posture sagging. 'I was in an accident.'

'What kind of accident?'

'Can I sit down? I need to . . .' He looks drained.

'Yes, yes.'

He heads into his room, dropping his backpack before sitting on the bed. His movements a little slow and shaky. I sit next to him.

'Jesus, what an evening,' he says. 'I feel a bit like Edward Scissorhands. Or an uncool Marty McFly.'

'What happened?'

'I was on my way home, just left the studio, when a woman was mugged by a guy on a scooter. Happened just a few paces from me, ripping her handbag off her shoulder. When I went over to help, I realised the asshole had stopped further up, so I tried to go after him. He zoomed off but someone was following on another motorbike. The bike half-hit me, scraping one side of my body, and I fell and . . . got a few cuts, as you can see.'

The grazes are dark on his skin.

'The girl was a bit hurt too and another woman who witnessed everything from her car insisted on taking us to A&E. I was bleeding pretty badly from one cut.' He indicates the bandage on his upper arm. 'Had to have stitches.'

I'm on the other side of him, by his good shoulder. When I touch his face, brushing his hair back, there's dried blood on his temple.

He gives me a weary smile. 'It looks a lot worse than it is. I don't know why they had to ruin my shirt like this. Though there was blood all over the arm anyway.'

I notice a blotch on the stomach area too. Bright red in the cloth, as if it's fresher.

'Hey,' Arran says after a moment.

I look up from the blood. I must have an odd expression on my face because his eyes are softer.

'I'm OK,' he reassures me. 'More of a shock than anything else.' His arm slides round my waist. 'Seems we're both good at having accidents.'

I try to level my head. 'Do you need anything? What can I do?'

'You can kiss me.'

I do as he says, letting my weight lean into his warmth. There's a strange smell on him. Chemical, like industrial soap. Must be from the hospital.

'Are you thirsty?' I ask. 'Or hungry? I can make you something. Or, if you want, there's some cake.'

'Cake?'

'Yes, I . . .' Suddenly I feel self-conscious. 'I made it this afternoon.'

He's smiling. 'What kind of cake?'

'Polenta and cinnamon. A recipe of my mum's.'

'That sounds amazing. Yes please.'

'Are you sure? I could make us toast or—'

'Tess. Cinnamon sponge sounds perfect. Right now, that's just what I feel like. Cake and bed.'

* * *

It's 10 a.m. and I've been awake for over an hour. I let Arran sleep and get up to make breakfast. Continuing the Spanish theme, *tostada con tomate*. Deceptively simple – grated fresh tomatoes on toast with extra virgin olive oil and salt.

When I go to check on him, he's sitting at his desk, doing something on his laptop. I go back to get the tray of food as a surprise. As soon as he hears me behind him, he shuts the lid – almost a snapping motion. As though he's been caught doing something. As though he doesn't want me to see the screen.

'Hey, what's this?' he says, twisting round and seeing the tray.

'Spanish breakfast.'

'In bed?'

'Well, it would be, if you were still in bed.'

He smiles and goes back to get under the covers. He's topless, in boxers, and it's only now, in the morning light, that I see the bruising on the side of his body. Pale purple blots in the skin like a map of islands. I stare at them, a flash of reminiscence gripping me without warning. The bruises on Rosie.

'Tess?' Arran says.

I blink and take the tray over. We bite into our tostadas.

His eyes widen. 'This is delicious. Why haven't you made me this before?' He wipes tomato off his lips with his thumb. After the next bite, olive oil drips down his chin. A drop of it landing on the duvet.

Twenty minutes later, after a shower, I watch him dress.

'I'm heading to the studio,' he says, pulling on jeans.

'Why? You need to rest.'

'I have to finish off some ceramics for a commission from a gallery in Glasgow. My first ever commission, as it happens.'

This is the first I've heard of it. And I don't want him to go – to leave me here in the flat for another day, alone.

'Why don't you just stay at home today,' I say. 'We could watch movies and order a takeaway.'

He smiles and kisses me on the forehead. 'I'd love to, but this is too important. Thank you for breakfast.'

He's gone before I can think how to persuade him.

I look at the drop of oil, a spot in the white of the cover, citron-yellow. Those bruises on his skin, down his ribs and on his hipbone. They looked painful. But he didn't show it, except for a couple of grimaces.

I feel that reminiscent grip again. Rosie lying in bed last year. Autumnal outside, November, I think. I sat on the mattress beside her, my weight shifting her body. She wouldn't talk for a long time. Just her bare shoulder poking out of the duvet. Eventually I got her to take a shower.

She finished towelling herself in her room. I came through with a cup of tea and that's when I saw her pulling on a top. Two bruise spots in the curve of her waist. Not only that but how thin she was. The groove of her ribcage visible, hipbones sticking out. I stared at my sister, wondering if she had an eating disorder. Or if she had just lost her appetite as she claimed.

'Here,' I said, handing her the mug of tea.

She sipped.

'Rosie, don't get upset, but how did you get those bruises?'

Her eyes dropped towards her stomach. 'What, these ones on my side?'

I nodded.

She sighed, her breath rippling the surface of the tea. 'A stupid runner knocked into me, made me fall against a lamp post.'

I looked at her, thinking, *Qué va*. Come on.

Rosie lifted her hand at me. 'Truth, Tess. She was really apologetic, asking if I needed help.' She slurped her tea. 'All a bit OTT, frankly. It took me a while to get her to go away.'

'Sounds like a kind person to me.'

She gave me a dark look. 'The weird thing was I thought I recognised her from somewhere. I asked if I knew her right before Carlota called my name and appeared behind me. You remember I bumped into her?'

I nodded.

'That was bizarre. What are the chances? Coming across a friend who went back to Spain two years ago. She was telling me how much she loves Madrid, saying I should move there.' Rosie sighed. 'Maybe I will. Maybe I'll just pack up and go.'

Soon after that she closed up again, a mussel shell, barely letting out a sound. That's what I hated the most. When she went silent.

I try calling her phone. It rings, then goes to voicemail.

I look for Arran's diary but it's not here. His laptop is on the desk. What was he doing earlier, when he could surely hear me in the kitchen making breakfast? Why did he close the lid so fast?

I open it up and there's a password box. I try a few words. Stoneware. Sourdough. Niyama. Joanna. None of them are right. I'm no hacker.

I give up and open my laptop instead. I'm thinking about catching up on some translation work when I see it in the news headlines on my home screen.

Joanna is missing.

41

Joanna. Missing.

I'm staring at the screen. Disbelief buzzing through my ears. I go onto BBC News and find the report flashing cold, clear reality at me. Its headline: APPEAL OVER MISSING BALHAM WOMAN JOANNA REYNOLDS.

The picture below is her, no mistake. The Joanna I've been following. In the image she's at a summer garden party, in a lovely floral dress, elegant, smiling. Protruding ears visible in front of tied-up hair.

The article was posted this morning.

Police are looking for a woman from Balham, London, after she failed to come home on Monday night, or turn up for work yesterday.

Ms Reynolds was last seen leaving her office on Fetter Lane, near St Paul's, at 18:15 on Monday. No one has heard from her. Her family and friends are extremely concerned.

Georgina Thompson, flatmate of the twenty-eight-year-old, said that she is a 'wonderful friend and person – everybody who meets her instantly warms to her because she puts you at ease.'

'Normally we are in contact at least every couple of hours via text or calls. Her silence since Monday evening is very out of character,' she said.

The Metropolitan Police are appealing for anyone with information to contact them.

That last line glares blackly at me. *The Metropolitan Police are appealing for anyone with information to contact them.* Does that apply to me? Am I someone with information?

My mind glides over the past few days. Joanna's phone call after Alice's yoga class when she told whoever was on the line that they couldn't keep ringing her and showing up places. Then in Apple & Adelaide, similar, about her ex-boyfriend refusing to accept their break-up, waiting for her outside her flat, following her.

Arran?

No no no.

That's all my brain can think. A stuck needle.

He couldn't have. I refuse to consider it even for a second. It's Arran. A man who makes sourdough and has a sweet lopsided smile and whose touch is gentle.

No. Impossible.

So why does it feel like there's something spiking into me, a tiny seed in a dark part of my psyche, countering my conviction?

I look at the news story again. *Last seen at 18:15 on Monday.* The night Arran got home after ten-thirty, sweaty and on edge, hair ruffled. About four hours between those two times. Hours Arran said he was working on his design project. Hours he could have been doing something else.

* * *

I'm on Hampstead Heath. It's getting dark. The sun dipped into the west twenty minutes ago. The sky still glowing with some of its orange light, burning the edges of cloud.

I'm sitting against the oak. Rosie's tree.

If I look straight up through the branches, there's a small gap in the leaves showing the sky. A single star, a faint speck in the grey-blue, though I feel like it might be a trick. You can never see the stars in London.

I couldn't stay in the flat. I kept refreshing the news page, looking for more information about Joanna. But that initial report is the only one. Other news providers saying the same thing: that the police are appealing for information.

I stared at my phone. I imagined dialling 101 and stating that I was calling about Joanna Reynolds. Telling an officer how I'd been reading about her in my bnb guest's diary and I'd started following him, then Joanna, and I'd purposefully bumped into her and made her spill smoothie all over me just so I could talk to her, and my bnb guest might have had something to do with her disappearance.

Even to my ears that sounds crazy. They wouldn't take me seriously. They'd snigger to their colleagues that they'd just spoken to some busybody.

I considered calling Pettiford. But he wouldn't believe me either. He'd probably just confirm that I was paranoid, making stuff up.

So I went out into the streets.

Somehow, I ended up here. I wandered the heath, looked at the ponds, a few swimmers in the brown water. One question clicking through my mind: What's happened to Joanna?

That sharp seed is still in my side. I want to rip it out, but it's nowhere specific. It is possible that Arran did something, that he's involved in Joanna's disappearance. But there are other possibilities. She could have gone somewhere without telling anyone. It could have been somebody else, a stranger, an abductor.

Overlooking the obvious – in correlation to my sister, to what I'm almost certain is true for her, as it is in most cases. That violent crimes are committed by someone you know. Most often by a spouse or ex-spouse. Especially crimes against women.

I'm still unsure whether Arran is the ex Joanna talked about. Or if it's another man. Either way, she knows Arran, which soaks him in potential liquid. Though it doesn't necessarily sink him in guilt. If something happened it might not have been intentional. It could have been an accident.

That word: accident. Last night. The cuts on Arran's arm and bruises in his skin. What if they weren't an accident? What if it was all a story, a lie, about the woman being mugged and the motorbike? What if his injuries have something to do with Joanna?

I get up from the ground fast. I feel sick, the slice of polenta cake I had hours ago stirring up. The taste of it is in my mouth, mixed with stomach acid.

Then I hear faint laughter.

I turn towards the sound. It's night now, the remains of the sun leaving dark. The heath is full of shadows. I can't see anyone, especially here beneath the trees.

Heartbeat in my throat, that fear creeps back. Wondering if it was my imagination. Telling myself there could easily be other people around, walking their dog, on the way home from a summer evening picnic. There are always groups of teens drinking and playing music here.

That little voice whispers again. *Isn't this what you wanted, Tess? The past four and a half months since Rosie was found? Someone to jump out at you, threaten you.* I thought so. But not now.

I walk away from the oak, out from under the trees. My footsteps seeming loud, crunching on bits and twigs.

A rustle behind me. A step.

My skin is prickling, hairs upright all over my body. I'm on grass now. My tread is quieter so I speed up. There's another rustle, a throat noise. Unmistakable human sounds. I stop and peer back towards the trees.

'Who's there?' I say.

A swish of leaves and a distant siren.

'Who the fuck are you?' My voice is louder – bolder than I feel.

No response.

I run down the slope. There are noises behind me. They're coming after me, I know they are. I trip on something and fall into grass.

As I scramble up again I can't help looking back. Expecting hands to grab me, a body to pin me down.

But over my shoulder there are no hands, no face grinning. Only black and gloom.

About to run on, my eyes detect a more defined shape. Up the slope, near where I was standing, there's a figure. Dark outline of body and legs. Hooded. Looking down at me.

42

I'm shaking as I open the door into my building's stairwell. The light switching on above makes me flinch, suddenly too bright.

When I saw that silhouetted figure on the heath, I ran. All the way to the train station and then again from the station to here. I'm not sure where the terror came from. After courting this kind of danger, being reckless, putting myself at risk – something's changed.

Joanna, I think. Arran. They've shifted something in me.

My throat hurts. There's mud on my jeans, and all over my boots. I go up the stairs into the flat. The rooms are all dark. Flicking on the lights in the living area, my whole body jolts. Someone's on the sofa.

'Arran,' I say. 'What are you doing sitting in the dark?'

He doesn't turn. Doesn't move.

'Arran?' I go round and look at the side of his face. It's white. His hands resting either side of his legs.

It's like he hasn't heard me. Hasn't noticed the lights or my presence. But then he looks at me, his eyes focusing.

'Tess. Where have you been? I was worried.' He doesn't seem it, except for something in his voice. An uneven note. 'When I got home and you weren't . . .' His head shakes. 'I went to look for you. In the streets around here, along the canal. Shoreditch Park.' His eyes float down my body, to the mud on my jeans and shoes.

'Sorry,' I say.

I can only manage one word. Feelings and uncertainties flying around my brain, all bumping into each other. Part of me thought the police might have come for him. But he's here sitting on my sofa.

See. It wasn't him.

'Please don't do that to me, Tess.'

Arran's eyes are gleaming. I go over and sit next to him, thinking, *You did it to me*, two nights in a row.

'Why the hell don't we have each other's numbers?' he says. 'That's what I thought while I was wandering the streets. I couldn't call you.'

'I know. It's stupid.'

I hug him gently, careful of his cuts and bruises.

He leans his forehead against mine. I can smell the coconut again, but there's something else too. A trace I'm unsure of.

'All that matters is you're here now,' he murmurs. His skin is hot. His fingers gripping my arm, a little too tight. 'You're my saving grace, you know that?'

He leans back and I look into his eyes. What's he implying?

Arran pulls me into another hug. And I catch that trace again. Almost tree-piney, or like soil. I look down and notice his shoes by the sofa. Normally he takes them off at the door. But his trainers are here on their side, laces strewn, the white of them stained with dirt.

He lets me go, sighing. 'Today's been ... Christ, I don't even know what. Like brown paint.'

'Brown paint?'

'Yeah, you know if you mix too many paint colours together, they turn brown.'

I do know, from the few times I've tried painting. Red, yellow and purple make brown. Green and pink make brown. I remember Rosie getting pissed off while trying to mix colours for her canvases. *Fucking brown*, she'd mutter.

I don't want to ask him what he means, what he's been mixing.

'Did you finish your pots?' I ask.

'Not quite. I got interrupted and couldn't really concentrate.'

I wish he'd tell me. Just come out with it all. I want the pith of him, but I'm hardly in a position to make demands. There are so many things I haven't been honest about. And I'm not supposed to know about Joanna. The only reason I do is through full-blown invasion of his privacy.

His candle's still on the coffee table, wax dribbled down the side of the tin.

'I just want to forget it all now,' he says, turning to look at me. 'Leave the day behind and be with you.'

His fingers slide my hair off my shoulder and he kisses my neck. I feel his hand slip under my top, then start unbuttoning my jeans. A tiny part of me resists. My body responding to his touch, yet my mind saying no, dimly repelled by the caress of his fingertips, uncomfortable beneath the weight of his body.

He's on top of me when he pulls off his shirt. I see the bruising again, and the cuts and grazes. A glimpse before I succumb. Before I think how those scratches, long and fine and red, could have been made by fingernails.

* * *

Arran's gone to the studio again and this time I didn't try to stop him.

Since he got out of bed he's been in a strange mood. Tense, rubbing his hair, stroking it down on his skull. In the night he was twitching. I woke up to body jerks and trembles. Sounds in his throat like moans, but deeper. He was dreaming. And when he fell quiet, I felt his hand on my stomach.

For breakfast I forced down granola, the coffee he'd made bitter in my mouth. I wanted to tell him what he'd been like in the night – ask him if he remembered dreaming. But I stayed silent.

His arms gripped me in a hug goodbye. The feel of them warm and protecting, yet unwelcome. I wanted him to let go.

He breathed in my hair. 'You smell like cumin.'

I didn't respond, holding him loosely, waiting.

'I'll see you later,' he said, hands slipping off my body.

I watched him disappear along Ravengale Road, his gait fast, without its natural ease.

Now, I'm in his room. Like his hair and general appearance, it's messier. But the diary's in the bedside drawer. In my hands.

Was it mine?

The question your eyes half-answered, but I waited for your mouth to confirm. 'I think so,' you said.

Think so? I almost repeated it, wanting to grab you, grip your waist, breathe tell me into your face.

'I can't be sure, but the timing . . . how many weeks along I was.' You stared at the floor, your voice a shell of its normal tone. 'It was yours, Arran.'

I moved back from you. I couldn't touch you then. I'm not sure why, just this wince. You saw it, the look on your face painful yet aggravating. The whites of your eyes somehow grey. It made my hands tense, the bones stretching inside the skin.

I looked at the ultrasound on the floor beside us. The colourless shape of a life.

When I got home, the anger came. Hitting me in a wave, breaking more than my stoneware.

I couldn't face you, despite the fact I wanted to be there for you. I wanted nothing more than for us to be together. But everything you'd done to me, everything you'd put me through — it hurt. I could feel it in myself, this growing resentment. Letting in the rot.

When I came to see you, you pushed me away. You said where the hell had I been, how could I just go silent on you? I asked you to forgive me. But you wouldn't have it. You slammed the door and wouldn't talk to me. I hated you then.

I waited until I couldn't wait anymore. I let you walk a few streets, then I stopped you and said we had to talk. You were surprised, drawing away from me. This coldness I hadn't felt before, ugly in you. I said we're not over. You hesitated and looked down at my hand on your arm. You tried to pull it away, but I wouldn't let you.

There's one more entry.

You were a screw in my brain. Difficult, stubborn, doing senseless things.

You called me, talking about some girl you thought was following you but you weren't sure if you were being paranoid. Please could I come. And I did. I held you in my arms. You said you loved me.

You'd burrowed yourself under my skin, and there was no way to dig you out.

I came to your flat to check on you. I watched your windows until I saw you were in there. I watched you leave. I cursed your back.

Still, after all this, I was the outsider. Unknown to everyone in your life. So well hidden, you'd made me the weasel in the dark.

I saw you with your family. Dinner in a smart restaurant. You arrived alone, sitting there, then through the window your dad taking your hand, trying to say something to you, your sister's back to the glass. Your mother's eyes birdlike. A hawk, unblinking.

You called me again, not making much sense. You said something about this girl, annoying you, seeing her in places like a cafe and on the street.

Shit. She means me. Of course she must have noticed, after I botched up my stalking by Liberty's. It would be strange for Joanna not to suspect or find it weird.

Way to go, Tess.

Putting my blunder aside, I keep reading.

You also said something about your ex-boyfriend and how he was bugging you, he wouldn't leave you alone. You asked to meet with me and your eyes were a little brighter, I could see that spark in you again. But then you retreated into yourself, saying you were sorry, you'd been stupid.

Before I could do anything, you'd left. You said you were going to the toilet and you didn't come back. I was going to give you an ultimatum. Either we're together or I'm leaving for good, because I couldn't do this anymore.

I look back over these two entries, something wriggling inside my gut. *You were a screw in my brain. You'd burrowed yourself under my skin, and there was no way to dig you out.*

These phrases are creepy, but what's more worrying is how relatable they are – I feel like that about him. Writing and man, the guest I've welcomed into my home.

All of it is floating in fragments, and something about them doesn't slot together, as I felt before. But now there's a whisper in my head, a strange voice that doesn't feel like mine. No words, just the breathy texture of it.

The book I'm holding in my hand suddenly feels something alien, yet there's a familiarity lying beneath. Between the pages. I put it back in the drawer.

I go out. I need to walk, feel air flowing past me.

When I'm a little cooler and steadier, I check the news on my phone. I don't want to look but I have to.

The headline that pops up: MAN ARRESTED ON SUSPICION OF INVOLVEMENT IN DISAPPEAR-ANCE OF BALHAM WOMAN JOANNA REYNOLDS.

A man has been taken into custody for questioning on the case of Joanna Reynolds, a woman from Balham who has been missing since Monday evening.

Police are not giving out the man's name, but they have confirmed that he was detained yesterday in central London. He has since been released on conditional bail while the investigation continues.

Ms Reynolds' sister, Lily, said: 'Our whole family is so worried about her, we're in a living hell.'

Detective Inspector Cadu, the Met officer leading the investigation, said, 'We continue to regard this missing-person case as a high-risk inquiry. As in any investigation of this kind, we are pursuing all possible leads with the objective of returning Joanna safe and sound.'

The man could have been Arran. They could have taken him in for questioning yesterday and released him again. When I look at the other coverage, the articles say similar things – *Man taken into custody over disappearance of Joanna Reynolds* and *Man detained in connection to missing Balham woman.*

The way he was last night, talking about brown paint. His pottery was interrupted. He couldn't concentrate. Sitting in the dark, silent, staring. As if something had shaken him.

My legs feel numb. I hurry home, dodging round people, a cat, a lamppost. A man in a parked car seems to stare at me, face expressionless through the open window. When I turn into Ravengale Road I nearly bump into someone.

'Sorry,' I mumble.

There are footsteps behind me. When I glance over my shoulder, the woman I bumped into seems to be following. I quicken my pace. A man zips past on a bicycle. On the other side of the road, an old man is walking a yappy dog on a lead. Is he looking at me too?

You're being paranoid, I tell myself. *Stop it.*

But as I approach my front door, there's someone standing outside it. A woman in a suit with a badge hanging from a lanyard. My core goes cold.

'Teresa Hartley?' she says.

I swallow into my tightening throat. 'Yes.'

'I'm Detective Inspector Cadu, with the Metropolitan Police. We'd like to ask you a few questions.'

43

There are two police officers in my living room. One of them is Pettiford. He appeared behind Cadu on the pavement. I saw the purple tie and I knew.

'Hello, Tess,' he said, with a strange smile.

They followed me up here. Both of them are near the sofa. Pettiford is looking at me, while Cadu's eyes flicker about, taking in the place.

'We thought it best if I accompany Detective Cadu,' Pettiford says. 'Since we're already acquainted with each other.'

Don't panic. I don't know what they want yet. I don't know why they're here.

Cadu is shorter than me but athletic-looking, like she could have abs. There's something feline about her flat face – narrow chin and wide jawbone. Blonde hair tied into a tight bun to match her stiff plain shirt and trousers. She smiled rigidly when she shook my hand, but she's not smiling now.

'How are you?' Pettiford's smooth fireside tone.

What kind of question is that? Everyone knows it's hollow. After a moment, Cadu steps forward.

'Ms Hartley,' she says, 'we're here because we're hoping you can help us with our missing-person investigation.'

'Missing person?' I repeat.

Silence for a beat.

'Why don't you sit down?' she says.

Suddenly, with police in it, my home doesn't feel like mine anymore. 'I'm fine,' I declare. 'I'd rather stand.' I just wish Cadu's eyes would blink and leave my face.

She looks at Pettiford and nods.

He lifts a wooden chair out from the table. One palm flat on his chest, keeping his tie and lanyard straight, he sits down.

'Can you tell us what you did on Monday, Tess?' he asks.

What I did on Monday. *Fuck.* 'I just need some water,' I stall.

I go fill a glass and gulp it down. At the sink, my back's to the police – maybe when I turn around they won't be there.

But they are, waiting and watching.

'Is this about Joanna Reynolds?' I blurt.

'It is in relation to her, yes,' Pettiford says. 'Monday was the day she was last seen.' His chin lifts a fraction. 'We'd like to hear from you about what you did that day, if that's all right. Could you describe your movements?'

I'm not sure what to say. Do they already know what I did and want to test my story? Or are they not sure and they've come to check? They must know something, to seek me out like this. They must be suspicious.

'Start at the beginning?' Pettiford prompts. 'The morning.'

'I went to work at the Barbican Centre,' I say. 'But I didn't feel well, so I had to leave.'

'Nothing too serious I hope?' He doesn't sound concerned.

'I just didn't . . . feel good.'

He presses his lips together. 'So, when you left the Barbican, what did you do then?'

It's unwise to lie to the police. Worse than unwise – it's wrong. I know it is. Especially after Rosie. What if someone they questioned about her had lied, and because of that, the police never caught her killer? But I don't want to mention Arran. It would be like pointing an arrow at his chest. So I skip over him.

'I went into central London.'

'You didn't go home? Since you felt unwell?'

'I was going to, but I felt like some air and some lunch.'

'Right,' Pettiford says. 'So where exactly in central London were you?'

I glance at Cadu, her face a plank of wood. 'Soho.'

'That's a little odd,' she says. 'To go to the busiest area of London when you're under the weather.'

I search for excuses. 'I wasn't physically unwell. I just needed to get out. I couldn't be in some stark gallery any longer.'

Pettiford's eyes veer towards Cadu's and they meet for a millisecond. 'What did you do in Soho?' he asks.

'I walked around.'

'Did you see anyone?'

I don't know what angle they're coming from, what they're after. I don't want to give anything away I might regret. My thoughts are running too fast. I'm still not sure about Arran – about anything. Though the one thing I am sure of, like cement at the base of my heart: I want them to find Joanna. I want her to be OK, however much I resent her. The idea of what happened to Rosie happening to her. The possibility that she's dead. It makes my hands go weak. I should tell them at least part of the truth – it might help their investigation.

'I saw Joanna,' I say.

'Ms Reynolds?' Pettiford asks.

'Yes, Joanna Reynolds.' Is there another missing Joanna?

Pettiford glances at Cadu again. 'Do you know Ms Reynolds?'

'Hardly.' I swallow. 'I mean . . . we met on Sunday, though I've seen her at a yoga class before.'

'Yoga class? Where was that?'

'Niyama, in Camden.'

Pettiford rubs his thumbnail on his cheek. There's a scribbling sound – Cadu is writing in a notebook.

'OK,' he says. 'So how and where did you meet on Sunday?'

My heart is flailing around. *Stay calm.* Keep going, parcelling out pieces of truth. 'By chance. We were in the same cafe having brunch and realised we'd both been to Niyama.'

'Which cafe is this?'

'Apple & Adelaide in Covent Garden.'

Cadu's pencil keeps scratching in her notebook.

'Why do you need to know about the cafe?' I say.

They ignore me. Cadu writing more as Pettiford asks, 'What about Monday? You said you saw Ms Reynolds that day too. Did you arrange to meet?'

'No. We . . . bumped into each other.'

The scribbling pauses. 'That seems a surprising coincidence.' Cadu's tone is mid-pitched and nasal. 'To bump into each other two days in a row, in London, one of the biggest, most crowded cities in the world.'

I can feel my pulse inside my skull. 'Yes, it was. It was really odd.'

Cadu's eyes are narrowed at me, slitty like a cat. She closes her notebook and puts it away in her pocket.

'Where was this?' Pettiford asks. 'That you bumped into each other on Monday?'

I can't look away from Cadu. Her eyes are freaking me out, the way she's assessing me. I pull my gaze to Pettiford, who's waiting for an answer.

'Ms Hartley,' Cadu says. 'We have CCTV images of you on Monday afternoon, so I would advise you to think carefully about your response.'

CCTV? *Shit*. 'Outside Liberty's department store.'

'Right,' she says. 'And what did you speak of?'

'We just . . . said how weird it was, the coincidence, and we talked about buying flowers.'

'Anything else?'

There's sweat on my upper lip. I can feel it gathering there. Pettiford is sitting still and silent, hands folded in his lap.

'Please answer the question, Ms Hartley.' Cadu's nasal voice again.

She's watching me carefully. Pettiford rubs his pointy ear with a finger then stands up, stepping closer to me.

'Tess, I know this must be difficult for you, having us come and question you about a missing woman. We understand that. But our priority is finding Joanna Reynolds.' His grey eyes are fixed on mine. 'Time is vital in a missing-person investigation, and you were one of the last people to see her before she disappeared, barring her office colleagues. So, if there's anything you can tell us, about what she said, or her frame of mind, or the things you discussed – anything that might help us, we would be grateful.'

One of the last people to see her before she disappeared. What about Arran? They haven't even mentioned him. I don't know if that's a good or bad thing. Surely they know he's my bnb guest?

I look into Pettiford's powdery eyes. *Focus on Joanna*, I think. Anything that might help the police find her.

'Outside Liberty's,' I begin. Pettiford nods encouragingly. 'Joanna seemed a little bothered about something. I barely know her, of course, but she wasn't in a completely happy, easy mood. I asked her if she was OK and she shrugged it off. But then she . . .' I glance at Cadu. 'Seemed to see something behind me and said she had to go and walked off suddenly.'

'What did she see?' Cadu asks.

'I don't know. The street was crowded. It could have been anything but . . . I got the impression she'd seen someone she knew.'

'A man?' she says.

I stare at her before my head shakes. 'I don't know. It was busy. There's no way I can say.' When I look at Pettiford his head is cocked to one side. Panicking, I speak again. 'On Sunday, in Apple & Adelaide, she mentioned her ex-boyfriend. How their relationship was a bit complicated and he was finding it difficult to accept their break-up. She said he called and texted her a lot.'

'She told you these intimate details about her life even though you'd just met?' Cadu says.

'Yes.' I frown at her. 'She got a text and seemed sort of restless and troubled, so I asked her if she was all right – as anyone would do, stranger or not.'

She hasn't blinked. She gets her notebook out again, the scratch of her pencil seeming too loud.

What about Joanna's ex-boyfriend waiting outside her flat and following her – do I tell them that? I should. But it could be more arrows pointing at Arran.

'Did she say who the text was from?' Cadu asks.

'No. But the implication was her ex-boyfriend.'

'Did she name him? Her ex-boyfriend?'

I shake my head. They must know his name. Or maybe they think there's a man involved but they haven't identified him yet. My pulse is throbbing stronger. What else would be safe to disclose?

'She just said he wasn't who she thought he was,' I say. 'He'd changed and they'd had a few problems in their relationship.'

More scribbling. 'OK, Ms Hartley. Anything else? Any other details?'

Why is there no air in here? I go to the window and slide it up.

'Ms Hartley?'

'I've told you,' I say over my shoulder.

Both of them are quiet. Once I've taken a few breaths, I turn to face them again. Cadu has moved further into the living area, looking at things. Can she size me up from objects? Deduce meaning? That's how this whole thing started, with objects and my snooping fingers.

Panic grips again. What if they search the flat? What if they go into Arran's room? The diary is in the bedside drawer. If they find it, it would—

'You look a little pale, Tess,' says Pettiford. 'Are you sure you wouldn't like to sit down?'

I take his suggestion and sit at the table. He brings me my glass of water but doesn't sit again. Cadu is still looking round the living area. Pettiford tilts his head at her, like a motion of assent. She comes forward, hands in her trouser pockets.

'What we're wondering, Ms Hartley, is how come you saw a woman two days running, allegedly each time by chance, who then went missing hours after your encounter outside Liberty's.'

I blink at her.

'Surely you can understand this raises one or two flags for us.' There's something in Cadu's tone I don't like, a note of scepticism. 'You expect us to believe it's all just coincidence?'

I stare up at her flat face and scraped-back hair. 'What are you trying to suggest? That I was involved in Joanna's disappearance?' My voice gets louder. 'That *I* did something to her?'

Her eyes don't leave my face, cat-narrowed again. I glance at Pettiford. Indignation and horror surging up.

'How dare you. I would *never*—'

Pettiford steps forward, frowning. 'That's not what we're suggesting, Tess. You misunderstand us. It just seems a little odd, investigating Ms Reynolds' case, that your face and name have come up, that you actually saw her the day of her disappearance, given that you have . . .' He hesitates. 'Well, given your history.'

My eyes are damp. My history. Meaning Rosie and what happened to her. Even though she didn't disappear like so many other women. She was never 'missing' like Joanna. She just died. Or maybe Pettiford means my history with Oliver. My stalking.

They both watch me with funny expressions on their faces. Cadu sits down opposite, hands clasped on the table in front of her.

'I'm very sorry about your sister, Ms Hartley.' Her nasal tone seems deeper. 'And for the details that remain unresolved.' She pauses, letting the silence stretch. 'I'd like to ask – do you feel distanced from people? Lonely?'

'What?' I look at Pettiford.

'Do you feel a need to get involved in strangers' lives?'

'*No*,' I snap. Even as that inner voice answers back: *Don't you? Don't you like to pry and meddle, Tess? To the extreme of stalking?*

Pettiford clears his throat.

Cadu glances at him, then takes a breath. 'I'm merely wondering if you harbour a misguided sense of overprotection for women. Particularly those who remind you of your sister, who you were unable to prevent coming to harm.'

My eyelids blink and blink, trying to stop the tears. I can't believe what Cadu has just said, her words like a serrated knife-edge. Then I think: do they know about it? The stalking? Do they have CCTV images of me outside Foxcoal or the hotel or even Niyama?

Cadu is watching me. I get up. I try to wipe away the tears but more drip down.

'Tess,' Pettiford says behind me. 'Please don't—'

I jerk away. 'Don't come near me. I've told you what I know. I've answered your questions. And now you ... you do this? Bring my dead sister into it? Try to make out I'm unhinged and desperate?'

Cadu gets up from the chair. My bitterness spurting out at her and Pettiford.

'It's insulting, especially since you failed before, with Rosie, and now you're obviously failing again.' I'm almost shouting. 'You're the police. You're supposed to protect us, catch the bad guys, the criminals. Not come into someone's home and accuse them of mental illness.'

'I apologise, Tess,' Pettiford says, standing in front of me. 'That was not our intention.'

Cadu has halted near the doorway and turned to look back at me, flat face impassive.

'We're grateful for your time and cooperation,' Pettiford says. 'And we're hopeful what you've told us will help us find Ms Reynolds.'

'Hopeful?' I scoff. 'Sure. That's why you're here looking for a new lead from Tess the nutjob obsessed with vulnerable women. Right?'

Cadu doesn't move a muscle, hands in her trouser pockets. Pettiford's palm is flat on his purple tie.

'It's not over yet,' he says solemnly. 'We're doing all we can.'

44

I can't settle. The police left two hours ago. I keep checking the windows, the street, the back garden. For someone. I don't even know who. The police again. A person sitting in a car watching my flat. Oliver. Elliot. Arran.

There's never anyone there. Only strangers. That old guy repositioning his doll in the window. Above, the net curtains. A ginger cat on the windowsill before a hand swipes it back. Elliot holding something and talking to Ivy.

I check the locks on the front door. I lie down on my bed, and I listen.

* * *

I must have fallen asleep. The clock says 17:16. I get up and feel more uneasy. I have this feeling someone's been in the flat while I was sleeping. That they've crept round touching things, tinkering with objects. Even though everything looks normal, in its place.

I want Arran to get home. And I don't. A sense of dread even as I keep thinking, *He's innocent. He has to be.*

Switching on the TV, I flick between news channels. They're all covering Joanna's story – it's gone national. There's a press conference. Detective Inspector Cadu is there, sitting on the left with her scraped-back hair. On the right, behind the desk, is another male police officer. Not Pettiford. And in the middle, speaking into about seven microphones all pointed towards her like rockets, is Joanna's sister.

Not as beautiful as Joanna, but still pretty. Breaking down during a public appeal at the Met Police's City of Westminster headquarters.

'Joanna is a lovely, charismatic and happy woman. She's my best friend,' Lily says before her face pinches up, crying. 'Joanna, we miss you so much. We all love you. Please get in contact if you can.'

Another pause. Journalist cameras snapping in the background.

'Joanna has the best smile in the world and she is the kindest soul. She always puts other people first.' Lily sobs, clutching her forehead. 'Joanna is five foot nine, slender, with dark brown hair and hazel-brown eyes. If anyone has seen her or if you're out there listening, Joanna, please get in touch. Please come home where you belong.'

I wipe my eyes, only noticing the water down my cheek once the broadcast is over. I wasn't asked to give an appeal or address journalists. Rosie's case never came into the public eye. Not like this, the media bloating the story, everyone slurping it up. Preying on beautiful women who go missing. Uninterested in those who are already dead. It's the speculation people relish, the suspense, knowing she could still be alive right now, something horrible happening to her.

I watch the appeal again. I think about calling Pettiford.

Why didn't he ask me about Arran? Why didn't he or Cadu mention his name, or bring up my bnb guest? It must mean he's not a suspect. Unless they were playing both sides. I don't understand the police. The things they do and don't do, say and don't say.

Just after seven o'clock, Arran comes through the door. I feel a shower of relief, mixed with suspicion and misgiving.

He doesn't look good. Exhaustion pale in his face, hunching his body. Something dark about his eyes. He sits at the kitchen table. He stares at the wood, at his stoneware bowl, empty now.

I don't want to speak. I'm terrified of what words might come out of his mouth. But I can't bear the silence.

'Arran, what's going on?'

His inky eyes lift to mine. He looks at me for a long soundless moment, then takes a breath, as if about to say something. Confess or come clean. Instead, he says, 'I'm really tired, Tess. Can we just go to bed? Just sleep?'

I nod. It's the easiest option right now, so I don't have to think or worry – the world blocked out for a few hours.

He scrapes the chair on the floorboards. He comes over. I can't move, magnetism filling my body. Both energies pressing against each other: attract and repel. His hand comes towards my face. I feel his thumb brushing my chin, then his fingers down towards my chest. A split-second imagining them clamping round my neck.

But then they take my hand and we go into his room.

*   *   *

He's dreaming again, his body twitching. I lie here, rigid. After a few minutes, he goes still. Then the duvet rustles and I feel him sit up.

I pretend to be asleep, keeping my breathing light and deep. My heart pounding as I wonder what he's doing.

The mattress shifts, wobbles. Footsteps out of the room. I hear him go into the living area. Opening my eyes, I look at the door. No lights. He's moving around, quietly, bare feet soft, but the night deepens sound. And my ears are reaching for it.

There's rustling. Then silence. A thud. A sound like something opening. Faint footsteps coming back this way. I put my head back on the pillow. The footsteps stop, but he doesn't come into the room. He's standing in the doorway. I can sense him there, his outline, a black shape in the frame.

Seconds, then the footsteps move along the corridor. Behind another wall – the one I'm facing.

He's in my room.

I stare at the wall, unable to move. I can hear him in there, his feet on the floorboards.

My heartbeat's on my tongue as I listen to him moving around. Then he stops. Silence. Minutes clicking by without sound. Part of me wants to leap out of bed and confront him. Creep up behind, demand to know what he's doing.

But I lie very still, listening.

A scraping sound. Drawers? Items being handled?

The footsteps go out into the hall. He's back in here. He comes round the bed, stopping beside me.

My eyes are shut, still pretending sleep, forcing myself to breathe. Fear fizzing through my body. I can feel him standing over me. What's he going to do? This impression he has something in his hand. An object.

I remember the clay cutter I found just after he arrived. Never seen since. But he could be holding it now, the wire taut. Tension fills my nervous system, muscles urging to spring. Fight or flight.

Then his whispered voice above me, 'Please forgive me, Tess. Please understand.'

I suppress a tremor, keeping myself rigid.

He goes back round the bed and lies down. His arm slides round my stomach, pulling me into him. I don't move, his breath on my ear. The paralysing pressure only ebbing once I feel the breath thin. He's asleep again.

The pound of my heart with dread – forgive him for what?

* * *

Arran's gone to get something for lunch. He only got up at one o'clock. At ten I carefully extracted myself from his arms, then crept out and scrubbed myself in the shower, lathering soap all over my skin.

I'd been sitting on the sofa for two hours when I heard his voice from the bedroom. 'Tess?' As if he'd just woken, wondering where I was.

I didn't answer. His words in the night whispering in my ear. *Please understand.*

He was quiet, then I heard his phone, ringing through the flat. The tone cut out, but he didn't speak, as though he'd rejected the call. A minute later I heard him exhale, this long sighing breath, followed by a hushed, '*Yes.*'

Sounds of clothes before he appeared in the living area. 'Morning,' he said, coming up behind me. A moment where I wasn't sure what he was going to do. Then he kissed the crown of my head. 'Have you eaten?' Not waiting for my reply, a springiness in his tone. 'I'm going to get something delicious, my treat.'

That was fifteen minutes ago.

I've been scratching at my chest. Unconsciously, I realise, when the skin is pink and sore. It feels like the walls are smaller, shrinking in towards me.

I looked all round my room, checked inside the drawers, the cupboard, scanned every object and possession. Nothing's missing or out of place. The question of what he was doing, what he touched.

There are shadows in the corners. The sun is out, gleaming through opal cloud, but the shadows are there.

I go into the guest room. I open the wardrobe. I'm not sure what I'm looking for. That wire cutter maybe. I check between the piles, but there's nothing. I try his rucksack. Inside one of the front pouches my fingers touch something soft. I pull it out.

A small piece of material. Thin and torn, white daisy print on pistachio green. Clearly a woman's fabric. Frayed all round except for one edge, as though it's been ripped off.

I press it under my thumb, trying to squash my thoughts, the image forming in my mind. Arran grabbing her dress, yanking her back along the ground as she tries to get away.

I close my eyes for a moment. When I open them again, the colour and pattern of the material nudges. Recognition somewhere. Was Joanna wearing a top or skirt with this print at Apple & Adelaide? Or another day I saw her?

I'm so absorbed, trying to remember, that the snap of the front door is delayed in my ears.

'Hey,' Arran calls from the hallway.

I push the material back into the pouch and go through to the living area, where he's breezing round the kitchen, taking out plates and opening little cardboard boxes.

'Pastry time,' he says. 'What do you fancy? An éclair? Quiche florentine? *Tartelette framboise?*' He's putting on a French accent, playing around.

I'm standing in the middle of the room. He notices my face and stops.

'Tess? What's up?'

He puts the éclair down, the humour gone from his face. He comes over and touches my arm. But I move it away from his fingers, drawing back from him. There's worry and hurt in his eyes.

I can't stand it any longer, can't hold it in. Conviction and mettle in daylight, which the night steals. 'What did you do?'

'What?'

'What did you do to her?'

He stares at me, puzzlement shading to something else. Deeper traces in his eyes I can't identify. He swallows, Adam's apple moving in his throat.

'Tess, I . . .'

When he steps towards me, I step back, keeping space between us. His eyes are scaring me.

'Just tell me,' I say. 'What have you done? Where is she?'

His brow knits. 'Where is she?'

'Yes. *Where.*' My tone grows higher. 'Where have you taken her, hidden her, or—'

'I don't know what you mean.' The puzzlement comes back.

'You have to tell the police. You have to let her go. Let her live. Please.' My voice is shaky.

He steps towards me again. 'Tess, I think you—'

'Don't touch me. Just tell me what you've done to her!'

'Who?'

'Joanna!'

His eyes are wide, gaping at me. 'Joanna?'

'*Yes.*' My body's shaking now. 'Joanna Reynolds, the woman who's gone missing.'

Arran doesn't move. A strange noise in my ears, like that back-ringing after a music concert, eardrums still vibrating.

His mouth opens and closes. 'Tess, I'm not sure what you ...' His head shakes. 'Joanna Reynolds is OK – she turned up alive this morning.'

'What?' The back-ringing falters.

'She escaped from where the guy was holding her captive – her ex-boyfriend. I read the news earlier.'

I feel as though I've walked into a glass door. 'What? No, that ...'

I haven't checked the news today. I forgot. After what Arran said in the night, working myself up to confront him. I grab the remote and press the buttons hard, flicking through the channels to BBC News.

Inwardly, I gasp.

It's there, the headline at the bottom of the screen JOANNA REYNOLDS: MISSING WOMAN FROM LONDON FOUND ALIVE. There are filmed images, flashing police vans on a track leading to a quintessential English cottage. White and blue tape and a policeman coming out of the indigo front door. Then Joanna. A paramedic dabbing at a cut on her cheek. Joanna walking towards an ambulance and getting in the back before it drives away.

An unseen female reporter is talking over the filming.

'In the early hours of this morning, Joanna Reynolds escaped from a remote house near Sevenoaks in Kent, which you can see here on screen. The residence is a holiday cottage, let out via a website.'

The reporter pauses as they show an aerial photo of the area, the rusty-coloured roof of the cottage clear among all the green. The screen blurs. No, not the screen blurring – my eyes.

The reporter continues, 'Ms Reynolds claims she was brought here against her will.' The footage shows Joanna with a blanket round her shoulders, speaking to a pair of female police officers. One of them is Cadu. 'A man who is reported to be Ms Reynolds' ex-boyfriend has been arrested and remains in custody.'

Ex-boyfriend, my mind murmurs at me. Not Arran. Another man. The TV has gone back to the presenter in the studio and she's talking, but I can't hear her. That back-ringing has got louder.

Arran's voice is coming from behind me.

'What?' I say.

'Why would you think I did something to Joanna Reynolds?'

I turn to look at him. His face is drawn, confusion and offence in the creases. No words come into my mind. I feel a little faint.

'Tess? Why would you think that?'

Then, with gritty frustration, before I consider what I'm doing, 'I saw you together.'

'What?'

'You and Joanna. I saw you in a restaurant in Soho, and then a hotel by Liberty's.'

He stares at me.

'I know you know her, Arran.' My tone is loud and accusatory. 'I know there's something going on between you two.'

Seconds tick by, Arran looking as if he can't believe his ears. 'Yes, I know her. I mean – I'm acquainted with her. Another graphic designer, a mutual friend, recommended me to her.

Joanna's company is hiring me for some graphic design work, through Cyan Clover, my agency. We had our first meeting last week and then we had another more informal meeting on Monday, to discuss branding and style.'

I stare at him.

'Which must have been what you saw,' Arran says. 'At Foxcoal? We met there because it's part of the restaurant group I'll be doing the design work for.' Pause. 'I don't know what hotel you're talking about though.'

I can't speak. *Oh shit* repeating in my brain like the same small wave washing on shingle.

'I saw you following her,' I blurt. 'From Foxcoal.'

His forehead is drawn in. 'No. I was heading to Cyan Clover's offices in Marylebone.'

I think for a moment. Marylebone would make sense in terms of the direction he was going.

Arran's eyes are filling with hurt. 'I don't understand why you would think that. *How* you could think I would hurt her, could do something to a woman, to even . . .' He trails off, gaze gliding sideways, as though something is dawning on him. When his eyes come back to me, they're blacker. 'Have you . . . ?'

I know what's coming. I know what he's going to say, I can see it in his face.

He forces it out. 'Have you read my diary?'

I open my mouth to say something but there's only cold air.

'*Have* you?' he breathes.

My face betrays me. I can't hide it. His expression feels like skewers sliding through my ribs, long and slow and unbearable. The disbelief in his eyes. The distaste.

'I can't believe this.' He turns and starts walking away.

'No, wait, Arran.' I try to grab his arm but he yanks it out of my grasp. 'Please, wait. I'm sorry. I can explain.'

He pulls away from me again. He's too strong, striding to the door.

'Please don't go.' Desperation clogs my voice.

He slams the door behind him. I stand there, staring at the wood, my muscles quivering. Four words ringing: what have I done?

45

I can't move for a minute. My hearing zoned out. Slowly I take in the TV behind me, BBC News still reporting on Joanna.

I look at the screen.

The reporter is talking, saying something about Joanna's ex-boyfriend, and they're showing that image of her again, smiling at a summer party.

My eyes lose focus as my brain tries to sift through what just happened. Distinguish all the dots and pixels. There's a pattern in them, a picture, but I can't see it fully. I'm too zoomed in. Like a photorealist painting of someone's face – up close it's a speckled blur.

I go into Arran's room. His diary must be here. He didn't take anything with him. Despite this feeling of how deeply I've breached his trust, I have to look at it again. I find it in the bedside drawer and flick through, going over old entries, trying to find the pattern, a way to zoom out and focus the details. *You you you* everywhere, on every page. A *you* that's not Joanna.

There's a new entry at the end. A short piece of writing.

And now everything has changed.

I've been playing with fire, crazy to do what I've done. She just looks so much like you, I wanted to see her, talk to her, because it might feel like I was seeing you and talking to you. Like I hadn't lost you completely. But that was a fucking fool's hope. To be so reckless, to lie, to mess with her feelings, without any consideration of the consequences.

Too late now. A whim I can't take back.

She was too easy to find online. Too easy to watch, different people in the flat with her, coming and going. Internet trails. There on that website, her picture unmistakable. A click away.

It's mad, this whole situation. Yet how can I regret it?

Something dawned on me a few days ago. After spending time with her, knowing her – familiar with her temperament, her skin, her steadiness, her soft flowing movements. It wasn't you in the cafe that day. Your physical features are so similar, I just presumed it was the same girl at the museum. But I know now it wasn't.

It was her I saw first.

I stare at this entry, the sneak of foreboding and disbelief in my gut. The dots merging into an image.

You. Rosie.

All this time I've been reading about my sister. About her secret relationship with Arran. The nausea surges into my throat. I've had sex with the same man as her. The man she told me nothing about, kept behind my back. Behind everyone's back. Even Oliver's.

Oliver, my brain repeats. *Hampstead Heath.* What if it wasn't him that night she died? What if it was—?

The ground feels like it's slipping out from under me. I put my head between my knees and try to breathe.

Something squirms in my stomach, refusing to accept this. Refusing to believe it. Maybe Arran and Rosie had a relationship. Maybe they met and fell in love. But Arran the one who hurt her? The man I've been searching for?

I feel sick. I can't be in here. His room. My sister's room.

I walk out fast, back into the living area. Pastries, sunglasses, recycling bin. That book *The Black Tulip* on the coffee table. His stuff is everywhere I look. As I stand in the centre of the room, hovering in open space, I realise what I'm still holding.

I drop it.

The diary bounces on its spine before it lands closed. A silent story. The truth of it smirking up at me.

* * *

I'm on the floor. The boards are hard and cold against my body. I don't know how long I've been here, half an hour, two hours. I'm staring at all the dust and dirt and hairs. So many of my dark hairs.

I lift my eyes and see a corner of Rosie's painting above the sofa.

And it comes to me with a sharp smack: Rosie's things.

I go into the drawer at the base of my wardrobe and find the pair of black socks amongst belts, swimwear, miscellaneous items. Somewhere no one would think to look for a key – the one to the little storage space attached to the guest room.

I walk in there, stopping in front of the locked door in the corner. I have no idea when Arran might come back. If he comes back. I can hear the T-Rex clock from here, in the silence, its hands like a time-limit ticker.

The key slips into the lock. I turn it, the bolt scraping across. As the door swings towards me, light falls on the boxes stacked up to the ceiling. Behind them are some of Rosie's canvases.

I grab the top box, my back bending under its weight. I put it on the floor and slide it into the living area. Then I do the same with the next four. I don't want to open them in the guest room – where Arran's been breathing, his presence and possession over the space.

Five big cardboard cubes strapped up with glossy tape. Holding most of a person's life, in objects.

I grab a knife and slit all the tape. Then I yank it off the first box, heart in my throat. I open the flaps.

Kitchen stuff I couldn't face using. Pots, pans, crockery, cutlery. I check inside all the pieces of newspaper and padding. Next box – books, some wall hangings, stationery, socks, sketchbooks. Beneath that I find underwear, bags and a backpack. I pull it all out onto the floor, the pressure inside my body pushing higher.

I kick that box out of the way and pull the third over. Art stuff. Paint tubs and paintbrushes. Rags. Pencil cases of crayons, pens. Glues, sprays, all of her materials and tools. Most of it stained or dirty. A mess of creativity.

Fourth box. Inside are clothes with a faint apple smell, from her body or her laundry detergent, or both. I hold a dress into my nose, breathing it in. I have to bite my tongue to stop myself crying.

Near the bottom are some things inside bubble wrap. Ornaments. A couple of heavy items on top of towels. I rip off the bubble wrap and a cup rolls into my hand. Rustic stoneware. Pale Nordic grey-green.

My fingers are white I'm gripping it so hard. An impulse to smash it on the floor. But it's too beautiful. Too solid. It might not even break. I put it down and unwrap the other one. A bowl, similar to the one on the kitchen table. This is where I've seen Arran's ceramics before – a glimpse in the haze of packing up Rosie's belongings.

I look at the final box, frightened of what I'm going to find.

I kneel down next to it. Then I rip off the tape, like a plaster from my skin, and look inside.

More clothes on top. A bag of jewellery, all of it gold. Rosie's purse. One ten-pound note and some coins, her driving licence. There are coats and jackets, a pile of old birthday cards. One from me, making jokes, exclamation mark jolly, signed 'I love you so much.'

Bathroom things. Her toothbrush still with toothpaste marks on it. Beneath this are scarves and hats. A *sombrero cordobés* like mine. I pull it all out over the sides of the box. I'm almost at the bottom. *There has to be something.* One more scarf, a bottle of perfume, a small box made of basket weave. Inside are photos. I take out a clump. They're old film-style, taken on a disposable camera. Landscapes, pretty streets, a group of her friends.

A few of me. One where I'm sitting in the sand, grains stuck to my wet swimsuit, sunglasses in my hair. Several photos of us together. Side-by-side in a park, both holding big bowls of salad, matching red ribbon-bandeaus round our heads. Us in maxi dresses beside bougainvillea at La Feria de Sevilla.

Another with Rosie laughing, nose scrunched up. That was last summer on a day trip to Brighton. I bring it closer, peering at Rosie's face. She's half-turned, showing her left cheek. There on the bone, right up near her ear. A sunspot. It could be taken for a mole, but it only appeared in the last couple of years, after all the Andalucían sunshine.

Unobservant again. Only seeing what I want to see. What else has my brain filtered out over the past few months?

But that's all there is. Just photos.

There has to be something. That can't be it.

I scan Rosie's things all over the floor. A bunch of her sketchbooks sticking out from beneath a jacket. I grab them, flicking through. Lots of plants, indoor scenes, palm trees, drawings of houses and rooms – practice for her paintings. An older sketchbook with life drawing and faces. In all of them there are loose bits, card sticking out, paper she slotted into larger A4 and A3 books.

The last sketchbook is filled with paintings of sunsets. I remember her doing those in Spain, using a particular orange or yellow or red for each one. *Puestas de sol.*

There's one that's loose. The sun dipping down over mountains. On a piece of paper with something stuck to the back of it, I realise. Made of thick brown paper. When I pull it off, I see a splodge of orange paint that must have dried, acting like glue. And I see that it's not just brown paper – it's an envelope.

My hand is shaking as I lift the flap and grip what's inside: more photos, I can tell from the glossy surface. I take them out and my heart stops.

Arran.

He's sitting in a chair, in his denim shirt, smiling cheekily with his chin lifted. I inhale slowly before switching to the next photo. Arran again. His back walking through the flower market on Columbia Road. Next, Arran and Rosie standing together with his arm round her waist, both of them beaming.

I drop the photos.

They land upside-down, and I notice the one that was at the very bottom is bigger than the rest. A dark image with a white border. I turn it over.

An ultrasound.

That part in Arran's diary. I'd shoved it aside. I didn't want it to be real, that Rosie was pregnant, that she had a miscarriage. The pain of it all too strong. The knowledge of that happening to her, but worse, tearing at me somewhere deep – the fact she didn't tell me.

Why such secrecy? With her own sister?

Perhaps she was going to tell me that night I missed her calls and she left a voicemail, saying she wanted to be honest.

I look at the distorted image of a baby in my hand. This is why – her behaviour in those last months, the grief she must have been carrying.

There's another pain, rawer, more present. It was Arran's. Nausea swirls through me. I taste bile and run to the bathroom, throwing up into the toilet. My stomach clenches again and again, retching until there's nothing left.

Coughing, I lie on the cold tiles. I feel as though I'm hovering high in the air. Like a kestrel, perfectly still with the wind roaring past my body.

Why hadn't the police found these images when they searched the flat? Arran's pottery. The ultrasound. How could they have missed them, with their training and equipment? Sharper in my heart – how could I? This envelope particularly. I looked through everything, including her sketchbooks.

I get up and fumble for my phone in my bedroom. I call Rosie's number. It rings. Nobody picks up. I call again. Then I hear it – a dim vibrating. At first I think I'm imagining it. But then I take my phone away from my ear and it's there, coming from somewhere in the flat.

When my call goes to voicemail, the vibrating stops. I press the button again and it comes back. I follow the sound. Buzzing louder, louder as I go into Arran's room. Buzzing beneath his bed. I crouch down and see the light glowing on the material of his duffel bag. My fingers grope inside, finding the hard shape.

I pull it out. Simple graphite plastic, compact, light in my hand. *Tess* flashing on the small square screen.

Rosie's phone.

She's in deep.

Like me, but in a different hole. Her head is still above ground. I feel like I'm scrabbling at the sides, skin on my fingers raw. Blood and earth in my mouth. No way out.

Except her hand. Appearing above me, stretching down from the dark. So beautiful. A warm brown against the silent trees, the pitiless sky.

Asking me to take it.

46

The robotic voicemail drones just as I hear feet on the stairs. Those light scuffing steps, climbing fast.

I go back into the living area, not wanting to be in that room – something in me searching for space.

His eyes, in the doorway. Pale and red.

'Tess, I want to—'

Arran sees the mess on the floor. His gaze sweeping over the boxes and Rosie's things everywhere. Then his eyes land on the phone in my hand. Alarm shimmers through them.

'Tess, I can explain.'

'Why the fuck do you have Rosie's phone?' I breathe.

'It's not what it looks—'

'Why was her phone in your bag?'

All this time, it was him. The faceless man, the one who killed Rosie, he's been in my guest room. In my bed. His bare skin on mine.

Arran raises his palms.

'It was you on Hampstead Heath,' I accuse. 'You were there.'

'What?'

'You hurt her.'

Arran's eyes are wide with shock. '*What?* I would never have hurt her, Tess.'

'Liar.' Venom infuses my voice. 'You're the reason she's dead.'

His head shakes, taking a step forward.

'Don't come near me.'

'I wasn't on Hampstead Heath that night. I wish I had been.' The pain in his face is marked. 'I wish she hadn't run out on me in that restaurant, but she was gone, and I had no way of contacting her or finding her, because she left her phone behind.'

'What?'

'That evening, the twenty-sixth of January, she messaged asking to see me. I agreed to meet her at some restaurant. We sat at the bar, and she seemed good at first, more like her old self, but then she slipped back again. Suddenly she said she needed the toilet. By the time I realised she'd gone, it was too late. Her phone was on the bar beside me, left behind.'

'That's a lie,' I say, clinging to my conviction.

Arran's face is damp – shiny with sweat. He sucks a breath in through his mouth.

'Tess, please listen to me. I came back because I had to be honest with you. I know I've fucked up in lots of ways. I shouldn't have done this – come here to stay in your spare room, lied to you about who I am.' The earnest urgency makes his voice a whine. 'When I realised you'd been reading my diary the shock was . . .' His mouth opens like a goldfish.

My teeth are gritted, pressure between the molars.

'I was angry,' he says. 'It was an intrusion into my privacy—'

'Are you kidding? Like you intruding here, into *my* privacy? My home?'

His expression drops, strained and white.

'You're the intruder here, Arran.' My throat's sore from my stomach acid. 'The imposter. Who even are you?'

He's quiet before he answers. 'You know who I am, Tess. I may not have told you the whole truth of my past, how I'm connected to you, but I never pretended. Everything here, our conversations, what we've shared – it was me. It's real.'

Fear is creeping up through the anger. This man who hurt my sister, blocking the door, the only way out of this flat.

'Like I said, I was angry, but then I was terrified.' There's a strange sound in Arran's throat. 'Because you'd read it all – you knew the story. Everything that had happened. Then I thought maybe it's not so terrible. I didn't need to tell you or describe what I found so hard to say out loud. It was all there written down.' He swallows. 'But you didn't seem to know who it's about. And I had to come and tell you—'

'What? That it's Rosie?'

His breaths are uneven. 'When I came in, I could see it in your face. You knew. And . . .' He glances down, noticing the photos on the floor. The ultrasound on top. His jaw muscles flex. 'You've seen for yourself. I always wondered where these photos were. And the . . .' He turns sideways, looking away from it. 'The ultrasound. Wondered how you hadn't seen them. Why you didn't recognise me.'

'Didn't recognise you?' I repeat. 'Well, that must have been funny, when I opened the door and introduced myself. Joke's on me, right?' I'm trying to deflect the fear, but it's in the beat of my heart. Closing in.

'There is no joke, Tess. I wish there was.' His voice is weighed down. 'I wish we could laugh it all away and go back to the way we were.'

'I wish you'd never written a diary. Why did you? Why did you have to write about my sister and leave it around for me to find? Didn't you think that was stupid, dangerous even?'

He steps towards me, but I move backwards. Instinct to keep him at a distance.

'It was,' he acknowledges. 'It was careless and stupid. Though I never wrote her name.'

'Oh yeah, wasn't that oh-so-clever of you.'

'I wasn't trying to be clever, Tess. It wasn't a calculated or intentional thing. It just came out that way. The psychiatrist I'd been seeing suggested I write to Rosie, write what happened, get it all out on paper, as a way of coming to terms with it.'

'Psychiatrist?'

'Yes. I thought I was OK, thought I was dealing with it. But since January, since she . . .' He struggles to get the word out. 'I haven't been myself. I couldn't come to her funeral – do you know what that was like? Nobody knew me. None of her family or friends. I was unwelcome, a stranger. I didn't get a chance to say goodbye.'

I can't speak, my throat burning, with him trying to make out how much he's suffered. I glance through the window. The sky has shadows. Arran is closer, shoulders above me. The depth and weight of his body suddenly there.

'I've been messed up, Tess. Really messed up. If it hadn't been for my sister—'

'Bullshit,' I breathe. 'You're full of shit, Arran. What is this – all an act?'

'*No.*' He looks wounded, like I just cut him. 'You have to understand.' He rubs his forehead then lifts his hands. 'I *was* a mess – until you. Until I came here and met you and felt something lift. Just to see you, talk to you, each moment felt like a piece of happiness I didn't think I'd ever feel again.'

My head is shaking. 'I don't believe you. You're lying.'

'I'm not. I'm telling you the truth.'

'You're a liar. And a coward. I may have been gullible, taken in by you all this time, but I won't be the dupe any longer.'

Arran comes towards me again, and I step back into the last bit of space. The wall's behind. I'm backed into a corner.

'Tess, please stop this. Please listen to me. I have been a coward, and I'm so sorry.' The veins in his neck are showing with the force of his feeling. 'But you've changed everything.'

I stare at him, heart pulsing through my raw throat.

'Do you hear what I'm saying? I love you.' The intensity coming off him is like a quartz heater. 'I just want to be close to you, I need to see your face, talk to you and . . . touch you.'

I want to back up further, get away from him, but there's nowhere to go. The safety of my own home taken from me. 'Stop it! I don't want to hear this.'

He doesn't listen. 'You're so similar to her, and yet your character – we're much more suited. We fit together so easily.' His face is inches from mine. His hands grip my upper arms. 'Your body against mine, your beauty. It feels so smooth, so close. With Rosie there were all these jagged edges, these spikes between us.'

I struggle against his grasp, but he's too strong. I drop one of the phones I'm holding, trying to pull myself away. Arran just grips harder.

'We couldn't help hurting each other,' he says. 'We weren't right for one another. But *we* are – you and me.'

'*Basta!*' I screech, still struggling. 'Let me go.'

And he does, his hands sliding off my arms. I dart round and whirl to face him. 'How dare you say those things about her. How dare you demean my sister like this, after she's gone.'

'It's the truth, Tess.'

Something about his face, the weak watery expression, inflames the grief and rage I've been keeping down all these months.

'Your soul, it's the same colour as mine,' he says. 'It's one of the only certainties I have, that—'

'You killed my sister.'

His features shift, something dropping over them. 'No. I didn't.' He speaks the words slowly. A harsh note in their hush.

'Why didn't you hand in her phone then?' I demand. It's the one I'm still holding. 'Why didn't you help the police?'

He doesn't answer, a flicker in his eyes.

My thumb feels for number 9 on the keypad, but Arran's in front of me, his hands clamping round my wrists. The sudden pressure does something to my grip, and Rosie's phone slides from my fingers. Landing with a dim thud.

'I couldn't do anything, Tess. I was in stalemate. *Listen* to me.' I'm struggling when his arm rings my waist and his other hand holds my face. 'That night, I came to her flat to drop her phone back, but she wasn't here. I waited for nearly two hours. It was freezing, so I went home, intending to try again in the morning.' His fingers are digging into my neck. 'But then I saw it on the news, a woman found dead on Hampstead Heath. Her name at the bottom of the screen, and everything crashed in on me.'

I try to turn my face away from him.

'Do you know what I've felt since that day? The guilt, the what ifs.' His breath is hot on my forehead. 'That I wasn't there to help her. It's been eating me alive.'

There's a smashing sound from the street, followed by a shout. Dark out there now.

Arran continues, firm and vehement. 'Since I came here, I realised it must have been the same for you. I've realised maybe no one could have helped her. We all tried—'

'No one could have helped her?' I echo in disbelief.

'Yes, I—'

'Get off me,' I spit.

'Tess.' His arms are solid around my body.

'Don't touch me!'

'How can you not believe me?' he asks while my hands push against his chest. 'It's me – you know me. You honestly think I could do something like that?'

Half of me believes him, wanting him to be innocent, to have never laid a hand on Rosie. But the other half tells me not to be so gullible. It says: *Someone you know*. Just like Joanna's ex-boyfriend.

I scratch at his arms. He's not letting go, his eyes bloodshot. I whack him in the chin. He's really not letting go, his fingers pressing hard into my skin. Hurting me. I grab his shirt, twisting the cotton up. 'Let go!'

'I can't. *Please*.'

We knock into a chair. We're by the kitchen table. I look sideways for something to grab, and I see his stoneware bowl. Just as I do his grip loosens. He's giving up. But then he tries to kiss me.

My fingers find the bowl as I rip my face away from his. I grip the base and swing it towards him.

The clunk against his skull is a deep hollow sound. A dull crack of bone.

Surprise clouds his face before he falls backwards. The bowl rolls out of my fingers, the weight of it tipping away, smashing just as Arran hits the floor.

Silence. Dark and sudden and sheer, like looking over a cliff-edge into still pitch water, and the only way is down.

He's on top of Rosie's clothes. Unconscious. Head resting on something creamy yellow. As I stare, the cream starts to turn red. A blotch seeping wider around his skull.

What have I done? What have I done?

I watch the blood blotting the cotton of Rosie's dress, a clump of his golden hair stained, thick and wet. I drop to my knees beside him.

'Arran?'

I put my ear to his mouth, but I can't hear anything. My fingers fumble for a pulse in his wrist. I can't find one. Frantic, I try his neck, pressing my fingers in. And it's there. The thrum of his heart.

A gasp of relief. But it disintegrates.

I've cracked his skull. What if I've put him in a coma? What if he dies from brain trauma?

I need to call an ambulance. I snatch up my phone and start typing 9. But something makes me stop. Something makes me delete the 9s and go into my contacts. My whole body's trembling, shudders through my spine.

Brr-ing in my ear. *Please pick up.*

It goes to voicemail. After the tone, 'Nalika, I need your help. I don't know what to do. I've done something awful. I think I should call the police, but I'm too scared to.' I look at

Arran. That halo of red. 'I'm at home and . . . Oh God, if you're there, please pick up.'

I hang up and feel cold air on the back of my neck. Like a draught or disturbance from somewhere. A breath of dried grass. When I look up there's someone on the window, reflected in the dark glass. A blurred figure behind me.

47

Ivy is in the living room doorway, looking down at Arran. There's a suspended moment, time somehow elastic. No oxygen in my lungs.

Her eyes are fixed on his bloodied head.

'Tess,' she says. 'What have you done?'

I can't speak, the panic feels like quicksand.

'Is he dead? Did you kill him?'

I find a voice. 'He has a pulse.'

'Just unconscious then?'

I nod.

She steps towards him, leaning over his feet. As though she doesn't want to get too close. Her arms folded and her face blank. She doesn't crouch down or check for signs of life. She just says, 'Hm.'

A strange feeling comes on, dark in my abdomen.

I stand up. 'What are you doing here?'

'I heard some noises, a big thump and crash, and came to check if you were OK.' Her tone reminds me of a child's. Casual, glossed with innocence.

'How did you get in?'

She points her thumb over her shoulder. 'Your front door was ajar.'

Why don't I believe her? It's her air, the flippant look in her eye. Always jesty, only now it seems shaded with something else.

'Where's Luke?'

'Dunno.' She sounds bored. 'We broke up. He wasn't worth the effort anymore.'

I feel my brow tighten.

'Though he's had his uses, the chump. Just as this one has.' She nudges Arran's leg with her foot. She's wearing those trainers again, rose-gold with a flatform sole.

The dark feeling in my stomach deepens. Something's very wrong. Something rotten. I can sense the mould – in her, in this whole situation, Arran bleeding on the floor, Ivy standing over him, scratching her collarbone.

'He's provided entertainment,' she says. 'And kept you distracted.' Sighing, she swings her arms. 'It got a bit much, all that reading, then the stalking. First it was amusing, the way you chased after him, metaphorically and literally. Then it became tiresome.'

Her words vibrate on my eardrums. That hand in the phone light on Hackney Marshes. The figure on Hampstead Heath. Glimmers and glints. Of her?

She looks at Arran, expression souring. 'Arran bloody Cole. He's like an insect, worming his way into the people I have a core connection to, an exceptional feeling, using his looks and charm to dupe them. Closer than I can ever seem to get.'

I feel like there's a muzzle over my mouth, hard to breathe as the feeling sinks into me – I've made a mistake. A terrible mistake.

'I'm thirsty,' she says. 'Mind if I have a drink?'

I twist over my shoulder to look at her. She's taking a bottle out of the fridge. One of my Alhambra beers. Subtly, I reach towards my phone. The cerveza cap pings off and tinkles onto the floorboards. I swipe to get the emergency keypad. Ivy slurps some beer, her steps sauntering back towards me. I start typing 9.

I'm about to press the call button when her foot stamps on my hand. Pain sears through my palm, her flatform squashing the bones.

'Uh-uh-uh, what are you doing?'

I gasp. Throbs of pain as she sways her weight over me.

I yank my hand out from under her trainer. She picks up the phone, sliding it into the back pocket of her jeans. Then she leans over Arran and sniffs. 'Are you sure you didn't kill him?'

A wave of nausea goes through my torso. He needs help – medical attention.

She crouches down and touches his hair. A finger feeling the blood.

'Don't do that,' I say.

'What? This?' She pokes him in the cheek.

'Don't touch him.' My voice is raspy but stronger. I step towards him, trying to back her off.

'Aw, no worries, Tess. He's not dead – yet.'

'Get away from him.'

'OK, OK.' She holds up her palm, sidling away. 'What did you hit him with anyway? He's really out cold.'

I crouch and feel his wrist again. He *is* cold. What does that mean? I shake his arm. I put my mouth on his, trying to blow air in.

Ivy's reedy voice comes from behind, 'I don't think that's going to help much.'

I don't know what else to do to revive him.

'*Bien hecho*,' she says, a smirk in her tone. 'Isn't that what you say in Spanish?'

'Give me my phone!' I screech.

'No.'

'I need to call an ambulance.'

She swallows beer. 'He'll be all right. Besides, he's not important.'

There's no emotion in her demeanour or body. No concern for another person's life. I think about sprinting for the door – try to reach the street or shout into the stairwell. But she'd catch me. And she does something that makes me go cold.

Ivy picks up Rosie's phone from the floor.

Since she appeared behind me, the mould has been growing, looming into shape. I watch her holding the phone, her thumb rubbing over the screen.

The whisper of how blinkered I've been, looking right through glass, not seeing the person behind it. Smiling at me, red hair blowing in the wind. How wrong I was, about Oliver, Arran, all of it. The realisation is like opening your eyes and finding yourself in a black room. A lightless space of your own making.

'Where's this been?' Ivy murmurs. Then her face shifts. 'Arran had it, didn't he?'

She hasn't looked at me, gazing at the phone like some precious object. A gemstone or baby animal, her thumb still stroking. I want to snatch it from her, sickened by her fingers all over it. But before I can, she puts it in the other back pocket of her jeans.

She looks around at the boxes and the stuff on the floor, as though she's only just noticed. 'I recognise that dress. That paintbrush, that necklace. This is all her stuff, isn't it?'

Her. Ivy's first reference to my sister.

More whispers. The jogger Rosie mentioned bumping into her, who she thought she recognised. Ivy stayed in flat 74c opposite last autumn, when Rosie was living here. And in Arran's diary, Rosie telling him a girl was following her around, annoying her.

My sister's killer. Here in my home, drinking beer.

For a moment, the idea injects fear into my limbs, scared of what this girl's capable of. But then it dispels. Another feeling beneath my feet, humming up from the ground they've been on since Rosie died. This is what I've been waiting for. Actively seeking.

To face the person who took her from me.

Ivy puts down the bottle and picks something up from the floor, its corner poking out under Rosie's scarf.

'The diary, I see. Which has had you *so* hooked.' She flicks through it.

I watch her, turning a page, reading. Eyes sliding over lines.

'Hm.' She glances up and meets my gaze, with a gleam of emotion. Cagey, yet exposed. Like that day she was clutching the aftersun. 'I considered writing about her myself, you know.' She looks at the pages again, sadness pinching into her face.

Ivy drops the diary onto Rosie's clothes and grips the base of her throat.

It's quiet. No sounds in the building, or from the street. The sun has gone. Beyond the lit-up room, there's no dusk. Only oil-black sky.

'Admit it,' I say.

Her hand drops from her throat. 'Admit what?'

My fingers curl into a fist, nails biting into my palm.

'That I like you?' she says. 'Fine. I do. And I know you like me too, Tess. I know enough about you to see it, in your face. Hear it in your voice. Other than Arran and that idiot friend of yours, Nalika, I can tell you find most people either a bore or disappointing.'

I stare at her, the extent of her surveillance becoming clear.

'You're not very nice to a lot of folk, you know,' she says. 'So when you were kind, when you smiled, complimented me . . . I knew.'

She's been watching me, in the flat, on the street, listening in.

I glance at Arran, still motionless on the floor. I swung the bowl into his skull, but she's the source. Ivy, just like the creeping plant, insidious, squeezing the life out of whatever it grows on.

'Rosie,' I say.

Ivy blinks her mascara-thick lashes at me.

'You followed her onto Hampstead Heath that night in January.'

Her eyes don't leave my face, losing focus. Like she's seeing something else. Her jaw moving – chewing the inside of her lower lip. 'Yes,' she says abruptly. 'I did.'

So simple. I can't believe I've heard it. *Yes*. An admission weighted and glittering.

'Owh, hold on a sec.' There's a vibrating sound. She takes my phone from her pocket and looks at the screen. 'Nalika calling.' She turns it so I can see. Then she switches it off.

My heartbeat feels like a mallet. Nalika trying to call me. Help blocked out.

'What did you do, Ivy? What the fuck did you—'

'Don't go jumping to conclusions, Tess. I can see judgement in your face, and what makes you think you're in a position to judge? Huh?' She's stepped forward, her reedy tone loud in the silence.

I hold my ground.

'What do you think? I'm the sinner, the villain in all this? My devout Catholic mother will get out of her grave before she hears such insult.'

'You hit her over the head,' I say.

'My mam? Believe me, I wish I had. She was callous, an evil crab of a—'

'Rosie! You killed her.'

A shadow grows into Ivy's eyes, rimmed by the black liner. 'It's *so* easy for you, isn't it? Everything just flows, light and lovely and effortless. What struggles or suffering have you ever had? What have you come up against in your life?'

Bitterness is rising to the surface, leaking out of her like gas.

'An emotionally abusive mother? Boiled carrots and rice most nights for dinner because my dad spent all our money on lottery tickets and sport bets? Going to bed hungry?' The words are spewing out of her, a run-on sentence. 'Bullied since I was seven, tormented year after year. Even when I changed schools, from female-only to mixed, the girls seemed to sense it straight away. The looks they'd give me, the things they'd do. Their words and laughter.'

I'm clenching my teeth. Pressure building through my whole body.

'As if there was a smell on me I could never get rid of.' Her voice quavers. 'Even at university, I never quite fit in. I had boyfriends, guy friends, but ... always this distance, this gap between me and women. Treated with indifference, if I was even noticed.'

Ivy rubs the back of her skull. Then she touches Rosie's velvet skirt hanging over one of the boxes.

'But not you,' she says, quieter. 'Not Rosie. She *saw* me. I remember the first time she looked at me – she really looked, into my eyes. She stopped me in the street and told me she loved my dungarees, asked where they were from.' Her face lifts with the memory. 'A week later, she sat down next to me on a bench and started sketching trees. Such beautiful drawings. She recognised me when I said hello, and smiled. Before she left, she ripped out one of the sketches and gave it to me. Just like that.'

The T-Rex clock is ticking. It feels like it's inside my chest. Hearing all of this, now, hearing her talk about Rosie, is winding into me.

'She was so warm,' Ivy continues, eyelids closing for a moment. 'Beautiful, confident, kind. Obviously part of the in-crowd, but nothing like the other "cool"' – she makes quotation marks – 'girls. It gave me hope, made me realise what's possible.' She bites her thumbnail. 'But then it wasn't so easy. I kept seeing her around, and she didn't seem interested, she barely acknowledged me, even looked right through me. I didn't understand.' Her complaining tone suggests Rosie was at fault. 'We were becoming friends. Why didn't she want to exchange numbers, chat, meet up?'

Maybe it's because she was going through something, I think. *Maybe it's because she was struggling, depressed, and you didn't even notice, didn't know her well enough to realise.* That's what I want to say, but I can't speak, can't interrupt, needing to hear this to the end.

'I was forced to go to extremes,' she says. 'Forced to follow her just so I could be near her, to wait outside her flat for a glimpse of her. She left me no other choice.' Her pupils seem too big. 'She'd made me feel even more hollow than before. I felt so sad, so angry, that what I thought was a real friendship was turning out to be a sham. The disappointment, the trick of it . . .' She shifts her head. 'And then she started doing stupid things. Out alone at night. I just wanted to make sure she was OK. To be there in case anything happened.'

She makes a sucking sound on the roof of her mouth. 'That night in January I was following her again, and she was all over the place, shaky on her feet, not wearing enough clothes. She fell down on the heath and I tried to help her up. She shrugged me off first, then she started telling me to get away from her, screaming at me, accusing me of stalking her, calling me a freak. She wouldn't shut up, she was really upsetting me, and I lost my temper.'

Ivy looks at me with gleaming eyes. 'I didn't mean to. It was only a little knock. Then she tried to run away from me. I went after her, I wanted to apologise, to make her understand, but she didn't give me a chance. When I reached for her, she lashed out. We were tussling. I shoved her. She tripped on a root and hit her head on that tree.'

It's quiet. Stark silence inside my head, as though all this time there have been voices murmuring at me, echoing on high walls. A background hiss. Suddenly hushed.

'It was an accident, you see?' she says, with more urgency. 'It wasn't my fault. She was just lying there and she wouldn't get up. There was no blood, like *this*.' She points her eyes at Arran. 'But I didn't know what to do. I was scared. I ran away. I assumed she was unconscious and would wake up. But she never did.'

I stare at this girl in my living room, standing among Rosie's possessions. Some clingy friendship turning to poison. Speaking as if my sister's death had nothing to do with her.

'It was so sad,' Ivy says, bowing her head. 'I couldn't believe she was dead. I had to go away, back to Ireland. But when I returned to London the anguish was still too much. I missed her, I wanted to get closer again, have that feeling back. It was too tempting, Elliot's spare room, to be across from the flat she'd lived in. So I took it. And then I saw you.'

I feel the rage crawling back up – from earlier, only misdirected, no longer aimed at the man on the floor.

'I'd seen you before, of course. Glimpses of you with her, snippets of conversation. I'd been so focused on her, I hadn't taken much notice of anyone else. But then ... it was like another Rosie. The pair of you with such shiny lives. Moving through the world with ease and confidence. And you were right there, across the street.' She looks out through the window, towards her flat. Then turns back to me. 'Here was my second chance. My redemption, maybe.'

My eyes are damp. I can't take much more, but while she's talking I glance at Arran, then at the window. My subconscious brain trying to figure out what to do. A way out of this.

'I tried to ignore you at first, telling myself don't get sucked in. But,' she opens her palms, 'that didn't last. Especially once Luke had introduced me to you, and you were chatting to me.' The rhythm of her words is lighter. 'Once we started becoming friends.'

'Friends?' I say.

She smiles. 'Yes.'

'Are you crazy?'

Her smile sinks. 'Don't call me that.'

'How could we ever be *friends* when you killed my sister?'

Her face changes then. Darkens.

'You're sad and jealous, Ivy, latching onto people. You could never have a second chance with me.' I feel a judder through my body. 'You're deranged.'

Ivy's glassy eyes stare into mine.

A moment of stillness before she lunges at me, her arm swinging into my face. The shock takes the breath out of me, though I half-knew it was coming. I fall to the floor and she's on top of me, twisting my hair up, locking my head back.

'How could you?' she spits. 'I told you, it was an accident. I'm not deranged. It's *you*. You only think about yourself, you don't consider how you impact others.'

She rams my head into the floor. My forehead conks on the boards, my nose squashed. A dizzy throbbing behind my eyes.

'Are you listening to me, Tess? You and Rosie are the ones to blame, blind and ignorant and disrespectful.' Her elbow is jammed against my neck, her weight firm on my back. 'All I wanted was to be part of your lives. Is that too much to ask?' She yanks my hair again. 'I should have known – should have learned my lesson from Rosie. Tearing me up like that. And here you are doing it all over again.'

Her weight lifts off me. As I'm about to scramble up she kicks me in the ribs. Even with the rubber toe of her trainer, the pain is piercing. She kicks again. I gasp.

She goes to kick me once more. But as her foot lifts I grab her other ankle, tugging with all my strength, sweeping her feet out from under her. She lands on her back with a shriek.

I jump to my feet. I look around for something to defend myself with. Arran's ceramics are among Rosie's clothes and ornaments. But then I see Rosie's phone on the floor. It must have slipped out of Ivy's pocket. Split-second decision to dive for it, but Ivy gets there first. She kicks it away before kneeing me in the chin. I go sprawling, a metallic taste in my mouth. Blood. A hunk of my cheek bitten off. I spit it out.

I feel Ivy's hand on my shoulder as she hauls me up towards her.

Her face is blotchy, mascara smudged beneath her lashes. She's twisting my arm, pressing it round my back. I manage to jab my other arm towards her, elbowing her in the jaw. Her grip loosens for a second. I yank myself away and use my body weight to swing back round with all the force I have, my knuckles crunching into her nose.

The pain in my hand is white, shooting through the bones. Way deeper than when I hit Oliver. Ivy lurches away, but her face is back too fast. I try to hit her again but she blocks my arm. Then her fist slams into my face.

The blow shoots through my skull before I hit the floor. The air knocked out of me. I cough, wheezing into my lungs. And when I look up, my chest turns to ice.

'No!' I screech.

Ivy is crouched over Arran, her hand on his face. Her nails digging into his cheeks as she presses her palm to his mouth. 'What's that? You don't want me to polish him off?'

I push myself up.

'You don't want me to do this?' She thumps him on the skull.

I run at her, tackling her off him. We land on one of Rosie's boxes, among her clothes and painting stuff. Within seconds Ivy has rolled on top of me, her legs clamped round my ribs. Her hands on my neck.

Her fingers jam into my throat, squeezing my windpipe. I can't breathe.

'Why are you doing this?' she shouts, tears down her cheeks.

Blood pulses through my temples. My legs are flailing beneath her. I try to scream. I scratch at her arms. She's biting her lower lip, her thumbs pressing harder.

Just as my vision begins to blur, I notice something beside us. A metallic sheen.

Poking out from bubble wrap is one of Rosie's kitchen knives. I can reach it. My fingers grope into the plastic and find the handle. Ivy is sputtering. I can't hear her words, but her lips are moving.

With a heave of strength, I pull out the knife and plunge it into her leg. I feel the blade slice through jeans, tissue, slide deep into flesh.

Ivy's eyes bulge. Her fingers loosen from my neck. My hand is blood-soaked. I yank out the knife and stab it in again, lower down her leg. She tips off me, her body twitching. It's only as I hear her howl that I realise I've been screaming. And that someone's hammering on the door. Blue light flashing through the windows.

I sit up, coughing, searing pain in my throat. There's blood all over me. Ivy is rocking and moaning, gripping her leg. Then she slumps down.

Police are yelling, banging on wood.

48

Andalucían sunsets are quieter than other landscapes. I remember one in Granada. From Mirador de San Miguel, standing at dusk with Rosie, watching the colours on the Alhambra palace fortress, and on the mountains. Another over an olive grove, the small trees black and still, not a murmur in the hills.

Now, the sun is dipping into the sea and the air is mellow.

Behind me, above the white buildings of the town, swifts soar – skimming over roofs, chasing each other, their calls a gentle hisk. Some people think it's a screech, but to me it's soothing, a far-off sound near the clouds. Summer-sweet from all the Junes, Julys, Augusts spent here since childhood, with my sister.

Not like those birds in England, when I went to visit Rosie's grave. When I took her ultrasound and buried it in the earth near the house we grew up in. She'd mentioned once she hated the idea of being in a cemetery, with some cold tombstone above her. She wanted to be near animals and nature. So we'd buried her in a field beside a wood, a tree planted above her. I hadn't been back since the funeral.

Her beech sapling was taller, its leaves a vivid green. I dug a hole and placed the ultrasound beside an earthworm, knowing that might bring a smile to Rosie's face. She loved them when we were little, putting one on my pillow once, finding it hilarious when I yelped and leapt out of bed.

Those memories came to me with an inner smile as I covered the ultrasound and the worm in soil. I felt the image of her baby belonged there, something that was no longer a secret hidden away, but returned to her.

Even as I felt a small release, something restored, there were remnants of the uneasy feeling I'd had since that night. Ivy creeping and clinging. She's been pulled down, ripped off mine and Rosie's skin.

When I stabbed her, she lost a lot of blood. The knife sliced an artery and her heart nearly failed. The paramedics managed to stem the flow, rushing her off to hospital in an ambulance.

Part of me wanted to stop them. Pull them off her and watch the blood leak out until it was too late. Let her die. But I didn't move, pity somewhere distant. A dim sheen of compassion among the anger and pain.

I watched them take her away, ginger hair dangling off the stretcher. One of her shoes left behind. The rose-gold colour was spattered with blood.

Pettiford arrived on the scene, followed by Cadu. I hadn't expected to see her ever again. The astonishment on both their faces was wide and pale. They took me to the police station. They needed a statement.

I don't remember what they asked. I couldn't concentrate. My throat was still stinging and my face ached where Ivy had hit me. I told them everything. About Arran's secret relationship with Rosie, him coming here, staying in the guest room without telling me who he was. His diary. What Ivy had done, how she was responsible for my sister's death on Hampstead Heath. How she'd attacked me and tried to strangle me. I had no choice but to stab her. She was going to kill me too.

Elliot confirmed my story. He got home and saw Ivy hit me through the window, then Arran on the floor, the blood – through his high-tech binoculars, which apparently Ivy had been using to watch me. He ran outside, calling the police while trying to get into my building. But the street door was shut and no one answered the buzzers.

It turned out that was the second call reporting an emergency in 77b Ravengale Road. Nalika had already dialled 999 and told them I was in trouble, though she didn't know the extent of it.

When the police said I could go, my statement complete, Nalika was there in the waiting room. She hugged me so hard it hurt, the bruising on my ribs beneath her arms. I said how sorry I was. She told me to stop talking twaddle. She was sorry, and so happy I was all right.

She sat next to me while I called my parents. Pettiford had said he would need to formally contact them too, but he'd let me tell them first. Dialling the number, after so long without speaking, I was worried they might not answer.

It was my dad who picked up. I made him put me on speaker so they could both listen. The words as hard for me to voice as they were for them to hear – the silence once I'd finished an indicator of that.

But then I heard my mum grab the phone, the rustle and clack of her hand on plastic, asking if I was all right, if I was hurt. Once I'd reassured her I was fine, her tone shifted. Wanting to know if the police had these two people, saying she couldn't believe I'd let either of them into my home. I stayed silent, allowing her to say what she needed. Then I told her about Rosie's pregnancy. I thought that part needed to be spoken in person. But I didn't know when that would be, and my parents deserved the whole truth.

I had to repeat it to my dad when she let go of the phone without a word. His response was he had to go. Before the line clicked, I relayed that Pettiford would be in touch.

Afterwards, Nalika drove me to the hospital. When I got there, they wouldn't let me see Arran. They said they needed to examine me first in case I had internal bleeding. Two hours later I was allowed into his room.

I hesitated as I touched the door. A medley of emotions thrumming through me.

He was lying on his back. Eyes wide, a blankness to the colour. I walked over, halting before I got too close.

'I need to . . .' I stopped, changed what I was going to say. 'I wanted to see that you were all right.'

He blinked and turned his head towards me. He'd woken up moments after the police broke down my front door. Eyes glazed but open. They took him away in a second ambulance.

'I'm sorry I hurt you,' I said.

He was staring at me, as though he'd lost his voice. His skin was drained of colour, and I thought how handsome his face was, even like that, with a bandage round his skull, half-shaved, scalp exposed. A face I wanted to be rid of, along with Ivy's. One day, I hoped they would fade back.

Suddenly Arran spoke. 'That girl fooled us all.'

Neither of us could say her name.

'I'm so sorry, Tess,' he blurted. 'I didn't mean to—'

'I don't want your apologies, Arran. Or your lies. I don't want anything. I just came to say goodbye.' My voice was as cold as my chest felt. 'I hope you find what you're looking for, whatever that is, because it certainly isn't me.'

He gazed at me some more, then his body sank further into the pillow, eyes dropping away. 'I understand. You won't see me again.'

Of course you won't, I thought. The police will make sure of that.

He wasn't looking at me. That's how I wanted it, for those eyes to never look at me again. Thinking how he didn't kill my sister, didn't hurt her physically, but he crept his way into her life. Into mine. A cream moth, silently fluttering. Hiding in our clothes.

I watched his face for a moment before turning and walking out.

Reflection is a strange thing. When things slowly sink and settle at the bottom, they're not what they were at the surface. For a time, conscious of Arran and Ivy's absorption, of that sense of being watched without knowing, I kept my gaze on the ground. I wouldn't meet anyone's eye.

But eyes are a window – into that person, and into yourself. Mirrors everywhere. In glass, metal, rivers. Even puddles and pools of light.

I passed a small lake on the way to Rosie's grave. Leaning over the water, her features were there, yet I didn't draw away. I looked carefully at my reflection.

Then I sat beside her tree and pressed my hand into the ground. The birds got louder, calling at dusk. Jackdaws and crows, I think. I wanted to be there with her in silence, so I had to wait until it was dark and the birds had fallen quiet.

Since landing in Málaga a month ago, walking into the Costa del Sol air, the anxiety has softened beneath the warmth and sounds of Spain. Laughter outside cafes, music in the plaza. The sun burning deep into the ground. Its heat is still here in the night, warm wind blowing through the window when I can't sleep. My body tense with memory. Ivy's fingers round my throat.

She confessed in the hospital, a few days after she woke up. Then came a hearing, with her pleading guilty for manslaughter and attempted murder. Her sentence hasn't been given yet, but it will be long – possibly life in prison.

'She won't be able to come near you or your family again,' Pettiford said.

I told him I was going to Spain. That I'd decided to move there and sell the flat in London. Nalika helped me with it. The agent, the legalities, and packing up all mine and Rosie's things. We took a lot of it to charity shops. They could be someone else's possessions, if they wanted them. I kept just a few important pieces. Her artwork, photos, a few ornaments, our jewellery.

Before I left, I wrote Oliver a letter. I couldn't face him. And I don't imagine he wants to see me again. Pettiford said that when he questioned Oliver about being outside my flat, he denied it. He said he was nowhere near Ravengale Road that day.

I'm not the only one who lies. Who twists the truth of the things they do, to other people and themselves.

Apparently Joanna's ex-boyfriend just wanted to talk. They'd met in Greenwich Park and he'd offered to drive her home, but instead he drove her to a cottage where they were supposed to have had a holiday, booked through a third-party website. He was trying to convince her to stay with him. He wouldn't let her leave until she agreed to get back together.

Desperation is a powerful state, it can stretch people, make us do things beyond explanation.

The flat on Ravengale Road got snapped up by a young family. Perhaps they don't know the story of 77b. Perhaps they don't watch the news. They didn't seem to notice the new patch of floorboards, replacing the blood-dyed wood.

It seems odd to think of strangers in my home, their footsteps through the rooms, their stuff everywhere. It must look quite different.

The swifts are swirling through the sky, darting shapes, smoky grey against the evening light. They'll be flying south again soon, through Africa, down beyond the Sahara, living on the wing.

The sand is warm under my feet. I can still feel the sun on my face. Shadows of palm trees stretch across the beach and there's the murmur of Spanish voices from restaurants further along the shore. A girl is silhouetted in the shallows.

Tomorrow I'm going to Sevilla, to see my parents. On the phone yesterday my mum's voice cracked, asking me to come, saying she needed me, she needed to talk about Rosie, she couldn't keep it all pressed down in silence any longer. 'Your father needs you too,' she said.

I think what we need most is the shared stories, the memories of her. It's not going to be easy. But I know I have to. For my sister, everything should be lit with clear colour. No more white shadows.

I stay here, sitting in the sand, looking at the water and the sky. A few wisps of cloud above the soft glow of sundown.

Acknowledgements

There are too many to acknowledge here on this page. First and always foremost, my mum, for your unconditional love and support, your unwavering belief and encouragement. You are the bedrock of my river. Thank you for being worried I wasn't reading much around age 10, and getting me hooked on Harry Potter. Three years later and the dream was alive: write stories, share them, be an author. I am so grateful to both my parents for giving me the space to tick along writing over many years, and of course the care and help, always there behind me. Thank you to my dad for your quiet steady support, and for consistently asking me about my writing. I know you are proud of me.

So much gratitude to friends and anyone in my life who's given the smallest inspiration or backing – from a smile to boosting chats. Most especially Emily Arbis ('If anyone can do it, you can' – words spoken one afternoon at The Central in St Andrews, which I've never forgotten), Olivia Acland, Susie Coreth, Joe White, Izzy Williams, Claire Askew, Annabel Hosford, Rosie Tasker, Gordy Wright, Will Grill, Lizzie Daysh, Ed Cox, Ellen Grieves, Hattie Lee-Merrion, Alicia Canteli, Dave Westwood, Giulia Spingardi, Aurora Moxon, Lucy White, Simeï Snyman.

To my agent Jemima Forrester, for seeing something in my writing back in 2019 and believing in me since that moment. This story wouldn't have reached this point or its highest potential without you – thank you for your advice and suggestions. I'm grateful to my agent in the US, Claire Friedman, for playing a key part in my book's chance of reaching readers across that amazing expanse of water we call the Atlantic. Thank you to everyone at David Higham for all your work.

Deep recognition goes to my editors Rosa Schierenberg and Shannon Criss for your clear-sighted editing, and your excitement and confidence, which kept the spark lit. Thank you to Jennifer Edgecombe for your incredible work too. Special thanks to the teams at Welbeck and Holt.

Thank you to my brothers, Ned and Jamie, and to everyone in my family – Jilly Bond, my grandparents, my great aunt Pam who turned 100 last year, and to the ancestors reaching through time. I take none of you or your stories for granted. Nor do I take for granted every being who has participated in my life's flourishing – most especially those involved in the growing of food, those who have contributed to anything I've ever eaten. What incredible beauty there is on every plate. Nothing would be possible without the plants, the insects, the soil, the animals. As Thich Nhat Hanh so beautifully said: 'If you are a poet, you will see clearly that there is a cloud floating in this sheet of paper.' Unending gratitude to trees, birds, water and land.

About the Author

Tasha Sylva is an aspiring small-scale farmer, with a focus on regenerative agriculture, community and localisation. She is currently based in the southwest of England, after time in London, Scotland and southern Spain. For her, the power of story is fundamental, as is the power of language. She regularly asks: How can we foster curiosity and imagination? And, importantly, human connection – to each other, soil, plants and all threads of our environment. When not writing, she can be found swimming in the sea or watching birds. The Guest Room is her debut novel.

WELBECK

PUBLISHING GROUP

Love books? Join the club.

Sign up and choose your preferred genres to receive tailored news, deals, extracts, author interviews and more about your next favourite read.

From heart-racing thrillers to award-winning historical fiction, through to must-read music tomes, beautiful picture books and delightful gift ideas, Welbeck is proud to publish titles that suit every taste.

bit.ly/welbeckpublishing

WELBECK

ANDRE
DEUTSCH

MORTIMER

MORTIMER

WELBECK